Praise for Lauren Clark & *Dancing Naked in Dixie*

"Get ready for a great time as you travel along with Julia as she yearns to fall in love with life, family, and syrupy Southern sweet tea..."
- Dina Silver, Author, *One Pink Line*

"Lauren Clark paints a realistic and often hilarious picture of what it's like for a traveling city girl to leave behind her ultra-hectic life and find comfort (and a bit of chaos!) in a quaint little town in Alabama."
- Juliette Sobanet, Author, *Sleeping with Paris* and *Kissed in Paris*

"Lauren Clark has blown me away!"
- Laura Pepper Wu, Author, *Wow! Glowing Bride in 30 Days*

"I read this book in a day and loved every second of it!"
- Kate Rockland, Author, *150 Pounds*

"Lauren Clark has definitely been added to my list of favorite authors."
- Trudi LoPreto, *Readers Favorite*

"A splash of humor and a healthy dollop of romance make this a fun read from beginning to end."
- Lynnette Spratley, Author, *Memory's Child*

PRAISE FOR LAUREN CLARK
& *STAY TUNED*

" Riveting and much recommended…"
- MIDWEST BOOK REVIEW

"A great read!"
- REBECCA BERTO, AUTHOR, *PRECISE*

"Realistic and refreshing!"
- MICHELLE, *BOOK BRIEFS*

"Clark's first attempt at story-telling—fiction story-telling—is a prize for any reader to have on his or her shelf."
- MACON EXAMINER

"*Stay Tuned* is a great read with vivid characters and an entertaining plot."
- JENNIE COUGHLIN, AUTHOR, *WELCOME TO EXETER*

"Kudos to Ms. Clark on a wonderful debut…I look forward to reading more of her books."
- KATHLEEN ANDERSON, JERSEY GIRL BOOK REVIEWS

"*Stay Tuned* is as faced-paced as a real-life newsroom."
- DEVON WALSH, WKRG-TV ANCHOR

"*Stay Tuned* is a great read! Lauren Clark writes so well you can feel what the characters feel."
- LAUREN DAVIS, WVLT-TV ANCHOR

"Loved it and you will too. The book will draw you in and leave you wanting more."
- ANNE RICHTER, WWNY-TV ANCHOR

Pie girls

Also by Lauren Clark

Stay Tuned
Dancing Naked in Dixie
Stardust Summer
*A Very Dixie Christmas (*Merry & Bright *Holiday Collection)*

Pie girls

LAUREN
CLARK

CAMELLIA PRESS

Copyright 2014 by Lauren Clark

ISBN 978-0-9906231-2-0

All rights reserved, including the right to reproduce this book or portions thereof in any form whatsoever. For information contact:

CAMELLIA PRESS

Camellia Press LLC
20 Lancaster Road
Mobile, AL 36608

Pie Girls is a work of fiction. Names, characters, businesses, places, events, and incidents are either the products of the author's imagination or used in a fictitious manner.

Any resemblance to actual persons, living or dead, or actual events is purely coincidental.

For Sarah

CHAPTER 1

This cannot be happening.
This cannot be happening.
I steal a glance at the clock. Where is my husband? And my anniversary gift, for that matter. The robin's egg blue box, the crinkle of the white tissue paper. The gasp of surprise, well-practiced, when I lift the diamond-encrusted pendant from its nest.

Alton, always the gentleman, will insist on helping. He'll clear his throat, looking rather pleased with himself, stand up, and sweep my long blond hair off to one side. With flourish, he'll ever so carefully drape the platinum chain around my neck, plant a soft kiss on my bare shoulder, and ease the clasp into place.

When my eyes blink open, the room's still empty. Alton, who's been on a business trip for a full week, *promised* he'd make it home for our anniversary. If he doesn't, he's going to be in huge trouble.

I fold my arms across my chest and walk over to our huge picture window. Elegant skyscrapers glow in the dark night, windows twinkling white and gold. Below them, steady streams of traffic wrap like ribbons around the maze of interstate highway.

Away from the roadways, Atlanta is surprisingly lush and dense, with rolling hills and trees—beautiful magnolia, dogwoods, old Southern pines, and magnificent oaks. The expansive green space, well-manicured parks, and flower-lined sidewalks remind me a bit of home.

Buckhead—where I live—is a mecca for shoppers, visitors and businesses, with its upscale boutiques, restaurants, and hotels. Trendy bars, dance clubs, and bistros all come to life when the sun melts into the horizon. A place to see and be seen. It truly is the Beverly Hills of the South, as my friend Phillipa likes to call it.

As I gaze out at the red taillights twisting and weaving toward downtown, I can almost hear music pumping from speakers, feel the afternoon's heat evaporating into the evening air, and smell the giddy, stiletto-heeled anticipation of an evening out on the town.

It's Friday night. Everyone's off at parties, mingling over dinner, exclaiming over the hottest gossip, and exchanging air kisses over martinis.

Everyone. Except me.

I brush off the thought and smile down at my new shoes, a teensy little anniversary gift to moi. The extravagant purchase did include a little guilt...until Alton decided not to show up for tonight's dinner. I turn, twist my ankle, and admire the curve of the heel, the absolute perfection of the arch.

Christian Louboutin is a genius. I should have married him.

That makes me frown, and I turn away from the glass toward our lovely art deco-inspired apartment. Pursing my lips, I blow out the tapered white candles, which are beginning to drip onto the tablecloth.

The oven's been off for hours. The lamb chops are completely overcooked, and the endive salad looks wilted. The green beans, beneath a sprinkle of shaved almonds, seem pathetic and lonely. I even made a special trip to the wine shop and splurged on a bottle of Alton's favorite—a yummy Shafer Vineyards Hillside Select cabernet sauvignon.

Best of all, for dessert, and with my own hands, I created a fabulous chess pie from my mother's secret recipe. Several sticks of butter and two cups of sugar, creamed together with heavy cream, vanilla, and egg yolks in a flaky crust. Pure heaven.

From the corner of my eye, I catch a glimpse of the pastry sitting on the edge of our kitchen counter. Alton allows himself the indulgence once a year, always on our anniversary. The other 364 days he swears off sweets, vowing raw sugar won't pass his lips. Alton says it's how he keeps his trim high-school figure.

But we both adore sweets, and I suspect his secret, though I'd never breathe a word. Every so often, after a particularly challenging day at the office, he comes home smelling of toasted pecan pie or seven-layer caramel cake. The finest bakery in Buckhead, written up in *Southern Living* and reviewed in the *Atlanta Journal-Constitution*, is only a few miles away from our three-story brownstone. It's an occasional treat. Therapy. There are worse vices he could have, right?

My legs buckle the slightest bit. All of this thinking about dessert has me positively famished. And parched. I glance at the wine and walk toward it. Without hesitating, I pull the bottle opener from a nearby drawer, and then twist, pull, and pop the cork. The cabernet, dark red and silky, looks lovely pouring into the crystal stemware—a wedding gift from my mother-in-law, C.C.

Swirling the wine gently, I pluck a dessert plate off the granite countertop and set it down in the center of the kitchen table. My eyes find the chess pie. Simple, timeless, and delicious, it's my favorite Southern confection. Under the soft light from our blown glass chandelier, the smooth cream filling glows up at me, lightly browned and perfect.

Delicately, I chew my bottom lip and consider the pie, its fluted crust, and exactly why my husband would be five hours late. On the wall, silver clock hands tick and move with precision. I study the stainless steel numbers. Is it possible that he forgot our anniversary? Or that a last minute, emergency assignment cropped up? Or that his plane was diverted to Australia?

I shake my head.

With one last-ditch attempt to reach Alton, I punch redial on my iPhone. The line connects. Straight to voicemail. My husband's voice—deep, a little Southern, and all business—fills my ear. This time, I don't leave a message.

Placing my phone down on the counter, I kick off my brand-new heels. Wiping the lipstick from my mouth with the back of my hand, I upend my glass of wine and take three large gulps. When I come up for air, my head buzzes and spins so much that I have to grasp the back of the nearest bistro chair.

A pleasant warmth snakes through my torso and thighs, making my skin tingle. Another swallow. I open a nearby drawer, grab a knife, and slice a teensy triangle of the chess pie. Dessert safely on a small plate, I settle myself on the sofa and click on the television.

I pop in a forkful. It melts deliciously on my tongue.

Re-runs of *America's Next Top Model*. Boring. I am so over Tyra Banks.

Another bite. Definitely exquisite.

Real Housewives of Beverly Hills. I'm momentarily intrigued and consider it, but decide to change the channel. Someone is probably wearing my anniversary necklace. If I see that, I'll be even more upset.

Another sip of wine, more slowly this time.

Homeland. The show is fascinating, but I'm not in the mood for Claire Danes and her crazy bipolar personality.

I need happy. I need playful.

I need my husband.

My phone rings, startling me so much that I drop my next nibble of pie on the floor. It bounces onto the white wool throw rug and leaves a dark smear. *Nooo. Not tonight. Not ever.* Alton will have a conniption fit of epic proportions. He's the neat freak in the relationship, and I'm not messy by anyone's standards.

In the Roberts household, there are never clothes on the floor, no dishes left on the counter. Everything has its place. Underscoring my point, Alton's dress shirts are organized by color on wooden hangers, each hung one finger's distance apart in the walk-in closet.

Face down, my cell continues buzzing and ringing. I mute the TV volume; fumble with the phone's touch screen, not bothering to check the caller's name. It has to be Alton. I take a quick breath, soften my voice, and answer, trying desperately not to sound anxious.

"Sweetie?" The word comes out as a squeak.

There's a squeal of girlish laughter on the other end. Definitely not my husband.

It's my best friend, Phillipa, and she's drunk. Or at least, a half-martini away from being totally inebriated. I would be, too, if I were married to her horses' ass -richer-than-Bill-Gates husband.

Techno music pumps into my ear and I can hear shouting and laughter in the background. "Happy anniversary!" Phillipa yells into the phone. "What are you doing? Come celebrate with us!"

I press a hand to my forehead, grimace, and close my eyes. There is no way that I can admit—even to Phillipa—that Alton is MIA. I think quickly, grasping for a viable excuse.

"Thanks, sweetheart," I manage to conjure up a believable giggle. "But Alton's downstairs grabbing a limo. I ran back up to get my clutch."

There's a pause, and someone chatters to Phillipa. More music blares into my ear.

"Well, I miss you," she shouts into the phone. "If Alton crashes early, sneak out anyway! You know we're more fun."

Even though it's partly true, Phillipa's comment still smarts. Alton is rarely the life of the party. He's cerebral and brilliant; the guest most likely to talk about the latest *Huff Post* stories, global warming, or environmental issues. His favorite subject is advertising, though—the work that he lives and breathes. Most of his accounts are prominent designers, brands like Tom Ford or Fendi. On a recent trip to Europe, he met Donatella Versace. Even Phillipa was impressed, and she isn't dazzled by much of anything, unless it involves the French Caribbean or flawless diamonds.

The techno beat thumps louder. I smile and imagine Phillipa on the dance floor, pressed together with equally thin and beautiful Atlanta socialites. She'll have one arm in the air, waving at someone she knows from private school.

I love her so much. We've been BFFs since the afternoon our moving truck lumbered up to our new brownstone. Within minutes, Phillipa had knocked on our door with a bottle of chilled Louis Roerder Cristal, thrust out the welcome gift, and plopped herself down on my sofa like we'd been friends forever.

Amused at our animated chatter, Alton had packed for his business trip, zipped up his suitcase, and rolled it to the front door. With a smile, he'd pecked me on the cheek and waved goodbye to my new friend on his way out.

"*Je pars pour Paris,*" he said in a perfect French accent. "*Au revoir, belles filles.*"

I blew him a kiss, a bit sadly, as he closed the door behind him. "I miss him already."

Phillipa nodded with empathy. "My husband's in Spain."

"I think mine's in Europe more than he's home," I said with a rueful smile. With a giggle, and more champagne, we dubbed ourselves "work widows" and bonded immediately. We stayed up half the night, talking on the balcony as stars glittered over Atlanta's skyline.

Raucous laughter pulls me back to the present.

"Searcy?"

I sigh a little into the receiver. "Phillipa, I'm horribly sorry to miss out on tonight. But, I really have to run, darling. I'm keeping the limo waiting."

"Sear-cy," Phillipa slurs. "Alton better be taking you somewhere wonderful. Not like that horrible Thai place near the Aquarium last year. If he doesn't whisk you off to a fabulous dinner, I'm going to—"

"I'll see you tomorrow, darling," I say, interrupting. "At Mimi's shower. You'll be there?"

"Of course, sweetie! Love you," Phillipa yells over the din.

"Love you, too." I hang up and press the phone to my chest, trying to compress the hollow space inside it.

In my beautiful apartment, in a city of nearly half a million people, loneliness permeates the space around me. In that moment, I almost believe that the emptiness might be the price I have to pay for having almost everything my heart desires.

I stare back at my reflection in the phone's glass coating. Tilting my chin down and to one side, I survey my complexion, the curve of my cheekbone, and my mascara-coated lashes. Green eyes, the color of sea glass, look back at me. My hair, straight and thick, hangs down my back in a glossy gold waterfall.

Tonight, though, even after a trip to the salon for a blowout, a facial, and a mani/pedi, my polished look and perfect nails don't bring me an iota of joy.

I slide my cell onto the end table and push it away with my fingers.

The television's still on. Of all things, a jewelry commercial flashes up. I can't look away as a man kneels down and proposes to his girlfriend. They embrace.

Swallowing hard, I change the channel, jump up, and cut a second piece of pie. This one is twice as generous. As I take my third bite, I decide that I feel a bit sick, actually.

It could be the chess pie. Or the red wine.

Most likely, it's being abandoned. Again.

It's not my imagination. Over the past year, my husband's trips have stretched from three days to five or six. On weeknights, I'm lucky to see him before ten.

Another glance at the clock. Alton is now officially six hours late.

My breath hitches in my throat. Music announces the evening news. I try to focus on the television anchors, looking buttoned-up and concerned as the camera pans closer. When I start to change the channel, I notice the headline.

She's talking about Andrews & Quentin, Alton's company.

My nerves prickle. I push the volume button a few times and strain to hear what the woman's saying.

I bolt upright when my husband's photo appears on the screen.

Beneath his name is one word. My heart stops beating. *Missing.*

CHAPTER 2

My iPhone rings. First, it's Phillipa. Then Mimi. Other friends follow. Soon, people on the periphery of my acquaintance circle join in. Locked into a state of panic, all that I can do is stare at the screen as each name pops up. Thirty voicemails in 15 minutes. And none of them from Alton.

Tears prick at my eyes and I blink them away.

I'm shaking. And freezing cold.

I can't believe he's missing. It's a mistake. I'm sure of it.

A firm knock at the door causes me to jump, knocking over the crystal goblet near my elbow. The glass shatters into a million shards, a glittery mess on the table's edge, spilling onto the hardwood floor. A few, scattered drops of wine punctuate the disaster like blood.

I shudder and raise a fist to my mouth, pressing it into my lips so as not to cry out. There's the knock again, harder this time. Insistent and firm. And my name.

"Searcy, let me in."

Conner?

Shaking off bewilderment, I stand and shuffle to the door, careful to step around the minuscule broken sparkles. When I reach the door, I twist the handle and pull the door open.

Sure enough, my husband's boss is standing there, disheveled and gorgeous. His black hair is wind-blown, his dark eyes are fiery and fierce. He brushes past without a hello.

"Please, come in," I say to the empty hallway. After a half-second, I step back, turn, and press the door closed behind me.

Conner Andrews is a multi-million dollar advertising executive, one half of the dynamic duo of Andrews & Quentin.

"What the hell, Searcy?" Conner sputters at me. His hands are on his hips. A faint sheen of sweat covers his forehead.

I gather my wits and remind myself that Conner is an Irish-Catholic hot head, famous for his explosive temper and hissy fits. Keeping my arms tight to my ribcage, I take a step forward. Despite my panic, I do my best to keep my voice even and level.

"I have *no* idea where he is," I say, looking into Conner's eyes for emphasis.

Alton's boss simmers, digesting this, and then launches into a conversation that doesn't seem to include me. "Does he realize what he's doing? All that's at stake? The Bergdorf account, for one. Burberry. And Trina Turk." Conner claps both hands over his eyes and shakes his head so violently that I debate calling 9-1-1.

He needs a distraction. "Can I get you something?" I ask. "A drink? Perhaps..." My eyes scan the room and land on the dessert. "A slice of pie?"

There's a beat of silence, but, somehow, this breaks the foul mood. Conner strides over to the dish and stares at the dessert. After I hand him a fork, knife, and plate, he extracts a thick slice and proceeds to spear and pop pieces into his mouth, one after the other.

"God, Searcy, this is delicious," he mumbles, stuffing in a huge bite. "I didn't know you could bake. Thank you. I haven't eaten since this morning."

"You're welcome," I murmur back and sink into the nearest chair, exhausted.

"He was in Beverly Hills, and then Los Angeles for meetings, as you know," Conner says, swallowing the last bite.

I nod.

"The best we can tell, he checked in at LAX this morning, and his flight arrived at Hartsfield around three." Conner runs a hand through his thick, dark hair. "But after working some major connections at Delta, they confirmed he never boarded."

I choke and start coughing into my hand.

Conner reaches out to pat awkwardly at my heaving back.

"H-he *wasn't* on the plane?"

Alton's boss draws back and levels his gaze at me. He doesn't joke. Or lie for fun. "I think something terrible happened. It's why we called the TV—"

The click of metal on metal reverberates through the silent space. It's the sound of a key sliding into and turning the lock of the apartment door.

I shriek and jump up, racing Conner to the foyer. When I fling open the door, a wide-eyed Alton is standing in the entrance.

Immediately, Conner and I take turns berating him with questions and accusations. *What were you thinking? Why didn't you call? Where in the world were you?*

At least one sleepy neighbor wakes up and pokes her head out into the hallway. Flashing an apologetic smile at the woman, Alton waves us both back into the apartment.

My emotions swing between disbelief and shock. I can't take my hands off of my husband, touching his arm to make sure he's real, checking his chest for bullet holes.

"Searcy," he says, after tolerating the examination for ten minutes. "Really." He gives me a squeeze. "Would you please stop handling me? I'm fine."

"I've been frantic, Alton," I insist. I scrunch up my face into a frown and shoot Conner a look. *Do something!*

Alton turns away from us, takes a small box from the cabinet, and reaches for the teapot.

Tea? My husband doesn't drink herbal tea. Ever. As I watch him fill the silver container, I realize he's not wearing his clothes.

No splashy Tommy Hilfiger tie, no khaki slacks, and no navy blue Armani sport coat. Tonight, he's sporting a Patagonia windbreaker, loose-fitting linen pants, and a long-sleeved organic cotton shirt. And are those...open-toed Birkenstocks on his bare feet?

I try not to gape.

Alton ignores us, proceeding to make tea as if it's the first thing he does when he walks in the door. The very same man who likes his coffee with three shots of espresso, steamed soy milk, and a dash of cinnamon.

Conner follows my gaze and clears his throat. "Alton. What is going on?"

In slow motion, my husband turns toward us.

"I quit." His face holds the slightest hint of amusement.

There's an appreciable gasp, in unison.

"What?" Conner demands, red-faced.

"As in, quitting your job?" I demand, slightly hysterical.

Alton nods, and goes back to stirring. "I'm not happy, Searcy. I haven't been in a long time."

Conner's face turns a deeper shade of magenta. "Just like that? After everything I've done for you? How dare—"

"Wait." I cut him off, tamping down my own hysteria, and trying to adopt an understanding tone. Drawing myself up taller, I force a bright smile. "You must be joking. Darling, go lie down. You're jet lagged. Everything will look much better in the morning."

But, as I say the words, I can't process the expression on Alton's face. He looks...content. At peace. Complete panic overtakes my brain.

Enraged, Conner makes an attempt at gripping Alton by the collarless shirt. His hands don't quite connect, which results in him pushing against my husband's chest. Alton backs up and Conner stumbles to regain his balance.

"Both of you. Stop it. Please," I cry out.

Conner freezes in place and my husband shakes himself free.

"We'll discuss this tomorrow," Alton says with a pointed look at his boss. "You need to leave, and I need to speak with my wife."

Breathing heavily, Conner frowns and slams a hand down on the counter. "If you quit—if you step away from the firm—it's your funeral." With that, he turns on his heel and stomps out of the apartment, not bothering to shut the door behind him.

I press a shaking hand to my lips.

"Searcy." Alton frowns and walks over. He cups his hand and lifts my chin a few inches. "We have to talk."

Petrified, I don't meet his gaze.

"Are you listening?"

His voice echoes between my ears, as if he's shouting into a megaphone. Alton never shouts. My mind is playing tricks on me.

"Yes," I whisper.

"This is so difficult. I owe you an apology."

A strained edge creeps into my voice. "For being late?"

Alton's hand falls away from my face. The movement startles me, and I finally meet his eyes.

"For not talking this over sooner. I'm sorry."

Sorry for what? I strain to listen to the words, now completely confused. Alton doesn't talk in circles. And this is complete nonsense.

His phone begins to ring. Alton retrieves it from his pocket and glances at the caller ID. His shoulder slumps.

"C.C.," he mouths, putting the cell to his ear.

My mother-in-law shrieks when Alton answers the phone. There's a flurry of maternal chatter, some chastising, and repeated admonishments.

While I wait, it feels as if someone's tying an invisible, thousand-pound anchor to my leg.

"Yes, I promise," Alton replies.

More tongue-lashing. I bite my lip, nearly drawing blood.

"I love you, too," he answers his mother.

He hangs up and stares at the tiled floor.

Now, inside my body, I am screaming. The anchor's being thrown overboard, chains clanking, to the bottom of the ocean. As I am being dragged away, I cling to a shred of hope. I wait for my husband to tell me that tonight—whatever this is—has all been a big mistake.

My eyes fill with tears.

I begin to shake. Out of confusion. Out of fear. Out of relief that he's home. With a trembling hand, I reach up and caress the side of his face. I tilt my face and smile. "It's all been a big mistake, right? You're sorry?"

I wait for him to grin back. I want to hear that everything's going to be fine. I want him to tell *me* he loves me, too.

He hesitates, knitting his brow.

"I-I know," I say, fingers fluttering to my throat. "You couldn't find the pendant from Tiffany's. And it was so important that you had to fly to another city to get it for our anniversary. Right?"

Alton stares at me like I'm a stranger.

"You know," I say, building enough confidence in my own fabrication to wink at him, "the Soleste Yellow Diamond necklace? I've only left a dozen catalogs open with the page marked."

Instead of laughing in agreement and pulling the blue box from behind his back, Alton pauses and delivers the blow.

"Searcy, I don't know if I want to be married anymore."

Chapter 3

After tossing and turning for hours alone, I'm a frazzled, nervous wreck. When the alarm chimes for the third time, I force myself to roll out of bed.

In my La Perla bra and panties, I catch my reflection in the mirror. My face is tear-streaked; my eyes are red and puffy. Even my hair looks matted and flat.

It's the morning of Mimi's baby shower. The glamorous party of all parties, planned down to the last detail by yours truly. I'm supposed to play demure hostess and adoring friend.

I'm an emotional train wreck.

And not at all certain that I can pull it off.

All because Alton's lost his mind.

As I peek into the living room at the sofa, I see that my husband's still snoozing, one arm tossed across his face to block the morning sun. I rub my temples and watch him. He never sleeps in. He never skips work.

As Alton dozes, I consider that last night might have been a terrible dream. A nightmare, or a temporary mid-thirties crisis. Perhaps Alton has food poisoning, or someone slipped drugs into his drink at the airport.

He did, after all, have a serious bout of cold feet before the wedding. Disappeared for a week. Didn't call, didn't send a postcard. His parents were wild with worry. Our wedding planner threatened to cancel the entire event. I suspected that he'd had a last-minute fling at a strip club, a wild guys' trip to Vegas or Atlantic City, but I held my ground, promising everyone that he'd be back.

Alton was on my doorstep the morning of the ceremony with a bouquet of gorgeous, fragrant purple and pink lilies. Once he came home, the reasons and excuses didn't matter. I pretended they didn't, anyway. I wasn't going to be humiliated. I wasn't canceling the wedding. I was getting married.

That was a decade ago.

I ease out of the living room, deciding not to wake him. We can talk later, when he's had some rest and his head clears. When Alton comes to his senses.

With my eyes, I trace the edge of his face, the contour of his jawline, and the way his hair falls across his forehead. We've been together since high school. I thought that I knew everything about my husband. I always prided myself in our open relationship—the fact that we share all of our family skeletons, dark secrets, and crazy, irrational fears.

Or do we?

My gaze lands on the open briefcase near his feet. With a cautious step, I ease my way toward the satchel, jam-packed with folders and papers. I crane my neck sideways and sink to my knees, holding my breath. With careful fingers, I flip through the files.

Excel spreadsheets, memos, and financial statements. I stifle a yawn. Work, work, work. Boring. Until my thumb pauses on several pages of parchment paper.

As I pull them out to look closer, my heart jolts. The title on the first page reads *Shri Ram Chandra Mission*. Blinking rapidly and wrinkling my forehead, I scan the *Request for Stay at Molena Ashram* and a release of liability. Weird. And the last page *is* signed by my husband. Or by someone who does a fairly good job forging Alton's handwriting.

The packet is an application to stay at an Ashram—a yoga retreat or resort—in Molena, Georgia. And it's dated last month.

My breath catches in my throat as I speed-read the rest of the papers.

The emergency contact doesn't list 'Searcy Roberts.' The name on the page is vaguely familiar. I wrack my brain, urging a connection.

Finally, I realize that it's a co-worker from the advertising agency. A male co-worker. *Whew*. I almost giggle out loud.

Alton just needs a vacation. That's it. Husbands like Alton don't up and visit Ashrams. Alton's never done a minute of meditation in his life. Yoga isn't in his vocabulary. Neither is vegetarian food.

He is having a mid-thirties crisis, poor guy. And I can remedy this. I'll suggest a trip to Turks and Caicos. Snorkeling in Grand Cayman. Or, heck, even backpacking in Belize.

Alton doesn't have to face this alone. And he doesn't need an Ashram.

Ever so slowly, I slide the papers back into Alton's briefcase, stand up, and smooth the buttery-soft leather.

We'll be fine. I nod to myself and smile at my husband. He looks so innocent. So peaceful sleeping on the sofa. With a smooth movement, I draw the spare blanket over his exposed shoulder and bend down to kiss his forehead. He stirs slightly when my lips brush his skin.

"Shh," I whisper. "I love you. We'll fix all of this, honey. We'll be back and better than ever. I promise."

Alton turns his head, smiles in his sleep, and snuggles deeper against his pillow.

I exhale, taking my husband's peaceful expression as a positive sign from the gods, and watch him for a few more moments.

With a deep breath, I return to my bathroom and get to work on fixing my appearance. After a thirty-minute, scalding hot shower, I begin to feel semi-human again. I scrub myself from head to toe, buffing and polishing my skin until it glows.

After slathering on lotion and dabbing Preparation H under my eyes (yes, it really works to reduce puffiness), I camouflage my blotchy face, bloodshot eyes and irritated skin.

After a moment's hesitation, I throw on a cute Gucci sheath and buckle on my favorite pair of Jimmy Choos.

Before I leave the apartment, I scribble off a loving note, reminding him of Mimi's baby shower and promising to be home soon.

Thirty minutes later, I cruise into the parking lot of a string of posh and popular boutiques and bistros in Buckhead. I've picked out a brand new place, one that offers outside seating, a covered patio, and tableside service.

I'm the first to arrive, but a very pregnant Mimi bustles in seconds later with an entourage of family and friends.

She squcals in excitement when she sees me and air-kisses both cheeks. "Searcy Roberts," Mimi breathes. "Bless your heart, sweetie. What in the world happened with Alton? Is he all right?"

Anticipating direct bombardment of questions about my "missing" husband and last night's semi-sensational television news story, I've rehearsed my explanation on the car ride over.

I let out a practiced giggle and hug Mimi gently.

"Oh, that silly husband of mine," I explain and roll my eyes. My brain goes into warp-drive. "Can you believe that Alton was so exhausted that he missed his flight at LAX? He forgot to check in at the office, and then fell asleep at the terminal."

Mimi claps a diamond-encrusted hand to her pink lips. "No."

I nod, taking my friend by the crook of the arm and leading her away from the crowd. "He's fine, now, and home sleeping..."

"Why the missing person story?" Mimi's eyes grow wide. "Did something happen in LA?"

"Oh, sweetie," I flush in embarrassment. "Conner Andrews freaked out. They have a huge presentation today. I think it's with...." I lower my voice. "Amazon. Or maybe Google." Of course, I'm completely making this up, just a tiny fib to deflect attention from my personal life.

Mimi raises an eyebrow and makes an "o" with her lips. "Wow."

"So, when Conner didn't hear from Alton, he assumed the worst. Kidnapping, terrorist attack, hijacking. You know Conner's always been a bit of a drama queen," I say, nudging her gently and winking.

Then, I take Mimi by the shoulders, turn her toward the head table, and steer her to a cushy seat.

"Put your feet up, sweetie. We'll have plenty of time to catch up later." I paste on a huge smile. "Today," I announce, "is supposed to be all about you, my dear friend."

Mimi rubs her rounded belly and glows.

"And the little munchkin, of course." I lean down and kiss Mimi's cheek. "Now, let me get this party started."

After three hours of gift unwrapping, exclaiming over baby booties, and pretending to eat sugar-encrusted petit fours, I am exhausted. My cheeks hurt from smiling so much, my feet ache, and I can't seem to push the worry about Alton completely out of my head.

For the fifteenth time, I slip a look at my cell phone. *Nothing. Nada. Not one call.* Where is my husband? Did he go to the office? Did Conner talk some sense into him?

I rub the back of my neck, trying to ease a muscle spasm. Surely, I'll come home to find that everything's back to normal.

Finally, Mimi's mother and her three sisters load up her brand new, baby blue Lexus SUV with gifts, boxes, and cards. The trunk is chock-full of Baby Bjorn, Peg Pergo, and two identical Louis Vuitton diaper bags. Mimi swears she's keeping both—just in case one wears out.

It takes six trips to the parking lot to carry out all of the presents.

Mimi, though tired, beams from all of the attention—completely hugged, cooed, and fussed over. A few remaining guests wave goodbye from across the parking lot.

She hugs me tightly before opening the Lexus door and easing into her SUV's leather seats. "How about I treat you to lunch tomorrow?" she asks. "We need some girl time before this baby decides to make an appearance."

I hesitate, worried about Alton. I can't say another word about my husband. And it's not likely Mimi will take no for an answer.

"Sounds fabulous," I agree.

We air kiss and Mimi shuts the door. She rolls the window down. "Thank you, Searcy. For everything. It was perfect. Really lovely. And you are a fabulous, wonderful friend."

"You're the fabulous one," I insist and wave goodbye. "Call me later."

As her Lexus turns out of the parking lot, I watch until Mimi drives out of sight. The moment she disappears, I slide behind the wheel of my BMW 325i and head home.

I call out to Alton after I turn the key in the lock and open the door.

No answer.

He can't still be sleeping. I frown and drop my keys into the silver dish on the table that sits in the foyer. I pause and listen.

Silence.

"Alton, I'm home, darling. Mimi's shower's over," I call out, shrugging off my Pashmina and laying it on the back of the nearest chair.

Still no answer.

Slipping off my shoes, I pad into the kitchen. The note I left my husband is sitting in the exact same place, seemingly untouched.

My pulse zips into overdrive. Chest tight, reminding myself to remain strong, I walk toward the bedroom. The hinges creak when I finally press my palm against the wood and push. With breath caught in my throat, I blink back tears. The room is empty. The bed is neatly made. And Alton's gone.

CHAPTER 4

My cell vibrates with an appointment reminder. I'm due for a date with my personal shopper, Lucinda, at Saks Fifth Avenue.

Lord knows I need the distraction, but how can I focus on my summer wardrobe when Alton's gone missing again? I rub my temples with my thumb and forefinger, trying desperately to soothe the thoughts ricocheting in my brain. *Where is he? What on earth is he doing? Why didn't he leave a note?*

Swallowing hard, I stalk into the foyer of our apartment, and stare at my face in the huge beveled mirror. I am shocked at my reflection. All of this nonsense is taking its toll. My usually creamy skin seems pale; my green eyes are bleary gray. I smooth a stray strand of my blonde hair and tuck it behind my ear.

Then, I square my shoulders, think quickly, and decide on a plan of action.

First, with a shaking hand, I speed dial my husband. The phone connects and rings endlessly. No Alton. No familiar cheery voicemail message. Not even a generic cellular phone message asking callers to leave a name and number.

My heart lurches when the phone clicks off. I stare at the black screen, desperately waiting for a message to appear. A quick text. An explanation. Anything.

The cell stays black.

Fine. I'm on to Phase Two: Alton's office. My husband doesn't leave loose ends. If he's pursuing this bizarre idea of quitting his job, there must be out-processing paperwork, forms to sign, meetings to wrap up. I squeeze my eyes shut and decide that Alton probably overslept, sprang off of the sofa, hair rumpled, and rushed into work without seeing my note.

I check my watch and decide there's enough time to make a brief stop at Andrews & Quentin first. Alton's advertising firm is housed in a glass skyscraper downtown, not far from Saks Fifth Avenue and my personal shopper.

I can be late for my appointment. Finding Alton is paramount.

The sooner, the better.

In the past hour, the sky has gone from bright blue to overcast and stormy. A few fat splashes of water hit my windshield as I navigate toward Buckhead's MARTA station. Dodging raindrops, I park my BMW and dash inside to grab the Red Line southbound to Five Points.

Secretly—and I'd never mention it to my friends—I don't mind public transportation at all; it's so much better than navigating the nightmare that is six lanes of downtown Atlanta traffic in the pouring rain.

As I settle against the hard plastic seat, I busy myself with the latest *People* magazine, absorbing the most recent Tori and Dean scandal.

We jerk to our first stop at the Arts Center and a rush of people zigzag in and out of the rail car. With a hiss and grind, the double doors slide shut again, and we bump along toward Midtown and North Avenue.

My nose twitches as the car becomes more packed with people at each stop. There's the distinct smell of leather and coffee, mixed with the scents of perfume and newspaper print.

Peachtree Center is the last stop before Five Points and I am ready to stretch my legs and walk a bit. I've been staring at the same page for the last five minutes, memorizing paparazzi pictures of the Kardashian sisters as if my life depended on it.

The Marta car lurches again and I brace myself, grabbing the metal pole next to my shoulder.

I hadn't noticed her before, but there's a cute little girl standing directly across from me. She's dressed in purple and yellow, with perky matching bows in her curly brown pigtails. I smile and wiggle my fingers in her direction. She mimics the movement, then turns and buries her head in her mother's lap.

"What a cutie," I say.

"She's a hot mess," the child's mother replies, flashing me an exhausted grin. "Up and on the go since the crack of dawn, and no nap."

"No nap," the girl echoes happily.

It's then I notice that there's a second child—a baby—in the mother's arms. She's less than six months old, I estimate, too tiny to walk or crawl.

"Oh, bless your heart," I say, nodding.

Then, I notice that there's no nanny in sight. No husband. No friend to help with the stroller, or a diaper change. I have no idea how she manages.

Mimi's baby hasn't arrived yet, and she's already hired two nannies—both of whom speak French and Italian—and there's a third girl on call for emergencies.

We continue along on the Marta, swaying as the train makes progress toward my destination.

"Hungry," the child announces and holds out both hands. "Please Mama."

I watch, expecting her mother to pull out Cheerios and a sippy cup of organic juice. Instead, her arm reaches into a huge plastic bag. She withdraws a tall fountain drink with a domed lip and red straw—a cherry Icee—and then retrieves a humongous blueberry muffin.

Alternating between sips, the girl manages to finish half of the muffin in the next three minutes, leaving a messy half-circle of crumbs around her feet.

As the train swerves to the right, the little girl nearly loses her balance. Her mother reaches out to steady her. I close my eyes, trying not to watch. I would switch seats, but there's not an empty space in sight. For a brief moment, I close my eyes.

Please, no.
Don't let her fall.
When I look again, it's too late.

A second later, she wobbles, then collapses. As the girl falls to the ground and rolls, her hand reaches for me, catching nothing but air until she hits my knee and pant leg. I feel a tug on the material, followed by the cold shock of Icee on my skin.

Instantly, I'm coated, head to toe, in freezing-cold red syrup. There's a drip from my shoulder, and then another. *Dang.* It's even splashed my hair.

Somehow, despite my shock, I realize that the little girl is crying, bent in a crumpled pile around my feet. She's still hanging on to my trousers, grinding blueberry muffin into the thin wool.

Poor thing. "Here now," I reach for her, trying to soothe her. She's sobbing, big heaving waves of tears, and I can't bear the sight of it. Her mother looks frantic, and is about to stand up.

"Stay right there. It's okay. I'll get her," I say to the child's mother. Slipping off my seat, I bend to pick her up. "All right, sweetie pie. All better."

As I tuck her to my chest, the little girl emits an eardrum-splitting wail, buries her blueberry-streaked face in my shirt, wraps her arms around my neck, and holds tight.

"Well, she's not frightened of strangers," I laugh, making eye contact with the mother, who apologizes profusely.

"I'm so sorry," she whispers. "Your pretty clothes; they're ruined."

"It's fine," I assure her firmly, trying desperately not to look at the damage.

The train eases to a stop at the Marta station, and mercifully, most of the passengers begin filing out. Still holding the little girl, now positioned on my hip, I stand up, and then do my best to help the mother and baby maneuver through the crowd.

"Here we are," I say brightly as we reach the sidewalk, trying to unwrap my new friend.

"Angelica, time to go."

She hugs tighter, practically choking me.

"Angelica," he mother repeats, this time more sternly.

Reluctantly, lip stuck out several inches, Angelica untangles herself and slumps her shoulders. With heavy feet, she stomps back to her mother, who takes her firmly by the hand.

"No more Icees for you, miss," she says, then looks up at me. "And I'm so sorry. We have to go. The baby has a doctor's appointment. Is there anything—*anything*—I can do?"

Think. I can't go to Andrews & Quentin looking like this.

"Do you have a blanket I could borrow?" I ask the mother sweetly. "Maybe two?"

"Of course." Her face is awash in relief. She pulls out a soft yellow sheet covered with baby chicks, and another, this one pink, with polka dots and kittens.

"Perfect," I say. "How can I get them back to you?"

She shakes her head. "It's the least I can do."

Angelica, still pouting, gives me a mournful goodbye.

I wink and wait for them to disappear from sight, trying not to look panicked. When they round the corner, I duck and race like mad into the nearest restroom.

My soiled pant legs are the most noticeable, so I grab a handful of paper towels, wet them, and do my best to clean off the semi-dried blueberry and Icee mess. I yank off my right shoe, balance on one foot, and thrust the leather pump under the automatic spray. I swallow hard, trying not to look as the water soaks into my chocolate brown Jimmy Choos. I repeat the process two minutes later with my left heel, holding onto the counter for balance.

My feet squish against the wet soles as I wriggle the shoes back on. I splash some cold water on my face for good measure and open the two blankets. After folding the first into a triangle, I throw it around my shoulders, letting the edges cover most of the red stains. I use the pink blanket next, folding it lengthwise and letting it drape over my legs.

Staring at the stranger in the mirror, I squint at my reflection.

I look slightly ridiculous.

But, for once in my life, I realize it doesn't matter.

My marriage matters.

Icee or no Icee, I am on a mission. And nothing is going to stop me.

CHAPTER 5

There is no sneaking into Saks Fifth Avenue.

"Darling," a salesperson greets me from the cosmetics aisle. I wave and ignore her curious stare at the yellow sheet around my shoulders.

"Searcy, sweetheart," another coos as I tug at the pink blanket and try to dash past the lingerie department.

"So great to see you," a manager calls out as I crouch low on the escalator to the second floor of the department store.

Head down, I make straight for the personal shopping area and practically dive into my favorite dressing room with Lucinda at my heels.

"I may have to move to Russia," I announce and slump into a cushioned lounge seat.

"What? How—?"

"There was this adorable little girl. Then a blueberry muffin, and an Icee…"

Lucinda clucks her tongue in disapproval.

"I know—" I roll my eyes. "Silly me. I was on the Marta."

"Oh, angel, what have I told you about *public transportation*? How perfectly awful," Lucinda clasps her hands under her chin and looks at me with worried brown eyes.

She's so perfectly serious, I almost giggle. Minus today's mishap, I like riding the Marta, being around regular people. It's a refreshing change from having to be perfect 24/7.

Lucinda pats my shoulder. "Wait right here, dear. We'll get you all fixed up."

While she goes on the hunt, I regroup and glance at my iPhone.

Nothing.

He's at work, I tell myself. *He's come to his senses. Alton had a good night's sleep and realized that he was being foolish.*

There's a knock on the door and I slip my cell into my purse. Lucinda is back with champagne, a luxurious, full-length Vera Wang bathrobe, faux fur slippers, and a pouch of baby wipes. She sets everything down on the table beside me.

"You get cleaned up and comfortable, Searcy. Just slip into these, and in a minute, I'll take those nasty clothes. We'll send them to dry cleaning and see what we can do."

"Shoes and all?" I ask meekly.

"Shoes and all," she says, smiling, and closes the door behind her.

I sink further into the chair and survey the small space. Seeing the champagne lifts my spirits slightly. Lucinda always remembers my signature favorite: Two raspberries in the glass. The bubbles swim and pop to the surface as I reach for the crystal stem.

With a deep breath, I down the entire drink.

There. Better. I stand up, shimmy off every stitch of clothing, and use half a dozen baby wipes before sliding into the white chenille robe. It's deliciously soft and thick against my skin. The slippers are equally exquisite.

I am definitely starting to feel human again.

Lucinda knocks. "Searcy, darling?" she calls. "Are you ready for me?"

"Come in."

With a swish, the door sweeps open, and Lucinda returns with another glass of champagne on a round silver tray.

"I thought that you might need a refill," she winks. "Nothing like a little release after such a traumatic experience."

"Thank you," I smile gratefully.

Lucinda bundles up my clothes, sorts them, and deposits them into two cloth bags. "Now then. What can I show you today?"

With a small sip of my champagne, I wave my wrist and shrug. "Anything at all. I am completely open. Surprise me."

This delights my personal shopper, who probably sees more dollar signs with every glass of champagne I drink. She's correct, of course. I do spend more when I have champagne. Alton goes positively ballistic those months.

I bite my bottom lip.

Alton.

He'll understand. I'll explain about the sweet little girl, the blueberry muffin, and the Icee.

I have to see him, and look my best when I do, so I need to take care of replacing my clothes and shoes.

It's the only logical decision.

After a third glass of champagne, I am back in my Zen place—surrounded by beautiful things, pleasant music, and a salesperson who will do just about anything to make me happy.

Lucinda knows my bra size, is aware that I detest lime green, and is sworn to secrecy about my left foot being half a size larger than my right. As my personal shopper, she has access to my Black American Express card, bank accounts, email, and personal cell phone number.

In the past five years, only my husband, my gynecologist, and Lucinda have seen me naked. After Alton, Phillipa, Mimi, and my mother, Lucinda might just be the most important person in my life. I'd almost compare it to a James Bond/Q relationship. Or maybe a superhero/sidekick team—if any of them had fashion sense.

Lucinda interrupts and breezes into the changing room, a stack of dresses swung over one arm. With grace, she hangs the frocks around the room, fluffs the skirts, then swivels back to face me.

"Now, Searcy," she chirps and flutters her eyelashes. "Remind me. Didn't you and Alton just celebrate your anniversary?"

"Um," I choke at the word "celebrate." With a toss of my head, I force a bright smile. "Yes. It was lovely."

Lucinda stares at me for a moment longer than is comfortable. My cheeks begin to burn and I grasp for the stem of my empty champagne glass. I am a terrible liar. The worst. But revealing this confidence may be my undoing. I can't bear the shame—the possibility of an affair. Of Alton leaving.

Her warm hand pats mine, and then she grasps my fingers and squeezes. "Oh dear, what's wrong? It's not that horrifying vice president of corporate relations, is it?"

Words fly out before I can suck them back in. "The Python?" I gasp, unwittingly divulging my invented nickname for the terror that rules Andrews & Quentin. A cold clamor creeps over my forearm and up to my shoulder.

But Lucinda is far from horrified. "That's a perfect name for her," she giggles and smothers a laugh behind a manicured hand.

The Python, aka Pamela Pryor, is one of the most terrifying women I've ever laid eyes on. I've always joked with Mimi that The Python was sweet on Alton, but the casual remark seems to hold weight—a lot of it—right now.

"Oh, it does make sense," I cry out in dismay.

Lucinda is still holding my hand, almost annoyingly so, but I am so distracted by the semi-revelation that I allow the patting and rubbing.

"She keeps him long hours and drags him along for every single meeting. There was one week, the Pyth—," I stop myself. "Pamela kept Alton at the office 24/7. The entire time. He didn't come home. She had his clothes picked up and cleaned. I had to drop off his shaving kit and razor at the front desk. They wouldn't let me see him," I whine.

Lucinda's eyes haven't left my face.

I blink and realize what I must sound like. The poor wife, left at home, while her husband wines and dines the boss. The room begins to tilt and swim a bit.

"Darling," Lucinda releases my hand. "It happens to so many of us..."

But. Not. Me.

With a huff, I stand and shake off any pity party intentions. I am stronger than this. I am smarter. I can win him back.

"La Perla, please," I say. "And a few Bebe dresses. Or Versace. Something shocking and short. Thigh-high boots. Stockings," I tick off. "And how about a garter belt?" That should get some attention.

Lucinda bounces to her feet and claps her hands. "Yes," she agrees. "And how about an overcoat?" She throws her hair back and gives me a wink. "Let's just take the dress in a bag, shall we?"

"How positively daring. Scandalous, really," I muse, thinking over my options. I imagine storming into Alton's office, pushing him against a wall of books, and clamping a hand on his private region.

"I love it." Lucinda says, breathless. "I'll be right back."
"Brilliant."

Thirty minutes later, I am decked from head to toe in the finest lingerie Saks Fifth Avenue has to offer. Wrapped in a lovely Armani overcoat, belted securely, I smooth the deep red cashmere scarf against my bare neck.

The sensation of wearing barely anything gives me a heady rush of power. The garter belt, slung low around my hips, allows a satisfying tug when I take a step. Silken stockings caress my legs, and Lucinda opted for a buttery-soft pair of black thigh-high boots to finish the outfit.

After smoothing and coaxing my hair into submission, Lucinda talks me into some lotion, and then a dusting of sparkly powder to highlight my décolletage. She wields a huge brush and swishes the iridescent flecks onto my skin with expert precision. The result is amazing.

"Perfect." I blink at my reflection. My skin appears softer and luminous, almost flawless. The glow makes my eyes seem brighter, even in department store lighting.

"You look fabulous," my personal shopper agrees. She steps back to survey her work and gives me a satisfied nod. "He won't be able to help himself once he sees what's under that overcoat."

We dissolve into giggles at that point and I sign the receipt. My brain does register the astronomical dollar figure. Three thousand dollars seems a little much for a bra, panties, boots, and a few dresses, but today, I don't care.

Lucinda squeezes my hand. "Good luck with everything. I think Alton will come to his senses." She pauses and frowns. "He'd better."

I lift my chin and flash a brilliant smile. "I'm going straight to the office. Right now. I'm going to get to the bottom of this. I'm going to *make* him want me."

As for Pamela Pryor, she'd better watch out.

This is war. No price is too high.

I am going to win my husband back.

CHAPTER 6

Alton's office is on the top floor of the Andrews & Quentin building. As I ride the elevator up, I notice some admiring glances from the businessmen standing next to me. The car makes several stops, and finally, I am the only one left when the bell signals the penthouse suite.

I wiggle my fingers at the tall, brunette receptionist, who's in the midst of a conversation with a client. She holds up one finger and tilts her head.

"Just a moment," she whispers, holding her hand over the receiver.

Ashley? Amber? Adele? I can't remember. She is always pleasant and professional, but relatively expressionless, which I chalk up to huge doses of Botox and Restylane injections. Her lips are bee-stung and bright red, full of plumping filler. Any more "work" and she might as well be a window display mannequin.

The receptionist frowns and begins rubbing her forehead with manicured fingertips. She looks like she's about to burst into tears. The client making the complaint is so loud that I can catch parts of the conversation.

"Not acceptable."

"Deadline."

"…talk to Conner Andrews now!"

Ouch! I turn away and walk to the other end of the long lobby so that the receptionist doesn't feel like I'm eavesdropping.

I focus instead on the Andrews & Quentin decor. The look is sleek and shiny, everything trimmed in silver and black. Addy awards and CLIOs line the walls, along with several display cases full of trophies for state and regional advertising excellence.

I pause in front of one of the cases and find Alton's name on almost every project. My heart swells with pride at my smart, talented husband's accomplishments. He's always been a star. So creative, full of ideas. The Python and higher-ups at A & Q must be scurrying to figure out a way to keep Alton in the firm.

"Searcy," the receptionist says, hanging up the phone with a clatter. "I am so sorry to have kept you waiting."

"Rough day?"

"You have no idea," she whispers, flicking her eyes around the office to make sure no one is eavesdropping. "It's been so terrible. We're all so shocked about the decision."

I bite my lip.

"So, how can I help, Searcy? You just missed Alton."

My heart stops.

"H-he's not here?" I choke on the question. My brain spins and twists like a tilt-a-whirl carnival ride. *But he has to be. I don't understand. He can't do this.*

I stop myself when I realize that I am on the verge of freaking out in my husband's workplace. With a deep breath, I steady my posture. "Are you certain? That's so odd. I was sure he said to meet him here for lunch."

The receptionist cocks her head. She blinks up at me with wide-eyes, lashes so long that they appear Tammy Faye Baker-esque.

"I'm sorry," she says, with a trace of genuine sympathy.

I shiver and debate running out of the building or having a complete nervous breakdown. Before I can decide, I feel a tap on my shoulder.

"Searcy?"

I whirl around at the sound of the familiar, high-pitched voice. Pamela Pryor regards me with a coy expression. She leans in, narrowing her dark eyes.

"I'm between meetings," she says, cocking her head and sliding a thin hand along the marble-topped counter. "Care to chat? It'll just take a moment."

I can't say no. Don't show weakness. Shoulders back.

"Sure," I reply with a slight shrug.

"This way, then," she says, clearly pleased with my reply.

Intrigued, I follow behind Pamela, trying not to gape at the swath of material that barely grazes her behind. Her long legs are toned and endless. The woman must spend three hours a day with her personal trainer.

She traipses easily in her five-inch stilettos, slowing only to wave at a client or deliver a gruff order to one of a dozen assistants. Her hair is short, cropped, and spiked, with bold eyeliner and red lips to match.

Intense. That's the only way to describe her. And she knows it.

As expected, her corner office is spectacular and overlooks downtown. Pamela closes the door behind us, and the skin on my throat begins to itch with anticipation. She glances in my direction, flashes me a smile, and walks over to the wet bar.

"Have a seat," she says.

I sink into the nearest leather chair, grip the arm rests, and watch Pamela. My eyes grow wide when, instead of flicking on the coffee pot, she pours two glasses of scotch, neat, and carries them back to her desk.

With a tiny, barely perceptible sigh, she sets the drinks down and nudges one in my direction.

I blink and try to decide if Pamela's lost her mind or if this is some strange ritual welcoming me to the Andrews & Quentin inner circle—if there is such a thing.

Pamela lets out a giggle and tosses back her scotch. "I think this will go much easier if we both have a drink," she says, motioning for me to raise my glass. "Bottoms up!"

I pretend to take a sip, tilting the glass back until the liquid touches my lips. I open my mouth the slightest bit, allowing a tiny amount to slip past my tongue and down my throat.

Ugh. *Yuck.* I gag at the taste. My throat burns like I've swallowed acid. I sniff back the tears threatening to spill.

When I regain my proper vision, Pamela is watching me, mouth twisted into an amused smile. "Not your thing?"

"N-not really," I choke out. I'm a chocolate martini kind of girl, a cosmopolitan-sipping, Kahlua and cream lightweight—none of which I plan to disclose to the very scary individual sitting across from me.

"Are you feeling all right?" she asks, getting up to pour herself a second shot.

"Fine," I reply brightly. "Couldn't be better. Why do you ask?"

Pamela swivels on her heels and gives me a knowing look. "You never come to the office," she says. "And, forgive me, you don't look like you're feeling your best."

Suddenly, I'm burning up.

She pauses, scrutinizing my face. "Are you sure you're all right?"

"Nerves," I tell her and raise a hand to my chest self-consciously. With my index finger, I touch the area along my collarbone. It does feel quite warm, like I've been sitting out in the sun several hours too long.

It's nothing, I tell myself, and focus my attention on Pamela.

I realize that I'm not obligated to tell her anything. But I'm insanely curious to find out what she knows about Alton.

"So, this isn't exactly a social visit?" she asks.

When I shake my head, Pamela leans back against the chair, exasperated. She moves the seat back and forth, shifting her hips as she thinks about this. With a sigh, she interlaces her fingertips and plunks her elbows down, leaning toward me. "What the hell is going on, Searcy?

You, of all people, should know something. You live with the man."

After several beats of silence, I reply. "I wish I knew."

Pamela rises from the chair, placing her hands on her slender hips. "Why would he want to leave? Is it money? Perks? Benefits?" She cocks her head to the side and looks at me. "Jesus. He has an enormous office, an expense account, and our best creative team. We lease him a BMW 5-Series. What more could he want? We have to figure out a way to keep him, and fast."

Again, I don't have an answer. I always assumed that this was Alton's dream job, he was happy, and everything would continue as planned. He's never talked about doing anything other than advertising.

"We're going to lose clients. A lot of important clients. No one pampers and spoils them like Alton can. He's like the goddamned Pied Piper." Pamela flicks an imaginary piece of lint off her sleeve and turns to roll her eyes at me. "Do you know how awful this is? Jesus, I've been lying for three weeks, telling everyone who calls that he's sick or on vacation. I don't know how much longer I can keep this up."

"Three weeks?" I repeat weakly. "I thought..."

Pamela stops breathing. "What? Oh, shit. You didn't know?" She sizes me up, obviously thinking that I'm the most naive person on earth. "What did he tell you? Business meetings? Working late?" She snorts with laughter.

I shake my head. *Three weeks. Where has he been? What has he been doing?*

When Pamela regains her composure, she sinks back into her chair, not taking her eyes off of me. "Sweetheart, you're in worse shape than I thought. You really *don't* have a clue."

The words sting and I cover my mouth with one hand to stifle the stunned gasp threatening to escape.

"I am sorry that I had to be the one to break it to you. I thought you could shed some light on this. But, you're just as screwed as we are."

I swallow. I had expected to storm into the office and confront Alton, not have a heart-to-heart with The Python. The woman he's supposed to be sleeping with.

"But I th-thought," I stutter. "That you and Alton…"

Pamela turns pink and begins to inspect the tips of her manicure. After a long, terrible pause, she raises her eyes slowly to meet mine. "No. I am not sleeping with your husband."

"But everyone says—"

Pamela starts to laugh. "I'd love to hear what everyone says, but maybe another time." She shakes her head. "Alton wouldn't give me a second glance."

I blink.

"Hell, he rejected me. So, why not be honest with you?" Pamela shrugs and takes another sip of scotch.

I summon the nerve to call her a home wrecker, but suddenly, my skin is on fire. A thousand tiny fire ants march up and down my legs. As subtly as I can, I reach down and run my fingernails along my skin.

"Searcy?" Pamela is still talking.

With my other hand, I reach inside my trench coat and scratch my belly. I can't sit still. Everything itches. Everything feels swollen, like the ants are now feasting on my torso, legs, and arms.

"Are you all right?" she asks, louder this time.

I can't sit still. I'm burning up. *Did someone crank the heat?* I begin to perspire, still dragging my nails along every inch of bare skin I can find.

When I can't take it any longer, I stand up, wriggling to unzip and kick off my new boots.

"You don't look so good." Pamela says. She's about two inches from my face. "What's wrong?" She's talking funny. I can barely hear her.

I'm so tired. My fingers ache from scratching. My skin is raw. My chin drops with exhaustion and I look down at my hands. Everywhere, on every tip and crevice, they sparkle.

Oh no. The lotion. The glitter. I'm having an allergic reaction.

I need water, a washcloth, and my medicine. I desperately need a shower, though I doubt that the office has one. I could set off the fire alarm and the overhead sprinklers, but I'd have to find a lighter in a non-smoking building.

At this point, I'd do anything to get the coating off my body. I'm so miserable in my own skin that I begin jumping up and down.

"Searcy? Have you lost your mind?" Pamela asks, trying to grab my arm. I wrestle away from her. I don't have time to explain. I'm not rational. I can't think.

"I'm calling a doctor," she tells me. "And an ambulance."

Thank you Jesus, I think.

Then, I remember the wet bar.

I run over to the counter, survey the inventory, untie my belt, and rip off the overcoat.

At that very moment, there's a rap on the door. Without waiting for a reply, Conner Andrews walks in.

Wearing only my new bra, panties, and garter belt, I grab at the first bottle of scotch. It's half-full and sloshes wildly when I unscrew the top, balancing on one leg to scratch the other with my toes.

"What the—?" Conner's voice echoes in the room.

I don't even bother to acknowledge his presence. I simply close my eyes and douse myself with the alcohol. It pours in rivulets down my chest, belly, and thighs.

"Umm. So, I had a wild idea to pitch Chivas Regal," Pamela says wryly. "Searcy and I are just doing a little brainstorming."

With a small sigh of relief, I shake the last few drops of scotch onto my skin. I move straight on to the second bottle. I crack it open, tilt my head back, and exhale as the cold liquid hits my hot skin.

"Well." Conner crosses his arms, grinning. "I think this particular approach might sell the heck out of any brand."

CHAPTER 7

After popping two Benadryl, scrubbing myself down with wet paper towels in Pamela's office, and being deposited into a waiting taxi by Conner, who was now eyeing me with quite a bit of appreciation, I survive the ride home.

Heaving all of my shopping bags over one shoulder, I totter into the building. After I skulk past the doorman, offering a little wave while I feign a headache, I practically throw myself into the elevator and sigh in relief when the doors close behind me.

I press my back against the sterling silver bar. Suddenly, all of the must-have dresses carefully wrapped in tissue feel weighed down with bricks. I let go of the dozen handles digging into my palm. They fall—thud, thud—to the floor as I hang on for the ride.

Although I'm desperate to see Alton and dying to hear about his day, I'm a little hopeful for a ten-minute reprieve. I can unpack my purchases, hang up my new frocks, store my new boots, and get rid of any evidence that I've just finished the shopping spree of the century.

As I make a mental note to intercept this month's American Express e-bill, the elevator dings, the car stops, and I slowly straighten up.

As the doors slide open, a whiff of Chanel No. 5 drifts through the opening.

Oh. No. That scent only means trouble, in the form of my mother-in-law.

Before I can jump back, whack the down button, or throw myself against the ceiling of the elevator—hoping I'll cling like Spider-Girl—she sees me.

Act normally. Breathe. Don't scream.

Our eyes meet and I plaster on a larger-than-life and so-excited-to-see-you smile. I clench my teeth together, forcing the corners of my mouth to the sky, while I reach down for my bags.

Shit. Shit. Shit.

C.C. doesn't pay house calls. She doesn't stop by uninvited. And C.C. never, ever, goes out of her way to see me.

I was actually hoping she'd forgotten where we lived.

But she's waiting. Staring right at me. Unblinking. And that can only mean one thing.

I'm a dead woman.

C.C. Anderson was a force to be reckoned with while she was still married to Alton's good-for-nothing father. After divorcing him and marrying up, C.C. resembles a Category 5 hurricane. Relentless rain, 160 mile per hour winds, and destruction of anything that stands in her way.

Of course, her strength and wrath are cloaked in genteel charm, a thin, elegant body, perfectly coiffed hair, and the most refined outfits from Atlanta's priciest boutiques. It's like ripping off a Cinderella mask to find a green, pockmarked ogre underneath.

As I've learned in the last ten years as a dutiful daughter-in-law, avoidance is the best technique. I try not to instigate, insinuate, or otherwise infuriate C.C.

Forcing one foot in front of the other, I push my shoulders back, lifting my chin.

"C.C.," I exclaim, standing on tiptoes for an air kiss. "What a lovely surprise."

My mother-in-law doesn't respond, just purses her lips and waits for me to open the door to the apartment.

She clears her throat, and I step back. "You haven't greeted my Precious," C.C. warns in a lilting voice, tilting her head toward the pink sequined bag hanging over her left forearm.

Precious? Like as in the Lord of the Rings? Surely she doesn't mean...

A tiny black nose and beady eyes poke out of the bag.

"Eek!" I jump back and squeal, clapping a hand to my chest and dropping the keys.

The dog—if you can call it that—begins yipping and complaining like I've just whipped it with a cat o' nine tails.

I freeze in place, flush a lovely shade of violet, and want to self-destruct; I'm certain that I've committed what equates to a mortal sin in the world according to C.C. Anderson. She's carrying her new puppy, a tiny Min-Pin, complete with a pink collar and matching pink toenails.

"I'm so sorry—"

C.C. waves her own pink manicured fingernails an inch from my face. I'm not to speak. My mother-in-law is completely involved in reviving the squirmy brown and black rat-creature.

"Mama's poor little baby," she coos in a high-pitched falsetto. "Are you okay, my sweetie-weetie, lovey girl?"

My jaw drops open slightly. I've never heard the woman utter a word of endearment toward any human being or living creature.

When I first dated Alton, I was almost certain that C.C., in fact, was among the undead. Five years ago, when she and Alton's father decided to move to Atlanta—under the auspices of being closer to their only son—I almost had him talked into buying some dove's blood from Marie Laveau's shop in New Orleans just to see if she'd drink it.

"Mama's Precious will be all right, won't she?" C.C. continues. "Searcy's just a bad girl. She'll do better, I promise, darling."

I can't bear to look. It's a good thing, because kissing sounds follow. Smacky, dry-lipped kisses. *Yuck*. The dog's head is now stamped with C.C.'s Chanel-red lipstick. If I was locked against her bony, cold body, I'd be frightened, too.

Shutting my mouth, and jerking myself into motion before C.C. sees the dumbstruck look on my face, I whirl toward the door, insert the key into the lock, and turn it.

The silence in the hallway is deafening. My heart thuds like a bongo drum in my chest.

My mind races. Why in the world is C.C. here?

She saw the news report, but talked to Alton right after it aired.

He told her everything was *fine*.

"Okay, here we go. Let me get the lights—" I make my voice sing-song and perky. The door swings open and we walk inside.

C.C. huffs in behind me, heels clicking on the marble floor.

When I touch the switch on the wall, the apartment is instantly bathed in a warm glow. Soft jazz begins to play. A blessing—any other time I might have been jamming out to Lady Gaga or singing off-key to CeLo. I bite my bottom lip to stifle a giggle. There's no way Alton's mother would approve of "The Lady Killer" or any of his other songs, laced with lyrics that would make Beyoncé blush.

"Can I get you a glass of water? Make some coffee?" I offer.

C.C. presses her lips together disapprovingly, as if I've offered her swamp juice with bits of twigs floating on top. She shakes her head and trots over to the sofa.

"How about some nice tea?" I don't wait for a response, just trot to the kitchen to retrieve two glasses, the pitcher, and a pile of sweetener packets. When I reach for the tray and catch my reflection in the mirrored silver, I remember I am still wearing the trench coat. C.C. must think I'm mad.

I chew on my bottom lip and shake my head. Thankfully, she's too preoccupied with Precious to care. And there's no time to change now.

When I return, C.C. sits on the sofa's edge and pats the cushion next to her. "Come now, Searcy, let's have a little talk. Mother-in-law to...daughter." She clears her throat delicately, looking as if the idea makes her ill.

I've never been good enough. No one could be. Not even Kate Middleton—before she married Prince William.

"Searcy," C.C. repeats.

Propelled like someone's lit a match behind me, I set down the tray and hurry to join her. I take a place across from her, a safe distance, I think.

With a sigh, she picks up a handful of Stevia packets, counts out eight and rips them open. I watch in horror as she proceeds to dump them, one by one, into the waiting glass.

Blech.

"But first, aren't you forgetting something?" she prompts.

I blink. My mind empties of anything logical. With a start, I reach for the teaspoon and hand it to her. "Here you are," I smile.

After scrutinizing me, she takes the utensil and stirs. C.C.'s carefully-Botoxed brow knits together a quarter-inch. Then, she lifts up the dog and holds her out to me.

I shrink back. Surely, she doesn't want me to take her.

C.C. clears her throat. "You need to apologize. This poor baby's feelings are hurt. You frightened her," she chides. My mother-in-law raises an eyebrow, waiting.

A giggle rises up in my throat. It starts to escape, but I make it into a cough. Of course, this scares the darn rat-creature a second time.

When I stop hacking and gather my breath, I swallow.

I can do this. I can talk to this rat-dog without laughing. I can do it for Alton.

"Precious," I begin. "I'm sorry for frightening you. I didn't intend..." My voice trails off. I have no idea what to say to a dog.

C.C. nods for me to continue.

What does she want, a whole speech?

Another beat. Of course she does.

I choke back any hold on reality and dive headlong into C.C.'s fantasy world.

"Of course, I will be more careful in the future," I hesitate, summoning all of the B.S. I can manage. "You are a sensitive, wonderful member of our...family. You light up a room when you enter it. Your...beauty is deep, inside and out." I want to vomit. "I am so glad that we are sisters," I finish with flourish.

"Sisters-in-law," C.C. corrects me. But her thin, pointy shoulders relax, and my ridiculous speech seems to pacify and soothe her. *Thank the stars.* I continue perching on the end of the sofa, hoping she'll get to the point.

C.C., instead, chooses to launch into a description of Precious's harrowing journey from her birthplace in Europe to the Atlanta-Hartsfield Airport. Apparently, she had to purchase Precious across the pond, as the American breed is much too common these days. She describes the pooch's bloodline, and explains that her real name is something having to do with "Queen of Rubies, Jeweled Crown of the Heavens, Precious Delight."

That might not be an exact translation, however, because I am too busy watching Precious ease out of C.C.'s bejeweled pink bag. First her nose, then one brown paw. Her head pokes out and she sniffs the air nervously. Precious, predisposed to a nervous condition, shakes all over as she slips from the bag onto my white couch cushion.

"Does Precious need to, um, tee-tee?" I ask, not wanting to use the incorrect terminology for puppy waste.

C.C.'s thin red lips twist. "Oh, darling, Precious tells me. Only the finest European trainers worked with her. She communicates her every need." My mother-in-law raises her chin.

I attempt to focus on C.C., nodding all the while, but can't help darting an occasional glance at the dog's quivering frame.

"One bark means she needs a nibble of food. Two barks indicate she's thirsty. And three barks means that Precious needs to use the potty."

The second C.C. says potty, Precious jumps from the sofa, squats, and relieves herself on our 100-year-old Persian rug.

A gasp of dismay escapes my lips and I wrench my eyes back to my mother-in-law, forcing a pleasant expression. *Damn that dog.* I have to get C.C. out of here.

"And these trainers?" I ask, leaning forward to get a better vantage point. Precious is now prancing toward the other side of the room, almost out of view. She pauses and sniffs the fringe on the edge of our brand new overstuffed chair. "How do they teach a puppy to behave?"

C.C. puffs up. "Oh, you can't imagine the hours they spend working with the animals. Weeks, in fact. Precious would never bite or scratch. It's not in her nature, Searcy."

From the corner of my eye, I watch the rat-animal latch onto the chair trim, pulling and tugging the edge of the stitching. It's all I can do not to scream.

"How marvelous," I chirp, digging my fingernails into the palm of my hand.

With a rip, the entire length of the trim breaks free. The sudden release sends the dog tumbling end-over-end, straight into a nearby table leg. For a moment, Precious doesn't move.

C.C., who's deaf in one ear, doesn't hear a thing.

"You must be so proud," I say, stealing a glance at the puppy.

After a moment, all four paws wriggle. Precious picks herself up, shakes, and trots away.

Oh. My. Lord.

"So, tell me," I say quickly. "It's such a wonderful surprise to see you and Precious. Are you in the neighborhood to visit friends?"

My mother-in-law shakes her head. "No, dear. I'm concerned about Alton."

Finally, we're getting somewhere.

"Alton?" I feign surprise. "What ever do you mean?"

I hear a slight scratching from the corner of the room. Where is that rat-dog? I sit up taller and crane my neck slightly.

"Alton's not calling me. He's so busy," she sighs, fluttering her fingertips to fix her diamond-encrusted bracelet on her emaciated wrist. "Traveling all of the time. Meetings. I haven't seen him in weeks."

Tell me about it. Then the thought strikes me. With the exception of last weekend, he's been over to his mother's every Sunday after church. It's their routine.

A chill streaks up my spine. He hasn't been with her, or home, or on a trip.

"I just don't feel as connected as we used to be." C.C. readjusts her slim frame and sighs. She seems honestly dejected. Maybe this is the moment I've been waiting for. Finally, a time that we can bond as mother and daughter. Oh, right. *Daughter-in-law.*

"Oh, I share..." I begin to say.

A gnawing sound interrupts my expression of empathy. There's a crash. Biting, growling, and grinding follow.

Precious. She's knocked over Alton's prized statue of a cowboy on his horse by Frederic Remington. The one that took him seven years to find at auction. We paid a small fortune for it.

When she realizes she can't sink her teeth into bronze, she goes after the antique mahogany pedestal stand.

"It's not a chew toy," I yell and jump up from the sofa, sending the sweet tea, my crystal pitcher, and the silver teaspoon flying.

The glass shatters everywhere.

From across the room, pausing from her destruction, Precious begins to yip and growl. Seconds later, the animal peeks around the corner, spits out a shard of wood, and stares at me.

I don't make a sound.

C.C., however, utters a howl of anguish worthy of a child getting his first shots at the pediatrician's office. She's covered with a splatter of tea on both pant legs.

Very slowly, her gaze travels from my toes to my face.

"How could you?" she lashes out at me, eyes narrowed. "What's gotten into you, Searcy?"

Precious begins to whine and duck her head.

"I didn't mean—"

"I know that you didn't come from much," she snaps. "Your mother's a hippie. You grew up in that strange little cottage. And Lord knows where your father is. Or who he is, for that matter."

C.C. might as well have slapped me across the face. Mama's always been kind to this woman. *Always*. I can't fathom insulting anyone about something this personal and painful.

She sniffs. "That's neither here nor there, really. But you're married to my son. You are a reflection on me, and the family name. I expect more from you."

I am appalled. Everyone knows that she thinks she's superior—I just never expected such hateful, awful words to cross her lips.

"And now, you're acting just as strangely as Alton. What is wrong with the two of you? If I didn't know better, I'd swear the both of you are taking drugs."

The rat-dog barks in approval from her hiding place. *Chicken.*

C.C. manages to stand up on her skeleton legs and balance. With a sniff, she brushes off the drops of tea, flicking the brown liquid on my white sofa. She stalks past me, searching for the animal. "Mama's Precious, where are you? Did that Searcy scare you again, darling?"

Precious takes a step into the open, sits prettily, and gazes up at C.C.

"Oh, there you are. Good girl."

I watch as my mother-in-law scoops up the puppy, deposits her into the bag, and turns for the door. C.C. changes her mind and faces me instead.

"Searcy, I did come here to talk to you. To share my feelings. To voice concern about my son and your marriage," she says, barely able to catch her breath. "And this is the thanks I get."

Flushing, I raise my eyes. There's not a smidgen of warmth on her face.

"This is your fault. Whatever's wrong with Alton," she whispers. "He's always been...a different boy. But something's really not right now. He's changed."

Ask him, I want to say. *Tell him your concerns.* But I say nothing.

"Fix it, Searcy," she adds. "It's all up to you. A wife supports her husband. No matter what. Know that I'm holding *you* personally responsible."

I wince.

"And one more thing." She sniffs dismissively. "If you think a garter belt under that trench coat is going to fix your marriage, think again."

Chapter 8

The door slams behind C.C.

"What a horrible, horrible woman," I exclaim out loud, pressing a hand to my forehead while I race toward the cleaning supplies. Any thoughts of owning a cute little pet are firmly out the window, along with dreams of vacationing in Madrid or the South of France with Alton's mother.

Armed with towels and a bottle of organic cleaner, I attack every surface in the living room, squeezing the trigger pump until my hand hurts. I blot the carpet and vacuum next, eyeing the ripped chair trim. Then, I pause and put a hand on my hip.

Alton can't see this. He'll freak—even if it's not my fault.
What would Martha Stewart do?

All at once, I have a flash of inspiration. I dash to a nearby drawer and grab the stapler. Bending down, I hold the silver trim in place and go to work. After puncturing the upholstery a dozen times, I stand back, barely able see the row of thin metal strips.

Yay! I practically hug myself in delight.

Now, for the statue and wooden stand. As I pull out the desk drawer to replace the stapler, my gaze falls on Super Glue and a brown Sharpie marker.

Brilliant!

Five minutes later, the antique stand looks almost brand-new. Carefully, I set the statue on top, hiding the bent parts as best I can. For added protection, I move one of the huge potted ferns, angling the fronds so that they drape lovingly against the statue and stand. *There.*

Flushed with relief, I sink into the nearest seat, tuck my legs up under themselves and pull a cashmere throw over my body. I'm almost trembling with exhaustion.

Just a little nap. I'll have time to shower and change in a bit.

I close my eyes and drift off.

In a sleepy fog, I think I hear the key turn in the lock.

My eyes blink wide open. I hear a footstep. *Alton's.* As is his habit, my husband puts his keys on the table, sets his briefcase on the counter, and slips off his shoes.

I know I must look a fright, but I sit up straight, pinch my cheeks, and smooth my hair, hoping it looks more sexy-tousled than complete bed-head.

"Searcy?" he asks, padding into the room. "What in the world?"

"Long story," I say, adjusting the belt of my overcoat.

Alton comes closer. He reaches out a hand and touches my cheek. "You look like someone scrubbed you with a scouring pad."

"Perfumed lotion. Saks."

He raises an eyebrow.

"I wasn't thinking," I explain with a shrug. "And it didn't happen right away. I felt fine until I stopped by your office and started talking to Pamela."

Alton makes a face. "Pamela?"

"I came to see you," I admit, lifting my chin slightly. "And Pamela wasn't so bad. We bonded, actually." I flash him a small, triumphant smile.

Now my husband really looks shocked.

"We were commiserating, actually." I cross my arms and give Alton a stern look.

Alton rolls his eyes. "Whatever, Searcy. She's a cougar. One of those insatiable, *Sex in the City* girls that eats men for dinner. And then has a few more for dessert."

This makes me grin. He's clearly not interested in the Python. I'm so relieved my knees practically turn to rubber.

Alton squints at me, then, finally taking in the outfit. "What's with the coat? Planning on going out?"

It's the perfect lead-in to my sexy seduction routine.

I shake my head. "Hoping to stay in," I reply with a coy wink. Slowly, I untie the belt, release every button, shrug off the sleeves, and let the material fall to the floor around my ankles.

My husband doesn't take a step. In any direction.

I'm wearing nothing but a teeny-tiny red bra and panties. The set is trimmed with lace, and accented with little bows.

Alton, completely unfazed, acts like I'm wearing a ribbed turtleneck and plaid polyester pants from a terrible sixties movie.

"Searcy."

"Alton," I pout. "Come and get me."

He still doesn't move.

"Searcy," he repeats. Alton's voice is husky. He grabs a pillow from the sofa and presses it to my chest.

Mistakenly, I think he wants to play. I take one of the pillows by the tassel and thwack him in the derriere. I can inject some *Fifty Shades of Grey* into our marriage, if that's what Alton needs. My mind buzzes with possibilities—toys, fur handcuffs, thigh-high Prada leather boots for me—it could all work out very nicely.

But when I inch toward him, Alton eases back further and puts a hand up.

"I thought I explained."

"You were tired," I argue. "I was exhausted and worried about you. I don't think either of us was thinking clearly."

"I was," he says.

"Alton, you're so funny," I say lightly. "Come to bed," I laugh and reach out a finger to poke him gently.

He catches my hand and squeezes. He doesn't let go. The pressure makes me stop and catch my breath. When I look up, his eyes are trained on my face, unwavering and serious.

"No."

Pressing my lips tight, I pick up the cashmere throw and wrap it around my body like a sarong. "Then what is it?" I plead. "Let's take an amazing vacation. Go to the islands." My voice rises. "We haven't had enough time together. We could go to the mountains or the Outer Banks. How about Savannah?"

My husband waits until I run out of breath.

"Searcy," he says. "Let's be honest with each other. Our marriage has been over for a long time. We want different things."

Blood roars in my ears and I fight to remain calm. "I don't believe that," I say, shaking. "We're a team. We've always been a team."

Alton stares at the floor.

I take my husband's cheek in my hand and make him look at me. "When people made fun of me because Mama worked three jobs, you stood up for me," I say. "When I had to wear thrift store clothes, you didn't care. And when Mama started *Pie Girls* to pay for my braces, you made sure the entire class hung out there after school—"

"She didn't need my help," Alton interjects. "Her baking is incredible."

"But you cared," I argue back. "You made everything better. You took me shopping, introduced me to everyone. You took me to parties and made me feel special. When I became your girlfriend, everything changed. I was popular. Suddenly, I was pretty."

"You were always pretty," Alton says, shaking his head.

A sob catches in my throat.

"You still don't believe in yourself, Searcy," Alton whispers.

"I believe in us," I retort stubbornly. "We had a plan—leave Fairhope together. Start our own lives and leave the past behind. Take the world by storm, the two of us."

Alton doesn't argue.

"See?" I plead.

"Searcy," he repeats. "I know what I said, but I've changed my mind."

I press my lips together and grip my hands together, trying not to burst into tears. This is not at all going like I planned.

"Where will you go? What will you do?" I ask, my pulse beginning to race.

Alton glances around the apartment and then, back at me. "This is my mother's place. I won't be able to afford it. And I can't afford to keep you in it. She'll have to have it back."

I let out a gasp. "What ever do you mean? You must be joking. Where will I live? I don't understand."

The room is ice-cold and silent after I've finished my rant.

"I'm not sure where you'll live, Searcy. But I'll help you." Alton leans back against the sofa. "This might be difficult for you to understand, but I've joined an Ashram. I'll be there—living and working—for at least six months."

Six months?

After finding the paperwork in his briefcase, I was prepared for Alton to spend a week or two away. A mini-escape. Get the whole yoga and one-with-nature thing out of his system. Time to refresh and recharge. But half a year?

"Living and working at an Ashram for six months?" I say slowly, wrinkling my nose. "Why would you do that? What ever for?" My head feels like it's been pumped full of helium, and my voice comes out in a squeak. "But what about your career and your clients? Don't you care about the firm and everything you've worked for?"

I can't even listen to my own questions. Nothing makes sense. *What is Alton thinking? Has he gone insane?* I begin wringing my hands.

"Searcy," Alton says, raising his voice. "Stop. You're acting hysterical."

"Just take a leave of absence. We can live on our savings, right? Maybe that's what you need to do—"

"Stop it, Searcy!" Alton cuts me off. "I'm not going back to advertising. I'm done. I've thought this through and I'll take care of you the best I can. It's not going to be easy, I'll admit that. There are going to have to be a lot of changes."

The room suddenly feels twenty degrees warmer.

"Changes," I repeat, thinking about my shopping spree.

"First of all, the credit card is a little out of control. So while we're in this transition, you can't go out to lunch every day with Phillipa. And no more personal shopper."

Is Alton trying to destroy me? *How will I live? What will I tell my friends?*

"I don't understand."

"I know this is very hard," Alton says gently.

I shake my head violently. "Let's go to marriage counseling, then. We can fix this," I plead, his mother's words from earlier today echoing in my mind. It's up to me.

Alton draws a breath. "Searcy, I think I'm in love with someone else."

My brain goes static, buzzing with white noise. I blink and try to focus on Alton.

It can't be. He loves ME. We're married. We promised forever.

"Are you saying that y-you've had an affair?" I ask, stuttering out the question. "Because we could go to therapy. Couples therapy. Plenty of people—"

Alton shakes his head. "I haven't been unfaithful."

Disbelief and desperation take over.

My stomach contracts. I press a hand to my belly, trying to quiet the churning inside my abdomen. I can't hold back. Tears run down my cheeks.

Alton heaves a sigh. He turns and strides over to his briefcase, extracting a thick envelope. "I've done a lot of thinking about this. About my promise to take care of you," he says quietly. Finally, he turns and walks back toward me. When he holds out the envelope, I see my name written in the center in dark, careful lettering.

I shake my head. "No."

"Please, just read it," Alton says. "It's my plan. You'll be fine, at least for a while. Until you can figure out what you want to do."

"What I want to do is stay married," I argue, practically stomping my foot.

With a sigh, Alton clutches the envelope tighter. "I'll leave it in the office."

As he leaves the room, my eyes skim the apartment. I'm desperate, seeking something, clinging to any memory or meaningful part of our life that will make him come to his senses. Across the room, I find it.

Mimi's baby shower invitation. It's adorable and yellow, with ribbons and scrolls across the announcement.

A surge of hope courses through me. It's the perfect solution.

Alton won't leave. Surely. Not with two people depending on him.

Holding tight to the cashmere throw, I walk toward my husband. With a deep breath, I form my plan.

"Please sit down for a moment and listen to me," I say. "Give me five minutes.

Alton turns toward me and wrinkles his forehead.

"I think I deserve five minutes," I continue. "It's important."

Surprisingly, he sinks into the office chair, looks up at me with red-rimmed eyes, and waits.

"Darling, listen," I begin. "I've had something to tell you for a while now. But we've been so busy, and I've wanted to make sure that everything was okay. That I was perfectly healthy."

Alton raises an eyebrow. I have his full attention.

"It's so exciting," I say, almost breathless. "You're going to be a daddy!"

CHAPTER 9

I wait, impatiently, for Alton to jump up, take me in his arms and kiss me full on the lips. It'll happen any second now. He's in shock.

"A baby, darling," I say, sliding next to him on the sofa. I give his leg a squeeze. "Can you imagine? The two of us, parents?"

Alton blinks at me, his eyes wide.

It's okay, I tell myself. He's just drinking it all in. Absorbing the news. Keep talking, Searcy.

"There's so much to do," I babble on, "we'll have to set up a nursery, buy car seats, pick out a stroller, and shop for baby clothes. Wait until we break the news to C.C. She'll be over the moon, won't she?" I beam at my husband proudly.

Alton swallows, shaking his head. I can tell he's calculating, running the timeline through his brain.

I press a hand to my heart. *Don't do the math. Don't do the math.*

"I'm so sorry I didn't say something sooner. With all of the risk of the first few months, and miscarriage, I didn't want to get your hopes up. You've been working so hard. You've been out of town. I didn't want to worry you," I say, rushing to explain.

"But what about your birth control?" Alton asks, his voice raising an octave.

My jaw drops slightly. Oh, that. *Crap.* My mind zigs and zags, searching for a viable explanation.

I drop my eyes. "Oh, I'm so silly. I stopped taking the pills a while back. Remember when I was so sick a few months ago? I thought it was the flu? Well, I went to the Ob/Gyn and she decided that the birth control was making me a little nauseous," I add. "So she asked me to take a little break, and we'd try something new once my body had time to regulate."

"Why didn't you share that with me, Searcy?" Alton asks, frowning.

"I'll do better, I promise," I say, sliding my hand into his and giving it a squeeze. "I won't keep anything from you ever again."

"It is important to be *honest*," my husband says, emphasizing the last word. He looks straight into my eyes.

"Absolutely," I say. My voice cracks a little bit and I cross my fingers under my leg, hoping the apartment doesn't get hit by lightening in the next few minutes. Surely a few white lies to save my marriage are well within my rights.

My husband shifts awkwardly on the sofa.

I remind myself to give him a little time to adjust to the idea. Meanwhile, I have to figure out whether to pursue an emergency adoption once we get our marriage patched back together. Perhaps I can talk Phillipa into borrowing her baby. I'll have to start padding my clothes soon.

Alton clears his throat. "Since we're talking about being honest," he says. "I have something that I need to share with you, too."

"Anything," I say, nodding emphatically.

"It's medical in nature," he begins, "And I should have talked to you about it before I saw my doctor."

I suck in a breath. "Darling, are you okay?" Worst-care scenarios fill my head. Cancer. Dementia. Bi-Polar disorder. Depression. All might explain his weird disappearance and his misguided unhappiness with our marriage.

Alton's lips twitch the slightest bit. "Healthy as ever. I'm fine."

My heart begins beating again. "Thank goodness."

"But are you sure that the baby's mine?"

I feel faint and the room starts to tilt and swim. "Whatever are you talking about?" I demand, doing my best to sound indignant. "Of course it's *ours*."

Alton turns his body to face mine. "I'm asking, because it's impossible," he explains.

My lips part. I try to form words. What is he trying to tell me?

"Searcy," Alton leans closer. "I had a vasectomy. Six months ago."

"What?" I squeak. "How? When?"

"You were in California with Phillipa."

My hands begin to quiver. I brace myself on the sofa. *Vasectomy?*

Six. Months. Ago.

I feel sick. I want to throw up. Or launch myself out the window.

My husband's gaze doesn't waver. He's serious.

"You see," Alton continues gently. "The baby can't be mine."

I can't speak or take a breath. All at once, I am furious. How dare he do this to me? Of all of the underhanded, rotten, selfish things to do to a wife. How could he take this away from me? From us?

Usually, I'm a calm, rational person. But without another thought, my right hand clenches into a fist. My fingers curl tight and the tips press into my palm. My arm bends at the elbow and I draw my body back, gathering momentum.

I take aim.

As my fist jets through the air, cutting a path straight for my husband's gorgeous face, everything screams to a slow-motion finish.

His face registers a mix of doubt, surprise, and then...in the last second...out-right terror.

I punch Alton square in the mouth.

Blood spurts everywhere.

In seconds, the living room looks like a movie set from the *Silence of the Lambs*, part II. The dark red stains his mouth and chin, drips over his hand. There are spatters from the initial blow, and when I look down, my trench coat is decorated with tiny droplets.

I don't register any sound until Alton shakes me.

"Searcy," he yells. It actually comes out more like "Smercee" because his hand's mashing his nostrils and mouth.

The reality of what I've done finally registers. I jump up and bang my knee straight into the coffee table. "Ow!" I wince, and then turn back to my wounded husband, who's now lying back against the white sofa.

I bend down, near his face to get a closer look.

"Alton, I'm sorry. Oh no, oh no."

He shrinks away.

Oh my Lord. I've really hurt him. In fact, his nose looks out of place and very swollen. The bridge is a bit off center, like one of those massive football player types.

"Smercee," he repeats, pushing me away with his free hand. "Call the doctor."

Of course. I crouch down and search for my iPhone. Where ever did I put it? On hands and knees, I begin crawling around on the hardwood floor. A peek inside my Coach bag reveals nothing. I do a quick-inspect of the outside and almost do a Hail Mary that none of Alton's blood stained the leather.

My husband moans again. I need to hurry.

"Can you call it, sweetheart?" I call out, taking a look under the sofa. When I poke my head up, expectantly, listening for the ring, Alton is glaring at me. He's holding out the phone and I reach for it in trepidation.

"Use mine," he grumbles.

My fingers wrap around the edges and I grip it securely.

Yes, I know this look. I think I've only seen it twice in my lifetime. The first was when I accidentally flushed my Tiffany diamond engagement ring down the toilet—in my defense, I was cleaning it! It cost him three hundred dollars to call the plumber on a weekend and fetch it out.

The other time was...oh, no!

His face has swollen to twice its usual size. And it's slightly purple around his upper lip.

"I'll get you some ice, first," I say and rush out of the room. As fast as I can, I snatch up a dishtowel, fill it with chips from the ice maker, secure it with a rubber band and sprint back into the room.

"Here you go, Alton," I whisper. His eyes are closed and he seems to have relaxed a bit. His shoulders aren't all hunched up around his ears like before. C.C. would have an absolute fit at the sight of her son sprawled out like he's just finished a drunken all-nighter.

I lower the ice onto his face.

At the touch of the frozen towel, Alton springs off the sofa. "Argh!" he roars, finally ripping his hand away from his nose and mouth. "Why did you do that? It's freezing."

I've somehow backed up into the corner by the wooden statue. "Um, I-I...the swelling. Everyone says that cold helps. I thought..."

He's staring at me, chest heaving.

"Alton, put the ice on your face," I point at the bag. Maybe if I move and talk really slowly, he'll do what I say. Kind of like communicating with an animal in the jungle. The tiger feels trapped. Maybe he's hurt. The safari person doesn't do anything scary. He moves carefully, talks quietly. The beast—Alton—calms down.

He finally acquiesces. Like a little boy, he pokes his bottom lip out and lowers his eyes as he draws the ice up to his face.

"There you go," I murmur. "Now, I'm going to call the doctor."

Gingerly, Alton sits. "Don't move," I say and concentrate on my husband's iPhone.

I stop. He certainly has a lot of calls from this Thomas person. And he makes a lot of calls to Thomas, also.

My finger hovers over the list of contacts. "Who's Thomas?" I ask and screw up my face into a frown. "Is he from the office? One of your new ad execs?"

"Smercee," Alton heaves a sigh. "Just call."

My head jerks up. "Of course." He's had to remove the ice from his mouth and nose to remind me to stay on task. I'm worried about some guy named Thomas when I've broken Alton's nose.

As I get ready to dial, Alton removes the ice pack, puts a hand on the side of his face, opens his mouth, and wiggles his jaw.

Oh my gosh.

I stare, horrified. I'm almost certain one of his front teeth is missing.

Horrible, awful thoughts ping through my brain. His gorgeous smile, ruined. All of that money that C.C. spent on clear braces and retainers.

The ice pack is back on his face.

But then Alton realizes that I'm mesmerized.

"Whamph?" comes the muffled question. His brow is knit together, tight.

My lips dry up like parchment. I don't think I can tell him. I'm not sure if I actually saw what I *think* I did.

I swallow.

Alton tips his head and narrows his eyes. His face is turning dark red again.

Do something, Searcy. Say something.

"Um, there's a slight possibility we'll need someone else in addition to the doctor," I mumble.

My husband raises his eyebrows and gestures for me to finish my sentence.

I can barely form the words in my mouth. No, I can't say it out loud. Not until I'm sure.

"Let me look, please," I say, trying to remain calm for Alton's sake as well as my own. No sense panicking if, well, there's nothing to panic about, right?

He doesn't move the ice pack.

"I won't touch you, Alton, I promise," I plead, making a sweeping cross-sign across my chest and pushing my palms into prayer position. "Cross my heart."

Behind the dishtowel, I see his mouth twitch a little at my fourth-grade reference.

"It's your teeth," I explain and scoot an inch or two closer. "I want to make sure that they're okay."

He nods and lowers the bag of ice from his face.

I conceal my reaction to the ghastly image his face projects. The bottom half of his face looks like a cross between Freddy Kruger and the Elephant Man. Heart beating almost out of my chest, I lean in.

"Now, can you open your lips the slightest bit?"

His mouth, encrusted with blood, parts a few millimeters. Like rusty hinges opening for the first time in a hundred years, Alton forces his jaw apart a little wider.

And I can't help it.

I gasp out loud.

His right front tooth is gone.

The ice pack is back in place before I can stop myself.

Alton presses a hand into my forearm. He tightens his grip for emphasis. "Wham isim?" *What is it?*

"I-I" I am trying desperately to not burst into tears.

My husband shakes his head in frustration and attempts to get up from the sofa.

"Don't," I cry out, clinging to his hand. My fingertips miss and he's across the room and striding toward the long hall mirror. The one with the perfect lighting. I know because I stop in front of it every time just before I leave the apartment. When I twirl the right way, I can catch even the slightest hair out of place.

I summon my strongest, sternest voice. The one I use when Alton's done something really wrong. Like the time he bought me pink roses instead of red for our anniversary. I was so angry.

"Alton, stop," I yell.

That works.

He turns and faces me, shoulders back, indignant. "Thell me, tlen." *Tell me, then.*

"Um," I begin, trying to decide how to explain it lightly, without injecting sheer panic into my explanation. "It's your tooth. It's missing."

Alton turns pale. He stands quite still, like someone's frozen him with a ray gun from Star Trek. Then, he wobbles a bit, just to let me know he's still alive.

My fingers grip the back of the sofa to steady myself. Another thought hits me. The tooth. If it's not in his mouth, where is it? I smother my own face with both hands, kneading my forehead. When I remove them and look up, Alton's staring into the mirror. Very calmly.

He's examining his open mouth, his jawline. He's looking at his nose, touching the tip of it. Carefully.

I squat down and check the floor for a shiny white piece of enamel and spots of blood.

"Smercee. Phone."

I stand up and scramble to grab it. "Here," I say and hold out his cell.

"Havmph to go."

"I'll drive you." Pursing my lips, I nod, still looking around the room desperately for a tooth to appear in a corner of the room or under a chair or table.

"Stop," he mumbles through thick lips. "I swallowph it."

I almost choke. "Let's go," I say, taking his elbow and starting to walk toward the door. "We'll call the dentist on the way. He'll know what to do."

"NO!" Alton shakes free of my grasp. He holds out his hand to block me.

"But, I want to help," I plead.

Alton clenches his fists at his side. "Haven't youmph done nough?"

For the second time today, the door to my own apartment slams in my face.

Chapter 10

I haven't left the apartment for three days. The weather's awful. It's stormed every day—giant, violent rain showers peppered by flashes of lightning and booms of thunder. People are driving like crazy maniacs. Every few hours there's the wail of another siren.

If I did decide to venture out, with my luck, I'd get hit by a car and end up in the hospital with two broken legs. I might run into someone I know. And they'd ask me about Alton. Or why I haven't been shopping. Or running to parties. Or gossiping at lunch with Phillipa and Mimi.

Besides, I haven't showered.

Really, I haven't needed to. I've barely moved off the sofa. Unless the door rings, and that's just to grab dinner—and lunch—from the string of delivery guys.

There are Chinese take-out boxes littered around the kitchen. I've had pizza, followed by sushi, and several orders of Thai food. I think the man from Won's True Thai Kitchen thinks he's my new best friend.

I've made microwave popcorn, finished off every can of Diet Coke in the Sub-Zero, and discovered a semi-stale bag of Fritos that Alton must have stashed in the back of the cabinets a few weeks earlier. They weren't that bad with salsa.

Also, so as not to waste it, I finished off the chess pie I so painstakingly made for our anniversary dinner.

In a valiant effort to forget about Alton, his vasectomy, and our failed marriage, I've also cut off all communication with society. I haven't checked my phone. I'm ignoring my email. I'm not reading happy updates about birthdays, anniversaries, and parties. I'm not staring at sappy pictures of loving couples gazing into each other's eyes.

Instead, I've watched re-runs of every Rogers and Hammerstein movie every made. It's a bit of a relief that I can finally sing the words of every song from *West Side Story*. It's always bothered me that I couldn't keep up with Anita in "America."

Unfortunately, none of it's helping.

I'm almost grateful when the doorbell rings.

I can think about lunch instead of Alton. I'm trying the new Indian place a few blocks away. After scanning their menu online, I ordered three different entrees. I can have one for lunch, one for dinner, and an extra meal in case I don't like one of the first two choices.

The delivery guy rings the doorbell again. He knocks. Impatiently.

I snatch up my wallet, snap it open, and count the bills.

Another knock. Someone is calling my name.

That's funny. I only gave the restaurant my *last* name. Roberts. And they've never been here before.

There's another muffled yell. "Searcy! Are you in there?"

Another voice, this one higher pitched. "Please come out. We're worried about you. You're not answering your phone."

Panic clutches at my heart. It's Phillipa. And Mimi.

What ever are they doing here? Then, my eyes mist over. They're worried. Someone cares. I sniff back tears and stride to the door, ready to throw it open and embrace my lovely friends.

Then, as I walk through the foyer, I catch a glimpse of my reflection.

I almost yelp in dismay.

Who is the creature staring back at me? I clutch at my chest, and the girl in the reflection does the same. I shake my head. She does, too.

Oh, my goodness. I'm puffy. My face is breaking out. My hair is absolutely hanging in clumpy, greasy strands. My eyes are red-rimmed and my skin is horribly blotchy.

My clothing is wrinkled and stained where I've spilled sauce and pie crust.

I can't answer the door.

Think. Think.

"I'm fine," I call out brightly, pressing a hand to the door as if my friends might come barreling through.

"Open up, then," Phillipa commands. "Stop being so silly."

"I-I can't, sweetie," I reply hastily.

"What ever is the matter?" Mimi calls through the wooden barrier. She's trying the doorknob.

"I'm really ill," I say, making myself hack and cough. "Some kind of terrible flu. I've been in bed for days."

"Let us come in, Searcy. We can help," says Mimi.

I press my forehead against the door and cross my fingers behind my back. I don't like to lie, but it's necessary under the circumstances. I can't let anyone see me like this.

"I'm contagious," I add. "You have to think of the baby."

This information gets met with silence. Then, I hear my friends whispering. *Ah-ha!* I've got them! *Whew.*

"All right," says Phillipa. "Get some rest, okay?" She's not totally convinced, from the sound of her voice.

I cough a few more times for good measure. My throat is actually beginning to hurt with all of this acting.

"Feel better," adds Mimi. She sounds absolutely dejected that I didn't let her in. She's probably crazy-emotional, being in the last six weeks of pregnancy. My heart pangs at the thought of hurting her feelings.

"I will," I promise, still crossing my fingers. "As soon as the doctor says it's okay."

"Is Alton there?" Mimi asks. "Is he helping?"

"Oh," I make myself giggle and then cough. "He had to fly to New York. Some emergency with a big account. He'll be home tonight, barring any unforeseen hiccups. You know how it is in advertising. Busy, busy."

"Right," says Mimi. She says it with a sharp edge, and then waits a beat. "Talk soon, then."

"Bye, love," says Phillipa. "Call as soon as you're better."

"Will do," I say and offer up another good round of hacking just to prove that I'm near death's door.

Holding my breath, I peer through the peephole. The two girls are walking toward the elevator, heads bent together. They're whispering, and Mimi glances back toward my door. She shakes her head, then turns back and presses the down button. I watch until they're safely in the car and the double doors close behind them.

My legs sag. What ever am I going to do? I start to sink down and sit on the floor. I want to collapse and go back to bed. Pull up the covers and not come out.

I'm not safe. They'll come back. And maybe C.C., too, wanting an update on Alton.

A vision of the envelope he left for me flashes in my mind.

I suck in a breath, hold my head up, and walk into the office, determined to be brave.

The envelope, when I pick it up, is heavier than I expected. It's bumpy in one place. I undo the metal clasp, open the flap, and turn the pocket upside down. There's a handwritten note from Alton and another envelope sealed shut.

I open it first. Inside, there's cash. Mostly twenties, a few fifties. In all, a thousand dollars.

The letter lands facedown on the desk. I flip it over and begin to read.

Dear Searcy,
I know that the last few days have been very trying for you. I understand that you are confused about my decisions. Hopefully, when we've both had some time apart,

we'll be able to sit down and talk calmly. I'd like to explain when we're both in a better state of mind.

Know that I care about you and will do my best to take care of you until you can find a job and get on your feet. You are smart and resourceful. I know that you will be okay.

We will need to vacate the apartment in thirty days, as I have signed the property back over to my mother. I will arrange to move your things to whatever address you choose.

In the meantime, I have left you the enclosed cash. I've also arranged to deposit an allowance for you into our bank account. Please, in the meantime, use the credit card only for emergency expenses.

I have asked my attorney to draft up settlement papers, which should be ready in the next ten days. Once you choose a lawyer, I will have them sent to his or her attention for review.

I'm sorry. I hope, someday, you'll understand that this is all for the best.

It was never my intention to hurt you.
Alton

I am speechless. He's actually going through with all of this.

How am I supposed to live? What will I do? Where will I go?

I begin pacing back and forth across the hardwood floor. I've never worked a day in my life. I wouldn't begin to know what to do. Besides, my degree is in hospitality management. I can't throw parties when my life is ending.

I'll never be able to face Phillipa and Mimi.

Now, I am furious.

I'm going to call Alton and give him a piece of my mind. He needs to come home and face me. He can't just decide all of this. Without a thought to my well-being or feelings.

I stomp through the house in search on my iPhone. I turn it back on and wait for it to power up, tapping my toe impatiently.

The screen buzzes to life.

Forty-one calls. Twenty-nine texts. Twelve voicemails.

I pinch my nose at the bridge and will myself not to be hysterical. Ignoring the messages, I dial Alton's number.

There's a strange clicking sound and a recorded message stating that the phone number I've dialed has been disconnected.

I bite my lip. I've just dialed wrong. Or the phone has malfunctioned. I take a breath and try again. Clicks. Same recording. This time, though, someone's beeping in.

My chest tightens with excitement. It's Alton. He's trying to call back. I click over and say a breathless hello.

"Searcy?"

It's not Alton.

"Searcy?" Mama repeats. "Are you there?"

"I'm here," I say brightly, my voice straining the slightest bit. "How are you?"

"Sweetheart! Oh thank goodness," she says breathlessly. "I called yesterday, and when I didn't get you again early this morning, I started to panic."

"I'm sorry." Guilt trickles through my limbs. When was the last time I talked to her? Three weeks ago? Four? Of all people, my sweet Mama doesn't deserve to worry.

I promise myself I'll do better. Call every week. Not be so selfish. She's alone in Fairhope, after all.

"You're okay, though?" Mama persists.

I press a hand to my forehead and look at the ceiling, forcing my lips into a smile. "Everything's great, Mama. Really."

There's a beat of silence. "Well, good. Like I said, I was worried—"

"We've been so busy, and Alton's been traveling. You know how it is," I rush to explain. "And Mimi's baby shower was this week."

Mama exclaims in delight and peppers me with questions about the baby's due date, decorations, and the restaurant.

As I give her the details, I realize that there's something odd about my mother's call. Underlying her cheery tone, there's more. I can sense it.

On cue, Mama changes the subject.

"Searcy, I wanted to ask a favor." She takes a breath. "I'd like you to come and visit, especially since Alton's traveling. Stay for as long as you like. It's our busy season at *Pie Girls*. The shop is a little crazy, even with Tobi and the high school kids pitching in. I could really use the help."

My knee jerk reaction is a total no. Absolutely not. I am not-not-not going back to Fairhope. I reserve that trip for Christmas, or a quick drive-by on the way to New Orleans.

But then, I hesitate. Tobi is my best friend from high school. I haven't seen her—really talked to her—in ages. And Mama is asking for a reason. Maybe she needs help at *Pie Girls*. Maybe not.

And—it is the perfect escape.

I can relax; spend time with Mama and Tobi. Enjoy the water, the beautiful sunsets. I can bake at the shop. I won't have to worry about questions from Phillipa or Mimi or C.C.

No one will bother me. In fact, I won't tell a soul where I'm going. And I don't have to decide how long I'll be gone.

Long enough to formulate a plan, of course. A master plan. Searcy Roberts' life: Part deux.

"I'd love to," I blurt out.

"Really?" Mama says, sounding flabbergasted. "I'm thrilled. That's wonderful. When do you think you can come? You'll have to buy airline tickets and pack."

I do some quick calculating. There's no time like the present.

"I'll be there tomorrow."

CHAPTER 11

After searching for the itinerary that will give Alton the least heartburn—surely he's not including airline tickets in the monthly budget—I book a flight leaving mid-morning. It's direct, Atlanta to Mobile. Knowing Hartsfield traffic, it will likely take longer to find a parking place, drag my luggage to the counter, and go through security than the forty-five minutes the pilot will spend guiding the jet from takeoff to touchdown.

As I won't have time when I wake up, I haul out my Louis Vuitton luggage, four pieces in all, and open my closets. It's spring in the Deep South, so the weather could range from cool sixty degrees in the morning to a steamy afternoon high of eighty-five. I have to plan for anything.

After examining my wardrobe, and not knowing who or what Mama's plans involve, I toss in several party dresses, a few silk blouses, and dressy pants. Eyeing my outerwear, I grab a denim jacket, a light jacket, and a few Pashminas. It's on to the jeans next. I grab six pairs, and then dig through my tops and belts.

Next comes the most difficult part: shoes. I choose my favorite Vera Wang wedges, slip-on Steve Maddens, and two pairs of Jimmy Choos. I hesitate, fingering my buttery-brown leather riding boots, and decide to add them, too, in case my mother decides we need to go for a walk by the Bay.

Purses line the top two shelves of my closet. I usually have to get our stepladder to fully examine everything I own and decide on a matching bag. With a little jump, I manage to knock down my Coach backpack, a Kate Spade clutch, and one Stella McCartney satchel. Perfect.

I finish off with lingerie, though I don't even pretend to try and match up the drawers full of La Perla and Victoria's Secret bras and panties. Just looking at the myriad of colors and lace makes me a bit seasick. I just throw in what I can find.

There's a bit of room left in my carry-on bag, so I pick out the pearls Alton gave me on our last anniversary, my sterling silver Burberry watch, and my favorite Chanel chain.

When I'm finished, I nearly collapse on the bed in exhaustion. I roll my head to one side and look at the clock. 9 p.m. This time tomorrow, I'll be tucked away in my mother's house. Safe from prying eyes, my mother-in-law, and overbearing bosses looking for my husband.

My husband.

Pressing my head against the down pillow that still smells of Alton's skin, I close my eyes, absentmindedly twisting my wedding band under my 3-carat princess-cut engagement ring.

Then, I stop.

Alton's wedding ring.

We'd promised each other we wouldn't take them off. Ever. Of course, I have to draw the line at the ocean and the spa where I get my massages. But even Alton doesn't argue with me locking it up for safekeeping. It's an hour, maybe two, then back on my hand where it belongs. I actually feel quite funny without it. Like a part of me is missing.

I sit up and stare at the facets of my diamond. I adjust my hand ever so slightly, and the stone glints back at me, winking in the darkening room. Like it's keeping a secret.

In an instant, I've rolled out of bed. In two steps, I'm standing on Alton's side of the dresser. His brush is there. His cufflinks. A few bowties. But, there's no ring.

Breath caught in my chest, I dash into the bathroom. Flicking on the lights, I scan the countertops, practically overturning my makeup brushes and perfume bottles.

No platinum band.

Heart thumping, I dash to the living room and check the desk where Alton left me the note. I run my hands over the edges, look under a pile of papers, behind the can holding pens and pencils. Nope. Nothing. It's not here either.

Maybe Alton's still wearing his ring.

Maybe, it's a sign.

My mind begins to race, full speed, with the possibilities.

Then, I stop myself.

I remember our talk. The vasectomy. His letter.

And I remind myself that it's real.

He's gone. And I have to stop living in fantasyland, where dreams come true, people keep promises, and people stay in love forever.

A lone tear trickles down my cheek. Wiping my face, I lay down on the bed and hug a pillow to my chest.

I have to reinvent myself.

And I have no idea where to begin.

The next morning, as if the travel angels are looking out for me, I breeze through my trip to Hartsfield, check my luggage, and walk without incident or pat down through airport security.

The flight's on time, and the plane loads like clockwork. As we take off into the clear blue, I settle back against the seat, close my eyes, and drift off. What seems like moments later, the plane touches down and taxis to the gate.

Within minutes, we're filing out of the jet, walking toward baggage claim and parking.

When we reach the second-floor lobby area, there's a small crowd waiting. Anxious children crowd the waiting area, as do grinning husbands with flowers, and girlfriends holding signs that say, "welcome home."

In a flurry, all around me, travelers embrace family members, hug loved ones, and high-five buddies. There's a positive energy in the space, undeniable happiness, and I can't help but feel a little wistful that Mama isn't waiting for me with an excited wave hello, a huge embrace, and a peck on the cheek.

But that's not Mama. If I have to guess, she's running a little late and has just pulled up outside.

I walk quickly, rushing to get to the escalator and down to the first floor. The moment I take my place in the furthest corner away from the baggage carousel, the lights hanging from the ceiling begin to flash and a horn starts blasting. The conveyer belt cranks to life and I strain to see if my suitcases are among the first pieces to emerge from the unloading dock.

Clutching my arms tight to my body, I scan golf equipment, one surfboard, brown leather satchels, navy blue duffel bags, and children's suitcases decorated in purple polka-dots and pink stripes. I watch, confidence waning, as the baggage makes a second lap. People pluck luggage from the belt, roll it away. The claim area empties. Soon, there is one lonely bag left. It's shiny bright red, plastic-coated, and definitely not mine.

Worry sets in. And I'm suddenly exhausted.

I take a ragged breath, limp over to the nearest official-looking airport person, and tap him on the shoulder.

He breaks into a broad smile and greets me with a slight bow.

"Yes, ma'am," he says with a thick Southern accent. "Lovely to see you, and welcome to Mobile." He pauses, letting the last word slip off his tongue. Moh-beel. "I do hope you had a pleasant flight. Now, how can I help you, sugah?"

I melt immediately at the man's impeccable manners. Though Atlanta sits well below the Mason-Dixon Line, the city is a melting pot of people from places as far-flung as India or Taiwan. While it makes for interesting mix of cultures and diversity, pleasantries about the weather or a polite inquiry about a person's day—customs intrinsic to the Deep South—are sometimes overlooked as unnecessary, idle chatter.

"I have a terrible emergency," I explain, wringing my hands for emphasis. "My bags are missing. Is it possible they're still on the jet? Flight 408 from Atlanta."

The airport employee doesn't break stride. "Oh, bless your heart. How awful. I'll check on that right away, my dear." He nods and scurries off.

I allow my shoulders to slump in relief. The nice man will fix it. He'll find my bags. I'll be on my way and out of this airport in no time.

"Searcy?" A voice calls out from across the room. "Searcy Roberts?"

I whirl around and scream in delight when I see Tobi standing right in front of me. She's my oldest friend, and it's been quite a while since we've seen each other, but I swear she doesn't look a minute older than the day we graduated. Same sleek chestnut brown hair pulled into a high ponytail, same pink cheeks, wide, brown doe eyes, and long lashes. She's taller than I am, with a curvaceous body born to stop traffic.

I have no idea how she's had three babies and still looks like a younger version of Sofia Vergara.

She squeals and throws out her hands.

"Tobi, oh my goodness!"

We embrace, hugging each other, rocking back and forth like fourth graders. I'm sure we're causing a scene, but I don't care. It's so good to see a familiar face, someone sweet and trustworthy. Someone who knows absolutely nothing about my train-wreck of a life.

"What are you doing here?" I demand as she releases me.

"I'm your ride," she says with a smile. "Playing chauffeur today."

"Ma'am?" The man from baggage claim rushes up. "It took some doing, but I finally located the rascal."

My luggage. I practically jump up and down. "Really? Fabulous!" I want to hug him.

The airline worker takes a step back and makes a tsk-tsk sound. "Oh, bless your heart. It's not the best news, I'm afraid."

Tobi, who's watching the exchange with interest, finally interjects. "The rascal?" she asks. "Did you lose your dog?" She glances around for dog carriers.

I shake my head. "My luggage."

"It's in Albuquerque," the man confesses.

Tobi and I exchange a long look of dismay.

"H-how is that possible?" I ask, feeling my skin break out in goose-bumps. "It was a direct flight. Forty-five minutes. How could my bag end up in New Mexico?"

"We can't stay," Tobi interjects, furrowing her brow.

The man clasps his hands together in front of his chest. "Of course not." He shakes his head vigorously. "It could be days."

"Days?" I squeak. "But it took less than an hour for them to get to Albuquerque."

The airline worker makes the tsk-tsk sound again. "I'm afraid not. The bags are still enroute."

I swallow hard. "Are you sure they're even on that flight?"

The man pauses and puts a finger to the side of his mouth. "Bless your heart, I know this must be terrible. It's our best guess, my dear."

Inside, I am screaming. *Best guess? Enroute?*

"Your mother has clothes," Tobi says abruptly. "Or you can buy some. Surely, Alton, of all people, won't care."

At the sound of my husband's name, I draw back. Yes, I think, as a matter of opinion, he will care. Although, if it's the airline's fault, I might be able to eek out a few hundred dollars and pick up a few things just to get by.

"Where is Alton, anyway?" Tobi interrupts my mental ping-pong, folding her hands across her ample chest.

I stop breathing.

If I start to explain, I'll burst into tears at the airport, in front of God and everyone.

"Oh, you know," I giggle, letting my hands flutter for emphasis. "South America this week, Europe the next. He's just back from Montreal and Beijing. I can barely keep up."

Tobi sighs and shakes her head. "I really couldn't be apart from Nick that long. We've been married forever, but he's my best friend. And the kids would miss him," she says. "I don't know how you do it, Searcy."

"Well—"

"Ma'am, sorry to interrupt," the airline worker says, taking advantage of the awkward pause in conversation. "I need you to fill out a few forms. Full name, contact number, description of the missing luggage." He checks his watch. "And an address where we can deliver the bags."

"If they get here," Tobi says doubtfully, hand on one hip.

I feel a twinge of worry, but refuse to think negatively. "*When* they get here," I say, making myself laugh a little.

What seems like an hour and five forms later, I have writer's cramp and Tobi is practically coming out of her skin. "We're going to be late. I have to get the boys from my sister's house."

"I'm so sorry," I say and rush to scribble the last answers on the page. Tobi is tapping her foot, her forehead creased with worry.

I push the forms back across the counter to the airline employee. "Thank you for your help, sir."

"Have a blessed day, ladies," he smiles and waves.

I link my arm in Tobi's. In less than twenty steps, we are outside. I long to take a deep, cleansing breath, but the air is heavy, humid, and still. Tobi digs in her purse and comes up with a humongous set of keys. There's a huge, dangly peace sign covered in sequins, a braided strap in rainbow colors, and a metal Cinderella's castle that says "Disney World" hanging from the ring.

Not exactly her usual style, but at least she won't lose those keys. Ever.

"This way," she cocks her head for me to follow. "My SUV's in the shop," she explains. "I had to borrow your mother's car. It's right over here. First row. On the end."

Tobi squints and points to the left side of the parking lot. I follow her gaze. There's a dark gray Ford Focus, a white BMW 300 series, and a bright Pepto-Bismol pink Cadillac.

I stop walking.

No. Way. My mother's taste in everything is eclectic, but this vehicle is another story. I say a silent prayer that she's somehow undergone a radical change in taste over the past year and has swung to the completely conservative side. I could even accept my mother in crisp, white, button-down shirts with plaid Bermuda shorts—if it meant this wasn't her car.

"She's something, isn't she?" Tobi jingles the keys for emphasis and winks.

"Um. Which one?" I ask hesitantly, slowing my steps.

There's a row of crystal beads lining the windows, pink rims on the tires, and a pink Cheetah print seat covers with a matching steering wheel. There are two dozen bumper stickers covering the tail end of the Cadillac, ranging from "Co-exist" and "Spay Your Pets" to

"DI" and "30A" magnets representing Dauphin Island and the highway leading to Seaside, Florida.

Tobi grins, knowing full-well that I realize we're about to climb inside the car that would best represent a pimp-mobile in the movies.

It strikes me, then, that I still don't know what exactly is going on. Why is Tobi chauffeuring?

"I really appreciate you picking me up," I begin, attempting to choose my words carefully so as not to seem ungrateful. "But, why isn't Mama here?"

Tobi unlocks the Cadillac and motions for me to enter. This time, she doesn't smile. "It's complicated, Searcy. I think, maybe, that she should explain."

We lock eyes for a moment. Feeling slightly like the worst daughter in the world, I nod. "But she hasn't said a word. Nothing. Not even a hint." My throat tightens.

"Hey, you're here. That's what matters," Tobi says, patting my hand. "Let's go."

With my heart weighing like an iron block in my chest, I slide in.

Tobi cranks the engine, backs up, then puts the car in drive. The Cadillac shimmies and hesitates, then quits.

"Oh my," I say, blinking in dismay.

I settle back against the seat and wait for her to turn the key a second time. The engine sputters again and Tobi punches the accelerator. After a slight whine, the Cadillac lurches forward, practically giving me whiplash. There's another jerk, followed by a second of hesitation.

After a moment, the car backfires. The sound, louder than a dozen firecrackers, makes me jump out of my seat. I grip the door handle and bite the inside of my cheek, drawing blood.

Tobi laughs at my reaction. "Sorry," she says. "Forgot to warn you. Happens all the time, especially when the engine's a bit cold."

I smile back and grip the armrest, hoping we don't launch into outer space next. We go another few miles, and when the car doesn't explode into flames, I allow myself to settle in and absorb the scenery.

As we enter Midtown Mobile, I gaze at the towering antebellum homes lining the street. We pass tall brick mansions and stucco estates with sprawling green lawns. Azealas burst with pink and purple blooms on every corner, shaded by a canopy of live oaks draped with Spanish moss.

Downtown, I note that the Bicycle Shop is still standing, and that Wintzell's Oyster House is bustling. A few cross streets later, I smile at Spot of Tea, one of the city's famous locations for a delicious outdoor breakfast. It's comforting that some things don't change.

We edge around people crossing the street and maneuver over to Government Street and the Bankhead Tunnel. We plunge inside and head underground, bumping along beneath the white-tiled ceiling.

We both exhale as my mother's vehicle emerges into the bright afternoon. Tobi turns right, taking the Bayway, and the car gains speed as we merge with 1-10 traffic. The pink Cadillac gets a few looks and at least one wave from a guy driving a beat-up Chevy pick-up. I smile back and turn my eyes toward the low-lying water on either side of the highway. The small waves shimmer in the afternoon sun, and pelicans circle overhead.

I crack the window slightly and smell the fresh air mixed with marsh and sea grasses. Above us, the blue sky is expansive and cloudless over the Eastern Shore.

We continue down Highway 98 until we reach the turnoff for Fairhope.

On the shore of Mobile Bay, the area boasts an eclectic mix of quaint, century-old summertime cottages and stately, newer homes.

By far, Mama's house stands out as the most colorful and memorable. Decorated in Key West style with plantation shutters, the exterior blends bright sky blue with coral pink and lime green accents. A few pink flamingos line the front yard, much to our neighbors' delight or chagrin. When the wind blows off the Bay, the air fills with the magical sound of Mama's wind chimes. More than a dozen hang from her back porch, by far my favorite place to spend a lazy summer afternoon.

When the cottage comes into view, I see that she's painted the door lilac to match her crepe myrtles. My heart swells at the sight of the front walkway.

Tobi parks the car, reaches over, and squeezes my hand. "Welcome home."

CHAPTER 12

As Tobi drives off, I pause, looking at the house. I am immediately transported back to my childhood. In that instant, I see myself as a six-year old girl in a dress and pigtails, trailing behind my mother up the path to our front door.

It was then, every morning, that my mother and I began baking. Mama would let me mix flour, sprinkle sugar, and drop ripe apple slices onto golden piecrust.

We'd eat piping hot blueberry tarts, fresh from the oven, burning our lips, and wash down the sweet goodness with tall glasses of cold milk.

It was a magical time, free of worry or care. My life seemed fairy tale-perfect, a melt-in-your-mouth confection.

How time changes everything.

I raise my hand to knock, but the door flies open before my knuckles touch the painted wood.

"Searcy, darling," my mother says, wrapping me in a warm hug. I allow myself to melt in her arms, inhaling the scent of jasmine that lingers on her skin.

Taking my hand, she leads me through the house, heading for the back porch, exclaiming all the while how wonderful it is to see me and how long it's been since I've been home.

We settle into the lounge chairs and I sigh in delight at being off my feet.

"Where's your luggage?" she asks. "And Tobi?"

"The airline lost it," I say, trying not to seem upset. "And Tobi—had to run and get her boys."

Mama smiles. "She's a busy girl. Between her husband, her children, and working at the shop, I'm not sure when she has any time for herself."

"I'm glad you have her," I say.

She nods. "I'm very lucky."

It's then, outside in the light, that I notice the changes in Mama. Well-known for her effervescent personality, today my mother is decidedly sedate. She's pale, thinner, and her skin seems almost translucent.

"Mama, are you okay?"

She stifles a yawn. "Sweetie, now that you're here, what could possibly be wrong?" Mama winks at me. "I'm positively tickled to have you visit."

Knowing she'll brush off any concerns, I ask again anyway. "I'm serious. You'd tell me if something was going on?" It's a broad question, but my point is well taken.

Mama waves a hand as if to make my inquiry disappear. "I'm a little tired, Searcy. Nothing I can't catch up on. I'm taking a few days off so that I can rest and spend time with you," she adds.

I'm not convinced at all, but I decide not to press her too much. "Tobi can handle things at the shop?"

Mama nods her head, yawns a second time, and lies back against the sofa. She draws up a throw over her legs. "So, tell me what's new," she asks. "How's Atlanta? How's Phillipa? Mimi? And where's Alton this week?"

Grateful for the change in subject, I gloss over the details, recounting Mimi's baby shower and my latest shopping trip downtown.

"What do you think?" I ask.

Mama doesn't answer.

I glance over. She's sound asleep.

Smiling at the sight, I draw the soft woven blanket over her shoulders. She's breathing heavily, and the light through the window hits her face just right, illuminating my mother's fine features. High cheekbones, full lips, a gentle jaw, and long lashes.

Her hair, still a thick, honey brown, is threaded with hints of silver. For anyone else in the Deep South, the sight would mean a one-way ticket to the hair salon—but Mama is far from conventional.

For as long as I can remember, and much to my own chagrin, my mother has existed in her own world, embracing life on her own terms, while somehow keeping a toe in the world of domestic, refined Southern women.

While my friends' fathers held jobs as lawyers, bankers, and business owners, and their mothers stayed home, Mama often held two or three jobs to make ends meet. As a teenager, I was mortified on a regular basis that she was forced to clean houses, cook meals, bake desserts, or run errands for local families. One summer, she filled in as a salesperson at a music shop. Another, she picked up weekend shifts at Page and Palette bookstore.

I realize now that she sacrificed everything—her time, her youth, even her talents—on making sure I had an excellent education, books to read, and food on the table. Looking back now, I know that there were evenings she skipped dinner so that my own plate would be filled with vegetables and fresh bread. I cringe at the thought of begging for a "real" shopping trip, when all we could afford was a walk to the thrift store.

At the time, I desperately wanted my family to be normal, with a father who wore a seersucker suit and a mother who volunteered at church. I wanted Mama to drive a sleek new car, not ride her beach bike with a basket hitched to the front. And if that didn't seem bad enough, there was Mama's flair for all things artistic and culinary.

Luckily for her, Fairhope, with its galleries, boutiques, and restaurants, couldn't be a better place for my mother to explore her passions. In the evenings, when she finished baking, Mama would spend her time in the backyard, facing a stretched canvas, a paintbrush resting in her right hand. She'd carry a thoughtful expression as she dabbed on midnight blues and heather purples. Her face would light up as she added a swath of poppy red or burnt umber.

Her paintings, abstract and bold, still grace our living room walls. A few pieces garnered regional attention, but the demand on Mama's time was too much.

Orders began to pour in for pies, cakes, and cookies—so much so that Mama had trouble keeping up with her other side jobs. One by one, they fell away. Eventually she packed up her paintbrushes as well, and opened *Pie Girls*.

Though I never asked, I believe Mama christened the bakery with that name because she dreamed of me joining her in the business, eventually.

And why wouldn't she? *Pie Girls* was successful from the start; she soon had to add half a dozen employees, mostly high school or college students with flexible schedules.

My own afternoons and weekends, as a given, were spent at the shop, and I'm happy to report that I wasn't embarrassed at my mother's occupation anymore. I rather enjoyed the work—rolling out dough, slicing ripe strawberries, and smelling the heavenly scent of toasted pecans.

But my head and heart were already gone, far away from Fairhope. Although it pleased me to see Mama happy and content, secretly, I didn't want her life. I wanted glamour, and a little excitement. I didn't *ever* want to struggle or work three jobs.

Since sophomore year, I'd made it my life's ambition to win Alton Roberts' heart. Alton, with his cute BMW, pressed khakis, and wealthy family. Alton, with his confidence that came from status and privilege.

Fortunately, once I managed to catch his attention, Alton and I bonded over our mutual desire to escape small town Alabama. He wanted to leave his overbearing parents behind; I wanted to be free of my past.

Senior year, we became the high school 'it' couple. My secondhand clothes suddenly became 'vintage.' Heads turned when I walked by. And I gained more new friends than I could count.

With all of the changes, my life also took on new meaning—improved status—as the daughter of the single, 'super' mom who owned *Pie Girls* bakery.

None of it, however, was enough for me to stay.

I stand up and shake out my hair, running my fingers through to untangle a few strands. As I wander around the cozy space, photographs beckon me forward. Smiling faces, groups of images, Mama usually in the center, me on the periphery.

There are several of Alton and me on our wedding day. He's handsome and dashing in his tuxedo, grinning into the lens, eyes twinkling with mischief. I'm by his side, holding tight to his hands. My Vera Wang dress seems to float as we pose for the photographs in Point Clear. We held the ceremony and reception outdoors on a perfect summer evening.

I held a bouquet tied with tendrils of thick white ribbon, dripping with yellow tulips and roses. My cheeks, pink from the sunshine, match the darker hue of my lips, curved into a smile. I'm glowing with happiness, set off by the sunset behind us—a burst of red below streaks of orange and purple across the Eastern Shore skyline.

The party lasted well into the morning. We danced under a netting of tiny white lights. Candle lanterns hung from tree boughs and fireflies buzzed their appreciation as music floated into the atmosphere. By the time the clock struck two, I'd lost my shoes and was swaying in Alton's arms, my bare feet smooth across the wooden platform.

After kissing Mama goodnight and bidding our guests a giddy farewell, we stole upstairs to the bedroom overlooking the waterfront. I'd saved myself for this wedding night, buying into the old-fashioned principle of forever love. Alton, who'd promised he'd done the same, awkwardly and sweetly undressed me, one tiny button at a time. After slipping off my dress and standing in the glow from the moonlight, he came to me, murmuring into my hair about how beautiful I looked.

Our lips met as we embraced, a cool breeze from the open window bathing our skin. I shivered at the sensation, and allowed Alton to lead me to bed, where he laid me on the sheets like the most fragile china.

He stroked my cheek, planted kisses on my forehead, ears, and neck. I clung to him, arms around his neck as he rolled me onto my back and pressed his weight into me. The exquisite tingle of his skin on mine was euphoric, and my breath quickened as his mouth sought mine hungrily.

"Searcy," he groaned, his lips traveling down my shoulder, finding my breast, and the small of my belly, back to the curve of my neck. In the blur of my emotion, I stroked his hair, closing my eyes.

In the next instant, Alton plunged inside me, taking me with a force and intensity that removed all reality except for the space we inhabited. The initial pain and fullness gave way to pleasure, and my hands clung to his back as we moved together, rising and falling like the waves outside our window.

My pulse sped as he drove deeper inside me, searching. His breath, heavy and hot, filled my ear. I cried out as he plunged one final time, rocketing to a finish.

Alton collapsed beside me, murmuring a desperate "I love you," and tucking his head into the space between my chest and chin. As my fingers traced the muscles on his arms and back, I sighed, content that his words were true.

Within minutes, we fell into a deep sleep, not stirring until morning light streamed through the sheer curtains.

I step back from the photographs, shaking my head against the memory. It was one of the few nights over the course of our marriage that we'd been intimate. That part stung, like the accidental scrape of a knee on concrete; the pain raw, open, and shocking.

Eventually, my heart compartmentalized the damage, healing through various forms of therapy. Shopping, lunch with friends, and exercise became my salve.

I made excuses for Alton. He was busy. He was tired. He was distracted.

Somehow, it was better than admitting defeat. It was my cross to bear, the burden that went along with the covenant of our marriage vows.

And I can't say Alton completely mistreated me. There were flowers on every anniversary, every birthday. Lavish gifts on holidays. Surprise weekend vacations at the beach, excursions abroad, and lovely dinner parties. A life anyone would envy from the outside.

I told myself it didn't matter. I ignored it, then tried discussing it, both to no avail. I cried myself to sleep on countless nights. After several years, I accepted it.

Alton had sought love and attention—whatever he believed was missing—elsewhere.

Until now, I'd been able to convince myself otherwise.

Chapter 13

With Mama asleep and no suitable clothes to change into, I decide a trip to the store is next on my agenda. After a quick inventory of the cupboards, I find most of them empty or close to it. The wooden bowl on the counter, usually brimming with fresh fruit, holds one lonely apple.

As I pull open the pantry, I find only a few cans of corn, beans, and peas, one box of grits, and a glass container of olive oil.

I realize she's only one person, but she's always enjoyed cooking and baking. I frown at the bare shelves. Why isn't Mama shopping?

With a swift movement, I find my purse, dig out a scrap of paper and make a list. No reason I can't fix what's missing—at least in my mother's house.

When I pick up my phone to call Tobi and see about getting the Cadillac back for a few hours, I notice she's already texted.

Car outside. Keys under seat. Back at shop.

I text back a quick thank you, check on Mama one last time, scribble a quick note, and leave the house.

Though I'd prefer to avoid Wal-Mart, it's the easiest option. And right now, I'm thankful Mama's car has a huge trunk and backseat. This shopping trip may break my bank account and damage the shocks on my mother's vehicle.

The second the automatic doors slide open, I'm met by a blue-vested woman. She smiles at me with a broad, open grin.

"Good afternoon and welcome to Wal-Mart," she says, close enough for me to clearly identify the gold-encased star cutouts on each incisor and one front tooth.

"Good afternoon," I say, checking the time on my cell. I don't want to be away from Mama too long.

The greeter steps in front of my path and tips her head. Her hand shoots out, palm open. "That's a nice phone," she says. "Can I see that phone?"

Taken aback, I grip the leather cover with my fingertips and maintain my breathing. The Louis Vuitton case was a gift from Alton, a buttery leather brown embossed with the signature LV.

The woman is staring at me and I feel my cheeks turn crimson. As if this happens every day, I calmly hand her the iPhone, staying within an arm's reach in case she decides to bolt from the breezeway.

"Oh, this is a nice phone case," she says with a slow slur. The woman holds the leather covering about an inch from her nose, so close I can't imagine she's seeing anything but a fuzzy smudge. "Where you get it?" she asks, her eyes darting to me, then back to her hand. "How much you want for this?"

I cough and shake my head, taking a second to swallow my surprise before answering. "Thank you, but it's not for sale."

This has to be the strangest experience of my life, and I'm certain her behavior is against store policy, but I'm so completely weirded out that I pluck the iPhone from her grasp. Grabbing a cart, I push my way into the store, blinded by the bizarre experience.

I increase my speed and head down the first aisle I find, wheels on the buggy rasping and squeaking when I turn. Tucking myself well out of sight of the doorway, I glance at my list, throwing Kleenex and paper towels in the cart, followed by cotton balls, Q-tips, and body lotion.

Glancing at my list, I round another corner, glancing behind me to make sure the gold-toothed greeter isn't behind me.

There's a crash and a jerk, followed by a yelp of pain and a shower of cardboard items hitting the floor.

"Lord have mercy, watch where you're going," a female voice snaps.

I blink in surprise and yank the cart to a stop. "Oh my goodness, I'm so sorry."

Through the metal cage of the shopping buggy, I can see a blond woman, dressed in a white linen pantsuit, crouched down and holding her ankle.

She's surrounded by black and purple boxes. A least a dozen packs have landed inside my cart. I pick up the colorful box and read it.

The label proudly proclaims "Trojan Condoms: Pleasure Pack." In a variety of colors, the smaller print reads "Twisted, Sensations, and Ultra-Ribbed."

Mortified doesn't even begin to describe it. I've knocked over an entire display of condoms. Someone, please shoot me. This would *never* happen in Atlanta. *Never.* I wouldn't be shopping in Wal-Mart, I wouldn't be running from gold-toothed greeters, and I wouldn't have mowed someone over in the personal hygiene aisle.

"Searcy Roberts?" the voice continues. The woman rises, and the familiar features make my fingers clench the cart's handle.

It's unmistakable. The petite features, perfect makeup, and coiffed hair. The haughty look hasn't changed one bit. As expected, she's dressed immaculately, and I fight the urge to swoon over her Gucci shoes and Roberto Cavalli jeans.

"Searcy. Roberts. Bless your heart. It is you!"

As best I can, I paste on a congenial smile and do my best to cover up the Trojan boxes with my bag. "How are you, Haley?"

Her syrupy sweet greeting doesn't fool me. Fairhope's former reigning beauty queen—even at thirty-five—has enough chutzpah to frighten Ellen DeGeneres into submission.

She bounces to her feet and rushes over to air-kiss my cheeks. "You're looking..." Her voice trails off as she takes in my rumpled outfit.

"Just flew in from Atlanta. Delta lost my luggage," I say with a forced laugh.

"Oh, sugar. How terrible, darling," she says, patting my hand. "You can't trust those airlines."

We stand there for an awkward moment.

"How's precious Alton?" she asks finally, batting her eyelashes when she mentions his name.

I cringe inside, but answer. "Good. You know, he's always traveling. This week, he's in Europe. For a conference. Of advertising executives." My voice falters, because I am a terrible liar. "They're doing advertising campaigns. And things."

She crinkles her nose and giggles. "Of course."

Feeling sick, I change the subject. "Your leg. Is it okay?"

Haley nods. "Oh, I'll be fine. I'll scoot on over to Jimmy's office and get it checked out."

I must look completely blank at the Jimmy reference, because she lets out another giggle.

"You know," she says, flashing a huge engagement ring and wedding band in front of my face, "My husband, Jimmy Richmond. *Dr.* Jimmy Richmond."

It's everything I can do to not let my jaw drop. Little Jimmy Richmond, class geek and fat kid is married to Haley Hill?

"He finished his residency a few years ago and we decided to come back here and set up his practice. I'm so proud." She clasps both hands together. "The Lord has blessed us. I have to thank Jesus, our savior, for all of our blessings. It's like God himself reached down and anointed Jimmy as a healer."

My throat catches, full of anything snarky or mean I ever said or thought about Haley. I still can't fathom the thought of her with Jimmy. And God anointing him is a stretch, but she obviously believes it and it makes her happy, so...*whatever.*

"B-best wishes. I'm so glad for you." I nod emphatically, forcing up the corners of my lips. "Again, I'm so sorry about your ankle. I have to run along." I begin pushing my cart, ignoring that I'm running over a few dozen Trojan packages.

"Tootles," says Haley. "Let's do lunch soon."

Wiping my forehead with the back of my hand, I disappear down another aisle, this one empty. With a guilty conscience, I stuff the remaining Trojan packs into a plastic sandbox bucket and pray some unsuspecting kid doesn't open them up, thinking they're a new sort of birthday balloon.

Paying close attention to the rest of my shopping trip, I make my way to the grocery section. With a burst of efficiency I haven't felt in weeks, I complete the list in less than thirty minutes and find a checkout lane with less than five people waiting.

As I unload my selections onto the conveyer belt, I group them into categories: paper products, refrigerated items, and frozen purchases. Keeping my head down, I concentrate on the beep of the price scanner and the rustle of plastic bags being filled.

When it's finally my turn, I look up.

"Find everything?" the checkout girl asks. I nod and move my empty cart toward the front of the store.

Hiya," the gold-toothed greeter says.

I almost jump out of my skin. She's bagging groceries. At the end of the register in my aisle. *Of course.*

"Hello," I say, trying to smile. I turn my attention to the register screen and my purchases. Bananas, raspberries, peaches. The checkout girl moves with amazing speed, her fingers flying over the keyboard as she enters SKU numbers.

We near the end of my produce and the checkout girl starts on the few items of frozen food. A half-gallon of strawberry for Mama, and another of Breyers vanilla, my favorite.

As the containers pass through, I breathe a sigh of relief that the bill is just a few pennies shy of one hundred dollars and that this shopping excursion has come to a close.

"Blue Bell ice cream's on sale this week."

I meet the check-out girl's dark eyes. She shrugs. "It is."

But it's not her who said it. The gold-tooth greeter continues, becoming a tad agitated. "It's buy one, get one free."

I stiffen and turn to face her. "Thank you, maybe next time. I'm getting Breyers ice cream for my mother."

She frowns and crosses her arms over her broad belly. "Don't ya like Blue Bell ice cream?"

"Yes," I say, backing up a step and trying not to make a face.

"It's buy one, get one free," she repeats in a louder voice. "It's on sale."

Ignoring the pitch as best I can, I stuff a crumpled one hundred dollar bill into the checkout girl's hand and don't wait for change or the receipt.

Maneuvering my wiggly, wobbly cart, I practically run out of the store and into the parking area. A few heads turn, but I don't care or slow down.

Breathing hard, I shield my eyes and pause to scan the blacktop. In the right corner of the lot, I find a flash of bright pink. Never have I been so glad to see my mother's ridiculously large Cadillac. I unload the groceries, slide the key into the ignition, and crank the AM radio.

As I drive away, I press the accelerator and shake my head in disbelief.

My high school nemesis, a Trojan condom display-crash, and a Blue Bell ice cream-obsessed Wal-Mart greeter.

And I haven't even been back in Fairhope for 24 hours.

CHAPTER 14

Before I go back to Mama's house, I decide to drive by *Pie Girls*, grab a coffee, and thank Tobi for the ride.

After I pull into a nearby parking space, I frown at the sight of my hard-won Breyers ice cream in the back seat, and decide to leave it in the car anyway. *I'll only be a minute.*

Pie Girls is on Section Street, sandwiched in between a gift boutique and the Downtown Fairhope Bicycle Company. The bakery's pink and white awning stands out against the bricks, and cute wrought iron cafe tables grace the sidewalk.

Inside, the smell is a heavenly mix of brown sugar and butter. Black and white photos of popular Fairhope locations—each dressed in a jaunty colored frame—grace the walls. White linen tablecloths are draped over every table, with black and white ribbon accents.

I notice that Mama still hasn't painted the walls, which alternate black and gold. I've mentioned more than once that brighter, lighter hues might open up the space, and Mama agreed, but never took a roller to drywall. It's a project that likely falls to the bottom of a long list of fundraisers, volunteering opportunities, pottery classes, and book club parties. With Mama, there's never a lack of to-do items.

My eyes continue to roam the shop. It's brightly lit, with a huge magazine and newspaper rack in one corner. Soft jazz plays through the shop's speakers, the notes adding just enough ambiance without overwhelming the atmosphere.

The bakery case is enormous and glows from inside, showing off the days' offerings. The pie selections are varied, depending on Mama's mood, and always displayed on the folding blackboard that sits outside the shop. Today, chocolate pecan, peach, and banana cream are written in pink chalk, using curly cursive letters.

I walk across the black and white tiled floor, noting a few familiar faces.

"Tobi," I call and wave her over when it's my turn at the counter. "I just wanted to say thank you again for picking me up today."

"No problem," she smiles. "How's Mama?"

"Tired," I reply thoughtfully. "Home taking a nap right now."

Tobi nods. "I'm sure she's glad you're here," she says. "Coffee?"

"I'd love some."

She fills a mug and slides it across the counter. "I've got to get back to it," she says, tilting her head toward the line that's filed in behind me.

The only other girl in the shop is scurrying around filling orders, slicing pie, and calling out names. I watch as she fills the espresso machine, tamps the ground espresso, and begins to foam the milk.

Tobi is a natural with the customers. She laughs and winks at the first couple while she rings up their order. She greets the next woman in line with equal warmth, taking a moment to point out something on the menu board. Another laugh and this time, she squeezes the woman's hand. This happy chatter continues with the next person in line, and the next. She knows everyone by name, remembers favorite drinks, and asks about spouses, children, and pets.

I've always known my friend to be sweet and personal, but I'm thoroughly impressed. It's then that I fully understand how much Mama appreciates Tobi.

Suddenly, an ear-piercing grinding noise resonates through the bakery. The screech is followed by the whine of machinery, and the familiar strains of "Sweet Home Alabama."

I stiffen immediately. Has someone in this normally serene little place gone absolutely crazy? Who in the world would make such a racket in a business district?

Other patrons around me shift in their seats uncomfortably when the noise waxes and wanes. A few couples get up, leaving their pie half-eaten and drinks untouched. What's most distressing is that Tobi and the other girl behind the counter don't seem to hear it at all.

When no one stands up and expresses that they're going to take care of the problem, Lynyrd Skynyrd gears up for the second verse of the state's favorite anthem, the beat grinding deep into my already-tense muscles between my shoulder blades.

Through the wall, there's a crash, and I jump out of my seat.

Not waiting for anyone else to react, I storm out the front door, turn right, and take ten steps to arrive in front of the Downtown Fairhope Bicycle Company. Through the glass door, I see a man in a worn navy t-shirt and a pair of Levi's, frayed at the heels. Though I'd rather not admit it, I can't help but notice that the jeans fit just right, and how his bicep and arm muscles contract when he reaches for a tool or tightens a bolt.

Dry-mouthed, I observe the noise-maker for another minute or two. He's singing along to the lyrics, pausing only for a brief air guitar solo.

He's either totally self-confident or doesn't care who in the world who sees him. I'm opting for the latter. I glance at the picture window, searching for a name of this proprietor with tunnel vision and few manners.

I take a deep breath and enter the bicycle store, coughing immediately at the acrid smell of oil and grease.

"Excuse me?" I say in a normal tone.

The guy keeps working, a shock of dark blond hair falling into his face as he removes one tire and replaces it with another.

"Hello?" I say.

He, irritatingly, doesn't hear me.

I take a few steps closer, reach for his arm, and tap. "Excuse me," I repeat.

The man jumps back and whirls around, grabbing at earplugs. "What in the—?"

"Searcy Roberts," I shout. I hate yelling and am uncomfortable being the only woman—the only other person in the shop at this time. "Could you?" I motion at turning a dial with my index finger and thumb. "Turn it down?"

The guy raises his eyebrows in acknowledgement, then nods and walks over to the stereo. With a quick motion, the music's clicked off and the shop falls silent.

"Thank you," I say, interrupting the blissful quiet.

"What'd you say your name was?" he drawls, looking me up and down.

"Searcy," I say, repeating myself. "Searcy Roberts. My mother owns the shop next door?"

He nods, taking a rag from his back pocket and swiping at his forehead and cheeks. It's then that I notice the bright blue eyes staring back at me curiously. I lose my concentration as I stare at his full lips and strong jaw line. I completely forget why I'm there as my gaze travels across his broad shoulders.

"Searcy?"

I shake my head yes, catapulting back into reality. "Yes."

"So, you're Maggie's girl from Atlanta," he says slowly. "I take it you're not here to buy a bike?" His face breaks into a huge smile and he chuckles at his own words. "I'm Luke Nolan."

I don't grin back. "Well, Luke Nolan, could you please keep it down?" I ask. "The radio? The music?"

He frowns and rubs his chin. "I thought the walls were insulated."

"I don't think so," I reply sharply. Confrontation isn't my strong suit, but I am defending Mama's business. That makes it my priority.

Luke's beautiful smile fades a little. He's either not used to someone questioning him, or he's just gathering ammunition for a smart comeback.

"So, can you alter your repair schedule?" I ask, pressing him. "Or put in that wall insulation?"

Knitting his brow together, he raises both arms and gestures at the bikes. "You're telling me how to run my business?" Luke snorts.

"Temporarily, yes," I say, nodding my agreement. "No one can have a conversation while you're over here dropping tools and clanging around with machinery."

"Is that so?" He asks. Luke runs a roughened hand through his casual mop of dark blond hair.

Despite my anger, I suddenly detect a flash of hurt. He rubs at a thin layer of stubble on his jaw line. And, for a moment, I think that I've won.

He draws in a breath, taking a moment to flex his muscles while he folds his arms across his chest. "It's funny. Maggie and Tobi haven't complained."

I purse my lips. Mama is too much of a Southern lady to complain, or suggest that he dial down the noise. Tobi, likely, doesn't feel like it's her place. It's not her shop.

And I tend to just be direct. But too late, I realize that I'm not in Atlanta anymore. Not in the big city, where folks are used to hard negotiations and scrutiny. I should have sugar-coated. Or at least made a little effort to soften my approach.

"I'm sorry," I begin. "What I meant to say was—"

He cuts me off. "Are you going to be working at your mom's place now?" he asks, keeping his tone even.

I shrug. "Not sure."

"Staying in town long?"

"I don't think so."

"Good." And with that, Luke turns and walks away from me, work boots clunking. Evidently, he doesn't care if I fly back to Atlanta. Or China. Or the Moon.

With a start, I realize that Mama's neighbor just intentionally insulted me. Red-faced and mind racing for a smart comment, Luke beats me to it.

"I'll keep it down. But only because I like Maggie." With a slam, his office door closes behind him.

CHAPTER 15

By the time I return the shop, my coffee is frigid. With a shaking hand, I take a sip anyway, trying to calm my nerves. It's rare that anyone other than C.C. unnerves me completely, but Luke Nolan has somehow stripped away all of my defenses, leaving me speechless and—temporarily—unable to offer a smart or witty retort.

Tobi wanders by with a tray full of dishes and glances at me curiously. "Searcy, you're as white as a ghost. Where'd you disappear to?"

I offer up a rueful smile. "Decided to go next door and investigate the noise issue. It was driving me crazy."

She screws up her face in surprise, but doesn't let on whether she approves or not. "And how'd that go over?"

Pressing my palms together, I rest my chin on my fingertips. "Let's just say that Luke Nolan and I are not going to be best friends anytime soon."

Tobi glances around the shop, which has emptied somewhat. She cocks her head. "I'm not going to defend him," she says. "The music alone is enough to make me come unhinged," Tobi smiles. "But he's a good person behind the gruff exterior."

My mind forms a picture in my head of Luke's face. His initial smile was so disarming I found myself catching my breath and unable to focus.

"I'm glad to hear it," I say, shrugging with reluctance. What proof do I have? One encounter doesn't mirror his true personality, but I'm still stinging.

"His whole life is that shop, and he started it with nothing, after his parents died," she explains. "In his spare time, he takes old bikes and fixes them up for kids in town—just gives them away," she continues with a wistful expression. He does all sorts of charity work. I don't know when the man sleeps."

I swallow another bit of gruffness.

She balances the tray in one hand. "He's kind of dreamy, don't you think?"

I gulp back a shocked look and nod. Tobi, my no-nonsense, very married friend, is absolutely swooning over the guy next door. And yes, in any other circumstance, I'd agree that he rocks the California-sexy surfer-guy look.

But I'm still reeling from Alton's confession.

"Give him a chance," Tobi says.

"I'll try," I say, making an attempt to smile. But in reality, the likelihood is slim. I'm not about to trust any man—Santa Claus and the Pope included. Alton's rejection has thrown me into a tailspin, and I can't seem to take the wheel and pull myself out of it.

"You must have done something right," Tobi adds with a wink. "No more music." She pauses and listens.

There's not a sound from next door.

I don't bother mentioning that Luke's probably gone to deliver meals to the homeless, after rescuing kittens from tree branches, or adopting puppies. Maybe he's delivering a bike to some deserving child in town—some kid who will forever think Luke Nolan walks on water.

My stomach twists, forming a tight knot of anxiety. Mama won't take kindly to me pissing off the town's own living, breathing saint. I'll have to explain. Make it up to him.

My phone jingles with Phillipa's ringtone. I hesitate before answering, summoning all of my strength to sound normal.

"Darling," she gushes with a slight squeal. "Where in the world are you? I've been calling; I stopped by the apartment again. I'm frantic with worry."

She is giddy with news, I can tell—brimming over with something gigantic to announce.

"I'm so sorry," I say, forcing the corners of my lips into a smile. It's good to hear her voice.

"You missed spa day," she scolds me. "And then you skipped lunch and girls' night. I'm beginning to think you're avoiding me. Either that or your sweet husband has stopped all of this mystery-disappearance nonsense and has swept you away to the Caribbean for a second honeymoon?"

Her voice takes on a hopeful tone, and I can tell she is on edge, waiting for me to fill her in on every last gossipy detail.

I laugh out loud at her guess, trying to sound jovial. The effort comes out stilted and forced. I cough to cover up my hurt and decide to just confess that I'm back in Fairhope.

"Oh, sweetie. Nothing nearly as glamorous as that," I reply. "Mama called and wanted me to visit. It's been forever, so I got on a plane and flew down."

"Bless your heart," Phillipa coos. "Such a good daughter. I hope she appreciates that your friends here miss you terribly."

"Thanks, sweetie."

We hang up with promises to see each other soon.

With a glance at my watch, I realize that Mama might be awake. A pang of guilt hits my chest. How long have I been gone? She might need me. I gather my purse and keys and head for the door. Before I can take three steps, a female voice stops me cold.

"Searcy? Twice in one day?"

I look up to find Haley Richmond staring down at me. This time, her children trail behind her, two little mini-me's in smocked dresses and matching hair bows.

"Fancy seeing you here...alone," she drags out the sentence and looks pointedly at the empty seat beside me. "When did you say Alton was arriving?"

My throat fills with ice. "He's so busy," I force out. "He's going to try to be here in a few days, but his schedule is crazy right now."

Haley regards me suspiciously. Her piercing gaze seems to penetrate my skin, finding its way into my brain, where all of my secrets are tucked away for safekeeping.

"Let's have dinner," she says suddenly, as if we've been best friends our whole lives. "It'll be such fun. We can catch up, share a bottle of wine."

The comment hits me center-chest. *Dinner? Wine?* Recovering, I muster up as much enthusiasm as I can for the thought of an evening with Jimmy and Haley.

"Thank you so much for the invitation," I say brightly. "I'll call you when I know he'll be free."

"Wonderful—"

"I have to run. Great seeing you."

Haley blinks at my abrupt departure, but I can't continue the conversation a moment longer. I swallow against the roaring in my ears and stumble away. I can't even manage to say goodbye to Tobi.

Tears prick my eyes. It's a wonder I can find the right key and manage to crank Mama's car. My eyes graze the back seat and land on the ice cream. When I touch the container, it's warm. I pick it up, and soft cream oozes down one side.

Dammit.

Wrapping it up as best I can, I manage to carry it over to the shop's trash can and deposit it inside the plastic bin. Standing there, shaking, my hand on the lid, I feel as if I might crawl inside too.

Like trash. Tossed away, discarded.

In the mile it takes to reach Mama's house, I settle my breathing.

Everywhere I turn, I'm reminded of Alton. Everywhere I turn, everywhere I go. It's like there's no escape.

A tear trickles down my cheek.

A big, wide future sprawls in front of me. I'm scared to death. Terrified.

If I'm not Alton's wife, who am I?

I don't know how to be alone. Especially if something happens to Mama.

More tears escape.

A crazy thought hits me as I make another turn. It's a desperate, very un-Searcy like idea.

I swallow hard.

I'll ask him for one more chance.

My hands are shaking by the time I pull the car into Mama's driveway and park. But I'm thrilled, and surprised, to see my mother outside—dressed and in the sunlight—talking to a friend over a row of blooming white rose bushes.

I grab the groceries, smile widely, and try to contain my jitters. With a wave, I greet the neighbor, and peck Mama on the cheek. "Be right back," I call over my shoulder.

Mama nods, smiles, and goes back to chatting.

Once inside, I set down my bags and scurry to Mama's laptop before I change my mind.

Mouth dry, I open my email, scanning the inbox for anything urgent or important before I begin. More than eight hundred messages greet me, varying from emails from Phillipa, reminders about birthdays, and advertisements for the latest in male enhancement products. I frown at the latter and click spam, sending it into cyberspace.

As the page refreshes, I see Alton's name. One message, sent a day and several hours ago. There's no subject line.

He's beaten me to it. He's written me first.

I hold my breath and click to open the email. Hungrily, I scan the first few lines.

Dear Searcy,
I hope this finds you well. Attached is my formal plan for our divorce settlement.

I did want to let you know that my mother has found a couple to rent out the apartment beginning the first of next month, so be sure to let me know when I can arrange to have your things moved.

Below is the number where you can reach me in case of an emergency. I no longer have use for my cell phone, but will continue paying your bill, as you will see outlined in the attached document.

Be well,
Alton

I can't think. The words dance and swim in front of my eyes.

A sob escapes my lips, and with a trembling finger, I hit delete.

CHAPTER 16

I wake from a wine-induced slumber what seems like minutes later.

The persistent sound of a honeybee buzzes in my ear.

Still half-asleep, I slap at the noise with my free hand, the other tucked firmly under my second pillow.

"Mmph," I mutter and roll over, an elbow over my face to protect from attack. Peeling one eye open, I glance at the clock, which reads 4:25 in glaring neon-red. The buzzing continues, relentless, now emitting from under my sheets. With fumbling fingers, I find my iPhone and press end.

Bleary-eyed, I squint against the intense screen light. While I don't immediately recognize the number, somehow it registers that the call is local and could be significant. Throwing off my covers, I race across the house and check on my mother. She's asleep, breathing evenly, her dark hair cascading off the pillow.

Thank goodness.

My cell buzzes again. I touch the number and press the phone to my cheek.

"Searcy?"

It's Tobi, breathless and rattling off something about the shop. I shake off any pretense of going back to bed, step away from my mother's bedroom, and ask her to slow down.

"It's everything," she says with a hiccup. "I didn't pay attention to inventory—the kids got sick, and I left in a rush. We're out of everything, or close to it. And there's no money in the cash drawer. We open in less than ninety minutes."

"What can I do?" I ask, picking my way through the house to the bathroom and stubbing my bare foot on the feet of my mother's favorite mahogany end table. *Ow!* I bite my lip and hunch over, grasping my big toe.

"I wouldn't ask unless I was desperate. Can you run to Wal-Mart if I give you a list?" Tobi asks.

An image of the gold-toothed girl appears in front of me, and crazy thoughts swirl in my head. Most certainly, she'd ask why I was buying White Lily flour and Daisy sour cream, as opposed to other brands. My reaction, compounded by too little sleep, would likely land me in jail.

"I'll watch the shop," I offer Tobi. "And reimburse you for the groceries. Don't worry about the cash drawer. I've got some money."

I'm basically paying to get out of an unpleasant task, but I'd rather spend my last penny than go back to the bizarre reality that lives inside that store. Besides, she knows her shopping priorities, and can probably race though the aisles in record time.

"Be here as *soon* as you can," says Tobi.

Tossing my hair into a messy ponytail, I rifle through my drawers and pull on an old Ramones t-shirt—left over from college—and shimmy into a pair of brand-new Wal-Mart leggings. I follow it with an old denim jean skirt and a pair of hot pink Keds. It's vaguely Madonna-esque, but considering I'll cover it with an apron, my outfit will have to do.

Oh, if Phillipa and Mimi could see me now...

I write Mama a quick note, urging her to call me at the shop if she needs me.

Minutes later, I am rumbling into the *Pie Girls* parking lot. Luke's truck sits to the side of the building. Seeing the flatbed and taillights makes my insides clench. *Does he live here?*

Pushing any thoughts of him away, I meet Tobi at the door, hand her a few hundred dollars in cash, and inhale a barrage of responsibilities about drinks and bakery racks. I am left alone in the space before I have time to scan the menu a second time. I jot down what I can remember, place the bills inside the register, and begin brewing coffee.

Dawn breaks early, casting a warm red glow on the sidewalk's edge. The street's hanging baskets drip with dew above manicured flower beds filled with lavender begonias, perky pink impatiens, and jaunty yellow daisy faces. A few solitary runners stride by, soundless music setting their pace. As the clock chimes six, I flip the sign from "Shut" to "Open."

In the minutes that follow, customers bustle in, asking for tea or a medium roast with a slice of today's featured selection, spinach and feta quiche. The first few customers offer momentary looks of surprise, and then order anyway, too busy to ask why I'm behind the counter.

Tobi slips in the back, the heavy metal hinges creaking with its own weight as she heaves and props open the massive door. Paper bags crinkle as she unloads.

"Searcy? Is that you?"

A deep voice resonates through the shop. I look up and see Alton's uncle, a distinguished man in his sixties with a shock of white hair and a tanned face.

Delighted, I rush around the bakery rack, throwing myself into his arms. "Pete!" I exclaim, as he holds me out to examine me from head to toe.

"Well, I'll never," he says. "Bless your heart, gorgeous as ever."

I preen just a little and pretend to blush. Inside, I am basking in the praise, thirsty to drink it all in. My self-confidence crashes a moment later at his next question.

"Where's my nephew?" he booms, looking past me, expecting Alton to pop out of the kitchen.

"Great Wall," I blurt out, "Of China," I add and follow it up with a mental slap on the head. *Think Searcy. There's only one.*

Pete pats me on the shoulder. "Y'all tell him hello," he says. "I assume you're staying with Maggie?"

I nod at my mother's name. "She's...taking a...much-deserved few days off," I bumble my way through the explanation.

A crush of customers enter the shop, and we're back to a chaotic give and take of coffee, money, and pie. Pete waves with his to-go bag in hand, and I allow my shoulders to relax as he exits the shop.

Next to me, Tobi slides a plateful of strawberry tarts across the counter. I can feel her eyes on the side of my face, but I don't look in her direction.

"China?" she asks. "What happened to South America?"

Caught in my own lie, I blush hard and don't reply, simply stride away, pretending to be insanely busy with an imaginary order. When I reach the back room, momentary shock hits me when I see Tobi's purchases on the countertop.

Betty Crocker cake mix, tubs of frosting, pre-made pie shells, and tall silver cans of fruit filling. There's more, but I snatch up the receipt and scan the itemized ticket. Hundreds of dollars, and we're not even offering my grandmother's recipes?

Instantly, I'm hurt beyond measure and confused. At Tobi, with my mother. *What sort of business is this?* It's false advertising, misleading sales techniques. I huff at the proclamation of "homemade" on the blackboard outside.

I'm so furious that I don't hear Tobi's footsteps behind me.

"Your mother hasn't cooked in six months, Searcy," Tobi says in a quiet voice. "And she won't share her recipes. Something about family secrets and preserving them for generations to come. Although..."

Her voice trails off and I realize what she's not saying. *Keeping the recipes to herself is foolish. There is no grandchild. There may never be. Who is Maggie kidding?*

"It's her choice," I flash to anger.

"I can't handle it all," Tobi retorts, clearly wounded. "I'm not a cook. I'm a manager. I can order, do the books." She stops. "I don't have your mother's gift for baking."

"Gift?" I sputter. "Buy Paula Deen's cookbook. Borrow the Lee Brother's recipes. Mix it up with some Giada DeLaurentes, for goodness' sake. But don't do this." I sweep a hand across the table, giving one of the Betty Crocker boxes a much-needed back hand.

The box tumbles to the floor, but instead of a satisfying thud, the cardboard bursts, sending up a cloud of cake mix around my bare ankles.

My skin twinges at the sensation and I jump.

Simultaneously, Tobi and I stare at the mess. Then behind us, a faint gurgle of water sounds. My eyes follow the sound to a trickle of water on the floor near the back of the shop.

"Oh no," Tobi squeaks out, flinging open a storage door. "A pipe burst." Sure enough, there's a leak, and what seemed like a spill moments ago now appears to be more along the lines of a hole in the Hoover Dam.

"Get Luke," she says, waving an arm in my face. "See if he's over there. I'm going to try and find a shut-off valve."

Instead of moving, though, I stand stock-still, water creeping closer to my pink Keds. *Ask Luke for help? Over my dead body.*

Tobi, apparently, isn't interested in my personal crisis. "Go!" She's inches from my face. "And let the customers know—calmly—that there's an issue. We'll re-open tomorrow."

With a push, she sends me toward the front of the store, where a small line has formed.

I clap my hands. "Everyone, we have an emergency. I'm so sorry. A slight water problem. We're getting it looked at," I pause. "And tomorrow, we'll re-open with..."

The faces all turn and look at me expectantly. I want them all to come back. I need a hook, a draw, something Alton would make up in one of his smash advertising campaigns.

"A free slice of pie for the first forty people!"

A small cheer erupts from the back and I flush from the excitement of my announcement.

"And if it's a big success, we'll make it an annual event," I add, finishing with flourish.

Herding everyone out the front, I rush next door. As I approach the bike shop window, I notice that while the music is still playing, it's thirty decibels lower. *Coincidence or respect for my request?*

"Luke?" I call out.

I wander through a maze of wheels and colored frames. The bicycle choices are endless.

But there's no sign of him at the register, and with Tobi's words ringing in my ear, I decide to press past, into the clearly marked "no customers" private area. I find him, bent over a workspace, one muscled arm pressed against the wall, the other holding a phone to his ear. Trying not to listen, I wave to get his attention.

"Yes, I understand. I know that. I'll be there soon," he says. "I love you, too."

He hangs up, stuffs the phone in his pocket, and faces me with a frown.

"No customers back here, Miss Roberts," he says without smiling, his tone frigid. "Wait, you don't follow the rules, in general, right?"

"I won't do it again," I say and swallow, trying to lighten the perceived offense. "But, there's an emergency, and I could use your help. I'm not sure what else to do."

I look pleadingly into Luke's eyes. For a moment, the darkness there softens. It disappears as quickly as it came.

"I have to go," he says and jabs a thumb at the door.

"We have a water issue. A broken pipe, or something," I add. "The shop's filling up."

This makes Luke pause, but his expression doesn't change. "Call a plumber." He turns away, rifling at the back of his hair absent-mindedly with one hand.

His brusque reply, his total dismissal, rips at my defenses.

After the way I handled yesterday's incident, I deserve the brush-off.

"I understand if you don't want to do it for me," I say, "but would you consider doing it for Mama?"

I let the idea float between us. I'm not one to ask for charity, and I have no earthly idea what health problems my mother is facing, but I intend to get to the bottom of them, and soon. "She's not well," I add. "You know that."

Saying it out loud makes me shake with trepidation. The words make it real.

"*Pie Girls*—it's her life. Her legacy. She built the shop from nothing. A single mom with no one to help her. And she's made it into a special place."

I put a hand over my heart to quiet the thumping.

Now, Luke is listening. I can tell.

"It's all she has."

CHAPTER 17

Luke doesn't say another word. He disappears into a back room, walking with a determined stride. I hold my breath, watching and hoping frantically that he'll decide to come back instead of returning to his phone call and the object of his affection.

Seconds later, Luke reappears, holding a toolbox in one hand and a stack of towels under his other arm. "Coming?" he asks, walking past me to the front door.

I follow behind, stifling the urge to jump up and down in delight.

The bakery has cleared out and Tobi is on her hands and knees, mopping up what she can of the growing lake on the floor. She utters a sigh of relief at the sight of Luke.

"Bless your heart, Luke Nolan," she says, sitting back on her heels and grinning up at him. "You're my hero!"

He immediately softens at the compliment, a flush of red creeping up his neck. "Aw, shucks, Tobi. You know I'd do anything to help you."

The comment pinches my ego just a bit, but I tamp it down. I don't care what it took to get him over here. He's here. He can fix this. And that's all that matters for Mama and her shop.

He clears his throat, re-focusing on the problem at hand. "So, ladies, want me take a look?"

Tobi waves him on and surveys me with interest. With Luke out of earshot, she perks up and cocks her head. "So, you must have done some fancy talking, Searcy, seeing that y'all were at each other's throats just a day ago." She wipes off both hands on her apron and lowers her voice after glancing in the direction of the water tank. "If I didn't know better, I'd think he was sweet on you."

I raise an eyebrow and laugh. "What?"

Tobi giggles at my expression. "Uh-huh."

"Now, wait just a minute. You heard him," I say. "He said he'd do anything to help *you*."

"But I'm not the one who asked," she half-whispers with a smirk. "And it took all of two seconds to get him over here. I'd call that motivation."

Furrowing my brow, I shake my head. "I told him that Mama needed the help. That's why he came over here. To help her—not me," I protest.

"Sure," Tobi says, unconvinced. She rolls her eyes.

I finally let myself giggle a little at her theory. As soon as I let down my guard just a smidge, Tobi zings me with a comment that sends my head spinning.

"Too bad you're happily married," she adds casually, getting to her feet. "Right? Still the blissful newlyweds."

I stiffen and stop laughing, unable to meet her gaze. My neck burns as I look away.

"Let's check on the man of the hour," I say.

The gushing water from the back room has slowed to a trickle, and there's only the occasional clank of metal on metal. Luke has certainly earned my respect, a big thank you, and more.

"So, since *your* hero seems to have come through and saved the day," I say, forcing myself to appear jovial and gesturing toward the back of the store, "let's get this place cleaned up."

An hour later, I'm exhausted. I've mopped up the floor with every available rag and paper towel, wiped down counters, and cleaned up tables strewn with coffee mugs and plates. I've chipped three nails, tripped twice, and discovered that the square footage of the shop is a lot larger than I ever realized.

After the shop is spotless again, Tobi shows me how to make cappuccino and espresso, then instructs me on the finer points of steamed milk and latte-making. She gives me a lesson on measuring and brewing coffee, runs through preparing the perfect cup of tea by using leaves and not bags, and makes my head swirl by zipping through ingredients for the dozen or more frozen drinks on the daily menu.

After a quick lesson on inventory and a tutorial on closing out the cash register at night, my head hurts and I'm ready to beg for mercy. Despite my fatigue, I have a new appreciation for the daily workings of the bakery.

"Sit for a sec," Tobi slides into one of the café chairs by the window and pats the table with one hand.

"Let me grab some water," I call over my shoulder. I choose two bottles out of the refrigerator, twist the caps, and sit down across from my friend.

We clink our bottles in mock celebration and sip quietly. After a minute, I feel the heat from Tobi's gaze grow more intense.

"Yes?" I look up and meet her eyes.

She tilts her head and lowers her voice. "I'm just wondering. How long you're here. It's usually home for a day and gone the next."

My shoulders sag and I swallow hard. I play with the label on my bottle, trying to choose my words.

"Alton?" she whispers.

I nod, choking up. "It's—I'm…"

"Don't," Tobi murmurs, handing me a napkin. "It's okay. I thought something was going on."

Sniffing back tears, I dab at my eyes.

"You've got people here who love you," she continues. "Remember that, okay?"

I manage a smile. "Thanks."

"Always."

Tobi's phone rings with a call from her oldest daughter. She jumps up, but motions for me to stay put and wait for her to finish.

While she paces and talks, I slide a little lower in my chair by the window, lean my head against the wall, and close my eyes. After a few minutes of listening to Tobi's conversation about school supplies and a missing book bag, I nearly doze off.

"Playing Sleeping Beauty?"

I jump at the sound of Luke's voice. My eyes fly open and I grab at the table to steady myself.

He laughs and reaches down to steady me. His hands, large and strong, grasp my waist and shoulder. "Easy now," he says, laughing.

"I—I was just..." At the heat of his touch, my skin melts. I can't speak or think.

"No worries," he chuckles, filling in the silence. "It's been a long day for everyone. I just wanted to let you know that I'm finished."

I manage to stand up, legs shaking. "Thank you," I say. "Really. I know you didn't have to—"

"You're welcome," he interrupts, waving off my appreciation. "Glad to do it." He smiles, his eyes crinkling at the corners.

"I'll let Mama know," I add.

"She doesn't have to worry," Luke says. "I can always make time to help."

I wince, remembering his phone call. "But I made you late and interrupted your phone call."

Luke nods, but doesn't move toward the door. "I texted her back. She knows I'm running behind."

The *her* makes me pause, but I don't ask.

"Okay," I reply, straining my brain for something casual and witty to toss back. I can't think of anything. I'm too busy wondering who she is. What she looks like. *Girlfriend? Wife? Significant other?*

I shiver and hug my arms tight to my chest.

A bang on the door interrupts the awkward silence.

There's a man in a navy blazer, khaki pants, and a red tie outside the bakery. He's peering inside, cupping his hands around his eyes and forehead.

"Expecting anyone?" Luke asks, taking a step back to survey the visitor.

I shake my head, then peer at an object sitting near the man's feet. An object that looks very much like my suitcase. A jolt of recognition courses through me. *Thank you, Jesus.* No more trips to Wal-Mart. No more wearing the same outfits. No more wondering if my clothes ended up in Sri Lanka.

Tobi, who's been watching my exchange with Luke, realizes my luggage is being delivered and makes it to the door before I do.

"Yes," she says after unlocking and flinging open the door. "Sure, I'll sign."

After she steps outside, I hear a gasp from Tobi, then a murmur from the delivery man.

Straining to see, I panic a bit as she scribbles a signature and snatches up the suitcase by its handle.

As she drags the bag into the bakery, I understand her initial reaction.

My lovely Yves St. Laurent suitcase, with its supple brown leather exterior and dark trim, is in no way the same bag that left Atlanta, Georgia.

The exterior looks like it's been in a bar fight, with slashes through the cover and sides. Duct tape, in varying shades of camouflage, wraps around the middle of the suitcase to hold it shut. There's a pink and black bungee cord attached to the top and looped around the bottom to hold the bag closed.

I swallow. Hard.

As Tobi rolls the suitcase inside, the lacy edge of my favorite La Perla bra drags on the floor. On the opposite side, the lace of my pink panties appear caught in the zipper. A white camisole drags behind the bag like a tail.

With a small shriek, I clap a hand over my mouth and run to grab the suitcase. My precious travel bag. My lingerie. *What else is missing or damaged?*

I can barely look as Tobi pivots the suitcase. My stomach flip-flops.

It's the exact moment Luke chooses to walk back into shop.

"Nice bag," he says, raising an eyebrow at the ripped and torn leather. "Going for the grunge look? Or are the airlines flying luggage outside the plane these days?"

Luke eyes my bra and panties carefully until I block his line of vision.

"The latter," I say. "Minor technical difficulties." With a quick sweep of my hand, I yank the bag behind me. Without bothering to apologize, I practically run him over to get my suitcase tucked behind the counter.

Suddenly needing to get him out of the shop, I smile brightly. "So, I've got to get baking. I promised a whole lot of people free pie tomorrow."

Luke raises an eyebrow.

"When the water leak started," I explain. "It just kind of...slipped out. First forty customers."

Tobi comes up behind me. "Yeah, and I'm wondering how you're going to pull of this little miracle. You'll need about ten, maybe a dozen pies, with our regular amount of customers. If word spreads…." She bites her lip.

I fight the urge to climb underneath the counter and hide for the next millennium. I raise my chin slightly and bit the inside of my cheek. "Do we have flour and butter?"

Tobi nods.

"Sugar?"

Another yes.

"And I can get fresh fruit from the farmer's market or the Windmill shop downtown?"

"Sure." Tobi, unconvinced that I can ever pull this off, glances at Luke, who's staring at me as if I've announced I've entered *America's Top Chef* and the competition is tomorrow.

"Then, I'm calling Mama," I say. "She'll know what to make."

As I turn on my heel, I notice that Luke and Tobi bend their heads together. A whisper prickles at my neck. He disappears, and Tobi begins wiping tables.

I straighten, yank out my phone, and hit speed dial. My mother answers on the third ring. She sounds stronger today. I don't tell her about the water leak or the clean up craziness. I don't want to worry her. I tell her the shop was busy this morning—not a fib—and that Tobi's been showing me the ropes, from cash registers to cappuccinos.

Mama sounds encouraged—happier than I've heard her in a long time. She gushes about Tobi's accounting ability and head for business.

I steer the conversation back to pie.

"Mama, since Tobi's not really into baking...she's better on the books," I say, "can you share a few recipes with me for the shop? I remember some things, but really could use your help to put together some of Grandma's homemade pies." I pause. "I know everyone will love them. And it would help Tobi out."

There's a pregnant pause, big and round, and for a moment, I almost believe I've made her angry. But the sound that comes through the phone is a happy one. It's a giggle. An almost gushing laugh of joy.

"Searcy!" she exclaims. "My darling girl, I thought you'd never ask!"

CHAPTER 18

I head home and take some of what is left from my meager stash of money, which should be plenty for fresh pie filling. I slide the cash into my wallet and head to the kitchen, where my mother is flipping through hand-written recipe cards.

Many of the thick index cards are yellowed with age, bent, and splattered with water, which blurs a few words. Some, decorated with blue and red stains from berry juice, have been placed to the side. Mama is dividing and rationing, decreeing which recipes can be shared.

She finally notices that I'm standing behind her and looks up. "Start with these," Maggie tells me, her fingers fluttering over the pile to her right. She stacks the recipe cards, making the edges fit neatly, and places them into my hands. "Fresh fruit, fully ripe, the brightest colors you can find," she reminds me as she offers up two tote bags for shopping.

I smile and nod, tucking the cards into my small backpack and zipping the outer pocket. I give the pocket a pat for good measure. Though the cards weigh little more than an ounce, they are heavy with importance. With a deep breath, I center the bag's straps on my shoulder, and lean down to kiss my mother's cheek.

Her skin is shockingly cold, and I draw back to scrutinize her face. "Are you okay?"

Suddenly, she looks exhausted. "Fine, fine."

"Mama."

She sighs. "All right. Maybe I'm feeling a bit under the weather," my mother admits. "I made an appointment with the doctor tomorrow, late afternoon. You can take me, if you like."

"Definitely."

Mama smiles. "Now, go on. Get your shopping done before they sell out of all of the best produce."

The Windmill Farmer's Market is rustic and bustling for a weekday. Immediately, I love the wooden building, the steps that groan a bit as they bear weight, offering a welcome. Inside, the space is cool and airy, with bare, raw wood ceilings that soar overhead. The structure is split into a mish-mash of rooms. I wander through, inhaling the scent of cinnamon and sugar, absorbing lively conversation, and soaking in the laughter of patrons and sellers exchanging pleasantries.

Almost immediately, I run across free-range, farm-fresh eggs in hues of light greens and turquoise. Calculating a few days' needs, I pick up three dozen, figuring I can come back for more if necessary.

There are gorgeous yellow lemons nestled inside a wooden crate. I pick one up and hold it to my nose, inhaling the sharp scent of summertime and citrus. Six go into my bag, and I move toward the smaller container of perky green limes. They are smaller, compact, compared to their sunshine-colored siblings. I choose two and continue wandering down the aisles.

As I walk, I run my fingertips over the displayed fruit, barely brushing against thick peach fuzz, the smooth, tight skin of nectarines, and the waxy bumps of bright orange tangerines. My eyes land on a spread of dark blueberries, edges shining almost black in the sunlight. They are piled high, spilling over a wicker basket jauntily tipped to one side. I smile and find a container to measure and weigh the berries, guarding against bruises to the juicy obs. Although it's one of the finest selections I've seen, I am still picky, choosing the largest and deepest blue fruit.

My bag is full to overflowing, so I grab a second bag, this one's bottom secured by a sturdier piece of plastic. Inside it, I place smooth red potatoes, yellow onions, several sprigs of rosemary, two sticks of cinnamon, and a loose piece of fresh ginger. As I glance back over the store space, I notice a rack of squash. I tilt my head, considering one of my grandmother's recipes. It could be fun. I smile to myself and tuck two of the twisted vegetables into the corner of my container.

The checkout line is short and I patiently wait, breathing in the fresh air. It's the first time in a while I haven't been urgently checking my calendar, rushing off to a luncheon, or waiting for Alton to drop dinner party plans in my lap at the last minute.

"Ready?" A young girl behind the counter asks me.

I jump at the question, not realizing that it's my turn.

She politely nods and gestures for me to place my items on the counter.

"Thank you," I stutter and hand over my purchases.

As she unloads, I regain my center. My heart pangs with missing Alton. Not the drama. Not the last-minute craziness, not the unpredictable schedule. But the knowing that he would be there. The promise that I had a husband.

Blinking away tears, I snatch a brochure from the counter and begin fanning myself furiously.

"It may be a hot'n," the checkout girl muses between ringing up my purchases.

I nod, smiling through the sting in my eyes. "Best get all of this home soon," I chirp, wanting to throw it all into my tote bags and run from the store. But there's no hurrying along things in the Deep South, let alone South Alabama.

Everything at its own pace and time, Mama always said.

I never was much good at listening.

There's a distinct ring from deep inside my Hermes bag. Ke$ha croons about brushing her teeth with a bottle of Jack. *Dammit.* I flash a wide smile at the clerk, ask what I owe for the groceries, and fumble for my purse's opening.

"Seventy-nine dollars and fifty-one cents," the girl replies, folding her hands at her waist. She waits for me to find and silence my iPhone. The screen flashes *Phillipa*. After stuffing it back inside the mouth of the yawning leather opening, I search through the jumble of Bobbie Brown cosmetic compacts, an assortment of Chanel lipsticks, an adorable hand mirror from Sephora, and a stack of receipts at least an inch thick, pinched together with a pink rhinestone clip. I swallow and ignore the mess, find my wallet and cash inside.

After handing four twenties into the checkout girl's hand, I hoist my bags into the crook of my arm. She drops forty-nine cents into my open palm.

"Have a blessed day," the clerk calls after me.

Ke$ha begins singing again. *Pedicure on my toes, toes. Tryin' on all my clothes, clothes. Boys blowin' up my phone, phone. Gonna get a little bit...tipsy...*

I am getting stares.

With as much grace as I can muster, I place the bags on the sidewalk. As fast as my fingers can find it, I answer Phillipa's call.

"What's up, sister-love?" she screeches into my ear. "I miss you!"

"Phillippa—" I begin to say.

She interrupts with flourish, chirping and insistent. "I have the most amazing news and you are not going to believe it. I was going to wait until you get back here, but then, I thought...I don't have your schedule. And there's this weird rumor going around about you and Alton..."

My heart lurches. "Phillipa," I say forcibly. "Hang on a sec."

Tilting my face up to the sun, I feel dizzy. Like an out-of-body experience. I'm not ready for this. Rumors. Gossip. Reality.

"Searcy?" she asks.

"I'm here," I swallow and straighten up, reaching a hand to smooth my hair. Normal. Act normal.

Through the phone, I can tell she is practically vibrating, tapping one leg furiously while checking the tips of her impeccably manicured nails every other second.

"So, how about the good news first?" I ask, forcing my lips into a smile. I lower myself gracefully, lacing my fingers through the bags.

Phillipa squeals in delight, the sound piercing enough to echo off Mobile Bay. I jump in pain, my arms jerking toward my head, trying to buffer my hearing from permanent damage.

In that same instant, I realize that I'm appearing to perform some type of writhing dance on the sidewalk. Mortified, my vision blurs and clears, and I find myself staring at a pair of large brown Merrell slip-on shoes. Men's. Distinctly familiar.

Luke Nolan.

Dammit. Dammit. Dammit.

I want to die a slow death. No, I want someone to shoot me and put me out of my misery. Now. Don't wait. Pull the trigger.

With my breath held, and Phillipa still blabbering on, I look up and meet his curious, amazingly sexy gaze.

Immediately, I am disarmed. My heart thumps. This is not me. I don't get flustered with men. Fighting to maintain my dignity, I exhale and grin, tilting my head to look up into the deep blue of his eyes.

"Need some help?" he asks, looking slightly amused.

I pause and mentally measure the tone of his voice. He's not being snarky.

"Maybe," I say with a small smile.

Phillipa is droning on in the background and I see him glance at my iPhone. From what I've gathered, the huge announcement is that she and her husband are adopting.

Luke gathers my bags before I can give him a definitive answer.

"Thank you," I reply, holding my cell out at arm's distance.

He raises an eyebrow.

I hold the iPhone to my chest to muffle the sound. "My best friend. She's a little excited," I reply. "She's adopting."

"Big move," Luke comments as we begin walking toward my mother's car. I don't have to point the way or direct him. No one in this town will ever mistake Mama's humongous pink Cadillac for anyone else's vehicle.

As I press the cell back to my ear, I catch the word 'Lowchen' and Germany. *OMG*.

"She won't let me get a word in," I add.

We reach the car.

"Phillipa," I say.

She keeps talking.

"Phillipa!" I repeat. "I have to go, sweetheart."

My best friend chirps something, says she loves me, and clicks off.

Luke loads my car.

"So she's adopting?" Luke asks as I toss my iPhone into my purse.

I nod. "But it's a dog."

Luke's jaw drops an inch.

I bust out laughing. "A Lowchen. From Germany." I pause, almost embarrassed by my friend's audacity and opulence. Then, I consider my own designer clothes. My gorgeous brownstone apartment. My over-the-top shopping trips. A few days ago, I was *that* person.

"That's a little high maintenance," he jokes.

I flush carnation pink. "It's actually…completely ridiculous," I say, laughing out loud.

Luke gives me a brilliant smile. "Hey, we do agree on something."

He closes the door after I slide inside the Cadillac, and waves as I drive off. As I turn onto the street and head for *Pie Girls*, I realize two things.

First—I'm actually starting to like this small-town life. Not the Wal-Mart trips, mind you. Or run-ins with crazy Haley Richardson. But a simpler, less hectic existence.

I also realize that I never did address Phillipa's concerns about the Alton gossip.

For the moment, I am perfectly okay with it.

I am going to bake instead.

Chapter 19

My alarm chirps, crickets in a field. I startle, gripping the sheets and flopping over to my right side. I squint at the clock, the numbers glowing red in the room's inky darkness.

Three a.m. came earlier than I'd ever expected. I swear, just minutes ago, my head hit the pillow, I closed my eyes, and I escaped into a sweet Peter Pan-Neverland of slumber.

The early hours weren't all bliss, however. My mind raced with thoughts of Alton. I dreamt about us traveling. Being left at various places around Europe and the Middle East. At the Taj Mahal, wandering. Outside Neusvenstein, climbing up the crest to reach the castle doors, only to find them locked. The last scene, in Heidelberg, Germany, Alton waves from a bridge, only to jump from the railing. There are no splash sounds.

It's at that moment that I wake.

Breathing hard, I press a hand to my chest. A sheen of sweat covers my skin. As the air conditioning kicks on, I shiver at the blast of air against the fine hairs on my arms and neck.

With a rush of determination, I throw off the duvet and sheets, thrust my feet from the warmth of the mattress and stand up straight. After a quick, lukewarm-at-best shower, I throw on clothes, and run a comb through my tangled hair. With both hands, I sweep and gather the thick strands at the back of my head and secure my ponytail with a sturdy holder.

I pack my groceries from the day before in the largest Lands' End tote I can find. Before I take another step, I catch a glimpse of myself on the way out Mama's door and almost stop short.

Face scrubbed clean, no makeup. A butter yellow t-shirt, albeit Polo, that's a bit faded, topping a dark, skinny pair of Levi 501s I picked up on a whim several months ago. I shove my toes into a pair of Born boots. They're slouchy, wonderful, and comfortable.

Dressed and ready, I examine my Bo-ho look.

It's me. But it's not.

In Atlanta, there would have been hours of preparation time. A trip to the salon for a blowout, a mani/pedi. Shopping, new makeup. All the while, wondering about my husband. Where was he? And with whom? When was he coming home? How long would he stay?

I accepted his excuses and promises without question. *We'd see each other soon. Next week. Tomorrow.* He spoon-fed answers–as needed—like children's medicine laced with cherry flavoring to make swallowing his words more palatable.

I wonder what I was thinking. Why did I just accept whatever he told me?

Pressing my fingertips to my lips, I shake my head. I wanted to believe in marriage. In Alton. In us. The white knight on the horse, rescuing me. A man who'd love me forever. No matter what.

I choke back a few tears and lift my chin.

For now, I must move forward with my life. My mother needs me.

First things first.

Still a bit sleepy-eyed at 3:30 am, I half-stumble out Mama's door and make my way to the bakery. The morning-air chill invigorates me, though, and my eyes adjust to the silvery-quiet of Fairhope far before dawn.

Walking helps. My decision to go on foot forces blood flow to my brain and extremities. It's all of a ten-minute trip, yet with everyone else in town asleep, no traffic, and no stopping to chat with neighbors, I arrive at the doorstep in half the time.

Unzipping my Armani backpack, my fingertips find cold metal. On my first attempt, the key slides into the lock; with a pull-and-jerk motion, the ancient mechanism groans and gives way.

I exhale as I take my first step on the hardwood planks. It is my first time in the bakery by myself, and the space takes on an ethereal quality. For a moment, I see Alton's face. Behind him, Phillipa and Mimi whisper over crepes and café au lait. In the far background, C.C. perches on a wingback chair, suspicious, assessing. Sneering.

Shaking my head at the images dismissively, they scatter to the corners of the room, bounce back, and stream toward the open door. Snatching at the wooden frame, I will the negativity out of the space. With a firm motion, I slam and lock the door behind me. Breathing hard, I lean against the wall just to the right, as if waiting for a microburst to blow out the glass, leaving me raw and defenseless.

There is only silence. I giggle at my neurosis and press a palm to my neck. My heartbeat throbs through my index and middle fingers, counting out my fear.

I straighten. Searcy Roberts. Mini pep-talk. Get over this. Get over yourself.

Pretend nothing else matters.

And, for now, I remind myself. It doesn't.

With the grace of an albatross swimming through corn syrup, I familiarize myself with the shop's kitchen. Mama spared no expense in putting in high-end cooktops, restaurant-grade ovens, and a freezer large enough to store Jimmy Hoffa and his entire extended family. I make a mental note to round out the necessary staples as soon as possible.

I crouch down, on a search for stainless steel mixing bowls, Pyrex measuring cups, and various tablespoon and teaspoon measures. With a bit of luck, I secure an array of wooden spoons, spatulas, pie plates, and cooling racks. Distributing them in order––the best I can—along the countertop, I attack phase two.

The pie crust is simple. Flour, salt, and shortening. I decide to begin small, with one attempt at the recipe, since it's been so long. Once I've made a satisfactory go, I can double and triple the process. At this point, however, I can't sacrifice quality for efficiency, even if I have to hand out the most miniscule slices of pie to anyone who walks in the front door.

Clanging the largest of the stainless steel mixing bowls against the counter, I center it in front of my torso, and measure out a cup of flour and salt. As I sift the powder, the white flakes fall like snow, drifting and settling in peaks and valleys against the curve of the metal.

Next, I grasp the container of shortening, peel off the plastic top, and scoop out one-third cup of the slippery solid, followed by an additional tablespoon. With vigor, I cut in the shortening with a fork, creating pea-sized shapes. I pause and fill a tablespoon with chilled water, sprinkling it, and then another, over and around the tiny spheres.

With a fork, I stir the mixture until the crust begins leaving the sides of the bowl. I drop an additional teaspoon of cold water into the bowl and continue melding. A few moments later, the crust appears the perfect consistency. With my fingertips, I pick up the now-solid dough and form it into a ball. After wrapping it in waxed paper, I pop it into the fridge to set.

Satisfied with the outcome, I repeat the process three times, tripling the recipe contents, and giving me a total of ten pie crusts after each section is divided and wrapped.

With renewed energy at this task finished, I tackle my fillings. With care, I slide the heavy tote next to my feet and begin unloading the lemons, limes, blueberries, and squash.

After glancing at Mama's recipes, I gather the remainder of necessary items, including eggs, milk, ginger, cinnamon, oil, butter, white and brown sugar, and tapioca.

I pause and regroup. Turning away from my task momentarily, I blink and stare outside. There's a slight red glow of daybreak on the horizon, reminding me I have minutes, not hours to refocus. Out of necessity, I stretch my arms over my head, interlace my fingertips, then turn and press my palms upward. Expanding my ribcage with a huge breath, I close my eyes, and reach my wrists closer to the ceiling.

A sudden banging on the door startles me out of any temporary Zen-moment I've reached. Stifling a small screech, I collapse out of my balanced pose, hug my arms across my chest, and squint at the offending noise.

The bulky frame of a person shifts outside the door. I swallow hard, right my balance, and take a step toward the entrance. My palpitating heart slows when I recognize the jaw line and shoulders. With swift movement, I untwist the lock and pull open the bakery's front door.

Luke Nolan stands on the doorstep.

Despite my every intention to show strength and nonchalance, I melt a little inside.

"Morning," he says, his voice rough and still laced with sleep. After examining my face, which causes me to flush hot-red, he looks past me, surveying the array of fruits, powders, and liquids.

When he doesn't continue the conversation, I force the issue. "What's up?"

For the first time, he fumbles for words. "Uh, saw the light on, thought you were Tobi," he says. "Then, it—you weren't—and then I wondered what was going on." He stops.

"Baking," I reply, waving a hand behind me. "Attempting to, anyway. I seem to have promised the universe free pie slices today, so I have to live up to some semblance of that," I explain. "Since Tobi doesn't cook much, and I made the deal, it's up to me to execute."

Inside, I cringe. I sound like a drill sergeant. Who bakes.

Luke's serious expression breaks open to reveal a grin. "Sorry I scared you."

"No worries," I say, brushing it off. I glance at the clock.

"I just..." he wrinkles his forehead.

There's an awkward space of nothing. He doesn't want to finish the sentence. Somehow, I can read his mind.

"You didn't think I'd get up and do this?" I ask sweetly. "Keep my end of the deal?"

Luke's mouth curves into a look of pleasure. He likes the honesty.

And I'm too stressed to play games or be coy.

"Maybe," Luke winks.

"I made a promise," I say.

He cocks his head and looks down at me, his eyes piercing beneath my skin, searching, probing. I'm not sure what—if anything—he wants to find.

Another beat of quiet.

"Look," I add. "Thanks for checking on me. I'm fine. And I have to get back to this. Or I won't be able to hold up my end of the bargain."

Luke nods, barely hiding a glow of surprised pleasure.

"Come back later," I say, shooing him out the door. "I'll save you some pie."

"Deal."

The door clicks shut behind him. I breathe out, my head spinning after keeping my total cool for the last five minutes. I'm not certain what Luke is doing to me. Or why he's so surprised about me keeping my word.

It makes me want to prove him wrong. And the rest of the world along with him.

Humming, I pick up a lemon. Back to work.

I decide, ultimately, that my pies of the day will be blueberry and lemon meringue. Though the temptation exists to cook up rhubarb berry, squash, or maple walnut custard, a sense of caution and good Southern tradition holds me back, at least temporarily.

As I retrieve the chilled pie crust and begin to smooth the balls into smooth, flat surfaces, my thoughts turn with the rhythm of my wooden rolling pin.

I am very much a stranger here, despite this being the town where I took my first steps, walked to elementary school, and kissed my first boyfriend. I'm also reminded that my nonexistent trust fund, my father's absence, and Mama's eccentricities kept me on the periphery.

Until Alton came along.

Fast forward to this moment. I've been away, and living the life of a queen—so everyone believes—high atop the bright lights, big city that is Atlanta. Married to a powerful advertising executive, surrounded by wealth acquired from dot-com-mergers, not Civil War lineage.

And despite my jewel-encrusted calling card, my absence means that I've become something of a foreigner.

I have not lived my days close to the waters of Mobile Bay, waves chasing the pebbled beaches of Point Clear and Battles' Wharf. I've not celebrated Mardi Gras, attending balls with the Maids of Jubilee or the Order of Persephone, though Alton and I had received yearly invitations. We'd not been among the faithful, returning home with a gaggle of grandchildren tugging at our designer pant legs.

If I'm going to start over, I have to re-channel my energy. Try to become part of Fairhope—for real this time. Take care of Mama. And keep *Pie Girls* going.

If so, it can't be about me.

My grandmother's advice echoes in my ear. *With baking—like life—there's no place to hide.* Her words tickle and remind me, then disappear into the morning darkness.

I didn't quite understand her meaning until now.

Grandmother's point was that all pies can be prettied up and finished in flaky-edged, fluted flamboyance. A cook can cover her work with careful, leaf cut-outs or a latticed crust. She can sprinkle the top with a buttery brown sugar and cinnamon mixture.

But it's what's on the inside that counts.

Just like a person.

Pies, grandmother, always said, must be made with love. Otherwise, there is no taste, no texture. The mouth cannot explode with happiness, taste buds dancing.

For a quick moment, I place both hands on the cold stainless steel of the counter and summon her memory—the crisp cotton of her dress, the way her hands held a spoon, and how her hair reflected in the window's sunlight like fine threads of liquid silver.

Inhaling her quiet resolve, I set about to begin my work in earnest, measuring out blueberries and sugar. In a saucepan, I combine both with flour, tapioca, butter, salt, and lemon juice. With a flick of my wrist, I light the gas flame on the stovetop and heat the double ovens.

Gathering a deep breath, I prepare a double boiler for the second set of pies. Again, sugar, flour, and salt, this time adding water and whisked egg yolks. Another blue flame ignites under the metal cookware. I watch closely as the consistency thickens. I remove the double-boiler from the heat, pour in fresh lemon juice and sprinkle in a bit of rind. The zest tickles my nose and invigorates my senses, giving me a surge of adrenaline.

The blueberries finish cooking, and I flick off the burner, turning in the remaining fruit, and pouring the batches into waiting pie tins. For what seems like the thousandth time this morning, I open the giant refrigerator door and make room. The pies need the chilled environment to set.

I tackle the meringue next, beating egg whites until my arm aches, ladling in sugar, and continuing the process until stiff peaks form. With care, I stop to pour the lemon filling, finishing off each with a thick, cloud-like layer.

With relief, I open the oven doors, allowing the open space to yawn their hot breath into my face. Drawing back slightly at the heat, I cradle my creations, sliding each onto metal racks.

Setting the timer for fifteen minutes, I rest for a moment, knees buckling, my muscles and brain fighting exhaustion. I smile to myself, thinking that the last time I experienced this much fatigue was a half-price sale at Saks, with Phillipa chattering non-stop about Prada pumps for the entire span of our day. It took me one hot bath and a deep-tissue massage to recover. I don't have that luxury anymore.

Giving in to the shouts from my abused feet and calves, in a most unladylike fashion, I allow myself to slide to the floor—just as the shop's front door slams, sharp and quick.

CHAPTER 20

Before I can gather myself properly and get off the floor, Tobi rushes into the kitchen, clutching her purse and a jumbo-sized bag full of Skittles. At first, examining the room at eye-level, she doesn't notice me.

"Where on Earth did she go?" she mutters to herself. The red Skittles bag's plastic crinkles as Tobi plunges her hand inside it.

I watch as her gaze grazes the countertops, the dirty dishes, and cooling trays lined near the stovetop. Tobi pops a few Skittles into her mouth—red and orange—and chews thoughtfully. Her expression fluctuates in front of me like a pendulum, swinging from dubious to semi-pleased, back to doubtful again.

"Tobi."

She squeals at her name and whirls around, sending a thousand Skittles flying into the air. Around us, yellow, purple, and green candies rain to the ground, bouncing off the ceramic tile like hailstones.

Wincing at the mess and Tobi's frightened face, I kneel and start picking up the small sweets. "So sorry," I say.

Both hands still clapped to her chest, Tobi's jaw finally moves. "Were you—sitting on the floor?" She is incredulous, I note, and not moving one iota to help me clean up.

"Yes," I reply, wrinkling my nose.

Tobi smirks and puts a hand on one hip, summoning her best Southern accent. "My Lawd, I just never thought I'd see the day," she says, pretending to fan herself. "Fairhope's own Searcy Roberts, sitting on the floor of a kitchen restaurant like a common citizen."

She winks, crumples the Skittles bag into a ball, and tosses it into the trash. The plastic unfolds loudly the moment it hits the bin—almost as if were sending applause for her comeback.

"Well, I said I'd be here," I say. "So, here I am." The Skittles begin to melt in my hand. Bright yellow bleeds into the crevices of my palm, mixing with a smear of grape and Astroturf green.

"And you've baked," Tobi says, staring at the oven lights, squinting to see what's inside.

I realize, then, that she's shocked. Flabbergasted that I actually showed up. Worked. Baked. Like a *common citizen*.

She and Luke both.

"There's more in the fridge." I say, and then realize I've neglected something.

Blueberry pie. Whipped cream.

"Hang on."

Throwing myself into the task at hand, I step past Tobi and grab the whole milk cream out of the refrigerator. Pouring the containers into the bowl, I secure the mixer in place and begin the process of whipping enough air into the liquid to make it as light as cotton candy.

Conversation now impossible, Tobi sets down her purse to make the morning's first batch of coffee.

The buzzer sounds for the lemon meringue pies and I rush to scoop them from the ovens. Steam rises from the doors, momentarily scalding my cheeks, but the delicious smell of citrus and sugar overpower my senses.

With utmost care, I place each on wire racks. The meringue is toast-brown tipped at the edges. The pies are glorious; I have my grandmother to thank for her years of perfecting the recipe.

I retrieve all of the blueberry pies and line them on the opposite counter. With a wide spatula, I spoon on the whipped cream, generous with my portions. On a whim, I search for some color, a bit of contrast to the white. I find a few loose kiwis, a handful of strawberries, and a bowl of blueberries. With a sharp knife, I peel the kiwis and slice the strawberries thinly, decorating the center of each pie with a splash of red, green, and blue.

As I stand back to assess my work, Tobi skirts by me with a large container of sweet tea.

"Very nice," she says.

A tiny glow wells back up inside of me. I follow behind her, carrying my creations to the bakery racks. All told, I've made two dozen pies, a personal-best record for me. I can't think of a time when I've made so many desserts.

I grab the sidewalk blackboard, pieces of blue and pink chalk, and write the day's specials in large script. With a gulp, I add the "Free slices today – first 40 people!" in bold strokes.

Tobi flicks a look at the clock. It's 6 o'clock, and already, a few customers are lingering outside. She walks over, flips over the sign, and turns the lock.

She picks up the blackboard and carries it toward the street, all the while calling out greetings.

Tobi is back within twenty seconds and assumes her place behind the counter. Without hesitation, she takes orders with precision, committing everything to memory.

The best I can, I follow along, pouring coffee into mugs, slicing into my lemon and blueberry pies.

We hand plate after plate to customers, some expectant for the gift, others pleased that they've stumbled onto a small treasure.

"Looks like you did good," Tobi nudges me with her elbow, assuming a redneck accent instead of her usual Southern drawl.

I can't help but laugh, maybe more out of relief than anything.

Outside the front window, a streak of color rushes by in a blur of wheels, helmets, and jerseys. I can't count how many bikers ride past, but apparently the group stops next door, as talking and laughter soon drift through the vents of Luke's shop and into the bakery.

When the bell over the entrance jingles merrily, Luke Nolan and five of his equally broad-shouldered friends walk through the front door. Tobi, having kept quiet the last few minutes to re-brew all of the coffee, lets out a little murmur of delight under her breath.

When I focus my gaze, I understand why, and try to stop staring. Not only does Luke look amazing in his spandex biker shirt and shorts, his biceps and thigh muscles glow from a light sheen of sweat. His friends, equally well-built and rangy, jostle for position in front of the counter, their biking shoes clicking and knocking against the plank wood floor.

"Where'd you go today?" Tobi asks, serving up coffee in mugs without missing a beat.

Luke glances over at me and I flush, quickly averting my eyes, re-arranging pies in the bakery case. I pretend not to listen, busying myself with the non-task of moving each slice a half-inch forward.

"Hey, Searcy," Luke calls out, grinning.

At the greeting, I raise my head sharply, immediately whacking it on the metal edge of the display. "Ouch," I whisper and look up, hoping no one's seen me.

"That's gonna hurt," one of Luke's buddies comments. Another whistles long and low, shaking his head.

"Oh, I'm good, y'all," I say, forcing a big smile over the pain of my throbbing temple. I want to crawl under the floor and disappear, but I stand there, making eye contact with six very attractive men, Luke the very last of the bunch.

"Morning, Luke," I add, backing up to allow Tobi in front of me. She grabs two slices of lemon meringue. "So, you were saying—your bike ride?"

My hurt head is forgotten immediately as Luke and his friends recount the sixty-mile round trip from Fairhope to Gulf Shores. Their early morning encounter included several armadillos, one flat tire, and an angry motorist.

"The dude's insane," one of the guys pipes up, wiping his brow with a spare napkin, "Total anger issues, laying on the horn, acting like he's going to swerve."

"Get his tag number," Tobi suggests. "Call it in."

Luke gives her an easy smile. "Aw, the guy probably had a bad cup of coffee or something."

"You're such a lover, not a fighter, Lukie," one of the other members of the group teases in a high-pitched voice.

The entire group pushes and pokes at Luke like a bunch of teenagers. I stand there, amazed at the camaraderie. The last time Alton and I did anything social with Phillipa and her husband, it was a stiff hour of tea followed by analysis of the day's NPR reports.

My only other recent witnessing of Alton with another X-chromosomed human being was dinner with C.C. and his step-father at their home in Buckhead. It was an equally formal meal followed by a glass of hundred-year-old port by the gas-burning fireplace they keep for show. It gets cold enough to use it about once a year.

A few of the bikers take seats at empty tables, but Luke lingers at the counter, chatting with Tobi. He is engaged in the conversation, and I hear something about her kids, their schoolwork, and the morning's steady stream of customers.

All at once, I picture myself as Tobi at school dances, backed up against the gym wall, chin down, eyes roving the dark, disco ball-lit room. Alone. Locked out of the conversation, a stranger despite known faces.

I am not a part of the conversation and am not being included. It's the first time in forever that I've felt exclusion this acutely. I'm a bit jealous. And sad. I wipe an imaginary speck off the counter.

Suddenly, I am wrenched back into the chatter. "Free pie helps," Tobi adds, giving me a wry glance.

"The shop probably won't be offering *this* special again for a while," I say, agreeing with a grin.

Luke is on his second piece of lemon meringue. Between mouthfuls, he grins. "It's good, Searcy. You'd probably go broke."

Before I can absorb a tiny bit of satisfaction from the compliment, the bell above the door rings sharply, and there's a definitive closing of the front door. Heavy boot steps rock the floor, and when Luke moves his shoulder, I can see an unsmiling man heading straight for the counter.

In a flash, Tobi disappears, and Luke drifts back to one of the tables, finishing off his last bite of yellow filling and golden crust.

He glances back and gives me a reassuring look, as if to say, *Don't worry, you've got this.*

I freeze in place. Got what?

The man, definitely attractive and self-assured, is about my mother's age. His hair, jet-black and impossibly thick, is threaded with silver flecks, making him look distinguished. His jawline, set firmly, gives his face a hard edge. Above his full lips sits a distinguished, sharp nose. What grabs my attention are his arresting, emerald green eyes, just a shade darker than my own. Instead of sparkling, though, they pierce through the crowd, his dark irises eventually landing squarely on me.

"Good morning," I say, not sure why I'm gripping the counter.

"So, a slice of pie for free?" he asks.

"Yes, sir," I reply.

There's an awkward beat of silence.

"All right," he says, eyeing the blueberry.

With a moment of hesitation, I slide a hand toward the bakery case. "Would you like a piece?" Hiding my nervousness, I force the corners of my mouth into a smile.

"Why not?" he shrugs, and his indifference settles over me with a chill.

The plate clinks down in front of him and I hand over a fork and thick white napkin. The man's looking past me now, his eyes searching for someone or something.

I shiver, despite the heat of the kitchen behind me.

"Maggie here?" he asks, taking the edge of the plate with his thick fingers. He's dressed in a red and blue flannel shirt, dark Carhartt jeans, and a University of Alabama ball cap. Grasping his fork, he cuts into the pie, spears the end, and shovels the dessert into his mouth.

"Not today," I say, and don't offer an explanation.

"Tobi, then?" he says, between mouthfuls of pie. He's not asking, I decide. He's demanding—under a veil of entitled pleasantries. If I had to guess, this man always gets what he wants.

My shoulders stiffen. I set my jaw firmly. "Your name?"

"Quinn Hillyer," he replies, finishing the last bite of pie. He sets the plate and fork down hard on the counter.

"Searcy Roberts," I say, extending my hand. A peace offering, though I don't know what anyone's fighting over.

The announcement of my name makes Hillyer pause, but only for a half-second. He recovers and nods, giving my hand a quick, firm shake. "Heard you were in town. Staying long?"

Brushing my long hair off of my shoulder, I shrug. "I haven't decided." It's the most candid reply anyone in this town's received since my arrival, and I've decided Quinn Hillyer deserves a vague, non-answer for being so darn presumptuous and arrogant.

He leans in and lowers his voice. "You'll give her a message?"

"Sure," I reply, unconvinced it will be anything remarkable. I reach for a pen and a pad of paper.

Hillyer eyes me carefully. "The rent's due. Six months of it. By the end of the month. Tell Maggie I need to collect."

CHAPTER 21

I arrive home in a rush, heart still thudding from the encounter with Quinn Hillyer. I don't mention a word to Mama—just help her into the car and drive straight to Jimmy Richmond's office. We pull into the parking lot with moments to spare. There's no rushing my mother, and no amount of cajoling helps.

My mind is still spinning.

How much money? Why hasn't the rent been paid? What about the utilities? How much does Tobi know about this and why hasn't she told me? What will happen to my mother?

The fill-in-the-blanks loom large and dark over my head, following me like a sudden storm filling a clear blue summer sky.

My mother, looking every bit the cute bohemian that she is, adjusts the twenty silver bangles on her wrist. She straightens her peasant top, embroidered at the loose neckline with greens and purples. Her purse, long-strapped and colorful, resembles a Rastafarian's slouchy gold and red hat.

At five minutes past two, we walk into the office and sign in at the reception area. My mother writes her name, the letters arcing over the page.

Mama makes pleasantries with some of the other ladies in the waiting room, re-introducing me as her daughter. Many of the faces are familiar, but after more than a decade of being away, most are faded and blurred in my memory.

"Miss Mason?" A scrub-clad girl of eighteen or nineteen calls my mother, standing on tiptoes to make eye contact over the dozens of heads. She smiles brightly, showing off wide, white teeth as we make our way across the carpeted floor.

"Searcy," my mother whispers. "Don't you have an errand to run?" She glances at the watch on her wrist. "Go get a cup of coffee and come back in an hour, sweetie."

I wrinkle my nose and shake my head. "Why? I'm fine, Mama." With a hand to her elbow, I guide her toward the waiting employee.

"Hey, y'all," she exclaims, putting a guiding hand on Mama's back. "How're y'all doing? Such a pretty day outside, isn't it? Just glorious."

Mama smiles while I ignore the employee's idle talk. I am not fine. I have six months' rent to worry about and about a million questions to ask the doctor.

Chattering away while taking my mother's height and weight, and then blood pressure, the nursing assistant's singsong voice reminds me of Sunday school or nursery rhymes. Pausing to jot down the numbers, the girl winks at Mama, still maintaining her over-zealous my-world-is-full-of-unicorns-and-rainbows attitude.

"So," the girl asks, "are we here today for a check up?"

My mother shifts and twists her mouth, uncomfortable. She covers up the action quickly. "Dr. Richmond asked me to come back in a month," she replies. "But everything's fine."

"Super duper!" the nursing assistant replies brightly.

"How are the numbers?" I ask, attempting to peer over the girl's shoulder as she leads us down the hallway.

"Room three!" the nursing assistant says brightly, as if we've won the lottery. She ignores my question, doing her best to focus on Mama.

The girl pats the exam table. "Now, Miss Maggie, hop yourself right up on here. Put on this cute little top."

The limp cotton wrap she's referring to is yellow and imprinted with ducks. I swallow a comment about farm animals and repeat my question.

"The numbers? Please."

For the first time, the nursing assistant loses some of her shiny-happy-people exterior.

I frown.

"Searcy, dear," Mama warns me in a sweet tone that used to mean "I'm going to put you in time out" when I was six or seven. "There's nothing to concern yourself with. Not a thing."

I immediately flick on good-girl mode, matching the other two in tone and wit. "Oh, y'all, I just want to know if Mama needs to trim up any before bathing suit season," I giggle and cover my mouth at the absurdity, but it works.

"Heavens," my mother says, blushing. "All right."

The nursing assistant pauses, glances down at the information, and turns to the computer monitor. "Just a moment," she says. With deft fingers, she types on the keyboard and finishes by hitting 'enter' with flourish. Frowning slightly, the girl hands me the slip.

"Dr. Richmond will be in to see you in a jiffy," she adds, then leaves the room. The door closes behind her with a click.

I glance at the paper and scan the numbers, masking a sharp inhale with a huge yawn, exaggerating the sound and opening my jaw widely. In my wildest dreams, I wouldn't imagine. I knew Mama had dropped weight, but this was ridiculous.

Both Mama and Dr. Jimmy Richmond have some serious explaining to do.

Fifteen years and five minutes later, my former classmate appears after a quick rap on the door. He still resembles the fictional TV physician from the early 90s, Doogie Howser—a younger version of the openly gay, hilariously funny, and still gorgeous Neil Patrick Harris.

"Lovely Maggie Mason," he greets my mother with an air-kiss on each cheek. "And, Searcy, it's been a long time," he smiles.

I've always liked Jimmy—blond hair, horn-rimmed glasses, and all. He was a brainiac, and I admired that quality. After landing a near-perfect pre-SAT scores, UAB, Vanderbilt, and Emory started courting him freshman year of high school.

He could have had his pick of big cities and huge salaries, but internal medicine and coming home to live in Fairhope won out.

"Let's see how everything's going," Jimmy says, consulting the screen of his computer. I watch his face for any signs of displeasure. "We've got your blood work. Thanks for getting that done before the appointment." His voice trails off as he assesses a long page of codes and numbers.

Blood work? When did you do that? I flash a look at my mother.

She smiles back at me, attempting a bewildered look, then focuses her attention on Jimmy.

My irritation level steeps, like hot water in a tea kettle, left to boil over an open flame.

Jimmy sits down on the circular exam stool and scoots it close to Mama. "So," he says, glancing at my mother. "I have to have your permission, Maggie, to discuss everything in front of Searcy. HIPAA regulations." His small hands make a dismissive, fluttering gesture.

My breath catches hard in my throat, making my lungs burn.

"Searcy, dear," my mother says in a quiet voice. "Please give us a minute." Her eyes flick toward the waiting room, nudging me to leave.

I don't move.

The silence in the exam room screams into my ears. I know the game—a Southern belle's way of pretending everything's fine—a bit of martyrdom, modesty, and manipulation. And even though Mama is more hippie chic than former debutante, the ideals ring true. Don't worry your family. Maintain a bright outlook. Fake it 'til you make it. Smile even if your heart is breaking.

I know the rules. I've lived them.

Dr. Richmond clears his throat.

About to acquiesce to my mother's wishes, I push myself out of the hard-backed plastic chair. It's then that I notice, under the harsh florescent lights, a butterfly wing-shaped rash across Mama's cheeks.

She'd done a fabulous job of covering it up with artful foundation and powder, but the stress of the moment drained the usually-cheery pink from her skin.

"I'm not leaving," I say, announcing it as if I've just decided to run for mayor of Fairhope. I sit, firm, unmoving.

Jimmy and Mama recoil.

I summon my thoughts, pushing them together into a cohesive argument. "Mama, you asked me to come home to help you. And now I'm here, but you're trying to shut me out from a major portion of your life."

"Now, Searcy," Mama protests.

"Please, Mama," I beg. "I care about what's going on with you. You're sleeping all of the time, you're not eating, and now, there's something funny going on with your skin."

Mama's hands fly to her face. She knows. Her eyes fill with tears.

"I'm sorry," I say, reaching for her hand and giving it a gentle tug. "Mama, I don't want to make you feel worse. But I love you. And I can't bear to let anything happen to you."

Jimmy waits, ever patient. Until Mama nods her approval, dabbing at her wet lashes.

"All right," Jimmy straightens in relief, likely worn to a frazzle with all of the estrogen and drama. "Searcy, your mother's been struggling with a number of symptoms for several years now. I've determined that she has a form of Lupus."

The room tilts.

He continues. "Lupus is a chronic inflammatory disease. It happens when your body's immune system attacks your own tissues and organs. It can affect a person's joints, skin, kidneys, blood cells, brain, heart and lungs."

I grab at the edge of my chair to steady myself.

"At first, we thought your mother was exhausted from managing the shop and had contracted a bad virus. But after running tests, all signs point to Lupus. What sealed it for me was the most distinctive sign of the illness—a facial rash, similar to what your mother has now."

Jimmy pauses to let me absorb this.

"And there's no cure," I say, the words painful and cutting.

"That's true," replies Jimmy. "There's research being done, but right now, all we have are ways to manage the symptoms, both through medicine and lifestyle. Lupus is particularly difficult, as no two cases are exactly alike. Signs and symptoms come on suddenly or develop slowly, may be mild or severe, and may be temporary or permanent. Most people have flares—symptoms get worse for a while, then improve or even disappear completely for a time."

I'm positively sick to my stomach. "Other symptoms?"

"Fatigue is major, sometimes accompanied with a fever. Joint pain, stiffness, and swelling are common, as is the facial rash," says Jimmy. "We also have to watch for skin lesions that appear or worsen with sun exposure, shortness of breath, chest pain, headaches, confusion, and memory loss."

"What about the medications? Can Mama take them?" I ask.

Jimmy purses his thin lips. "We've discussed a variety of things that could help, from over the counter Advil to steroids and chemotherapy."

I glance at Mama, who is looking terribly white and guilty. "And?" I prompt.

Jimmy tugs at his tie and hesitates.

All at once, I have the sense of being a teenager again. I feel certain that my mother and I are about to be called to the principal's office after being caught with a can of spray paint on the school grounds. I wish Alton was here, ready with a joke or witty comment to break the tension.

But he's not.

It's only me. And Mama. Who's apparently very ill.

I wait patiently for Jimmy's reply. When it comes, the reality of it hits me square between the eyes.

"Maggie's refused any treatment."

CHAPTER 22

The ride home with my mother is a mixture of frustration and familiar longing—I ache with a sudden need to have Mama throw her arms around me and tell me everything is going to be okay. But now, it seems the tables are turned, and it's up to me to shoulder the responsibility.

As has been the case my whole life, there's no father figure to lean on, and no Alton. He's always been the logical one. Calm in a crisis, levelheaded in a bad situation.

As furious as I am with Alton, I miss him. It's so very hard knowing he'll never really be a part of my life again.

I have to be strong.

I have Mama to worry about.

And *Pie Girls*.

There exists an urgency in my belly now, a burning need to make things right.

Without consistent, fresh homemade goods, the shop won't make money. Without cash, we can't pay Mama's bills and buy her prescriptions.

The shop had to offer better. *The best.*

I decide to stop at the pharmacy first, but I don't want to leave Mama in the car for a moment. Luckily, the drive-through window is still open. There's a car ahead of us, so I pull up and wait.

I am so lost in my swirl of thoughts that, a few moments later, the squawk from the pharmacy window frightens me to death.

"May I help y'all?"

After recovering my breath, I ease the Cadillac forward look up at the girl in the glassed window. She's all of 18, with lacquered-into-place, larger-than-life Southern hair, a red vest, and long-cat-claw fingernails. She's chewing gum. Bright orange gum.

"Maggie Mason. Two prescriptions, please," I say, biting my lip.

What Phillipa and I couldn't do with this young lady. A few hours at Macy's and my favorite salon, and the girl would be transformed. She has the skin and the bone structure of a natural beauty. I can tell—even beneath the layers of war paint and false eyelashes.

Reading my mind, Mama injects her thoughts. It's easier to talk about than the real reason we're visiting the pharmacy.

"Bless her heart, she's from way outside Robertsdale, from what people say," my mother whispers. "Nice as can be. Her mother waits tables at the Fairhope Inn."

I lean back against the car's seat and smile. Small town Alabama. Everyone knows everything about everyone. Or, at least, they think they do.

As we drive away with Mama's prescriptions, I consider this.

I think about Atlanta, with its glittering skyscrapers, busy sidewalks, and endless traffic. In the big city, it's easy to have secrets. It's possible to get lost in a crowd or disappear for a while.

Here, people notice.

They pay attention.

They care.

And that's wonderful and comforting, especially when it comes to Mama.

Considering my own situation with Alton, everyone will find out soon enough.

I'll confide in Mama when she's feeling better.

Mimi and Phillipa will have to wait.

At home, Mama takes her medicine and falls asleep before I can fetch a blanket. Covering her from shoulder to toes with the softest throw I can find, I write a quick note, lock up the house, and walk down the driveway.

I'm wired. I can bake, but feel the need to do something physical and productive. Something to make Mama happy. I get behind the wheel of the Cadillac, drumming my fingers on the seat, and drive aimlessly. When I round the corner, I see a sign for Jubilee Ace Home Center on Fairhope Avenue.

Heading straight for the paint colors, I am immediately drawn to the warm blends. My fingertips find a mellow gold Caramel Ganache, a creamy pomegranate Terra Sol, and a cheery pink named Hibiscus.

Feeling bold and dangerous, I opt for the bright color palate and pray that Mama will like it as much as I do. I choose Mocha Icing, Vanilla Latte, and Gooseberry, a name just silly enough to make me laugh out loud. I pick up pints of Hibiscus and Hot Cocoa for accents.

Satisfied, I add rollers, brushes, drop cloths, and other supplies. Minutes later, I am helped out the door by an enthusiastic salesman who carries my purchase to Mama's Cadillac.

"Good luck," he tells me and tips an imaginary hat. "Hope Maggie loves it."

It's past dinnertime now, so *Pie Girls* is closed and dark.

I open the shop, flick on the lights, and carry my load in the front entrance. With a final look around the gold and black walls that were probably last painted during the Madonna music-craze, I set up to work.

The paint I've chosen combines primer and topcoat, and I calculate that this should cut my time in half. I tackle the trim work first, taping off windows so that I can edge quickly. It's been years, college maybe, since I've painted walls, and a feeling of accomplishment wells up inside me as I roll on the brand-new coating.

Music, something folksy with an edge, begins to murmur next door. The sound increases with the song's intensity, and I immediately recognize the artist. Matt Nathanson's album, *Last of the Great Pretenders*. He's one of my favorite performers, and I hum along to *Earthquake Weather* and *Kill the Lights*, which has me swaying in time to the sultry, sexy beat.

When someone knocks at the door, I jump and whirl, sending droplets flying. They land mostly on me, pink pinpricks against dark blue denim.

Luke stands in the fading afternoon light and waves at me through the thick doorway glass. Grasping the knob, he turns and walks in. Keys dangle in his hand. "You left these outside. I figured you might want them."

Flushing, I set my brush on the open paint can and take the dozen steps to cross the room. I can't look at him, not directly, as he dumps the metal into my palm.

"Thank you."

"So, pie and dancing?" he asks, his eyes teasing me.

Dammit. He saw me. As I notice the backdrop—an expanse of windows—I think probably everyone else in Fairhope was in on the show.

"Only after hours," I say, blushing.

"I see," he says, cracking a smile. I can't help but be drawn to the way the curve of his lips light up his entire face and the room. His teeth are perfect, I note. My heart contracts and expands. I am drawn to him, inexplicably, despite my brain fighting it.

I break our gaze and look at the floor.

"Need any help, Searcy?" Luke asks, clearing his throat.

I exhale and nod. "Have a ladder I can use?" With a trembling hand, I grab the wooden back and give it a shake. It groans and creaks like an old, rusty wagon. "This one isn't very stable," I laugh.

"Sure. Be right back."

My body sags in relief as he exits the building and goes next door. Rubbing my forehead, I remind myself to keep my cool.

Luke's back in no time, ladder hoisted on one shoulder. He doesn't bother to knock to warn me this time, and unfolds the wooden frame close to where I'm working.

"Thank you so much," I say brightly.

When he doesn't leave, I position the rungs so that my back faces him. As I ease the paint can to one side and dip in my brush, I peek over my shoulder.

He's texting or replying to email, and doing so intently, head bent so that I can just make out his long, sandy eyelashes and the sprinkle of cute freckles on his nose. His hair, which curls just a bit, is messy. Sexy and windblown. The sight of it makes me want to drop everything and sit in his lap, wrapping my arms around his strong shoulders, pulling his mouth down on mine.

"Searcy?"

Luke's voice breaks my fantasy into pieces, and I slosh the bristles into the bucket, almost knocking over the dangerously full can. The ladder rocks from side-to-side, an inch or two, and I hang on until the motion stops.

"Yes," I say, trying to recover.

When my eyes meet his, a little guiltily, he brings my attention to the FedEx man outside the door. How I missed the arrival of his huge diesel-powered truck is beyond me. The white expanse of it is parked behind him, blocking the street.

"Oh," I say, startled, and begin to climb down.

"No, you stay," he says, holding out a hand as if to brace me from ten feet away. "I was just checking email. I'll grab it."

"Thanks, Luke." Saying his name makes the tiny hairs on my arm stand at attention. I force myself to turn back.

What is it about this guy? I'm definitely starved for attention. Wanting a man's touch. But you need to be careful, a tiny voice in my brain reminds me. Don't get hurt.

I shake my head at all of it, trying to get rid of the thoughts. Forget Luke. Forget Alton. My arms are tired, my shoulders ache, but I raise the wooden handle and hold my hand steady, moving it across the ceiling's edge in an even stroke.

I hear Luke return as I continue, moving the ladder a few feet. It's not as heavy, as I've used quite a bit of paint.

"Hope you don't mind, but I signed for it," he says.

"That's great. Just set it on the counter," I say, pushing one elbow at the bakery case. "I'll take it home to Mama or give it to Tobi in the morning."

"It's for you," he says.

Me? I stop myself from uttering the syllable.

Luke ambles over and sticks the envelope under the ladder, just within my line of vision. "It could be important."

My skin prickles as I scan the address. *Darn FedEx.* And darn Luke for being so helpful. "Nope."

He frowns, completely confused, and turns the package around so that the writing faces him. "But isn't this from your husband? It says Roberts." He pauses. "I thought he was in Bangladesh or somewhere exotic," he says, persisting.

"Um, Thailand," I say, choking on the reply and needing to change the subject. I want to jump down, snatch the FedEx delivery, and throw it in the trash. Instead, I maintain my decorum as a Southern-bred girl, and try to step gracefully down to the floor.

Of course, in my attempt to maintain a semblance of aloof detachment and dignity, I manage to wrap my leg inside the bottom rung, catch a thread of my pant leg, and panic.

"Don't!" Luke warns me.

I jiggle my foot, then pull with my leg, twisting away from the metal frame. I lose my balance, and pitch myself backward, taking the ladder, brush, and paint along with me. In an eruption of deep, lovely pink, the can upends and becomes airborne. In seeming slow motion, the metal edge catches me squarely in the middle of my nose.

CHAPTER 23

The impact blinds me momentarily, stinging and cutting my skin, and I can't help crying out in pain. Continuing its tumble, the container makes another half-rotation and dumps over me, coating my shirt, jeans, and shoes.

"Searcy," Luke crouches next to me, his face awash with concern.

Tears squeeze from the corners of my eyes. My nose throbs. I don't move from my sprawled out position on the floor.

"It's a good thing I like pink," I say, cracking a smile to hide my embarrassment.

Luke laughs. "It's a nice look for you," he teases, helping me into a seated position.

Gingerly, I touch my nose. "Is it as bad..."

He tilts his head with a degree of serious inspection, rubbing his chin with one hand. "It could've been worse."

The pain radiates from the center of my face. "Blood?"

"A little."

"Stitches?" I wince and force myself to sit cross-legged on the floor. I'm dizzy.

"I don't think so," he says.

I exhale in relief, then turn my head and survey the mess. It's not too bad, mostly on the drop cloth and me. With a quick motion, I slide off both tennis shoes. Ruined. With another small giggle, I check the pink tips of my hair. "Nice," I add. "Maybe it'll be the new trend in Fairhope."

"Somehow, I don't know if it'll catch on," says Luke wryly.

I narrow my eyes in mock frustration. "Non-believer."

He chuckles. "And they say I'm a little crazy for running a bike shop here." He stops himself and puts one strong hand on my elbow.

Letting out a breathy, small groan, I straighten, allowing myself to lean against Luke. He's so close that I can smell the clean, soapy scent of his skin.

"Let's get you cleaned up," he says, still holding tight to my arm.

I glance up and raise an eyebrow. "Here?" I have a flash of stripping down in the back room, tossing my clothes in the trash, and driving like crazy to make it to Mama's before the Fairhope Police Department spots a blond, female driver in only her bra and panties.

Luke smiles down at me. "Next door," he says. "Come on, I'll show you."

With a deft hand, he unlocks the shop and allows me to go inside. Luckily, the paint's almost dry and doesn't drip. I pad, barefoot, across the smooth pinewood floor. I don't ask, though I wonder exactly what he has in mind. A hose in the back? A utility shower full of tools?

Through two more sets of doors, we enter a small room. It's pleasant, with unfinished bricks and dark wood, emitting the distinct feel of a man's space.

"There's a shower in here," Luke says, gesturing. "Go ahead. I'll grab a bag for your things." He disappears for a few seconds, then reappears with a large, frayed yellow towel and a black plastic trash bag.

I hesitate. "Should I give you the keys to Mama's house? She can get me some clothes." My head hurts at the thought of Luke being caught sneaking into Mama's house and grabbing intimate apparel from my bedroom. I think I'd rather die.

He laughs again at the look on my face, a deep, delicious sound which fills the room. Luke rolls his eyes at me. "I have stuff here, Searcy."

This time, I cross my arms and squint up at Luke.

"In. The. Store." His body shakes with laughter, and he doubles-over slightly, wiping a stream of tears from his eyes. "For bicyclists."

Obviously, the bump on my nose is affecting my brain. "Oh, gosh," I reply, my face getting hot. "Of course. Thank you."

"No prob," he says. "Take your time. No one will bother you."

Before I can protest, he's gone.

After adjusting to being alone in the foreign space, I focus on getting cleaned up. My clothes are definitely ruined. As I peel off my shirt and pants, they slop together and squish.

I fold them into awkward triangles and set them on the ragged towel. The edges of the towel are embroidered with white daisies. It looks like a pre-teen girl's beach wrap, ten or twelve years old. The corners are faded and worn, and the body of the fabric is marred with faded smears and stains.

Old girlfriend? Donated by a shop employee for the rag pile? Something left there by a customer and never claimed? There has to be a good explanation.

With a jolt, I remember Tobi mentioning a girl named Sarah in Luke's life. That she had special needs, whatever that meant. It could equal high-maintenance, for all I knew. If she was his girlfriend, I'd never seen her.

Perplexed, I reach over and lock the door. Not that it would help if Luke decided to barge in. He probably has a key, I remind myself.

It had been a while since I'd seen someone so finely muscled. Not in a hulking, gym-obsessed way, either. Luke exuded athletic and outdoorsy. Different from Alton's toned body. Both were attractive, but Luke made me weak-kneed in a way my husband never had.

As I strip off my bra and panties, I realize the difference. Pure, unadulterated attraction. A yummy, tear-your-clothes-off physical need. Plus, as a bonus, he's genuinely nice.

Focus, Searcy.

I shower as quickly as possible, letting the scorching-hot water cascade over my body. The tile surface is lovely, and paint rinses from my hair and bare skin in bright pink rivulets. As my eyes graze the Travertine tile and gleaming stainless knobs, I'm thankful that the space is more than a glorified truck stop rinse-down.

Scrubbed clean and refreshed, I step out, grab the towel and dry off. Tiptoeing across the floor, I unlock the knob, and crack open the door. As promised, folded clothes awaited me, tags still on.

Back inside the bathroom, I examine the layers. A Bella short-short with an adorable halter with artsy bike wheels and sprockets decorating the chest. Luke included a matching Xenon 2 AS Lady Jacket, a pair of Terry logo pink and red socks, and Tourmaline shoes to finish off the outfit. Tags still on, I was looking at close to $400 in bike wear, more than I could afford.

Preferring the alternative, which is streaking to Mama's in only a towel, I rationalize that I can always trade pie for apparel.

The pieces fit perfectly, and I relax into the feel of the fine fabric snug across my body. Luke is waiting for me in the main bike showroom, eased back against a modern black and silver chair. He gestures to the one next to him.

"You look like a professional," he says, cracking a wide grin. "Ready to ride?"

I sink into the open chair, my body collapsing against the padded leather back. "Rain check?" I ask, biting my lip and tossing him a weak smile. It's been years since I've ridden a bike, let alone anything with more than three speeds. The idea slightly intimidates me, but I like a challenge.

A challenge.

I sit bolt upright, remembering the paint-spattered mess in the shop.

"Relax," Luke says, reading my mind. "I finished and cleaned up."

Gaping at him slightly, then closing my mouth with a snap, I struggled for words. "Th-thank you so much." The kindness of his action overwhelms me.

"I figured it was the last thing you needed to worry about," he adds. "It didn't take long, though pink really isn't my color." He holds up his arm and points at a smear of pink. "Missed a spot when I washed up."

The sight makes me giggle, until I see the FedEx package next to his feet. Luke followed my gaze and picks up the envelope, handing it over.

"Great," I say brightly, my fingers trembling as I feign nonchalance and tear at the strip to open the cardboard holder.

I peek inside, allowing myself the most cursory glance at the cream linen paper and official legal letterhead. My vision blurs as a read a string of last names broken by commas and ending with LLC. Breathing erratically, I pinch the envelope shut, press it to my chest, and press a hand against the nearest wall for balance.

Luke reaches a hand to steady me. "You're white."

"I don't feel so well," I say, not willing to admit that the contents are making me ill. "Let's go next door?" I ask. "I'll make us some coffee? Get you a piece of pie—if there's any left."

He nods and leads the way, staying close enough to touch. The nearness of his body makes me tingle. I am, at once, aware of the way his arm and legs move with athletic grace, how quickly a smile forms on his face, how willing he is to help without the expectation of being paid back or owed.

Inside, I put the sturdy white envelope under my purse for safekeeping and survey the pie shop walls. They are bright, cheery, and perfectly finished. The drop cloths lie folded in the corner, and the floors shine. "Wow," I say. "It looks amazing. Thank you for cleaning up."

Luke glows at my appreciation and takes a corner cafe table while I grind and brew the beans. The movement soothes me, as does the noise, which blurs out the whirring worry in my head. As the coffee percolates, the scent of dark-roast Columbian permeates the small space, invoking notes of wood, warmth, and chocolate undertones. Minutes later, I carry two steaming mugs and a lone slice of lemon meringue to the table.

"So, want to tell me about it? The delivery." Luke asks, his eyes piercing into mine.

I fold inward, and then consider the worst outcome, which isn't much better than my current reality. *Might as well start somewhere.* My confession rushes out.

"The truth is, my marriage is not in a good place." Unsmiling, I raise an eyebrow and pick up my coffee, taking a tentative sip. Despite the unpleasant topic, in a small way, I am relieved. Telling another human being somehow eases the stress.

Luke murmurs an acknowledgement between bites. "I'm sorry, Searcy."

"Don't be," I say and hold up a hand. "Please, I'm not even sure what's going on. He's disappeared, kind of, to an Ashram. Quit his job, turned the lease on our apartment in Atlanta back over to my mother-in-law. He's...spending some time...finding himself."

"With someone else?" Luke asks.

Pausing, I swallow the nausea that accompanies the thought of Alton being with another woman. "I think so, yes."

Luke frowns. "And so you're here. For how long?"

"I'm not sure." I stretch both legs out straight, cross my ankles and tilt my head back to rest on the chair back. "I was supposed to come for a week. Get my bearings, have some breathing room."

"Right," Luke says, finishing his last forkful.

"But, with what's going on with Mama, I could be staying a lot longer." I run a hand through my hair. "By the way, Tobi knows about Alton, but not Mama. I didn't want to worry her with anything else."

Luke eyes me thoughtfully. "I won't tell her."

"Thank you," I say.

There's a pause, and Luke pushes away from the table a few inches. He gives me a long look.

"This may be none of my business, but what's up with Quinn Hillyer?"

Exhaling, I bite my bottom lip. Do I tell? Do I say anything? I weigh the harm. And that Luke may already know.

"The rent's past due," I say in a hushed voice. "By about six months. And I was so flustered I haven't even asked what that means, in terms of an actual total. I think I'm afraid to."

Luke runs a hand through his blond hair, calculating in his head. The bike shop's about the same square footage. "So, why the painting?" He asks, his eyes trained on me.

Half-smiling, I shrug. "Didn't care for the gold and black much. And I needed some stress relief," I touch the bridge of my nose. It's so tender I wince. "Not sure it was the best outcome."

Luke looks around at the walls and then grins back at me. "It's good. The place was way overdue for a change."

We're both quiet for a few moments, sipping our coffee. It's comfortable and nice, like being wrapped in a soft, fleece blanket near a crackling fire.

Setting down his mug, Luke clears his throat. "So, what does your mother say?"

"About the rent?" I raise an eyebrow.

Luke nods.

My face flushes. "We haven't even talked about finances," I say. "We had a doctor's appointment today," I say, meeting Luke's gaze. "I-I hadn't realized she's so ill. Being in Atlanta, I missed more than I should."

He leans closer, putting both elbows on his knees. "I knew something was wrong when she stopped coming in." Luke sits up straight, thinking. "About six months ago? Maybe more."

Guilt tightens around my chest. Tobi knew. Luke knew. Everyone knew, except me. I was too busy shopping. And socializing.

Luke leans back. "She didn't say anything about not feeling good? No explanation?"

I shake my head. "I had to practically force her into taking me to the appointment to figure out what's going on," I explain, trying carefully not to break Mama's confidence. "And not surprisingly, she isn't taking her medicine."

Luke nods, but thankfully, from good manners or Southern graces, doesn't push me for more. "Stubborn," he says.

"Yes, a bit," I reply, managing to smile. "I may have some of that."

We share a look of amusement, which fades into silence.

"The scary thing is that the doctor has some answers, but Mama's condition can change," I add. "Weekly, sometimes daily. It makes her really tired."

We both walk to the counter, Luke carrying his plate and fork.

All of a sudden, I am overwhelmed. My arms and legs begin to tremble and the porcelain mugs fall from my hands, smashing into sharp bits on the ceramic tile. I let out a gasp at the sound and cover my eyes quickly to hide the tears that have escaped.

Luke grabs me to his chest, pulling me in tight. Before I realize what he's doing, his hand is around my waist, the other buried in my hair. I'm pressed against his chest, inhaling deeply to catch my breath, my cheeks wetting his shirt. After a second, I sag against his body, allowing myself to relax into the embrace. The feel of his arms around me is delicious, yet foreign.

How long has it been since Alton held me, offered an impromptu hug or caress for no reason? And what about Luke's girlfriend? My shoulders tighten. Struggling to compose myself, I sniff back my tears and wriggle free. "Wait. Don't," I murmur, fighting him.

He releases me and steps back, giving me a wide space. "I didn't mean," he begins, running a hand through his hair. "Please accept my apology," Luke says stiffly. "I couldn't help myself. You seemed upset. I just—"

"Really. I'm fine." I lie, trying to straighten my shirt and act nonchalant. "There's the Alton mess, which I have to deal with sometime soon. And there's the small issue of your girlfriend," I say, blinking up at him.

Luke frowns, confused. "What? What girlfriend?"

I redden immediately, wishing I could swallow the words. "I don't know her name."

Luke frowns and rubs his chin. He's perplexed. Then, realization dawns on his face and he lets out a booming laugh. The sound is rich and full, echoing in my eardrums.

Searcy," Luke says, trying his best to contain his amusement. "That's my sister."

Chapter 24

My heart skids to a stop. *Sister.*

Between laughing at the assumption and wanting to vaporize myself with a sudden blast from the sun, I stand there, looking up at Luke, blinking into his bright blue eyes.

I stumble for words. "I—I had no idea."

Luke nods and leans against the wall, thoughtful. "Well...it's not like *we* were friends in high school."

I allow my breath to exhale. *We graduated together?* My face flames hot and red. I want to fan myself but force my hands to stay close to my body. Instead, I rock back on my heels.

I gulp back some guilt and tuck my arms across my chest, hugging my body tightly. No. It's probably the truth. "I'm sure I'd remember..." I wrinkle my nose, trying to recall ever seeing or speaking to Luke or his sister. Nothing sparks my memory. "I'm sorry."

"Searcy," he says, voice quiet. "It's not like I was even on your radar." He shrugs. "Different universe. And Sarah's a lot younger."

My defenses perk up and I feel the skin on the back of my neck prickle. "I wasn't popular until I met Alton," I say. "And that was because he was in the right crowd. Before that, Tobi and I were friends, but otherwise, I kept to myself." I stand up, feeling the sudden urge to do something. Anything. I walk over toward the kitchen.

Luke nods thoughtfully.

"So, not that either of us need another jolt of caffeine, but could I make you an espresso or cappuccino?" I ask, feeling slightly self-conscious in the skin-tight bicycle shorts. With a glance over my shoulder, I check his reaction before reaching for the beans. "I desperately need the practice," I add with a roll of my eyes.

Luke nods and gives me a sexy smile. "I'd love some."

"Great," I nod and make myself busy at the machine. "So, tell me more about you and your sister."

After a few beats, he continues. "My parents died the summer after junior year. Semi-truck hit them head on. They never had a chance."

A chill jars my body. "I can't imagine. I'm so very sorry." I say and swallow as the large stainless steel machine purrs to life and the water inside heats. Though I've never known my own father, and have often acutely missed having that adult figure in my life, I can't fathom the pain of losing my mother.

"Thank you. It was a long time ago," he adds, bringing his gaze back to me. "My sister is the one who got me though it," he says. "She's deaf. My mom home-schooled her—until she died."

"And then you took care of her—by yourself?" Incredulous, I think back to my senior year and the following, fun-filled, carefree days of college. No responsibilities. All I worried about was which outfit I was wearing to class and where Alton and I would meet on the weekend.

"I have some family in Gulf Shores," he explains, remembering. "And they were great. Did the best they could. My aunt stayed with us for the next two years."

"So you didn't have to move?"

"Or change schools," Luke adds. "Of course, my sister was another story. We found a tutor, temporarily, but when I went to college, she ended up at the Georgia School for the Deaf. It's in Cave Spring, northwest of Atlanta. I was at Georgia Tech, so I could see her sometimes."

I nod, overwhelmed with the logistics of a college student managing the life of his hearing-challenged high school sister at least an hour and a half away.

"We were both homesick, though," Luke says with a rueful smile, "and once she finished up with high school, we came back to Fairhope."

Before I can stop myself or filter the thoughts ricocheting around in my brain, I blurt out a question. "Does she live with you now?"

Luke cuts me off with a booming laugh. I join in with a giggle because it seems to have amused him so much. When he catches his breath, he shakes his head emphatically.

"Are you kidding me? We'd drive each other crazy," Luke says. "She's very headstrong. She's smart. And pretty independent."

"Of course," I murmur. I am quiet for a few moments, thinking about how I would miss the sounds. Birds chirping, lawns being mowed, children's laughter. Hearing the tone in someone's voice.

When I look up, I realize that Luke is staring at me intently.

"Sarah doesn't like anyone feeling sorry for her," Luke warns, the look on his face measured and serious. A bit protective, despite his sister's expressed need for independence.

"I wouldn't either," I reply, emphatic.

He nods.

"Believe me, I don't need anyone pitying me about the shop—the rent past due—or Mama," I add, ticking off the list of issues like I'm heading to Winn-Dixie for groceries.

"I get that," Luke says, studying me with interest. "You don't have to worry about me saying anything."

My cheeks turn pink and my shoulders relax slightly. "Thank you."

Inside, the core of my body warms appreciably. I know Luke is watching me, and my stomach flip-flops, mixing nerves with the enjoyment of some innocent flirtation. I push it aside, determined that I am simply giving Luke a proper thank you for helping out with my accident in the shop.

"You know, we could use some extra help on Thursdays and Fridays, in the afternoon," I say suddenly. "Do you think she'd be interested in working a few hours?"

"Sarah?" Luke brightens. "Sure. I'll mention it."

"Great," I reply. "Just tell her to come by anytime. Tobi or I can talk to her."

I pour the dark, glossy beans into the grinder, then empty the grounds into the portafilter. With the movement becoming second-nature, I tamp the espresso. Satisfied with my progress, I shift over to foam the milk. After pressing the steam button to ready the machine, I reach into the small refrigerator beneath the counter for a chilled pitcher and pour the milk. After checking the temperature, I lower the steam wand into the pitcher.

And nothing.

Frowning, I readjust the wand and hold my breath, listening for the ch-ch-ch sound.

The machine doesn't budge. Placing a hand on my hip, I stare at the button, dismayed. When I turn to face Luke, ready to explain, I run straight into his chest, bumping my tender nose for the second time.

"Oh," I squeak, hand flying to protect my bruised face. Tears sting my eyes as the pain re-awakens.

Luke's hands grip my upper arms, holding me steady. For a moment, I press my head against his chest, allowing myself to catch my breath. He smells divine, masculine. After another moment, I wrench myself away, stepping back to put some space between us.

"Sorry," he says, ducking his chin to check my expression. "I was just coming over to take a look. Didn't mean to re-injure you."

Forcing a wide smile, I touch my nose and wince at the throbbing. "It's all good. I'll live." In an attempt to distract from my paint debacle, I shoot a bemused look at the failed cappuccino attempt before meeting his gaze. "But I'm not sure you'll get your drink now."

Luke shrugs and grins. "So, let me help."

I raise an eyebrow, a smile playing on my lips. His confidence is contagious. "So, you fix espresso machines, spilled paint messes, and bikes?"

"Maybe," he says. "I'm a pro at the last two. Haven't tried coffee makers, but I love a challenge." He winks at me.

I hold myself back from saying an immediate 'yes.' Despite how appealing this sounds, and how much I'd adore Luke swooping in and fix everything, I don't want him to feel obligated.

"Listen," he says. "I have the time."

I hesitate and then exhale. "Thank you. I'd be eternally grateful."

Luke smiles suddenly, the expression lighting up his whole face. "Will work for pie," he says with a deep chuckle.

It's my turn to laugh. "I can probably do that..."

Before I can say another word, he walks over and plants a kiss on my forehead.

The brush of his lips on my skin warms me to my toes. I swallow hard, fighting the urge to swoon.

"I-I'm…"

Luke puts a finger to my lips. "Don't."

I blink up at him, unsteady, overwhelmed with emotion and unsteady with attraction.

"I care about you, Searcy Roberts," he whispers softly. "I don't know how or why, but I've fallen for you. I think it was the moment you stormed into my shop. All sassy about my music."

"It was loud," I argue softly.

Luke laughs and hugs me tight. "I like your spunk and no-quit attitude," he continues. "You're a good friend to Tobi, and you care about your Mama's store. You've worked hard since you got into town—despite whatever's going on back in Atlanta."

I close my eyes. *Alton*. I have to take care of that part of my life. And soon.

"I'm not going anywhere, Searcy," Luke murmurs into my hair. "Work things out. I'll wait." He takes my face in his hands. "Especially if I know that you care about me, too."

Gazing up at him, I take in his handsome features. The curve of his lips, the line of his jaw, the way his blond hair falls on his forehead. I want to blurt out that I've fallen, too. That being around him is magic. Instead, I simply shake my head.

"I do."

Luke beams. "Well, then, let me tackle this and see what I can do. And you go home and get some sleep."

I stand on my tiptoes and kiss him lightly on the cheek, inhaling his soapy-clean scent. "I'm too tired to argue."

"Won't do you any good," Luke says, his eyes sparkling with mischief.

"Call if you need something?" I say. I grab my keys, find my bag, and slip the strap over one shoulder.

"Searcy, go," Luke says, checking his watch and jabbing his thumb toward the front door. "You have to get up early and bake. I've got your mama's house number."

Still semi-flustered, I turn to find my keys. Biting my bottom lip, I make my way to the door, feeling odd and strangely relieved at leaving Luke in charge at the shop.

A thought nudges me.

"So, what's your favorite? Just in case I have time to grab some ingredients this week," I ask. "Apple, pumpkin, pecan?"

Luke grins back at me, delighted with the question. "How very kind of you to ask," he laughs. "Let's see if you can find out."

CHAPTER 25

As I make my way back to Mama's house, I'm still smiling at Luke. The feel of being in his arms. Knowing that he cares. That he believes in me.

It's later than I thought. Ten-thirty, according to the clock in the Cadillac, which may or may not be accurate. If I'm judging based on the gas gauge, it hasn't moved off the empty mark since I arrived into town.

The sky's turned a midnight blue with stars pinpricking through the treetops. Without the warm blaze of summer sun, the night air cools off the blacktop streets. I make a second turn under the glow of streetlights, admiring the large baskets of cheery red geraniums and the immaculate landscaping, overflowing with impatiens and verbena. In Fairhope, I swear the city workers and shopkeepers don't allow a single flower to droop.

I cut the engine and sit, enjoying the solace. Crickets chirp while cicadas buzz, and if I listen closely, there's the faint lap of Mobile Bay in the distance.

With a deep exhale, I reach for my bag and manage to tangle the strap. The contents upend, scattering lip gloss, mascara, and a variety of pens on the floor. As I reach to gather them, pulling the bag toward me, I uncover the envelope from Alton.

After a moment of hesitation, I reach for the delivery and pull it onto my lap. Though it weighs a few ounces, the weight of it presses into my thighs. With a furtive glance at the light burning in Mama's window, I reopen the envelope and reach for the paper inside.

A wave of regret washes through me.

Despite the glow of happiness from Luke, I'm still sad over my failed marriage. Over the loss of so many years.

All of that time spent with someone I might not have ever really known.

A rush of thoughts jumble my head—Alton and I dancing at the senior prom, our first kiss behind the football stadium. Earlier than that, he rescued me after I wiped out on my bicycle, and carried me back to Mama's house without complaint.

Years later, he laughed at the Halloween outfits I chose for a party, saying that Cinderella and Prince Charming were much too predictable. Of course, after a little arguing, I wore the tiara and baby blue dress while he carried around a glass slipper on a red velvet pillow all night.

A stray tear escapes my eye, and I brush it away with a swipe of my wrist. With shaking hands, I unfold the linen paper. Blinking at the letterhead and formal type below, I realize that the letter isn't from Alton at all. There's a foreign signature at the bottom, scrawled in black ink, and the words "Attorneys-At-Law" printed in bold type under the firm's name.

I scan the sentences. With only a bit of legalese scattered throughout, the gist of the letter is clear. It is Alton's wish that we negotiate a property settlement in ten days, including temporary alimony.

My breath escapes in a rush as I read the next line. According to Alabama state law, this mediation would allow us to be divorced right away, as soon as the paperwork is signed and delivered to the courts.

The tears return, and this time, I don't bother to try and stop them. Salty drops hit the letter as I continue to read. My other option and legal right, it says, is to retain counsel of my own and schedule a court hearing. Of course, this is not his client's desire, the attorney writes in the next paragraph, and he only wishes for a fair resolution.

The last sentence says something about Alton taking care of all of the lawyer fees and mediation expenses. It asks me to review the enclosed property settlement, mark any changes to be considered, and mail it back within the allotted timeframe.

I am crying in earnest now. The sum of my relationship with Alton—a decade of my life—has been reduced to a piece of paper.

With a deep breath, I wipe my eyes with the back of my hand. I blink back any tears threatening to fall.

There's a different way to look at this.

I will, instead of being sad, be happy that I have the rest of my life. I will count blessings. I'll smile and be thankful for Mama and Tobi. And Luke. And I'll forgive Alton. Maybe someday, we can be friends.

Carefully, I open the car door.

If I'm lucky, I can make it into the house without waking Mama. One look at me and she's likely to launch into a tirade of questions, then want to drag me to Dr. Richmond's office in the middle of the night. It wouldn't be the first time she's done it, although it's been years and years since the sprained ankle during cheerleading camp and the pulled hamstring after attempting a round-off back handspring at gymnastics camp.

Gingerly on the gravel driveway, I tip toe my way toward the front door, make my way up the steps, and insert the key into the lock. It turns and releases, allowing me entry into the small foyer.

I pause and listen. *Nothing.* I exhale and let my shoulders sag. I slip off my shoes and pad barefoot across the hardwood. Before I round the corner, I hear a soft groan.

"Searcy?" From the other room, it's Mama's voice, weak and thready.

My heart palpitates with fear and I lose any sense of my own pain. Rushing to the living room, I find Mama sprawled on the floor in an awkward tangle, her hair splayed to one side.

A cry escapes from my lips, and I sink to the floor next to my mother. Her skin appears gray and translucent, and she's so tiny and frail that I'm afraid to handle her too roughly. With careful hands, I hold her arm steady and feel for the pulse on her wrist, somehow remembering the basic lesson from first aid class in high school. Her heartbeat is weak and slow, barely registering on the tips of my fingers.

"What happened?" I ask, whispering the question.

My mother, almost imperceptibly, shakes her head and tries to smile. "I'm fine, Searcy. I just tripped and fell," she explains between ragged breaths. "Can you be a dear and help me back on the sofa?"

Typical Mama. Flat-out denying her condition. It has to be related to Lupus. A flare-up. She needs medical attention, and soon.

"Let's get you to the hospital," I say, taking a moment to smooth a stray silver hair from my mother's cheek. "They'll figure out what's going on."

Mama's eyes flash indignantly. "I'm not going anywhere at this time of night." She tries to struggle to her elbows, but collapses back against the thick rug covering the living room floor.

Panic rises in my chest. "Mama, I'm sorry, but I'm scared, and we need help," I say. "Please don't fight me. If I have to, I'll call an ambulance and they'll take you out of here in a stretcher with all of the noise and flashing lights."

I pause and let this digest. When my mother refuses to meet my eyes, I know she's resigned herself to going.

A fleeting thought—calling Luke—crosses my mind, but I push it away. There's no time.

Assessing the situation, I thread my arms around Mama, easing her to a seated position. I prop her body up against a chair, letting her head settle against the padded seat and armrest.

Taking a deep breath, I find the keys, bend down, and pick up my mother. She's much lighter than I expect, and it takes me no time to carry her through the house and deposit her onto the front seat of the Cadillac. She begins to shiver, so I retrieve a blanket from the house before I crank the engine and begin driving.

As seems to be my luck, we hit every red light. I do my best to pay attention to the road and Mama, glancing over every few seconds to make sure she's breathing. We stop at the large intersection at South Ingleside, waiting for the signal to change. In the distance, I can almost make out the lights from Thomas Hospital.

"Searcy?" Mama's voice floats over the front seat in a whisper.

I turn my head and check on my mother. She's awake now, and staring at my face with great interest.

"What in heaven's name happened to your nose?" she asks, her voice making a little squeak as she squints at me through the darkness.

I almost laugh. Leave it to Mama to scrutinize my altered appearance three seconds before we reach the hospital.

"It's a long story," I say with a smile. In my rush to take care of Mama, the throbbing of my face had dulled. "I had a little tussle with a paint can at *Pie Girls.* But I'm fine."

As the words leave my mouth, we pull into the Emergency Room parking area. Street lights overhead illuminate everything. Mama shrinks back in her seat, closing her eyes against the glare.

I park quickly and hurry to the passenger side door, easing Mama out as best I can. A bit of pink has returned to her face, and she's able to stand with help. We head for the sliding glass doors, and with one arm around my mother, we make it across the threshold.

Mama's breath comes in short bursts now, and there's a low wheezing sound coming from her chest. She sags against me, her face flushed with the exertion. Keeping my arm around her waist, I guide her to the nearest chair. She sits carefully, easing herself back against the cushions.

We're greeted almost immediately by a perky employee in scrubs. "Hi, y'all," she chirps.

"Hello, we're here—"

"Oh, bless your heart," she cuts me off with a voice loud enough to make half the heads in the ER waiting room swivel. The girl, who looks all of 18, stares at my nose. "You look like you've been in a nasty bar fight and come out on the losing end. What happened, sweetheart?"

Before I can retort that she has the wrong patient, I catch a glimpse of myself in the large mirror hanging on the opposite wall. In the bright light, there's nowhere to hide. I didn't think about makeup, and my face is far worse than what I thought.

Dark purple streaks, accented by patchy blotches of brick red, now ring each eye. My nose, formerly a small and delicate facial feature, has ballooned to twice its normal size.

Doing my best to ignore my own horrifyingly embarrassing reflection, I give Mama's hand a squeeze and turn back to the hospital worker, who's eagerly awaiting my reply.

"Please, I'm fine," I say, leaning forward and shaking my head to emphasize. "It's my mother. I think she's having a Lupus flare."

After what seems like forever, we're placed in an exam room, and a kind, older physician arrives to examine Mama. After a preliminary check, he asks his nurse to start an IV, and orders some medication that I can't even dream of pronouncing.

"Your mother's very dehydrated," the doctor says, finally glancing at me over tiny spectacles that sit on the bridge of his nose. "The IV will help, and I'll give her something so that she can rest." With a curious look at my nose, a reassuring smile, and a fatherly pat on my shoulder, he disappears between the curtains.

Anxiety wells up inside my chest as the nurse wipes Mama's hand with an alcohol prep and inserts a needle. I fight a wave of nausea, but thankfully, she finishes and bandages my mother's hand before I can start hyperventilating.

Clinging to the wooden armrest for balance, I breathe through my nose. The last thing anyone needs, including me, is a fainting spell. The way my luck's run, I'll break my collarbone and end up in the hospital with Mama, unable to help with the shop or deal with the finances.

"Are you okay, love?" the nurse asks. She's impeccably made-up over her plump, round body. The seams of her red scrubs strain as she holds out a stack of official-looking hospital papers and a pen.

"Yes, thank you." My voice cracks on the last word, though, giving me away. Quickly, I take the wooden clipboard and examine the top page so that I don't have to look at the woman.

Despite my attempts not to look, from the corner of my eye, I see the nurse fish a purple business card from her scrub pocket. "It's normal to be in denial, sweetheart," she replies in a hushed voice. "Especially when the ones we love hurt us so much."

My brain's fuzzy from exhaustion. "The ones we love?" I repeat, glancing up.

Oozing pity, the nurse takes another step toward me, tilts her head, and purses her lips. "You poor, poor dear," she says, clucking her tongue.

"I'm fine," I insist, shaking my head, and setting down the stack of paperwork. "If you're talking about this," I point at my nose, "It was an accident. I was painting and the bucket—"

"Of course, of course," the nurse cuts me off, waves her hand to stop me, and turns to Mama. "They'll be transferring you to a room in just a few minutes," she says.

My mother nods and does her best to smile as the woman pads across the floor. From across the room, I can feel her gaze burning on the back of my neck.

When I look up, the woman tips her head toward a purple card she's placed on the table. She spreads her thumb and pinky finger into the symbol of a phone and holds it up to one ear.

Tightening my jaw, but still smiling as widely as I can, I nod my chin up and down.

The nurse gives me a big thumbs up. "Good girl," she mouths. "Promise you'll call?"

I balk, but realize that it's the only way the nurse is going to leave the room—other than me calling security.

"Promise," I echo weakly.

"God bless you," she whispers, almost looking tearful. With a gentle wave, and one last backward glance, she's gone.

I soften a bit at her emotional reaction, but don't change my mind that the woman is suffering from some sort of delusion. I remain perfectly still, and wait a beat to make sure she's not going to pop back in. When I don't hear footsteps, I allow myself to collapse against the stiff-plastic covering of the hospital chair.

Of all the bizarre nights.

With a heavy arm, I lift the purple card, turn it over, and read the print.

Domestic Violence is REAL
Are you a Victim of Abuse?
Call 800-Get-Help
24/7 Shelter, Food & Clothing

CHAPTER 26

After retrieving makeup from my bag, and applying a thick layer of MAC StudioFix, light lipstick, and a sweep of mascara, I'm able to face the team of nurses on the hospital floor who'll be taking care of Mama. My makeup shield allows the perfect cover. I can breathe and ask questions without any of them looking at me strangely, pulling out purple cards, or insisting that I need domestic violence intervention.

"There's nothing you can do right now, ma'am," Mama's nurse tells me with a pat on my hand. She's perky, smiles a lot, and wears pink and green scrubs so bright they make my brain hurt. "Best that you get home and get some rest. You'll be happy you did."

I hesitate, not wanting to leave Mama.

"We'll call if anything changes," the nurse adds.

With a final glance in at Mama, so as not to wake her, I take the stairs and head outside.

Sleep sounds fabulous, but I'm wide awake when I leave the hospital parking lot. It's another two hours until I need to begin baking, but the night's bizarre twists have injected me with an unexpected burst of energy. My mind buzzes like I've downed four espressos, and I hardly notice the Cadillac bumping and hesitating as I urge it forward.

After being closed up inside the hospital for what feels like days, the night air is deliciously cool and refreshing. I roll the windows down along the drive, letting the breeze caress my hair and skin. Along the road, the glow from streetlights illuminate my path; overhead, hundreds of stars glitter like diamond chips sprinkled on plush black velvet.

I decide to stop at the open-all-night Wal-Mart, park quickly and jet inside for fresh vegetables and fruit. After perusing the selections, I add fresh spinach, tomatoes, peppers, squash, onions, and garlic to my basket. On the next section of the store, I pick up apples, bananas, peaches, blueberries. Keeping my head ducked low, I pick up butter, cream, eggs, feta cheese, and shaved dark chocolate. By some miracle, I avoid any employees, use the self-checkout, and pray that Alton's credit card won't get rejected because I've skyrocketed over the limit.

I hold my breath, one hand on my chest, fingertips tapping my collarbone. It's taking forever. I glance at the lone cashier six lanes away. Still nothing. Maybe it's broken.

The screen blinks back at me, waiting. Finally, it dawns on me to hit 'enter.'

Silly me. I press the green button and hold it down, biting my bottom lip. When the card reader shows 'approved,' I snatch up my bags and practically run out of the store, gleeful not to be accosted by Bluebell ice cream fanatics or anyone with gold teeth.

The parking lot is empty, and I'm thankful that no one is around as I make my way to the car. Though Fairhope is very safe, there's no telling who might wander up.

Fumbling with the keys, I unlock the Cadillac door and slide inside, now breathing heavily with thoughts of serial killers and mass murderers rolling around in my head. I lock myself in, then double check the seat behind me, the floorboard of which is large enough to hold a three hundred pound man.

Empty. I breathe a sigh of relief. My heart pounds with relief.

Searcy. Get a grip. Calm down. Reel in the imagination.

As I rumble toward *Pie Girls*, I promise myself that shopping will now be a daytime activity, threat of strange employees or not. Mama needs me. And I need to be there for my mother.

It's a comfort when I see Luke's truck parked in the usual space. I have a sudden urge to talk with him and wonder if he's still awake. As I ease Mama's car to a jerky stop, the Cadillac backfires twice, I wince and close my eyes, trying to block out the sound echoing down the street. Quickly, I turn off the engine, praying Luke—and any nearby neighbors—are able to sleep through the obnoxious noise.

Now mortified, I quash any idea of knocking on Luke's door. He'll think I'm crazy, if he already doesn't, and will wonder why I'm out shopping in the middle of the night. I could tell him about Mama, but the emergency's over for now. The last thing Luke probably wants is a slightly hysterical, sleep-deprived female knocking on his door at one o'clock in the morning.

Once outside the vehicle, I hesitate and hold my breath, half-wait for a light to flicker on inside his store. When the windows remain dark, I exhale and head inside the bakery.

My shoulders relax as I enter the kitchen. I shrug off my jacket, grab for an apron, and tie the long straps around my neck and waist. Smoothing the thick linen striped material, I consider my next move. Though the pie shop has been known for its traditional sweet treats, I think it's time to mix up the morning offerings. New selections tend to get people excited, and there's nothing better than getting customers in the door, all vying to try the latest breakfast dish. Tarts and quiche are the perfect alternative for those people who want a heartier entree— more of a real breakfast to carry them all the way through the morning hours.

Excitement begins to bubble inside me. If the idea catches on, I can expand the menu to include heartier dishes for the lunch hour, and later, freeze the selections so that customers can stop in, pick out a quiche or tart, and take it home to heat up for dinner.

Ingredients and ideas swim around in my brain as I make my way to my recipe stash in the back office. Flipping through the cards, my fingers hesitate on the directions for making a gorgeous roasted red pepper and feta tart. I pull out the card and set it aside, continuing my search.

To balance out the morning's selections for meat lovers, I choose a delectable spinach, artichoke, and bacon tart that includes a cup of Swiss cheese and heavy cream. The recipe isn't complicated, but seems to please even the pickiest of male palates. Even Alton's. My heart twists a little as I gaze down at the index card in my hand. I made the dish as an anniversary surprise several years back. Alton was touched and pleased.

"Darling," he said. "You're the best." We clinked glasses of champagne and dined over candlelight as Alton caught me up on his week. He'd been to Munich, Germany, and then Paris, stopping in London for a day or two on the return trip. As was his nature, he was excited about new clients, new projects, and was busy brainstorming campaign strategy from the moment he walked back into the apartment.

Hoping for some romance after an extended dry spell, I poured more champagne and encouraged him to drink up. "Have a little more, honey," I urged, taking my own flute in hand and downing the crisp, bubbly liquid.

Alton paced himself carefully, but my head swam after three glasses. I was giddy with desire, and took his hand, leaving the dinner dishes for later. We moved into the living room and curled up on the sofa together. I pulled a blanket over my legs and snuggled against his body.

With my head on Alton's shoulder, I began rubbing his chest, hoping to get him in a playful mood. When he suddenly became quiet, I'd hoped my roving fingertips had stimulated his interest.

Unfortunately, my attempts at enticing Alton into a hot, spicy evening in our king-sized bed fell flat. He began snoring moments later.

Not even the ding of his cell phone, signaling a text message, disturbed his snoozing. When his iPhone rang a second time, I looked at my watch. Ten o'clock at night. A crisis at the office wasn't likely.

Ever so carefully, I slipped out from under his arm. My escape didn't even register. Alton's head lolled to the right, and he sighed and settled back against the sofa cushions.

Eyeing the cell phone across the room, I considered my options.

Investigate. Or leave it alone.

For the moment, I stood still. I'd never considered myself a jealous person—one of those wives who call the office incessantly, demanding to know her husband's immediate whereabouts and the intimate details of his desk calendar. After all, I had my life, he had his. I shopped, ate out, enjoyed friends, and kept myself fit with our personal trainer.

Alton worked. And worked more.

Up until that night, I hadn't given a thought to Alton having an extracurricular love life. He had a life. Our marriage and his job.

Contrary to most of my friends' philosophies about suspicion and snooping, I'd never checked Alton's email, searched his credit card records for suspicious charges, or scoured his pockets for a telltale sign of cheating.

Naive or not, I simply trusted him.

Easing myself off the edge of the sofa, I inched along the floor, keeping my eyes on the phone screen. My focus was so intense that I forgot to navigate around the coffee table and decided to go straight through it instead. The sharp corner met my knee with a crunch.

"Ooo," I moaned softly, covering my mouth with one hand. Tears welled up in my eyes, blurring my vision. My knees buckled slightly, and I had to press my fingernails into the palm of my hand to keep from crying out in pain.

Despite the bit of noise, Alton didn't move.

Tiptoeing closer, I reached out for the phone. Straining to reach the cell across the wide table, my fingertips brushed the metal edge. Instead of grasping the corner, I fumbled, sending it sliding across the remaining few inches of the table. In seemingly slow motion, the thin black iPhone tumbled end over end. With a sickening crack, the corner hit the floor, bounced, and fell flat against the hardwood.

For a moment, I couldn't breathe. Turning my head an inch, I stole a glance at my husband. He hadn't stirred. Wincing, I bent to pick up Alton's cell. Biting my lip, I turned it over to examine the front.

The screen now displayed a spider web of broken glass.

Through the kaleidoscope of slivers and shapes, I could make out the name on the text message. "Thomas."

In my rush—in my certainly that I would find a woman's name, I almost laughed at the absurdity of my discovery. Though I didn't know of a particular Thomas, it didn't mean the person wasn't a new hire. Or a client. Or a friend. The possibilities were limitless.

Behind me, Alton coughed.

Gripping the iPhone tight, I whirled around, not realizing that the shards of glass would immediately penetrate my skin. I gasped in pain and watched as pinpricks of blood rose to the surface of my palm.

My husband jumped to his feet, now wide awake. "Searcy!"

Within ten seconds, he'd grabbed a hand towel from the kitchen, wrapped up the cell phone, and sat me back down on the sofa. He flicked on a nearby lamp, pulled my hand into the light, and adjusted his glasses.

"What ever were you doing?" He scolded me as he turned my palm under the bulb.

Tiny shards of glass were embedded in my skin amongst the red pinpricks of blood, and the sight made me nauseous. I couldn't focus on Alton or make myself answer coherently.

"Wait here," he instructed. "Don't move."

There was no chance of that. Trembling and clutching my wounded hand with my useable extremity, I leaned back against the sofa until I heard my husband's footsteps.

He returned with tweezers, antiseptic, and Band-Aids, as well as a small dish from the kitchen. Painstakingly, he positioned my hand and began extracting the tiny pieces of glass.

I didn't move or make a sound for the next ten minutes while my husband worked.

"There," Alton said finally, setting the tweezers on the table beside us after pulling the last visible splinter from my index finger.

After spraying on some antiseptic and bandaging the holes, Alton took a deep breath and frowned. "So, I think I deserve an explanation."

"I-I..."

My husband tugged at his ear, clearly uncomfortable with my lack of willingness to confess exactly how and why I'd destroyed his brand new iPhone.

"It was an accident," I said, rather guiltily, avoiding his gaze. "You were sleeping. The phone was ringing with a message. I was afraid it would wake you."

"And so," Alton continued, "did you see who was trying to reach me?"

I shrugged, feeling like a five-year-old with her hand caught in her brother's Halloween candy bag. "Thomas."

My husband nodded, never breaking eye contact. "And..."

I swallowed hard. "I don't know who he is."

"And does it matter?" Alton asked, a bit sharply. "You'd assumed it was a woman?"

Sheepishly, I nod.

"Searcy, I'm not Phillipa's husband. I'm not interested in other women." He reached out and touched my chin, tilting it down with his thumb and forefinger. "There's nothing to worry about. I'm right here."

CHAPTER 27

The rumble of tires on pavement, a lone truck, and the glare of its headlights jolt me back to the present. Back to the pie shop, my mixing bowls, and the long hours stretching before me.

Alton, Atlanta, that incident—they all seem so far away.

At the time, I wanted so desperately to believe Alton still loved me that I quashed my self-doubt. I packed it away, along with the nagging sensation that something was desperately wrong.

But I knew, deep down.

We didn't kiss passionately. We didn't communicate.

We weren't a couple.

Alton wasn't in love with me.

We were roommates. From the start.

And—out of fierce, stupid pride, a quest to escape Fairhope, and my desire to live a glamorous life—I ignored it all.

We'd both pretended.

I shake my head.

The truth was bittersweet.

It's in the past, Searcy. Move forward. Live for today.

As I begin to measure and pour, I inhale deeply, letting my body find a smooth rhythm. The familiarity of it is comforting, and I feel my shoulders relax as I drop in a pinch of salt and add tablespoons of ice cold water.

I yawn widely, going through the steps of forming dough, watching the industrial-sized mixer churn. The hum lulls me, soothing my mind. The scent of the pie crust wafts up, tickling my nose along with a dusting of pastry flour, which billows from the bowl.

The vegetables come next. I retrieve them from the pantry, pausing only to grab a heavy wooden cutting board and Mama's best chopping knife. I go to work on the Vidalia onion first, then garlic and spinach.

I add a splash of extra virgin olive oil to two cast-iron skillets and flick on the gas-stove burners. They catch and light immediately, blue flames licking the bottom of each pan. I fill the first surface with the chopped onion, garlic, and spinach, the other with slices of smoked bacon.

In a small mixing bowl, using a large stainless steel whisk, I whip together the cheese, cream, and eggs together to hold the savory ingredients.

After adding cracked pepper and a dash of salt, I set the bowl aside, pull out wrapped pastry balls, and place the first onto a floured section of the counter. Pressing and rolling, the dough expands and stretches. Once I'm satisfied with the thickness, I nestle each crust into glass pie dishes.

When I stand back to look at my work, a larger, longer yawn escapes. I have to shake my head against the growing sleepiness in my body. With renewed determination, I crumble the bacon and add the vegetables from the skillet to the egg, cream, and cheese. Tipping the bowl over each pie crust, I pour in the mixture, watching it settle, and then slip them into the oven, making space so that each can rise and bake evenly.

As I close the door with care, my limbs take on a leaden feel. I lean against the stainless steel edge of the oven space and let out a sigh. Eying the fruit on the opposite counter, I reach for Mama's handwritten recipe. The ink letters bend and swim as I peer down at them. Rubbing my eyes, I look again, only to have the words twist and turn.

With a sigh, I wash my hands and dry them, and then walk out of the kitchen, rub at my face and throat, trying to wake up.

I pull out a chair at the nearest cafe table, worrying about Mama and wondering whether she's sleeping. As I sink down, I give into my weariness, and place both hands and elbows on the table. I let my head rest between them, my cheek on my hands.

My eyes close immediately, slamming shut with heavy lids. I allow my body to relax and lean against the tablecloth, breathing in the fresh linen scent. My breath becomes slow and heavy, warming the skin on my arms. Within seconds, I am drifting.

I awake to a voice saying my name. Softly at first, then becoming urgent. There's a hand on my shoulder, and I jump at the touch, emitting a tiny scream as I jerk to sit up straight.

Luke's eyes are inches from mine. "Searcy," he says, breathing hard.

Bleary-eyed and confused, I move my chin from side to side like a robot, saying no.

"You could have been hurt...the oven was on," Luke adds, semi-scolding me as he glances back at the kitchen.

"Oh," I squeal and leap from my chair, sniffing the warm, sweet air. "The pies."

Luke steps in front of me, catching both arms. "Whoa," he says. "Everything's fine. I caught it in time. We were lucky."

He's right. There's no burning smell. No smoke. No blackened tarts in the trash nearby.

"How-how did you know?" I ask.

Luke rubs his chin. "I don't want you to think I was watching you—or stalking," he says. "But when I heard your Mama's car—"

"Sorry," I murmur and roll my eyes at the ceiling. I'm pink-cheeked, remembering the vehicle backfiring and shuddering to a stop.

He laughs and runs a hand through his hair. "And you don't think I'm used to it?"

I blush harder.

"I know the routine, generally," he adds, "and I'm a light sleeper. So when you pulled in so early, I was curious, and checked on you after a while."

"Mama..." I begin to tell him about my mother, but catch myself starting to cry.

"Shhh," he says. "I know."

Wrinkling my forehead, I give him a curious glance.

"My sister works as a clerk at night," he says. "She's not supposed to give out patient names, but she knew I'd want to know right away." Luke pauses and gazes down at me, searching my face. "She's in good hands. I know the staff. They'll take care of her."

I can't speak. My eyes are welling up with tears and my throat is thick with words I can't say. My heart hurts for everything that's happened and what I can't change.

Luke reaches out and folds me into his arms. "Come here," he says into my hair. I think I feel his lips brush the top of my head, but I can't be sure because I'm crying in earnest now. All of the stress and anxiety of the past few weeks spill out and my body shakes against his chest. He holds me tighter, drawing me close, and with one hand, strokes my shoulders and back.

He lets me sob silently against him until I am worn out with emotion. I brush my wet cheeks, dab at my eyes, and duck my head. With both hands, I untangle myself from his embrace.

"Thank you," I say in a soft voice. I'm slightly mortified to be found sleeping on the job, and the thought of burning up the pies—let alone the entire bakery and block of shops—is enough to make me want to faint dead away.

"I'm just glad I was here," Luke answers, still close enough to touch. He's watching me closely, concerned.

"I can't imagine..."

"Don't go there," he says, quick to cut off my thoughts. "You're exhausted, Searcy. Let me help you. I'll call Tobi. The two of us can finish up the morning while you get a little rest."

I try to argue, but Luke is firm. He's already dialed and is talking to Tobi before I can begin to mount a reasonable defense. When he hangs up, he grins and nods. "Taken care of. Now show me what else you had planned for the morning."

I can't help but feel buoyed and safe. He walks me to the kitchen, one hand lightly guiding the small of my back. It tingles where his fingers rest, and I'm not sure if I'm imagining it from sleep deprivation, or if my entire body is just longing for more of his touch.

I stifle another yawn, covering my mouth. All of a sudden, I realize that I must look a fright, and smooth down my hair without a mirror. The movement catches Luke's attention, and he turns to face me. After a moment of scrutinizing my appearance, he reaches up and twists a stray hair gently, bringing it down toward my neck. "There was only one really wild piece," he says, laughing. "The rest was mild, in comparison."

Biting my lip, I resist the urge to run to the restroom and check my makeup, also. I can only imagine the streaked mascara and partially rubbed-off lip gloss.

Luke is reading my mind again. "You look fine," he says, giving me a stern wink. "Under the circumstances, you're still gorgeous."

"You're awfully sweet," I whisper, covering up my face with both hands.

He laughs and throws an arm around my shoulder. "I'm just getting started. Come on, sleepy girl."

We step outside onto the sidewalk, and through the front door of Luke's shop. In the back, he brings out and unfolds a cot, throws down blankets and a pillow. After easing the bed against a wall, he gestures for me to lie down.

He glances at his watch. "It's still early. We have plenty of time before the morning rush."

I nod, still groggy. I take a step back and gingerly sit down on the hard edge of the bed.

"Rest, okay?" he urges. "And don't worry. I'll take care of things. Tobi will be in shortly. And I won't check on you unless a few days go by." He pauses.

"Thank you."

Gripping the pillow for comfort, I lie down. The blankets smell like Luke, as does the down filling where I'm now pressing my cheek. I close my eyes tight, still absorbing his touch, the way his arms felt around my body.

He's everywhere. Inside me and out.

CHAPTER 28

My eyes flutter open and I'm immediately disoriented. I sit up, fast enough that the room spins. Pressing my fingertips to my eyes, I inhale deeply and try to think straight. The last twenty-four hours rush back. Paint, Mama, my almost-burning-the-bakery-down. Luke rescuing me and the shop. Oh. My hands drop to my knees and I squeeze my eyes shut.

There's more. Me completely falling apart. Luke touching me. The feel of my body against his. My face flushes immediately.

I shake my head and glance at the clock. Seven o'clock. With a jolt, I throw off the sheets and fly out of the cot.

I'm late. Tobi is going to kill me.

In a frantic panic, my eyes dart around the room. There's a pile of fresh clothing—Luke's, I assume—on the counter. Folded jeans. A soft flannel shirt. I eye them doubtfully, but grab them and stuff them under my arm on the way to the bathroom, where I do my best to splash water on my face, run my fingers through my hair, and inspect my nose. The swelling's gone down, thank goodness, but the bruising's traveled under my eyes, making me resemble a semi-human punching bag.

I shimmy out of my shirt and pants, jumping up and down to kick off the legs. I reach for Luke's shirt and jeans, hesitating for a moment. I clutch them to my chest and debate running home. Another glance at the clock confirms there's no time.

With a sharp intake of breath, I pull on the jeans, which swim around my waist, then thread the leather belt through the loops, and secure the buckle. With flourish, I shake out the flannel shirt, which carries the same soapy-clean scent of Luke's skin.

My fingers fumble as I button the shirt, which billows and settles around my body in giant folds. I tuck and fold it as best I can, then reach for my socks and tennis shoes, tying them up in double-knots for good measure.

Pulling my hair into a ponytail, I give one last glance at my reflection. For a few seconds, I actually don't recognize myself. Sans makeup, and despite the purple and red marks mottling my face, my skin is clear and bright. I pat on a bit of foundation to cover my nose, but don't bother with anything else.

There was a time, not very long ago, when I wouldn't have left the house looking like this. Phillipa would take the first look and let out an ear-piercing shriek, followed by dragging and/or carrying me back inside the house at the first glimpse of my wearing anything flannel—unless it carried a prominent Ralph Lauren or Stella McCartney label.

And the shoes. I glance down at the beat-up gray and pink Nikes from high school gracing my feet, tied up with decidedly un-bright white laces. It's an entirely new layer of *What Not to Wear* that would throw my girlfriends into a full-blown heart attack. I close my eyes, remembering the last pair of shoes I purchased. And the pair before that, and the heels before that. Three hundred dollars each? Four hundred? I shake my head, remembering. Sometimes, I spent more. Without blinking. Laughing about price tags, then gleefully going for a thirty or forty dollar lunch afterwards.

I wince, inwardly.

Nothing mattered unless it was pretty, and expensive, and could be carried home to fit in my closet. There was no purpose, no higher meaning, and no giving to others.

My eyes sting a bit, and I fight to blink back tears.

I don't have time for this, I remind myself.

I am good enough. I am better than that.

I've grown here, being away from Atlanta. Being home with Mama. Sucking in my breath, I smooth down Luke's shirt, feeling the cotton against my fingertips. It soothes me, momentarily.

I like who I'm becoming. A month ago, a year ago, I couldn't say that.

Another deep breath. I blow it out in a rush. As the warm air escapes my lips, I admit to myself that I'm scared as hell. I don't know how I'm going to fix everything. But I'm determined and resourceful. I'll figure it out. The shop. Helping Mama. And, as difficult as it will be, wrapping up my life with Alton.

We both deserve happiness, in whatever form it takes. And much as I've fought it and hated to admit it, that happiness will only be found apart.

I bite my bottom lip. I can do this. All of it.

One last glance in the mirror. This time, my reflection smiles back.

Time to go.

I'm in such a hurry that I run smack into a line of customers so long that it snakes half-way down the block.

I slow my stride to a stop and take in the scene. Across from the shop, I count two television news vans, camera equipment, and a small horde of reporters.

My mouth dries up as my mind races with possibilities. A murder? Has someone been robbed? What about a car accident? A hit and run? My feet begin moving again and I tap on tall shoulders to inch my way through the crowd and toward the front door.

My eyes dart from face to face, taking in the emotions. No one's unhappy. People are smiling. In fact, many of them are making casual conversation and laughing. I blink several times and rub my eyes to make sure I'm still not asleep.

Then, when I open my eyes, through the crowd, I see Tobi carrying a large round tray close to her shoulder. Small, insulated Dixie cups fill the space, all steaming hot. Wisps of steam evaporate from the mini-servings as she pauses to hand out the samples.

Still weaving and moving through the mass of people, I wave to catch her attention, but to no avail.

"Searcy!" someone calls out over the steady noise of small talk and muffled giggling.

I stop and stand on tiptoes, searching for the source of the voice. Arching my neck, I strain to find the person who wants my attention. As I catch eyes, I see plenty of familiar faces. I get a few waves and nods, lots of smiles. There's Mama's friend, and the post lady, and I recognize the girl who works at the bank. I lower my tennis shoes back to the ground and resume making my way to the front door.

Suddenly, like the Red Sea parting, a huge gap appears in the mass, and I move toward it quickly. Elation fills my chest. I can reach the front door! But before I can take more than three steps, a large, masculine hand grasps my elbow, stopping me short. The hole closes, leaving only a wall of people again.

I whirl around and body slam into Luke. "Whoa," I gasp. Shaking off the impact, I gulp oxygen.

"Sorry—I was trying to get your attention," he says, holding my shoulders steady.

"You have it now," I joke, all of my senses heightened. His breath is on my face, and his hand is still resting on my arm.

Luke jabs a thumb in the direction of the news vans. "They want to talk to you."

My wits return in a rush. "What? Why?" I wrinkle my nose. "I have to go to work."

Crinkling his forehead, Luke shakes his head and holds up a finger. "In a minute."

I ignore the signal and lean in to whisper. "Help me get through this crowd. Who's working the counter? And what's going on with all of these people, anyway? Please tell me we're not giving away free pie again."

With a grin, Luke puts a hand on the small of my back and steers me away from the shop. I drag my feet purposefully, protesting the whole time. "Luke! Stop it."

A few yards away, Luke looks me squarely in the face. "The TV stations?" he says. "They're here to talk to you. About the free pie day."

I start to cough, violently. "Um, what?"

Luke slaps a hand in the middle of my back to quiet my hacking. "It's a huge deal. Everyone loved it. Someone called the TV stations and told them about giving away all of the pie. They talked about how you promised to make it into an annual event."

"Uh oh," I say, clapping a hand over my mouth.

"Yep," Luke laughs. "They love the whole 'giving love back to the community to make customers happy when you're on your last dime' kind of story. How the pie is made from scratch, from old family recipes. That you're the second generation pie girl and that your mom is sick and you might lose the store because your landlord is demanding back rent."

All of this spills out in a rush and roars into my ears.

"Searcy," Luke looks at me apologetically. "It's a small town. Everyone knows everything."

I melt just looking at the pleading expression in his face.

"Just go talk to them," he urges. "They want to know about the free pie. Why you did it. If you're going to make it an annual thing."

"Pie for the masses, huh?" I ask, blinking out surprise and deciding that I adore the idea of a catch phrase.

Something in the back of my mind tickles at me. Alton would be proud.

"Pie equals love," Luke quips.

"Everything's better with pie?" I ask, raising an eyebrow.

"Make pie, not war," Luke winks.

I giggle. "*Pie Girls* for humanity," I giggle.

Luke puts both hands on my shoulders and squeezes. "Go forth and talk about pie," he whispers, locking eyes with me. "Tell them you're going to do this every year."

Crossing my arms, my stomach starts to twirl and twist like a ballerina before her first Nutcracker performance. "Am I?" I ask him.

Luke nods emphatically. "And the second time around, it'll be bigger."

"Because we're not going out of business," I add, feeling a surge of courage. "Because I'll figure out a way to pay off the shop."

"Exactly."

"This is crazy," I state and stand up a little taller. "And I look like someone beat me up."

Luke leans back to survey my appearance and brushes a stray hair from my forehead. "You're beautiful. Go for it."

CHAPTER 29

The instant I walk toward the small crowd of reporters and camera people, I am bombarded with questions.

"Searcy, how did you come up with this idea?"

"How many pies did you make?"

"What's your most popular pie?"

"How many pieces of pie did you give away?"

I swallow hard and paste a smile on my face. With a big breath, I dive in and answer each question, trying to smile at each and every one of the TV reporters.

"Searcy?" Another voice calls out.

Directing my face toward the sound, I search the crowd for the person who said my name.

He's a taller man, with bushy eyebrows and a shiny-bald head. He's holding a small pad of paper and a pen, poised to write. When he sees that he has my attention, he begins firing away.

"So, Quinn Hillyer owns the shop. He's calling for back rent. Are you in danger of closing?"

Other reporters begin to chime in.

"How much money are we talking, exactly?"

"Do you have a deadline for returning the payments?"

The crowd of cheerful people becomes somber and quiet.

The cameras are still trained on my face, and I do my best not to balk and bolt for the nearest doorway. Below the surface of my skin, every muscle in my body tenses.

For several moments, I say nothing. The silence is deafening, until a bird chirps overhead.

"Searcy," the man demands, not unkindly. "Can I get some answers?" Every pair of eyes is laser-focused on me.

Waiting. Watching. And then, out of the corner of my eye, I see Luke. He smiles and gives me a nod. I can do this.

"I'd love to share the numbers," I answer, trying to keep my voice from cracking. "But I'm relatively new to the operating side of our business and we're still assessing our finances."

This seems to appease most of the reporters, and the man jots something on his paper.

A breeze kicks up, momentarily taking my breath away and sending stray hairs flying in my face. As I pull them back, the diamond in my ring catches the sunshine and winks back at me knowingly. I've been wearing it on my right hand, with every intention to lock it away in Mama's safe when I get a spare moment.

I stare at the perfectly cut facets glinting in the light.

An idea forms in my head. Jewelry, I think. And my mother's artwork. And my horrible, horrible '80s clothes.

I clear my throat, wave an arm, and grab everyone's attention a second time.

"We'll also be holding a fundraiser. The date will be announced…tomorrow," I say with flourish, before I can change my mind. "All of the proceeds will support *Pie Girls*. We'll account for every penny. It'll be a huge, lovely event with all sorts of glamorous items to buy. Women's clothing, shoes, jackets, and jewelry. Some furniture, perhaps. Decorative items for the home," I add, my mind racing with possibilities.

"And pie?" One of the reporters pipes up.

"Oh yes. Definitely pie."

I'm breathless with excitement as I turn to head back to the shop. Tobi catches my arm, and Luke breaks into a jog to keep up with us.

"How in the world are you going to pull this off?" Tobi whispers close to my ear as she smiles and waves at one of our customers.

"What do you mean, you?" Luke interjects, more loudly than the both of us. "Don't you mean 'we?'"

The force of his voice causes me to stop mid-step and turn to look into his eyes. The deep blue of his iris flashes with intensity as he smiles down at me. My body reacts instantly, like a hummingbird to the sweetest nectar. I tilt my chin back up at him, absorbing everything—the look on his face, his soapy, outdoorsy smell, the way his shoulders fill out his shirt.

For a moment, Tobi just stares at us, her face locked into something between surprise and disbelief. After a few seconds, her mind begins responding again. She glances from me to Luke, and then back, again.

"Oh, my Lord," Tobi says, clapping a hand over her chest. Her mouth forms a little 'o' as her fingers begin tapping. "Lord, Lord, Lord. You two. And I missed it. Somehow, I missed it."

"You did," Luke says before I can deny anything. He nods at Tobi, breaking out into a grin. He lets out a boyish chuckle, and runs a hand through his hair. His arm reaches out and grazes the small of my back.

I swallow hard, fighting every crazy, goofy, infectious, loving feeling resonating from my body. I want to throw my arms around Luke's neck. I want to kiss him hard and not care that hundreds of people see. I want to hold his hand and stare into his eyes, run my hands down his muscled chest.

But, there are people around. Lots of them. And they're watching and listening.

"Come on, you two," I plead, inching away from Luke's touch. His fingertips burn as they fall away from my back and graze the bare skin of my arm.

The two of them stare at me for a moment and simultaneously burst into laughter. Tobi's shoulders shake as she covers her mouth. "I'm happy for you."

I bite my lip hard, trying not to smile. Out of the corner of my eye, I notice that Luke almost glows. His face, in the sunshine, is heavenly.

It's all within reach.

The shop.

Happiness.

Love.

A real life without lies or half-truths. Without a high-maintenance lifestyle and friends who judge you by the shoes you wear, the labels on your clothes, and the year of wine you drink.

But romance, right now—without me fixing the shop and my own life first—will only stir up trouble and give Quinn Hillyer ammunition. The gossip, if it hasn't started already, will swirl faster than hurricane winds on a hot August night.

I inhale the warm sweet air and focus on the exterior of the shop. My shop, if I'm very, very careful. If I can pull off the yard sale of the century. I'll have to channel a bit of Alton's advertising magic to get it done.

Catching Tobi's eye, I tilt my head toward the bicycle shop and begin walking. I tug on Luke's sleeve to get him to follow. It's quiet there, and we can talk for a moment without fear of anyone overhearing.

In a few steps, we're inside. When the door closes behind us, my shoulders lose a few ounces of tension.

"Umm," I interrupt, red-faced, and try my best to address them with a serious look. "Everything else aside, please, let's think about this." I pause and take a breath. "Logistics, time, day, location. Can we pull off a huge yard sale in a week? Can we make the kind of money we need to?"

Luke crosses his arms across his chest and looks over at Tobi, who's busy calculating in her head.

"I—don't know, Searcy," she says slowly, eyes meeting mine. "It's a good idea, but…"

I clap my hands together for emphasis, then rub them hard. "What if—I get Alton to ship everything from the apartment?"

The idea hangs in the air for a moment.

"Like, furniture?" Luke frowns.

"Sure," I say, nodding my head vigorously. "But, more than that. I have clothes and shoes. Coats, belts, accessories. And jewelry. And it's all…expensive."

Tobi brightens. "Right! Oh my goodness. And all of that stuff in your house. The vases and trinkets and antique things."

"Yes," I say, smiling quietly. "All of it. We can put all of it up for sale."

"Are you sure?" Luke asks.

I shrug, feeling freer than I have in a long time, as if letting all of it go will unburden my life. "When am I going to need Gucci purses and Diane Von Furstenberg dresses? Prada shoes and Burberry coats?"

Tobi snorts and wrinkles her nose. "You didn't need them in the first place."

I give her a playful shove and examine my trim shorts and t-shirt. "I live in these now. If we can keep the shop open, I don't see that changing."

"Maybe Alton will let you have his stuff, too?" Tobi says out loud, her head cocked to one side. "All of his fancy suits and ties. The leather belts." She presses two fingers to her lips, thinking. "That would be amazing. What a wardrobe."

I close my eyes and see our huge walk-in closet with shelves full of pressed shirts and cashmere sweaters in every shade and color. A dozen Armani suits. Rows of

Italian-made shoes, laces tied neatly. Rich mocha and black leather belts hanging side by side.

"That's his business," I say quickly, averting my eyes on the hardwood floor. "If he offers to donate it all to the shop, that's great. I won't ask, though. It's not my place, anymore."

With that statement, we all fall quiet for a few moments.

When I finally force my gaze from the raw wooden planks to Luke's loafers, then up his legs, past his chest and chin, I see that his face has taken on a distinct, distant expression.

My heart twists and a bit of panic rises inside my chest.

I start to reach for his hand when my cell rings. Luke steps away and motions for me to take it. He turns and walks toward the counter as I draw the iPhone out of my pocket.

"Probably another reporter," I say under my breath and wink at Tobi, who's still calculating a donation from Alton.

When I check the screen, it's not a reporter at all. It's the hospital, calling about Mama.

My eyes blur with tears as I listen to the nurse, catching her report in snippets.

"Fatigue and nausea. Refusing to eat. Fever."

I hang up, shaking, and relay the symptoms to Tobi and Luke.

"Go!" Tobi says. "Do what you have to. We'll be here," she assures me.

I hug her tightly, my eyes catching Luke's during the embrace.

He's halfway across the room, behind the register, fingers on the keyboard. He rises to his feet, but doesn't make a move toward me.

"She'll be okay, Searcy," Luke says. "She's tough." Something in his words doesn't convince me, though.

This time, they are hollow. He's not certain about Mama. Or me. Maybe he's not certain about anything.

I take a step toward the door. I have to leave. My nerves are jangling with fear and trepidation. Is Mama okay? What's wrong? Why can't they fix it?

Gripped with a thousand questions, I leave Tobi and Luke behind, jump into the Cadillac and crank the engine. Thankfully, the old girl sputters to life instantly, seemingly spurred on by the amount of tension and panic emanating from every pore of my body.

Luke's face burns into my mind as I ride to the hospital.

CHAPTER 30

I park the Cadillac's extended body haphazardly across two spaces, leaving the end precariously hanging out into a lane. I don't have time to correct, or re-adjust. I don't even lock the door, just race into the building.

Inside the elevators, I gasp for breath and punch the button for Mama's floor. A bell dings and the double doors heave open wide. I sprint to the nurses' station, skidding to a stop on the white linoleum floor.

A tall, slender nurse, someone I don't recognize, gestures for me to follow her. We fall into brisk step down the bright hallway, our shoes making a muffled shuffle on the buffed surface.

"She's really taken a turn," the nurse says, "just within the last few hours. The doctor's been in a few times. He's trying to keep her hydrated and pain-free. Doing his best to get her fever under control. She's fighting an infection, and her poor body's having trouble."

My knees buckle slightly at the words. Pain. Fighting. Infection. Fever.

The nurse touches my arm when we reach Mama's room. "She might be sleeping. Let her. And the doctor should be in to check on her before nine o'clock. He'll talk to you then. Answer your questions."

She leaves me in the private room. Mama looks small and frail in the large, padded hospital bed. I step closer, allowing my eyes to adjust to the lone, soft light coming from a sole lamp in the room's corner.

I take the seat closest to my mother, and position myself directly across from her face. There is tubing everywhere, connected to machines that blip and beep. Colored lines dance across screens, rising and falling, then disappearing all together. Clear liquid drips from IV tubes overhead, the substance snaking through clear plastic into the back of Mama's bandaged hand.

On her cheeks, her eyelashes rest, dark fringe against cool, pale skin. Despite the illness, and the telltale butterfly mark across her nose and cheeks, my mother's face is flawless and appears peaceful.

I fight the urge to smooth her hair or touch her face. Disturbing her would interrupt the moment, cut into the temporary peace and freedom from pain. Easing back against the smooth leather of the easy chair, I watch Mama closely, my eyes following the microscopic rise and fall of her chest under the crisp linens.

At least an hour passes before there's a soft knock on the door. The opening to the hallway widens, allowing more light to shine in. A dark figure appears, and quickly takes the shape of my high school classmate and Mama's doctor, Jimmy Richmond.

Tonight, I'm almost shocked by the haggard look on his face. He's unshaven, with a rumpled shirt and tie, quite unlike the usual department store-perfection I'm used to seeing.

"Searcy," he breathes in my direction, grasping my hand tightly in greeting. His eyes light on Mama, tracing her outline. After a moment, he directs his gaze back to me. Jimmy doesn't sit.

"We've talked about flares," he begins, "and this one's a rough one. Fast, strong. Out of nowhere." He breaks off and shakes his head, disgusted with the disease.

"But I thought she was getting better," I say, swallowing hard. "I thought I'd be taking her home."

Jimmy nods, but can't meet my gaze. "We all thought so," he finally answers. "Systemic lupus is tricky, though. This time, it's decided to go full-force and attack. Her skin, her blood, kidneys, joints." His voice trails off. "She's in a lot of pain. We're doing what we can to manage it, and fight the inflammation."

"And so far?" My voice cracks when I ask.

"Searcy, we're throwing everything we've got at it. Nonsteroidal anti-inflammatories, corticosteroids, antimalarials, and chemotherapy. Those are our best tools, and they have to be used judiciously, as they can cause her immune system to break down even further, which can make her susceptible to other infections."

The lump in my throat expands, choking my words. "What else can we do?" My mind jets in different directions. "Should we take her to UAB? Mayo Clinic? M.D. Anderson?"

Jimmy looks over at Mama. "Certainly you can take her anywhere you feel is best. My nurse can put you in contact with anyone at any of those hospitals. We'll arrange for whatever you need."

"Will it help?" I blurt out, my voice catching.

"Anything we do is risky at this point. She's fragile. The more exposure she has to people could mean putting her at risk for more infection, but that's always a consideration when we transfer a patient. It's not a given."

"Will the treatment be different somewhere else?" I say, stopping myself from saying *better*.

"I've trained with the best. We follow national protocols. The medicine is the same. But, Searcy, it's up to you."

"And Mama," I add, not able to consider the alternative.

Jimmy straightens. "Of course, your mother's prerogative is first."

There's the slight rasp of a sheet moving. Jimmy and I jump at the sound. Mama lifts her head and coughs weakly. "And my prerogative is not moving. I won't allow it."

"Mama," I cry, tears rushing to my eyes.

"How are you feeling, my dear?" Jimmy asks, leaning forward to touch Mama's arm.

Ever the Southern lady, my mother tilts her head to one side and considers this. "Dr. Richmond, I wish I could tell you that I'd have the next dance, but my body doesn't seem up to it today. Let's think about tomorrow."

Jimmy manages a chuckle and I wipe wetness from my cheek while Mama graces us with a small, satisfied smile.

"How about you get back to your lovely family," says Mama. "And leave us to catch up on some girl talk?"

On cue, Jimmy steps away, takes note of the numbers on Mama's machines, checks the IV levels, then turns to leave. He offers a little bow, and blows Mama a kiss. "Tomorrow then," he says. "I'll bring my dancing shoes."

When the door closes behind him, Mama's face loses a bit of vitality. She raises a hand to smooth the sheet, and it trembles with the effort.

"Tell me all about what's going on, darling," Mama whispers and closes her eyes. "Have you heard from Alton?

I fall silent.

"Searcy?" Mama prods.

"He sent divorce papers," I admit, flushing hot and red despite the room's chill. "A few days…maybe a week ago."

"Ah," my mother whispers. "And then what?"

"I-I've been in denial," I say. "Ignoring it with the shop. I'll have to face it sooner or later. It might as well be now."

"Darling," my mother says softly, "you've been needing to see this for a long time." She hesitates. "I knew—before you were married—that he wasn't truly the right man for you."

I inhale sharply. "And you let me—"

"Searcy," Mama retorts, a bit more strongly. "There was no stopping two headstrong Southern children determined to run off to the big city and make a wonderful life for themselves. Holding you—or both of you—back would have been a disaster."

Again, I can't think of a single thing to say. She's right.

"And you would have argued. Not believed me. Accused me of trying to destroy your happiness." She clucks her tongue. "And besides, you were already gone. In your hearts and heads. The only thing left was your body."

I nod.

"That's what parents do," she adds. "Let their children go and have lives. Pursue their dreams. Letting go of the best thing that ever happened to me is the biggest act of love I can think of."

The tears are coursing down my face, hot and thick now.

"I didn't think it was a mistake," I sob. "I thought he loved me. And I thought it was forever."

Mama holds her head up. "Searcy, dear, he loved you the best way he knew how. Until he grew up and realized what he really wanted and needed." She pauses. "And despite how lovely and talented you are, you could never give him that."

I choke back my tears and wipe at my cheeks with the back of my hands. With another sniff, I nod.

"Sign the papers, dear," she says, eyeing me carefully. "Set yourself free. I think you'll find there's someone special out there—who'll fit your life even better than you ever imagined Alton would."

My thoughts jet to Luke immediately.

Mama, thankfully, steers the conversation away from love and relationships. "And, so, how's the shop?"

I decide that it's now or never to talk about Quinn Hillyer and the money he's owed. At least now I have a solution in mind.

"Well, as a matter of fact," I begin, "I had a strange visitor a little while back. I've been meaning to talk to you about it."

My mother absorbs this quietly.

"Quinn Hillyer," I add.

Mama nods. "I'm sorry. Tell him to come and talk to me."

"I will not," I argue. "Besides, I think I can handle it. I have an idea for making up the shortfall on the rent. A good one."

Mama's eyelids flutter open wider and she peers at me, interested. Though she's exhausted and in pain, her eyes brighten as I describe my plan in detail.

"Tobi's in favor of it, but," I add, "Alton will have to work with me. And I'm not sure if he's at the Ashram, or where in the world he is at the moment."

"You'll find him," she says softly. "I have faith in both of you to make this work."

"Thank you," I breathe into the air, saying the words to my mother and the universe, which seems to be smiling on me, despite all of the struggles ahead.

Mama agrees to donate artwork, a few antiques in need of refinishing, and a portion of her extensive book collection, which includes many signed first editions.

Drawing in another breath, I fill myself with hope and my mother's love. She believes in me. In the future. That the shop will be there.

And then I picture a scowl, the one on the person standing between success and failure. In dollars and cents, I understand money is owed. It's business, his livelihood. But in a town of sixteen thousand people, a place where tranquility trumps tension, and friendship and neighborliness is valued, his angry demeanor seems out of place.

"Mama, the landlord," I ask. "Why is he taking this so personally?"

My mother turns her head. For the slightest instant, her face tightens, then relaxes again. It's clear from her lack of response that the situation hurts. And it's deeply personal.

A thought dawns on me. Maybe, just maybe, he loved—or he still loves—my mother. I shake my head at the idea, trying to picture Mama with Quinn Hillyer. The very idea sends icicle shards up my spine.

Questions race through my mind on warp speed. If they were together, how long ago was it? And what happened?

Thoughts and questions ping back and forth like electrical currents in a lightening storm.

"So? What happened?"

Mama yawns. "Searcy, the past is the past, darling."

I sit back on the chair and watch my mother as she closes her eyes.

There's no telling how many attic boxes I looked through in my childhood, digging for clues. *Who was my father?* But I never found a thing. It was as if she'd erased every trace of that part of my life. As if he never existed.

Easier for Mama, maybe. But there's still a void for me.

I just want a name. And a face. A photograph would be better than nothing.

Nothing is what I have now.

Mama breathes in and out, resting. I know she's exhausted. The conversation is over. My mother can't be forced into talking about sensitive subjects, and this one's hit a nerve.

In many ways, Mama is correct. The past is the past. Whatever happened can't be changed. With the landlord or with Alton. What's done is done. All I can do now is go forward.

Pay off the debt. Get divorced. Move on with my life. Make it better. Be happy. Be thankful for what I have.

In time, maybe it all won't hurt quite so much.

CHAPTER 31

I wake to the sounds of crickets chirping outside my window. If I listen closely enough, holding my breath, I can hear the water lapping on the shore of the Bay. It's so early that even the shrimpers and fishermen haven't ventured out.

Eyes closed gently, I think of Luke, still sleeping, eyes closed, arms hugging his pillow. I say a quick prayer that Mama has a peaceful day—a better one. She has to get better, for my sake. I can't lose her.

Within seconds, the alarm on my phone chimes out a melody under my pillow. Mission bells. Heart beating a bit faster, I feel with my fingertips to find the slick case, turn it off, and lay still, basking in the stillness and cool air with my bare legs wrapped in the sheets.

It's a new day, and there's so much to accomplish.

I throw off the covers, dash through the shower, throw my hair in a loose ponytail, and pick out a fresh pair of shorts and an "I Love Fairhope" t-shirt. I am feeling the love today, and want to exude it from my pores. I want everyone to feel it—in the shop, when they bite into a slice of pie, when they walk by the store and smell golden crust browning in the oven.

It takes me all of three minutes to slide into the Cadillac, start the engine, and rumble up the avenue. Street lights glow on empty sidewalks. On every cottage and bungalow, Soft lamps illuminate front porches and steps.

The shop is dark, and I flick on the lights after closing the front door behind me.

I place my iPhone in its stereo cradle and search for one of my Norah Jones albums. I need sweet music; a lullaby for the morning, and her voice effortlessly soothes the soul.

Though I'm not terribly worried about calling Alton and asking my favor, my heart flutters when I imagine hearing his voice on the other end of the telephone. Will he be all business, happy, uncertain, or dismissive? Will we make small talk, or will we talk like old times? Will the parting be a business deal, or will it splinter apart like firewood left too long in the elements?

Though I am ready to move on with my life, I believe the latter is true. Though I can't speak for Alton, and he's much further along in the second chapter of his life, I can't help but think that the final goodbye might conjure up a bit of sadness.

As I sift flour, cream shortening, and a pinch of salt, mixing my pie dough, I make a mental note to call him after the breakfast rush and before the lunchtime madness. The lull between—a sweet spot of thirty minutes—gives me just enough time to brew coffee, pour myself a cup, and gather my thoughts. It will have to be enough today, no exceptions. Neither Mama nor the shop can wait.

The berries I've cleaned and washed for today sit ripe and ready on the counter in a sieve. The mountain of fruit is shiny and glossy in purple-black, nautical blue, and deep red. After rolling out my pie crust, I heap the berries into each baking pan, careful to sprinkle enough sugar and some lemon to balance out the tart flavor.

Once the first batch is safely inside the stove, I flip through my mother's recipes. I'm in search of something savory and comforting; a pie that melts on the tongue and delights the senses with spice and flavor.

My fingertips run over the recipe cards, many worn on the edges. There are watermarks and smudges in the ink. Mama's impeccable handwriting is distinctive and flowing, with a light touch on each line. From her grandmother and mother, to my mother and me. Four generations of women tied through the bond of taste and touch and fresh ingredients. It feels magical and I feel privileged to share in this legacy. Something created entirely by hand. With love. Near perfect, but never quite the same.

I could never get this feeling with a pair of Jimmy Choos or a Trina Turk dress. Sure, the memories would be there—a party, a wedding, or a celebration. But it wouldn't be something born of my own hands and time, created from nothing. And it would give happiness only to me, not to the rest of the world. To strangers. To friends. To loved ones.

I am overwhelmed with gratitude at this moment, and my eyes fill with tears. As I pause to control my emotions, I grip the counter and look around the shop.

In a short, short amount of time, this space has become my home. Fairhope and its people have become my family again. Tobi feels like my sister. My mother and I are closer than we've ever been. And there's Luke.

I am blessed. And I must make it all work. For everyone's sake. Not just mine. There is much more than my happiness riding on this shop. Lives and livelihood, legacy and love. Happiness. My future. New beginnings.

Dabbing at my eyes, I decide to make an old-fashioned favorite, chicken potpie, in the traditional, comfort food style my grandmother used.

I check the cooler and pantry for ingredients, gathering most as I go from memory. Bright orange carrots, firm potatoes, green sugar snap peas, white mushrooms, pearl onions, and cloves of fresh garlic. From the refrigerator, I take out butter, heavy cream, an egg, and the Tabasco sauce for a dash of flavor.

Tobi, in a moment of extra energy, cooked a whole, four-pound chicken last night and chopped it into even chunks of dark and white meat, perfect for this recipe.

As the sun begins to break over the horizon, nearly an hour later, I assemble the potpies for baking. After heating the ovens and sliding the tins inside, I measure and brew our coffee—a Columbian dark roast, a Costa Rican medium roast, and the day's flavored selection: salted caramel.

As I grind the beans, the unmistakable scent of nutty aroma fills the shop, mixing with the scent of baking vegetables and chicken. I pause to inhale and close my eyes, allowing myself a second of rest before striding to the door and turning the sign from closed to open.

If I'm lucky, Tobi will make it in the back door and have time to tie on her apron before our first customers arrive. Stacey Howell, regional artist, and her husband, an amazing woodcrafter and physician named John, are usually among the first to stop by. Luke isn't far behind, with his rumpled hair and t-shirt, grinning over the day's first dark roast.

I unlock the door and turn back toward the counter, eyeing the room. I straighten one or two of the chairs, move a tiny vase of fresh white and yellow daisies to the center of one of the lacquered wooden tables.

A knock on the door interrupts my work. Peering through the glass to the sidewalk outside, I can only make out a bright, lime green sleeve. Odd. Why wouldn't the person come in? The knock sounds again, harder this time.

Pursing my lips and wrinkling my nose, I stride toward the entrance and turn the knob, opening the door wide—and gasp in surprise.

CHAPTER 32

I'm standing face to face with C.C.

Alton's mother gives me an apprising once-over, her top lip twitching with dissatisfaction, and then saunters past me, her thin, fine nose in the air, holding a squashed Precious under one arm. The dog notices me, sniffs the air, and emits a shrill, squeak of a bark, announcing her displeasure.

"I heard you were in town helping Maggie."

Before I can ask who told her, or process that there cannot be a D-O-G in *Pie Girls*, C.C. stops in the middle of the shop, turns exactly 180 degrees, and settles herself into the seat, catching the table linen with her thigh and nearly yanking it to the floor.

Dumbfounded, I rush over to release the cloth and smooth the covering in place before the coffee cups and silverware smash into a million pieces. C.C. shrinks back at the proximity of my apron to her matching lime green pants, and I make quick work of adjusting the table top.

"C.C.," I manage to gasp out. "And Precious. What a lovely surprise."

Precious growls under her breath, baring her sharp white teeth. She's anything but ferocious, but I don't dare laugh at my tiny challenger. Attempting not to choke, I swallow and step back from the table.

"We're in town for an appointment," says C.C. "We've had to wait three months—and that was the best they could do."

C.C. reaches up a hand and pets the dog, offering soothing murmurs.

"I hope everything's all right." I say, scrutinizing my mother-in-law from head to toe. Despite her caustic personality, C.C. has always been healthy. I don't even think she takes a multi-vitamin.

"We're seeing a specialist," she sniffs.

"Goodness, what ever for?" I ask, suddenly a bit concerned.

But my line of questioning is cut short when I hear the familiar jingle of Tobi entering the building. There's no way in the world I can warn her of the impending doom about to be unleashed.

"Tobi," I say in a high falsetto, "Look! Alton's mother is here with Precious."

C.C. narrows her eyes and gives Tobi a look that would make the Wicked Witch of the West melt—sans water. My insides twist like a kitchen towel being wrung out tight.

"Good morning," Tobi says cheerily, waving from the counter.

C.C. balks at the enthusiasm. "Hello."

On cue, Precious offers an offended yip.

Tobi gives me a sidelong glance with a discreet, tiny flick of an eye roll. She turns on her heel to disappear into the kitchen.

I lower my voice. "A specialist?"

Alton's mother draws herself up dramatically. "Precious has been having nightmares. They've caused her to stop eating. She's lost weight. Her fur isn't as shiny."

I stop myself from gaping. "Precious?"

C.C. nods. "Oh yes, it's been going on for months."

Slowly, I nod. "And there's someone here, in Fairhope…"

"A canine psychiatrist," she replies primly. "One of the best in the country. She does hypnotism and teaches relaxation exercises. Her office is a block away."

"You don't say?" My mouth twitches, but I manage to keep a straight face.

C.C. strokes Precious around the ears. "We mustn't talk about it too much around her," she whispers. "We've been warned it might make things worse. She's very sensitive."

I raise an eyebrow. "Of course."

"Now, Searcy," she adds, dropping her eyes to admire her own coral-red fingernails. "We talked before, but it hasn't seemed to make a difference."

Stiffening for the impending onslaught, I try to play dumb. "About Precious?"

C.C. purses her lips. "No, darling. About Alton."

With a flash of brilliance, I decide to beat my mother-in-law at her own game. "There's nothing that I'd love more," I say sweetly, "but in Precious' fragile condition, I'm worried we might add to her stress. Let's wait until after her appointment."

This stops C.C. short.

After a very pregnant pause, she acquiesces. "Oh, I agree."

"How about a nice White Chocolate Mocha?"

C.C. narrows her eyes knowingly, as if she's just caught onto my game. "The calories," she breathes out disapprovingly.

I walk to the counter. "We can make them with non-fat milk and no whipped cream," I offer, gesturing at the cappuccino machine. C.C. looks doubtful, but gives into the temptation. "Hmm," she taps at her bottom lip thoughtfully. "Can you make a Venti Iced Skinny Hazelnut Macchiato, Sugar-Free Syrup, Extra Shot, Light Ice, No Whip?"

I bristle a little, but smile anyway. "Of course."

Before I can turn to begin, she shakes her head. "No, that's not right," she murmurs. Precious utters a sharp bark. "I know, darling," she coos. "I was thinking the same thing."

"No problem," I say, staying rooted in place. "What sounds better?"

"Um. Let's see. I'd love a Caramel Macchiato, Venti, Skim, Extra Shot, Extra-Hot, Extra-Whip, Sugar-Free." C.C. kisses Precious on the head, mashing the pink bow flat.

I cringe at the list of 'extras', knowing full well this high-maintenance drink is nothing but a show of power.

From the corner of my eyes, I see Luke amble up the sidewalk. He gives me a wave before opening the front door and stepping inside.

"Good morning, barista," he calls out with a smile, and no trace of last night's slightly distant behavior. As he walks toward the counter, he greets C.C. then turns his head back in my direction, eyebrow raised.

"Alton's mom?" he mouths.

I offer a quick nod of confirmation and get started on C.C.'s drink.

"One Caramel Macchiato, Venti, Skim, Extra Shot, Extra-Hot, Extra-Whip, Sugar-Free," I say, and carry the steaming hot mug to her table.

Luke hides a grin. And instead of playing it cool, as I expect, he begins to flirt, flashing a wide, white smile as he walks over to C.C.

"That sounds like a very interesting drink," he winks down at Alton's mother.

"Oh, my dear, it's so delicious," she widens her eyes in mock ecstasy.

Luke presses a hand to his chest. "I've always been a 'Quad Grande, Non Fat, Extra Hot…"

I am watching him with narrowed eyes. He's barely containing a smirk, and slides me a mischievous look. He doesn't care a thing about fancy drinks or gourmet food. He loves dark roast coffee, no cream, no sugar. And pie of any kind.

"…Hazelnut Cappuccino. Upside down," Luke finishes loudly and with gusto, pumping his fist in the air.

By this point, Tobi has walked to the front to check on the conversation. She's placed one hand on her hip and is holding an oven mitt in the other. "Quad Grande? Upside down?"

"Four shots," I say, clarifying the insanity that Luke's about to drink. "And I guess he's going to stand on his head and drink it." I shoot a pleading look that clearly says "*The idea is to make her leave, not make her stay.*"

But Luke, clearly entertained by the whole situation, orders more. "And two slices of lemon sponge pie." He winks at me.

"Your favorite?"

"Yep. I'm starving," Luke says, rubbing his belly.

"This," Tobi smirks, "I've got to see."

I roll my eyes, smother a giggle, and start the espresso machine, making sure the temperature gauge and controls are set in exactly the right places.

With a click, I set everything in motion. The huge stainless appliance hisses and whirs into action, and I begin pouring and mixing.

"All right," I say, "here we are." With a big smile, I push the drink and two slices of pie across the counter to Luke.

C.C., who still hasn't uttered a word of thanks, keeps staring at Luke, who picks up his mug, plates, and a fork and heads for her small table.

When he sits, much to my dismay, Precious decides she loves Luke too, and begins inching her way toward his hand, sticking out her pink tongue to give him a kiss.

I bite my lip and shake my head, thinking that this is not exactly how to get C.C. out of the shop, but that I can allow myself at bit of amusement at her expense. Luke is, after all, playing the part of Southern gentleman and admirer.

And he's doing it for me.

The bell above the door jangles loudly, signaling more customers. A party of six files in, laughing and talking. Another two follow, an older couple holding hands.

As they order hot coffee, iced Mochas, and slices of pie, I toss a grateful smile in Luke's direction, and he sees it. He grins back, then winks, pretending he has something in his right eye. Luke even feigns interest in the fluffy animal, all legs and tails and pink bow. He nods thoughtfully, rubbing his stubbed chin, as C.C. tells him a story, waving her diamond-encrusted fingers around to emphasize her point.

Tobi sidles up and whispers behind a cupped hand and she slides open the pastry case. "What in the world is the crazy old bat up to now?"

"Going to a pet therapist," I hiss back. "Or hypnotist." My words trail off as I see a plump uniformed woman with a clipboard pause outside the front pane-glass window.

"Oh my gosh," Tobi says, a bit louder this time. She freezes, one hand still in the case.

"Is that...?" I say, feeling panic prickle in my chest.

"Yes."

"Oh no, oh no," I blurt out, starting to walk-run toward Luke and C.C.

"Don't," Tobi whips out a hand and drags me backward. After whirling me around, she puts both hands on my shoulders and stares me directly in the eye. "Breathe," she says. "We have to be smart. We can't tell her to go away."

I inhale dutifully and wait for some brilliant plan to come out of Tobi's mouth. She's probably dealt with dozens of visits. She knows the routine.

Tobi's eyes dart across the room as the door creaks and the bells jingle. A few remaining customers, thankfully, file out, as the woman steps inside the shop.

"Tobi?" I ask as goose bumps rise across my arms. "What's the plan?

Her pink cheeks flush a shade deeper. She blows out some air, lets go of my shoulders, and offers a stricken look. "I don't know," her voice squeaks.

"All right," I say, assessing the woman ambling toward the table. *So far, we're golden.* Precious hasn't barked, and C.C. is somehow doing an excellent job of blocking her pooch with her rail-thin body.

With my left hand, I reach over and twist the dial on the Sirius radio. The sudden change in volume startles a few people, as we usually keep the music low and sedate.

I turn and face Tobi, lowering my voice to a murmur. "Convince Luke to get C.C. out of the shop."

Tobi frowns and hisses back. "She's not going to listen."

"Make something up. An emergency," I mouth, walking backwards.

"Umm," Tobi wipes at her damp brow.

I urge her, a final plea of desperation. "Anything."

There's a squeal of displeasure as I take another step, directly on the toe of someone's shoe. I whirl around and find myself face to face with the health inspector, who is less than happy to see me.

"Searcy Roberts," I say and stick out my hand. "Bless your heart. I'm so sorry about your foot. Are you okay? Maybe we should see a doctor? There's one right down the street."

The inspector inches back and turns her head to one side. "I'm fine," she says, unconvincingly putting all of her weight on the other foot.

"Excellent. Yes, ma'am," I say loudly, almost saluting.

She offers me a curious look at the military response. "So, shall we begin?"

"Of course," I agree. "Although, next week is good, too."

The inspector, clearly not amused, raises an eyebrow and glances past me, her gaze lingering on Luke and C.C.

Tobi is talking quickly and pointing toward the sidewalk.

Oh no. I jump in front of her, wide smile on my face. "How about some coffee or cappuccino? An iced drink?"

"No thank you," the woman replies, giving me a strange look.

"It's a hot day," I explain. "I'm a little dehydrated." I begin fanning myself with both hands.

"It's 75 degrees and partly cloudy," the inspector replies flatly. "I think it's rather pleasant."

"Oh," I say, searching for an explanation. "I've just gotten over an illness." I pause to cough into my elbow for emphasis. "Eboli-Conjacka-Dissentary."

The inspector wrinkles her nose. "That's...not something I'm familiar with."

"Oh, of course. Brand new virus. Very contagious. Only found in Kenya," I rattle off, trying my best to look weak and bacteria-ridden. "On safari, in fact. They quarantined me."

"Really?" the health inspector moves away from me.

I smile and adjust a chair, dragging it across the floor. Under the sound of metal scraping against wood, a sharp, distinct bark pierces my ears.

The inspector and I both straighten up like we've been shocked by cattle prods.

"Ruff," I cough again, this time making my whole body shake.

"I thought I heard—"

"Ah-ruff, ruff." I make myself sneeze and offer a shrug to the inspector. "It's the virus. Makes your throat close up. I've been coughing like this for days."

She shrinks back even further, clutching her clipboard in front of her chest for protection.

I bark again, several more times. From the corner of my eye, I can see Luke linking arms with C.C., half-lifting her and Precious out of the seat.

Tobi, behind them, is furiously gathering up C.C.'s rhinestone-studded sunglasses, a huge key ring, and this season's Nancy Gonzalez bag, a raspberry applique crocodile tote with a four thousand dollar price tag. Enough to pay off a good chunk of the shop's debt, I think ruefully.

When she turns to wave, C.C. loses Precious. In slow motion, I see the dog leap from her arms, its sharp, beady eyes fixed on a slice of pie sitting half-eaten on a nearby table.

There's a sudden scramble as Luke leaps to catch the wiggling Precious, who's three steps ahead and gaining fast on the leftover delicacies. I hold my breath, praying that the inspector doesn't turn around. Tobi's mouth hangs open and her eyes lock on mine.

In desperation, I reach out and grasp the inspector's sleeve, wrenching her toward me.

"Medicine," I wail.

Tobi rushes over, on cue. "Eboli-Conjacka causes fainting spells."

"I'm calling 9-1-1," the inspector announces—just as Luke makes it outside with Precious under one arm and C.C. in tow.

As the door slams behind them, I sink to the floor in relief and loll my head to one side. *Not* my most attractive look.

"Searcy?" Tobi yells in my face.

I don't answer at first. I can't catch my breath, for real this time. The truth is, all of this cavorting around is hard work. "I'm okay," I finally manage to croak out.

The wail of a siren sounds in the distance. Another follows, and there's honking and tires squealing as the emergency vehicle gets closer.

"I'll let them know what's going on," the health inspector tells Tobi.

I don't move a muscle until she's safely out of the building.

"Well, there you go," Tobi says, sitting back on both heels, a satisfied smile on her face.

"I need some Advil," I reply, sitting up to rub my head. "That gave me a headache."

Tobi elbows me in the ribs. "You had it easy. Try dealing with C.C." She shudders.

"What happened with Luke?"

Catching her breath, Tobi nods approvingly. "He told her the dog psychiatrist had an earlier opening. Can you believe he knows the woman? She's an avid biker."

"Oh, I am going to owe Luke big time," I say, smirking to myself. "He saved me."

"Of course he did, silly," Tobi rolls her eyes. "He's crazy about you. The man would probably walk a tightrope above Section Street if you asked him to."

"Quit it." I elbow Tobi, trying to frown.

We burst into laughter as a stream of emergency workers, all wearing protective facemasks and gloves, careen inside the shop.

"Ma'am," one says from under the brim of his cap. "Who needs medical attention?"

Tobi stifles a giggle, wiping tears of mirth from her cheeks.

"I'm so sorry," I choke out between bursts of laughter. "False alarm." I get to my feet and wipe my hands on my apron.

The EMTs all shuffle their feet, looking confused.

"That lady said you had Eboli-Conjacka-something-something? I never heard of that one," the team leader scratches his head.

"Nope," I say. "No Eboli,"
"Just pie," Tobi replies. "Lots of pie."

Chapter 33

The next morning, there's a steady line in the shop just before lunchtime. It's Sarah Nolan's first day at Pie Girls, and between filling orders and ringing up slices of pie, she's learning how to make iced coffee, mochas, and the occasional cappuccino.

As the cash register sings, I glance at our quickly depleting inventory.

"When we slow down enough for you and Sarah to handle things up front, I need to do some baking," I tell Tobi. "I'm thinking spinach, red pepper, and feta frittatas and lemon sponge pie?"

She nods.

"What do you think, Sarah?" I ask, making sure she can read my lips. "Something cool and sweet to balance out the frittata?"

"Sounds delicious," she agrees. Sarah is petite and small-boned, and very much on the quiet side. She's adorable—with her long strawberry-blond hair back in a ponytail, clear blue eyes framed with long lashes, and a smile that lights up her face.

Sarah's smart, observant, and a quick learner—a great addition to *Pie Girls*. She's had years of speech therapy, so her voice is almost as clear as mine. I told her this morning that I'd love to learn sign language if she was willing to teach me. With a bright smile, she made a fist, then raised and lowered it at her wrist—signaling a "yes."

As Sarah heads over to clear dishes from a table, Tobi confers with me.

"She's really nice," Tobi says under her breath. "Polite, sweet. Super cute."

"Exactly," I wink at my friend. "I like her a lot."

Tobi fortunately, is also a blessing to work with. Even-tempered, reliable. A dream employee, for all intents and purposes.

"Thank you, too." I say suddenly. "I don't think I say that enough."

Tobi pauses and turns to look at me with a raised eyebrow. "Umm, okay," she answers slowly, blinking in confusion. "But I haven't done anything."

"You have." I reach over and squeeze her hand. "You're here every day. You could have quit, or left. You could have gotten tired of my never-ending drama."

Tobi snorts a little. "Well, that's a given." She winks.

"I mean it. Thank you."

"No problem," she replies, wiping down the counter. "I like this place. I love your mother. Fairhope needs us. We're employing hard-working young people, like Sarah."

I smile.

"And we can't let Quinn Hillyer win," she adds. "Under any circumstances."

I nod, biting my lip, feeling as if I've won the lottery of being surrounded by the best people in the world. A tear stings the corner of my eye. I'm so incredibly lucky.

"Have you seen C.C. today?"

My mouth dries in an instant. I swallow and cock my head, looking out the window at everything and nothing. "Not yet," I say. "I'm not sure how long she was staying."

"You have to call Alton, you know."

I wring my hands and frown. "I know."

She returns a steady gaze. "Searcy…"

"I will," I say, summoning courage. "Today—"

There's a commotion at the door, and we both look up simultaneously.

Haley Richmond storms in on stiletto heels, followed by Jimmy, and their two children. I try not to stare. They all belong in a Ralph Lauren magazine advertisement, with the broad expanse of the Caribbean ocean and a forty-foot, gleaming white yacht behind them.

Without a greeting or smile, Haley scans the pastry case under long, blackened lashes.

Sarah, who's closest, approaches with a smile. "Can I help you?"

Haley tosses her perfectly coiffed hair back over her shoulder, frowning slightly.

"Birthday cake," she says.

Sarah wrinkles her forehead and glances over at Tobi for clarification.

"Ma'am?" Tobi asks, motioning for Sarah to come back behind the counter. Or run for cover. We exchange a glance as Haley continues to stare at the shelves, moving across each one with a critical eye.

A reddened Jimmy Richmond steps next to his wife, putting one hand on her elbow. "Sweetheart, they don't have birthday cake. I told you."

Haley huffs. "That's ridiculous. What sort of bakery doesn't have birthday cake?"

"A pie shop—" Tobi begins with a smart edge to her voice, but I catch her hand and squeeze gently. *The customer's always right.* Make her happy. Try to, anyway.

"We'll make anything you like," I say, smiling from Haley to Jimmy.

This gets a Cruella De Ville worthy smirk.

"What's your favorite?" I ask, trying to read her mind. I picture something flowery, maybe with sparkles and bows. I admit that I'm at a loss when it comes to cakes. Pies are my forte. Quiche, tarts, anything with a crust. But I'm not dissuaded. How difficult can it be?

I choke on those words when she gives me her answer.

"Well, it's always been my dream to have a very special cake. One that no one else would ever order." She motions for me and Tobi to lean closer, as if she's about to offer up some top secret Al Qaeda information that might save a thousand lives.

I hold my breath.

"A Tiffany gift box. With a bow." She squeals and claps her hands in delight. Behind her, both children cover their ears and close their eyes. Jimmy looks pale and tired, exhausted to have a wife who's insatiable. The kids shift uncomfortably; the girl pulls at the hem of her dress, completely bored.

A Tiffany gift box. Exactly something I would have selected—a month ago. Or something equally as difficult and ridiculous. For a moment, I see myself reflected in her mood and actions, and wince.

Was I this demanding? This impossible? Did I lift my chin and look down on others? I tighten the knot on my apron and remind myself that I'm not that person anymore. Jimmy's wife is a customer, and it's my job to make her happy.

I shoot an uncomfortable glance at Tobi. *This may never end.* Jimmy's children begin playing tag in the shop, taunting and teasing. Both parents seem oblivious, Haley focused on her cake, and Jimmy focused on Haley. I hold back from commenting, not wanting to lose a big sale.

"Can y'all do that?" She squints at us, prompting.

"Sure. I'd love to," I say, trying to look enthusiastic. Tobi grabs a pad of paper and a pen to take the order.

"Almond flavored cake, raspberry filling, buttercream icing, but with reduced fat and calories?"

All the butter. No calories. That makes me smile.

"Oh, but what about fondant?" She brightens again. "That might be amazing. It would look so real. And I could have chocolate inside. With a cherry filling. Or vanilla."

Tobi starts to falter. "Uh, Searcy?"

The two children are standing on the café tables, each balancing on one leg. Disaster waiting to happen.

"Sarah," I call out. "Can you find out if they'd like cookies?" I gesture toward the budding gymnasts, and pick up a pad and pen.

She nods.

Ignoring the commotion, Haley smiles broadly and lets her eyes travel around the shop. "It must be quite a change in pace for you," she says, letting the words settle. "From Atlanta to here, taking over your mother's business, her illness—"

"We're fine," I insist, making myself smile broadly.

Haley leans closer, her lips curling into a Cheshire cat grin. "But you're not," she retorts triumphantly. "You're stuck here. From what I hear, you're *this close* to losing the business." She holds up her index finger and thumb, showing me a space of less than 5 centimeters.

I balk at her attack; glad Sarah can't hear the remark.

"That's enough," Jimmy cuts in, standing as tall as he possibly can in his 5' 2" frame. He puts himself between his wife and me. "It's time to leave."

Thankfully, Sarah, in an absolutely brilliant move, herds the kids outside to eat their cookies.

"I don't know where this is coming from," I reply. My voice is a bit shaky but firm.

"You were always the princess, the special one, the prettiest, the smartest," Haley snips. "You got everything you wanted. And you got to move away and leave this place." Her eyes glitter with hatred and contempt.

I start to argue, but let myself fall silent. What would it be worth…fighting some deep-seeded angst left over from high school? Wracking my brain, I try to come up with an incident that would have caused Haley to despise me. What did I have that she didn't?

If he was mortified earlier, Jimmy looks aghast at his wife's behavior. "I'm sorry, Searcy," he murmurs.

Haley whirls around. "You've had a crush on her since you were ten years old, and you've never gotten over it."

"That's ridiculous," I sputter, red-faced at the confession of Jimmy's unrequited love.

The door jingles. I don't even look up to see who's entered the store. I pray that it's Luke. Or the fire department saying there's a gas leak and total evacuation of Fairhope is necessary.

Haley doesn't seem to hear me. She's lost in her rant.

"Speaking of married," she adds, laying the groundwork for her final one-two punch. "What is going on with you and Alton? He's in Spain, he's in China, he's in the South Pacific." Haley flutters her fingers. "What outlandish excuse will you come up with next?"

I can't reply. I'm rooted in place. This time, I truly don't have an answer. I can't keep up with the lies I've told and the excuses I've made to cover up the breakdown of my marriage.

"The truth is, Searcy," Haley looks down at her own diamond engagement and wedding bands. "He doesn't love you anymore. He's found someone else, and you're here because you don't have anywhere else to go."

I summon every ounce of courage in my body. "You're right," I say, leveling a gaze at Haley. "He's not in any of those places. I made it all up because I was embarrassed."

Haley smirks in triumph at Jimmy.

"My marriage is over," I clear my throat. "It has been for a while. Yes, I think Alton has found someone else. He doesn't love me anymore. And as much as it's hurt me to accept that, I want him to be happy and move on. I want us both to be happy, if we can't be happy together. Alton's a good person, Haley. I'll always care about him."

There's complete silence in the shop.

"And as far as being in Fairhope," I continue, getting braver with each sentence. "At first, I thought I didn't have anywhere else to go, but now, I love it here. I'm with Mama. I have my friends. I have *Pie Girls*. And despite people like you who seem to want it to fail, I'm going to do everything in my power to keep it going, even if it means I have to sell the shoes on my feet."

I've run out of air, and breath, and words.

"Not the Prada shoes." Comes a voice from behind Haley. "They're your favorites."

CHAPTER 34

Everything in my body screams to a halt. My blood quits pumping momentarily. That voice. That tone.

Alton walks up to the counter, reaches for my hand, and looks down to examine my shoes. Today, I'm wearing a very non-glamorous pair of white Keds. Scuffed. With red laces.

He smiles at them, then back up at me.

"Hi," Alton says finally.

I choke back tears at the sight of him. I'm overcome with emotion. He looks wonderful, and content. And I'm glad.

He turns to face Haley. "Before you go, since you've made my life and Searcy's your business, you should know the truth," Alton says carefully.

I suck in a breath, my skin prickling.

"I care about Searcy. And her happiness. She's bright and funny and loving. She can do anything she sets her mind to," he adds. "And she doesn't need you telling her differently."

There's no response from Haley.

Jimmy reaches out a hand to shake Alton's. "Good to see you, man. We were just leaving." With that, he puts his hand on the small of his wife's back and steers her toward the door.

"So…" Alton smiles. "Typical day at the shop?"

"Most are a little less dramatic," I reply, letting out a sigh. We stare at each other.

"I wasn't expecting you to drop by," I say, lowering my voice. "Must be the week for the Roberts family. Your mother was here yesterday. She's on the warpath and wants some answers. She believes she's owed an explanation."

Alton smiles ruefully. "Of course," he says. "Confession time. More than she's bargained for."

More? More than the divorce? Quitting his job? Wrinkling my forehead, I don't press for details.

"What's the occasion? Stopping in out of the blue?" I ask. "It's a bit unexpected."

He considers this; looking at the floor, then back up at me. "I figured since you haven't responded to my letters, that we needed to talk in person. Could I have a few moments of your time? Later, now? Whenever."

Tobi jogs back in, breathless. "Oh my gosh, Searcy, are you all right? She's lost her mind." Seeing Alton, she skids to a stop "Whoa."

"Hey Tobi," Alton says, embracing her. "Great to see you."

"Y-you too," she replies, her voice unsure. She finds my eyes and pierces me with a "What in the heck's going on?" look.

"Could you watch the shop, please? We need a few minutes."

"Of course," Tobi says, nodding emphatically. "Good. Yes. Go ahead. Sarah and I've got this. No problem." She waves us out the door.

"Thanks," Alton says.

"Don't rush back. I can handle things."

I bite my bottom lip as we leave the safety and comfort of the shop. I'm suddenly clammy and chilled. The thought of talking, of sharing the same space with Alton unnerves me. I'm so lost in thought that I don't pay any attention to where we're walking, and run straight into Luke, who's making his way back up the sidewalk.

"Hey there," he steps back and grabs me to keep me from toppling over. When I've steadied myself, Luke sticks out a hand to greet Alton. "Long time. What? Ten, fifteen years?"

"At least," Alton nods. "How've you been?"

"Great," Luke replies, forcing a smile. I can tell he's not happy at all with my unsolicited visitor. "I own this place now; have for several years," He jabs a thumb toward the store window full of bicycles.

Alton looks up and takes in the proximity to the pie shop. "Convenient. Right next to Searcy. Enjoying her cooking?"

Gulp.

Luke doesn't miss a beat. "Sure am."

Alton lifts his chin, considering this. He doesn't look jealous, or bothered. Just thoughtful. He rubs a bit of stubble on his chin.

"Um, so we need to go, Alton. Catch up on a few things," I interrupt before the conversation gets more complicated.

I can't do it.

Stand on the street with the two most important men in my life—one who wants me, and one who doesn't anymore—pretending that everything's normal. My head's swimming and I need to sit down and get my bearings.

"Don't let me hold you up," Luke steps back to let us pass. He doesn't look at me, only past my shoulder.

"Right," I say, for lack of anything else.

"See you around," Luke mutters, offering another handshake to Alton. He doesn't say goodbye to me.

Alton and I walk in silence, down toward the waterfront. It's a relatively quiet afternoon, and we're likely to have more privacy here than anywhere in town. I'm glad for the breeze, the open air, and the water lapping against the shoreline. I need to focus on something, anything other than Alton's face. It's too difficult. He's familiar and a stranger all at once.

We stop and sit on a concrete bench in the sunshine. The wind ruffles my hair, catching the edges, and I watch in the distance as seagulls dive and play on the Bay's surface.

Alton clears his throat. "How are you?"

"Fine," I reply too eagerly and quickly. "Good. Really. Great."

"Truth?" Alton puts a hand on my arm.

"Don't, please," I say, shrinking back.

We both fall silent.

My head swirls with everything I want to say. From moment to moment, my emotions change. I want to yell and accuse, I feel like sobbing. There's a part of me that wants to slap him in the face, hurt him. Make him think about how much he injured me.

Then, there's another voice, smaller and softer—one that encourages sanity and self-control. I have a million questions, and yet, none of them matter. It's over, our marriage. The reasons don't count so much anymore.

"I have a favor," I blurt out suddenly. I might as well throw my plan out on the table, get some buy in and help. Surely, Alton can do this. It's the least he can do.

"Name it," Alton replied, seeming relieved that I've offered to speak at all, let alone allow him to make up—in a tiny way—for his transgressions.

"Send me my clothes, and shoes, please," I ask. "From the apartment."

"Of course," Alton replies.

"But, I mean, all of it, and as soon as you can," I add trying not to sound terribly desperate. My heart begins to pound in my ears. "Anything at all that you can't use or that you don't want. Anything that you'd donate to charity. Furniture, books."

A flicker of confusion crosses Alton's face. "I can do that," he says, his words measured and careful. "Can I ask why so soon?"

I hold up both hands in defense and shake my head, smiling at him. "I'm not keeping it, any of it," I reply. "I need the money—"

"But our agreement," he protests, interrupting. "It's generous. More than fair. It'll keep you going for several years until you figure out what you'd like to do with your life. You can go be a clothing designer, or a personal assistant, or go back to college. Teach or get a degree in marketing or public relations."

I'm quiet, holding back my amusement that he's naming off careers like they're ripe and ready for the taking, like apples in an orchard.

He's a solution kind of guy. A problem-solver. But this issue—my life—isn't going to be righted by running an Andrews and Quentin advertising agency brainstorming session.

"Thank you, Alton," I say gently. "But I've found what I need to do with my life. It's here, in Fairhope. At *Pie Girls*. With Mama and Tobi. For the first time, maybe ever, I feel happy and fulfilled. My life has a purpose. And I'd like to think I'm good at it."

Alton looks down at the ground and then out across the water. He's lost in thought.

And at first, I think he's going to argue with me. I can hear Phillipa's voice in my head, almost immediately. Telling me I've lost my mind; it's beneath me, and I can find someone else to take care of me.

But then, I look at Alton. His cool cotton shirt, linen pants, Birkenstocks, the slightly grown-out hair. And I remember that he's given up most material things, his home, his job, and me. Alton's voice cracks when he begins to speak.

"I'm really proud of you, Searcy,"

"Thank you," I reply, my eyes beginning to fill with tears.

Alton reaches out and puts an arm around my shoulder. I inhale his scent, notes of sandalwood and a hint of vanilla.

I lean into him and let my body relax. For a moment, I close my eyes.

He hesitates, then taps my shoulder with one finger. "And I so I guess you'll be setting up a house? Have you found a place to live?"

Sitting up straight, I inch away from Alton, letting his arm drop away from my skin. A boat chugs close to the shore, trailing fishing lines. The captain peers out under his ball cap and shouts something to his companion. We exchange a wave.

"I'm staying with Mama," I say. "She's not well. The doctor diagnosed her with Lupus a while back, and she's in the hospital."

"Lupus," Alton echoes. "Is there something she can take? Will she get better?"

"She's been refusing treatment, which made everything worse," I explain as I tuck my legs up on the bench, lacing my fingers around my bent legs. It feels safer this way, talking about my mother. "Mama hasn't been able to work for a while, so when I got here, I started helping out in the shop. I didn't know she was so sick until I practically forced her to tell me."

I give Alton a rueful smile.

"Good for you," he whispers in approval.

"She's failing, though, even though we've finally managed to get her on some medicine this week," I say, my voice catching in the slight breeze. "She looks so tiny and weak now, when I see her. She tries to act like it's nothing, like she's going to walk out of that hospital tomorrow…"

The words choke me. I swallow and wipe at my cheeks with one hand. The tears are blinding me, salty and wet.

Alton finds my hand and squeezes it.

I summon the energy to continue. "That's not all," I say. "Her landlord paid a visit to the shop recently. He's not the nicest guy on the planet. When Mama wasn't there, he pressed me to tell him what was going on with her."

"Odd."

"I thought so," I agree. "Way too personal. When I told him I was her daughter, he got even more perturbed and told me that Mama owed him some back rent. Quite a bit, in fact. And that he was calling in his favor. Needed it all."

"How much?"

I hesitate, but then give him the number.

Alton sucks in a breath, contemplating the amount. I can see his brain working, rolling around the options, working the angles. "I'll give you the money."

"No."

He sets his jaw. "Searcy—"

I soften my voice. "Thank you, but it's not for you to fix. My life is not your problem anymore."

"It was never a problem," he argues back with a fierce edge.

This makes me smile and I touch his lips with two fingers to make him stop talking. "Liar," I tease him. "The shopping trips, dinner parties, gifts, wine, spa days, and all of the mini-vacations. Admit it, you'd occasionally go a little ballistic."

Alton softens then and chuckles, remembering. "Maybe."

"I can do this myself. I have a plan," I say. "That's why I need the clothes. And whatever else you're not going to use."

"You're going to consign it all?"

I inhale deeply, filling my lungs and puffing up my chest proudly. "Not fast enough. I'm on this crazy deadline. So, I'm having a yard sale."

Alton stops breathing and his eyes grow huge. "A. Yard. Sale?"

"Yup."

We both dissolve into fits of laughter. After a few moments, I start to hiccup. Alton coughs and pounds at his chest. I dry my own face with the edges of my apron, which I just now remembered I'm still wearing.

I glance down at my watch, remembering the time. Composing myself, I run my fingers through my hair and smooth my shirt. "I have to go," I tell Alton. "Get back to the shop and check on things."

He sobers up immediately. A shadow, ever so slight, crosses his face. There's something else. Another detail. Something big.

I realize then, that it's no accident he's in Fairhope.

He needs closure.

It's then that I realize, finally, I want it, too.

"I'll sign your papers, if you can give me a few minutes to find them," I offer quickly.

Immediately, Alton looks relieved. "Thank you so much," he adds, flashing me a grateful smile and pulling out his cell phone. "I've actually got them in the car. I thought, that if we were able to talk, and you were willing, it might make things easier. Hang on, just a sec." He reads a message, types a few words on the screen, and presses send.

As he's texting, I examine Alton. His profile, his body. The way he sits. There's a contented air about him. A peacefulness I've never seen. He's almost glowing with happiness.

I swallow. It's more than the Ashram. Or the yoga, meditation, or clean eating.

He's in love.

"So, do I get to meet her?" Oddly, I am completely okay with this. Sure, there's still the sting and ache of loss. But any sense of regret or anger has faded. Totally. It's time for us both to move on. I want him to be happy.

Alton clears his throat. There's a long, pregnant pause before he responds. "Are you sure, Searcy?" He meets my gaze. "I don't want to do anything else to hurt you. I've done enough."

"Alton, you've given me a gift," I say. "You've released me to grow up and find out what kind of person I can be. Without relying on you. Or anyone else."

He nods.

"And we weren't happy," I add. "Not really. Not the way we should have been."

"Searcy..."

I shake my head. "I'm fine. Really."

Alton tilts his head. "Then, okay," he says with the faintest smile.

"Yoo hoo," a woman calls out from a few yards away. "Hello! Alton! Searcy!"

Alton and I jump at the voice. It's C.C.

Before we can stand up, a cloud of perfume envelops us. There's a yip from Precious. And Luke behind them, looking awkwardly upset.

"My darling son," she scolds, yanking Alton to his feet and crushing him in her embrace. She peppers his face with kisses, leaving streaks of pink lipstick on his cheeks and chin. As he struggles to get free, C.C. peppers Alton with questions.

"Where have you been? Why haven't you called? Are you eating? When are you two moving back to Atlanta? It's high time you stopped this nonsense. Just kiss and make up already."

"Mom," Alton interjects.

"There's a dinner party next week, and the Millers are having an engagement party for Stella. You have to come, it'll be the social event of the decade," she coos. "And Searcy, dear, we can go shopping and I'll buy you some new dresses. There's the most darling Trina Turk in lavender, and you'll just look divine."

"Mom," Alton repeats, a little louder and more insistent.

"I'm so happy," C.C. squeals, ignoring him. "I think you should have a renewal of your wedding vows, and we can do it in the Methodist church. I know just the caterer. They do these incredible canapés, and we'll hire the best florist in Buckhead—"

"Mother," Alton yells, startling everyone into silence.

C.C.'s bottom lip trembles.

A car door slams, interrupting the awkward moment. "Everyone all right?"

A handsome man of about forty walks over from a shiny Silver BMW, smiling broadly. He reminds me immediately of Antonio Banderas, with his curly black hair, twinkling dark eyes, and sexy air. He walks up to me and pulls me into a hug.

"Alton! She's even more lovely than in her pictures," says the man, kissing me on both cheeks with spicy cinnamon lips. He has a delicious Latino accent that I can't quite place, and blinding white teeth. Dizzy from the embrace, I fight to think straight, his accent dancing in my ears.

When he lets me go, I sag a bit. "It's um, nice to meet you," I say, wriggling out of his grasp and smoothing back the hair from my face. I fan myself to cool off, trying not to notice the way his biceps strain under the cotton of his white button-down shirt. He, too, is wearing linen pants, in a brick red, which sets off his mocha latte complexion to perfection.

By the time I've recovered and breathing semi-normally, he's moved on to C.C., winning her over with a little bow, murmuring something in Spanish, and kissing the back of her hand. Thankfully, she looks even more enamored with the attention.

A seagull squawks overhead, swooping close to our group, and I duck instinctively. When I stand up straight, I notice that Alton looks ready to make an announcement.

"Searcy. And Mother," Alton says, gesturing for both of us to come closer. His eyes are sparkling now, like he's keeper of the biggest secret on Earth. Whatever the news is, he's bursting to tell us. "I'm glad we're all here together so that I can share this with you."

I inch forward, and obediently, C.C. moves toward Alton, taking her place at his side. She keeps a protective hand on Precious, who's sniffing the air suspiciously.

Alton puts an arm around the Antonio Banderas look-alike, pulls him close, and smiles broadly. "Both of you, I'd like you to meet Thomas. My boyfriend."

CHAPTER 35

Two days later, the shock of it all still hasn't worn off. I've been in a daze, going through the motions of cooking and baking.

Yesterday, Tobi rescued three cherry pies from burning when I neglected to set the timer. I brewed decaf coffee in the dark roast pot, and filled the lemonade container with unsweetened iced tea. In the middle of mixing up roasted red pepper and feta frittatas, I had to stop myself from adding sugar instead of salt.

This morning, I'm doing much better. Since sunrise, I've only charred two-dozen mini quiches, which Tobi promptly rushed outside and threw into the trash cans.

"The shop would've smelled awful—like burned ham and cheese sandwiches," she announces when she comes back in, letting the screen door slam behind her.

"It's not that smoky," I protest, waving the clouds of gray from in front of my face. "We can open a few more windows."

"Even Luke wouldn't eat them," she retorts.

The mention of his name catches me off guard. I can't speak.

"Where's he been, anyway?" Tobi asks, wrinkling up her forehead. "He's been MIA for days. What's he eating? *Where's* he eating?"

"I-I'm not sure."

"It's awfully funny," she rubs her bottom lip with one finger. "You don't think he's…jealous?"

"Of Alton?" I want to snort, but I'm too sad to make the effort. "That's just plain silly."

Tobi purses her lips. "Maybe, maybe not. You pretty much ditched him when Alton rolled into town."

"I did not ditch him!" I exclaim. "I had to talk to Alton. I had to sign the papers. And then there was the whole thing about meeting Thomas."

"Hmm."

I pretend to ignore Tobi's I've-got-to-solve-this-mystery face and focus on the feel of the pie dough. The repetition is soothing, and I allow myself to get lost in it.

Luke, however, manages to creep back into my thoughts. The line of his jaw. The deep blue of his eyes. The hurt look on his face when Alton was next to me on the sidewalk.

"What are you doing?" Tobi's voice jolts me back to the present.

I stop kneading, look down, and realize that my usually lovely pie crust is now a crumbly, pebbly mess of flour. "Whoops," I murmur, biting my lip.

With a roll of her eyes, Tobi strides over, pushes me gently out of the way, and sweeps the bits of dough into the nearest trash container. "I'm going to give you a hammer and nails, girl. You can work out some of that frustration. Or nervous energy. Whatever it is."

"I'm not really sleeping much," I admit, not wanting to look at the dark circles under both eyes. The past two nights, I've lain awake in Mama's house, staring at the ceiling, worrying, wondering, and pondering everything that's brought me to this point in my life.

Tobi wipes down the counter with a damp cloth, scraping at the bits of flour with her fingernail. "I know you're on edge," she says, balling up the washrag and tossing it into the sink. It lands with a solid thud against the stainless steel basin.

"Nice one," I say, managing a small grin.

"Take the day off," Tobi suggests, giving me a halfhearted nudge at the door. "Really, you're not much good to me screwing up everything around here."

"Thanks," I protest, but smile, knowing she's half-right.

"Next thing you know, we'll be serving someone Oleander tea or replacing the mushrooms with beetles from the backyard," she teases.

"I'm not that bad," I retort, trying to give Tobi a mean look. Reaching for the shortening and a new bowl, I resume my dough making. "I'll pay better attention this time. Besides, what will I do at home? And Mama will shoo me out of the hospital."

"No better?" Tobi asks.

I shake my head, trying to measure out ingredients. "Her blood counts are all messed up. She's lost her appetite. She can barely keep her eyes open because she's on so much pain medicine."

"I'm sorry," Tobi says. "You know if there's anything…"

"You're already doing it," I reply. "You're here. Every day. Without fail," I add. "I really, really don't know what I'd do without you." My shoulders sag, and I catch myself from beginning to cry.

Tobi rushes over, catches me in her eyes, and squeezes me tight. "It'll all be okay," she whispers into my hair. "She'll pull through. She's tough."

I pull away and look Tobi straight in the face. "I've lost Alton. I never had a father," I say. "I can't lose her, too."

"Let's not think like that, okay," Tobi says, leading me over to a bar stool in the corner. She picks up where I left off on the pie dough, measuring and mixing carefully. "And besides, Alton was gone a long time ago."

I allow this to sink in.

"How long?"

Tobi's hands rest in the mixture. "Maybe even before y'all got married?"

I nod.

"Now that he's come to town and brought Thomas," she says with an air of confidence. "It all fits."

"It fits," I repeat, letting the words slip and slide around in my mind.

"Searcy," she says, "Alton loved you. I think he still loves you. But not in a married way. Not in a husband and wife way."

"I know," I say stubbornly. "I guess I didn't want to know, back in high school. Or college, or after the honeymoon…"

Tobi blinks at me. "You knew."

I shrug and don't meet her eyes. I stare at a speck on the floor, thinking back. "Maybe. It was easy to ignore it, though, especially at first. Planning the wedding, moving to Atlanta, Alton's new job, dinner parties, shopping. All the excitement."

"You kept busy."

"I didn't ask," I say and rub my temples. "The long trips, the nights out of town, and so many late dinners. We rarely had alone time. No sex to speak of." I wince. "Maybe for years.

"Years?" she squeaks, incredulous at my confession.

"Big sign," I try and joke. Neither one of us laughs.

"Speaking of signs, how about right before you came here—that time he went missing and was on the news?" Tobi presses her lips together and tilts her head.

"Oh my goodness," I exclaim and slap myself on the front of my skull. "Of course."

Tobi raises an eyebrow.

"And three years ago. Our anniversary. I suspected he was cheating on me…with a woman," I say, gesturing. "I was snooping and dropped his brand new iPhone. Smashed the glass, but could make out a text message from "Thomas." Surely, you don't think—?"

"Umm. Well," she stutters.

"Yes, right?" I demand, my blood pressure spiking.

"Whoa. Wait. Think about this. Really, does it matter?" Tobi asks, putting one hand on her hip. "Right now?"

Biting my bottom lip, I think this through. "I'm not angry. I'm not even jealous. In fact, I'm happy that Alton seems so in love. But he should have told me."

Tobi nods. "Yes, I agree. But maybe he couldn't. Or he didn't know. Or he didn't know how to tell you and didn't want to hurt you."

"He did, though," I say, swallowing. "Hurt me."

"Of course," she agrees, pressing both hands on the counter before rolling out the pie crust. "But think about this." Tobi taps her fingers on the table. "What if you'd had children? What if you'd stayed married for forty years and he'd decided then? What if he'd never said anything? Isn't that worse?"

This knocks the breath from my body.

"And you stayed, too," she continues, challenging me. "You must have gotten something out of the marriage, if you weren't getting love or sex. Right?"

"A great place to live. Fabulous parties. Nice vacations. And shoes," I answer, almost embarrassed to admit it. "A lot of really, really expensive shoes."

There's the blast of a horn out front, followed by a banging on the front door of the shop.

"What in the world?" Tobi scrambles to look at the clock. "It's 5 a.m."

"It must be an accident," I say, "Or an emergency."

"Or a serial killer," Tobi says with a wink.

"They don't come to the front door. Or knock."

"Good point." She nods and grins.

The banging starts again, and this time it sounds like a Gorilla getting ready to rip down the heavy, solid wooden frame.

"Keep your pants on," Tobi yells.

We race to the front. I can make out the outline of a huge moving truck. As the knocking continues, I scramble to turn the lock.

"If this guy wants some coffee and pie, and can't read the hours sign, I might knock his block off," Tobi threatens.

I can't help but laugh as I swing open the door.

"We're not really open," Tobi blurts out before I can say a word.

"Delivery for Searcy Roberts," the driver says, looking between the two of us. He's wearing a uniform and looks decidedly un-serial killer like. The man thrusts a clipboard, paper, and pen close to the screen. My name is definitely on it, printed in large capital letters.

"Who's it from?"

The man sighs and turns the clipboard back around to examine the originating address and name of the responsible party. "An Alton Roberts. Buckhead, Georgia." He rattles off the apartment address, Alton's phone number, and a back up number that could be C.C.'s.

"That's my—" I stop myself from saying husband. "That's the one."

I crack the screen door, scribble my signature, and wait for instructions. "My clothes," I murmur to Tobi under my breath. "For the yard sale." I size up the truck as the man walks away to open the back of the moving truck. "Probably a few boxes. Think we can handle it?"

"Sure," she nods. "Perfect timing. We can do it tomorrow. Or Sunday, depending on how much you've got." Tobi raises her chin expectantly.

"Aww, not that much," I say, brushing off her question.

In the distance, I hear the mellow rumble of a truck. The sound, the chug of the engine, the crunch of tires on pavement, is familiar as Alabama sunshine. Luke.

A minute later, he pulls up, parks, and hops out of the truck. For a moment, I think he's going to duck inside without offering a greeting. He rounds the end of the bumper, turns toward the front door of the bike shop, and glances in, but he keeps walking towards us.

"Special delivery?" Luke watches as the uniformed delivery man raises the door. "Lord, Searcy," he exclaims.

"It's not all mine," I protest, not even glancing at the contents. "It's got to be multiple families. A couple of stops."

"Nope," the delivery man says, overhearing me. "My instructions say it all goes here. Every box. Every piece of furniture. Down to the lamps and dishes."

Tobi elbows me. "Oh my."

I turn and feel my jaw gape open.

Alton has sent everything. Every chair. Every table. Every dress, shoe, belt, and book we owned. The boxes are labeled neatly in his handwriting. "Men's shirts." Then, "Suit jackets."

"So, your husband," Luke says, his voice thick. "Is he moving here?"

The delivery man clears his throat.

"One second," I plead, holding up my index finger while taking Luke's hand and dragging him close to the shop.

"What is it?" His eyes are stormy and dark. Cold.

"He introduced me to Thomas."

There's a long silence and I watch Luke's face for a reaction.

"So," he starts. "He's not—"

"No." I shake my head. "I signed the divorce papers. This delivery is all for the shop. The yard sale."

The stress and anxiety on Luke's face fades away. "And Thomas is?" He almost smiles.

"Alton's boyfriend," I reply. "He's cute."

"Cute?" Luke rolls his eyes.

"He's not my type," I jab him in the ribs gently, making him break into a chuckle. We begin walking over to the moving truck.

"Thomas isn't your type?" Tobi asks. She shrugs, exaggerating. "Yeah, me neither. Not at all. He's almost too good-looking. You know, he looks exactly like Easi Morales."

"Really? I was thinking Antonio Banderas," I exclaim.

"Easi," Tobi says firmly. "Hands down."

The truck driver folds his arms in mock disgust, giving Luke a knowing glance. They grin at each other.

"Ladies, I know the fate of the female world rides on your discussion, but can we have the Antonio Banderas debate later? I need to unload this delivery and get back to Atlanta sometime this month."

Chapter 36

After two days and nights of feverishly tagging and pricing every purse, trinket, and pair of shoes I own—well, almost every pair of shoes—I am thoroughly exhausted and running only on black coffee and slices of Key Lime Pie.

Tobi's attempts to get me to sleep, including threatening me with a spatula, haven't worked. I'm too excited, and nervous, especially after hanging dozens of signs all over Fairhope at nine o'clock last night. There are pink sheets of paper announcing the sale on every street corner, from Pine and Oak Streets to Pecan and Laurel. Even the Fairhope Inn and the owner of Camellia Café allowed me to tape signs on their doors. Of course, I begged and traded pie for twenty-four hours of advertising time.

After our run across town, I began baking as Luke dozed off for a few hours last night. After all of his hard work, no one bothered to wake him as he snoozed in the corner of the bike shop. He was adorable in his wrinkled shirt and cotton shorts, breathing deeply with his head propped against the rough-hewn brick wall.

Tobi's husband, under semi-duress, agreed to handle the swing shift. After forty minutes of instruction on coffee making and the cash register, I left him with firm instructions to text if there's an emergency. Sarah's coming in soon to help him out, thank goodness.

When I reenter the bike shop, I note with satisfaction that Luke hasn't moved a muscle.

"I don't know how he can sleep sitting up," Tobi says, picking up a Stella McCartney fringe dress worth well over nine hundred dollars. She holds it up and raises an eyebrow.

"Um, fifteen dollars?" I say, rubbing sleep out of my eyes. "Twenty?"

Tobi holds the frock to her chest. "I'd buy it, but I don't have anyplace to wear it. Heck, for this price, I might wear it around my house to vacuum."

We erupt in giggles, which makes Luke stir and half-open his eyes. I shush Tobi and select a pair of Miu Miu Mary Janes with the heel covered in black glitter. "I loved these shoes," I sigh. "New Year's Eve, four years ago. I haven't worn them since."

Tobi's marking a pair of black and red Christian Louboutin peep-toe pumps. "Last ones," she says, waving the shoes in the air in celebration.

"Thank you, Lord," I breathe, collapsing against the back of the metal folding chair. My neck aches, and my fingers are tired from gripping a black Sharpie marker. I stretch my arms overhead and glance at my wrist. We have only two hours until people begin showing up.

Long folding tables flank the two adjoining storefronts, and our plan is to fill the space with handbags, jewelry, and knickknacks to entice shoppers. There are more than a hundred re-usable bags and totes on hand, donated by the Chamber of Commerce. Luke has calculators, four changing rooms, and enough designer dresses hanging in the window that his store might surely be mistaken for a high-end women's boutique, if one didn't notice the Ultralight, Orbea, and Masi bicycles lining both walls.

"I'm taking five minutes to put my feet up," says Tobi, limping over to the nearest chair. "If I don't, there's no way I'll make it through the afternoon."

"Then, I'm going to run over and see Mama," I say suddenly, with a burst of energy I didn't know I had. She needs an update. It might buoy her spirits to hear about how industrious we've been. "Be back in a jiff."

I grab for my bag and cell phone, heading for the front entrance, thinking about talking to Mama. The instant I open the door and step outside, Quinn Hillyer fills my field of vision.

"Searcy," he greets me flatly, his voice void of any emotion. He glances past me, into the wild array of colors and fabrics. "Is this your idea of a Hail Mary pass?"

"Anything that works," I say sharply, and try to edge past him.

Quinn catches my elbow, but is quick to release me when I whirl around to glare at him. "Please, don't touch me." My skin burns where his palm connected, and there's a sudden urge to shower or scrub every inch of my body. I want to rid myself of every reminder of this man.

"It's never going to work," he sneers. "Not in twenty-four hours."

"That's not for you to say," I reply, facing him with my chin lifted in defiance.

He shakes his head, murmuring under his breath. "Just like Maggie. Same attitude. Same spirit. Spitting image."

"I don't understand you, Mr. Hillyer," I say. "You're determined to destroy the only thing that makes my mother happy."

The expression on Quinn's face changes from nostalgic to nasty. "It's business, girl. You should know that, marrying into the Roberts family."

"Not anymore."

He reels a little at the news.

"Just signed the divorce paperwork. And I'm staying in Fairhope to run the shop."

"And Maggie?" Quinn tries to recover. "Where's she in all of this?"

"That's none of your business," I retort. "Why do you care, anyway?"

Quinn grits his teeth. "I don't," he replies, but his tone does nothing to convince me.

"You'll have your money, Mr. Hillyer," I promise. "Sunday by eight sharp." This time, I walk away, not bothering to look back.

Mama's sleeping when I creep into her hospital room, trying not to disturb her. Despite my efforts to shake off the latest attack by Quinn, his interrogation has left me unnerved.

The moment I sit by her bedside, a nurse comes in to check my mother's vital signs.

"Good morning." She smiles at me, then makes note of numbers on several monitors. "Good news today. It seems she's getting a bit of strength back."

A surge of hope courses through me. "That's wonderful," I say under my breath.

"She's still on heavy duty pain meds, so, if she wakes up, expect her to be groggy," she warns.

"All right," I say, trying to tamp back a flicker of concern.

When she finishes examining Mama and checking her IV, the nurse pauses and looks at me. "She loves you very much. You're all she talks about. She's proud of what you're doing."

"Thank you," I say quietly, my eyes filling with tears. "We only have each other."

"Make the most of it," she adds. "Every day you have."

I sit in the silence after the nurse finishes her tasks and leaves the room. Watching Mama breathe in and out calms me. A bit of pink has returned to her face, and she doesn't seem quite as drawn and gaunt as a few days earlier.

"Today's the day, Mama," I whisper. "The big yard sale. You should see Luke's store, all covered with dresses and purses. And Tobi's husband and Sarah, Luke's sister—they're both filling in at the shop. I tried to get Tobi's husband to wear an apron, but he wouldn't do it," I joke. "Even for me."

My mother doesn't move or open her eyes.

"Quinn stopped by," I continue. "I think he's worried we might actually pull this off. He's firm about the deadline, and I pretty much told him we'd have the money. Whether we do or not."

I pause and check for some reaction. Any stirring. The flicker of an eye. Nothing.

"I keep thinking there's a secret," I say, pressing my hands together in my lap. "Like he's got an agenda. Some vendetta against us." I pause. "I wish I knew."

With a sigh of resignation, I stand and brush off my pants. I stare down at Mama, wishing I could penetrate her brain and see to the past. What happened? How did we get to this place?

I bend over and press my lips to her cool cheek. "I love you. Wish us luck."

There's a line on the sidewalk at least a block long, with stragglers walking up, cutting in line, or standing around to gawk at the shoppers. By the time eight o'clock rolls around, the women are restless, and the men have filtered back into the pie shop for a second cup of coffee.

Luke's back among the living, and looking animated and excited at the turn out. "This is huge," he says, nudging me. Sarah's just ducked in from the shop and is standing back and taking in the crowd.

"Good luck," she tells me, her voice just above a whisper. Her cheeks are flushed pink and she's tied on an adorable apron, ready to help.

I wink at Luke's sister. "Thank you so much for pitching in today. It really means the world to me."

"I wouldn't have missed it," she says.

A long, shrill whistle from Tobi breaks everyone's anticipation.

Tobi catches her breath. "Thank you for coming out and supporting *Pie Girls*. It means the world to us," she announces. "I promise that you'll find some amazing deals, and you'll be supporting a great cause. So, without further ado, let's get shopping!"

At the stroke of the top of the hour, we open the bike shop's front door and cut the long thick red ribbon separating the tables from the shoppers. With a surge, ladies of all ages rush forward, grabbing at items, exclaiming over jewelry, and reaching for handbags.

Watching the fray, I'm nervous a fight might break out over my favorite pair of Gucci sunglasses, or women might argue over who seized my Versace knee-high riding boots first.

But an odd rhythm settles over the room, and happiness seems to exude from every corner. Bags fill, calculators sing, money changes hands. My head swims with the amount of items each person carries out of the store. Within a few hours, nearly half of the merchandise is cleared out. Customers have carried out coffee tables, lamps, wine glasses, and table linens. To my embarrassment, there are still new items galore, a testament to my need for consumption.

How different my life is now.

Simple, easy. I haven't been shopping in weeks—save the necessary trips to the farmer's market and grocery store. I can't think of a new article of clothing that's been purchased, and my current wardrobe consists of shorts, t-shirts, and cute pink aprons.

There's a part of me that watches the activity and mourns the money wasted. But the joy that's being generated outweighs any regret. I'm helping Mama; I'm securing my future, Tobi's, our employees.

I'm overwhelmed with the generosity of friends and neighbors. Many round up the purchase prices, donating an extra few dollars to "the cause." It's all Luke can do to keep up. As our executive cashier, he hasn't had a moment to breathe or stand up.

I catch his eye, and he winks and offers two thumbs up.

"Amazing," he mouths.

I flush pink with happiness, admitting to myself that all of my things that once seemed important, almost crucial, to my existence, seem trivial now. I'd steeled myself in the wee hours of the morning, prepping myself for a tinge of sadness or a longing.

Instead, the sight of teenagers trying on my BeBe blouses and stately women holding up Donna Karan dresses to their necklines, admiring their own reflections, doesn't bring me the slightest bit of unhappiness. The joy in their faces, the little squeals of delight make me smile.

One girl in her twenties discovered a white chiffon evening gown, classic Vera Wang, that she intends to wear for her wedding next winter. Another woman in her thirties exclaimed over a retro Ralph Lauren swing coat with a faux fur collar. Sarah helps her slip it on. It fits her like a dream, and she practically dances out of the bike shop on air.

Several of Alton's wool suits go home with a distinguished man in his fifties. He spent fifteen minutes examining the cut and drape of the fabric at different angles in the mirror. The gentleman is taking so long that Luke finally nudges me.

"He's holding up the works," he murmurs, gesturing under the table at the line of ladies queuing for a turn at the mirror.

"Armani," I say, finally approaching him with a bright smile. I don't want to seem pushy or like I'm rushing him, but something stops him from deciding. "What do you think?"

He glances at me, reddening. "The price," he confesses, lowering his voice so that it's barely audible. "I can't read it."

I peer down at the white tag in his hand. There's a scribble of numbers, but nothing decipherable by my standards. From the corner of my eye, I see three identical suits, in different shades of gray, lying carefully on the back of a chair.

"They all fit?" I ask.

"Beautifully," the man agrees, breaking out into a huge grin. "I feel like a king," he adds, squaring his shoulders.

"How about," I lean closer to his ear and whisper a number that's one-eighth the price he'd pay in any department store, even if the items were on sale.

We shake on the price and I send him off to Luke, who raises an eyebrow at my wheeling and dealing. I'm not about to let a soul walk out empty handed, even if I have to give things away for pennies on the dollar.

Like a butterfly, I am shedding my cocoon. The wrappings are no longer needed, heavy and weighing me down. With every shirt, belt, and hat that leaves the store, I feel lighter, almost weightless.

I scurry over to help two young teenage boys pick out ties for a school dance, then zip the back of another dress, this time an elegant DKNY black cocktail sheath on a thin woman with a smart gray bob. "Wait here," I motion, and scramble to find a set of thick pearls and a matching bracelet. "These are Celine, vintage faux pearls that will look smashing with this outfit." I drape the necklace around the woman's neck and secure the clasp. She holds out her wrist for the bracelet.

"The champagne color is lovely," the woman tells me. "I'll take them. Thank you." She doesn't glance at the price, just nods and disappears back into one of the changing rooms, reappearing minutes later, her arms loaded down with a dozen more dresses and blouses.

Several people are waiting in line to pay Luke, Sarah's helping a young girl pick out shoes, and Tobi's busy assisting two ladies with scarves and belts.

"Searcy?" I hear my name being called across the room, and I poke my head around several shoppers, trying to match the voice with a face. The tone and pitch are familiar, and before my brain fully matches the two, I see Phillipa's tanned arms outstretched. She shrieks with pleasure at the sight of me and practically jumps into my arms. Mimi's behind her, waving excitedly.

"Oh my goodness," I exclaim, hugging her tight and inhaling the strong scent of Joy, Phillipa's signature perfume.

When she releases me, I hug Mimi, and then step back, inhale deeply and catch my breath. Phillipa looks amazing: toned and manicured, with perfect highlights and a white linen pantsuit trimmed in the faintest hint of silver rickrack. Her shoes are goddess-like, stacked pumps held together by crisscrossed threads of silver leather. Mimi is decked out equally as well, with a bright pink, one-sleeved top made from silk and a pair of tight gold pants that would look ridiculously garish on any other human being. Somehow, the both of them pull off the look, as if they'd stepped straight off the cover of Town and Country magazine.

Six months ago, I remind myself, I would have matched.

"What's all this?" Mimi exclaims, picking up a Fendi handbag and pausing to run her hand over a red Valentino gown hanging overhead.

"Nothing," I say quickly.

"Is it a charity fundraiser?" Phillipa asks, putting a perfectly polished fingertip to her bottom lip. She frowns.

"Searcy, didn't you have some of these?" She picks up a pair of black leather Dior pants.

I can't tell her that they're the ones we bought together. In New York. Last year.

"Let's step outside," I yell. "I can barely hear myself think." I take Phillipa's hand and wave for Mimi to follow. Thankfully, they don't argue.

"Mimi and I are just on the way to the beach," Phillipa announces as we weave our way through the crowded room, "and decided we'd swing out of the way for a few hours and visit. The husbands are out of town."

Luke raises an eyebrow as I half-drag Phillipa and Mimi by his makeshift desk.

I toss him an apologetic look.

"They're on their fourth golfing trip this year," Mimi adds. "How horribly boring."

"Right. I mean, of course," I exclaim as we burst out onto the sidewalk.

Phillipa runs a hand over her perfectly coiffed hair, still staring at the stream of people coming in and out of the bike shop. "So, where's Alton? I thought he'd be spending part of the summer here. And your mother? I expected to see Maggie, at the very least."

"I'm sorry I haven't called," I say, "to update you about everything."

Mimi steps off the sidewalk to let a group of shoppers through. "Heavens, you'd think people were giving away this stuff."

I try not to laugh.

"The truth is, girls," I say, taking a breath and letting it all out at once. "Mama isn't well and I'm managing the shop. Maybe permanently."

Phillipa raises an eyebrow accusingly and starts to open her mouth.

"Wait, wait." I hold up one hand. I lower my voice. "And Alton and I have split up. I signed the divorce papers a few days ago."

"What?" Phillipa shouts, making at least five people on the street turn their heads.

"Bastard," Mimi says, putting both hands on her hips. This gets several more glances.

"Shh!" I say, motioning for my friends to lower their voices.

"He *was* cheating, Searcy," Phillipa says, ignoring my attempts to shush her. "I knew it. Didn't I tell you that a few months ago—"

"It's okay." I keep my voice soft and even. I nod emphatically.

Both women stop talking to stare at me.

"Really. We talked. He was just in Fairhope," I add with a small smile. "And I met his new…"

"You did not," Phillipa rolls her eyes.

"Yes, I did."

"Really? Well. What's she like? What's her name?" Mimi demands, folding her arms across her chest defiantly.

"Thomas."

Mimi huffs in frustration. "The next time I see that two-timing—"

Phillipa's head whips around. "Thomas?" she interrupts.

Mimi scrunches her nose. "That's a funny name."

"It's not, really. Thomas is a man."

"Umm. Yeah," says Phillipa. "And I'm Princess Kate and have a baby named George."

"Me too," echoes Mimi.

"I'm serious," I say. "And I'm happy for him."

Phillipa rubs her forehead with her palm. "Wait. Does your mother know?" she asks, wide-eyed. "And what about C.C.?"

I nod.

"O.M.G." Mimi claps a hand over her mouth. "I'm surprised she didn't kill him."

"She's dealing with it," I say. "And Thomas is quite charming, by the way."

Phillipa walks closer, taking both of my hands. "And you're really okay? That's all that matters."

"I am now," I assure her. "It's for the best." I sigh. "I didn't think so at first, but I'm proud of him for telling me he wasn't happy. For not hiding his true feelings. And letting me go."

My friends let this settle in.

"You're going to be just fine," Phillipa says. She scrutinizes me. "I actually think that small town life agrees with you."

I laugh. "Yes, I do, too."

After another few moments of contemplating, Mimi perks up. "All this has put me in the mood to shop," she says, linking her arm with Phillipa.

"Go for it," I say, smiling. "Knock yourself out. I've got to get back to my duties, managing the 'charity' sale."

They both kiss me on the cheek, and Phillipa gives me another hug.

"I think we should go back in here first," chirps Mimi, steering Phillipa toward the bike shop. "These prices are ridiculous."

"I don't know," Phillipa shakes her head. "We don't know where they've been. Someone else has worn them."

I follow them inside and sneak next to Luke, who's watching the two of them with an amused grin. "Friends of yours?"

"You could say that," I admit. "It seems like a century ago. Maybe two."

"So, that was your life?" he asks, still watching Phillipa and Mimi giggle over a Dolce & Gabanna sequined top.

"Yep," I reply. "I might—just might—have been a tad high maintenance."

"I'm not sure I would have liked you," Luke says, giving me a sly wink, "back then."

I nod, continuing to watch, and then inch my chair closer to Luke. Slowly, I slip my hand into his and squeeze.

"Me neither."

CHAPTER 37

We've counted the money three times. All of the twenties, tens, fives, and one dollar bills. There's a sole hundred and two fifties—from Mimi, who bought out my Gucci purse collection. I've made Luke pin the bills to my shirt because I'm afraid we're going to lose them.

Each of the quarters, dimes, and nickels have been stacked and rolled, ready for a bank deposit. In a pile, we've scraped together spare pennies, extras from the shop and the ones I've found on the sidewalk.

Luke punches in the numbers a third time, carefully. I watch, holding my breath, as the total number jumps ahead, gaining in leaps and bounds with each entry. It slows, then, adding the change. Smaller gains are made, creeping closer to our goal. And then, letting out an exasperated breath, he taps the keyboard once more with his index finger.

We both stare at the number.

The exact same number he's come up with the two previous times.

"Damn." Luke runs a hand through his hair. It's sticking up at odd angles.

"No," Tobi exclaims. Her ponytail is sideways and dark rings are visible below her reddened eyes.

I'm mute, unable to express my disappointment at being so close to the finish line. It feels as if we've run the finest horse in the Kentucky Derby, only to have him stumble inches from the finish line.

To be fair, we'd expected a victory. Anticipated it. Tasted it. Smelled the red roses.

It's like the trophy's been stolen from us; ripped from our waiting hands.

Except it hasn't.

We're ten thousand dollars short.

"What are we going to do?" Tobi says out loud what we're all thinking.

I don't reply right away. The fan overhead beats out a rhythm, tick-tock, mimicking the hands on the wall clock.

"Luke, the bank's not open. Can you lock the money in your safe?"

He nods.

Tobi hugs me close. "We did so well," she says in my ear. "I'm proud of you."

We survey the room together. There's almost nothing left, save a pair of fuchsia leather gloves I'm secretly glad didn't sell, a pashmina in a wild leopard print my mother might adore, an antique Asian-inspired black coffee table, and a red Prada clutch Tobi's been watching since we unpacked it.

"Please take it." I pick up the clutch and hold it out to Tobi.

Her eyes widen in appreciation. "I will. Thank you." She takes it from my hands and tucks the red purse close to her chest.

"Would your sister like the coffee table?" I ask Luke.

"I think she would."

"Good," I say. "Then it's settled."

Tobi yawns, rubbing her eyes. "I'll check on the shop."

"When do you have to talk to Hillyer?" Luke asks, unfolding himself from his chair and stretching.

"I've got four hours."

Luke nods gravely.

"I'm not giving up. I've got some people to see."

Mama's hospital room is my first stop. She's awake, sitting up, and waiting anxiously for news.

After kissing her cheek, I grasp her hand and squeeze gently, sitting next to her on the bed. "We've sold everything," I say. "And we're still short"

Her face remains impassive as the news settles in. "How much?"

"About ten thousand."

Mama works this through her mind. "We can try and sell the Cadillac, though we don't have much time," she suggests, and then gets a devilish look on her face. "Or trade it to Quinn."

I roll my eyes. "Oh, he'd love that." We both manage a giggle, despite the grim situation. The idea of Quinn Hillyer driving the long, pink sedan down Section Street would boggle anyone's mind. "The man's too caught up in appearances to have any fun. I don't think he's smiled for the last decade."

Mama's lips part, and she looks thoughtful, like she wants to say something. Instead, she shakes her head. "You're probably right."

"We need a slam dunk," I say, standing up and pacing. "Something amazing. Something he can't refuse."

Mama's face brightens momentarily.

"What is it?" A spark of hope lights inside me.

"Um. Alton came to see me," she says.

"He *what*? When?"

"The other day. Just for a few minutes, with Thomas. I met him. He seems…nice," she adds.

I blink back surprise, though nothing that Alton does these days should give me pause. As I replay the afternoon of his visit, it makes sense. It's his way of wrapping up loose ends. Of showing respect to my mother.

"He apologized," Mama says, searching my face.

"That was noble of him," I reply, nodding. Alton and my mother were always fond of each other.

"It was the right thing to do," she says. "He wanted to make sure I heard everything from him. And that I understood…"

"He's happy," I finish her sentence.

"Right," she agrees. "And he wanted me to give you something."

I stop.

Mama lifts a hand and waves it at the corner cabinet. "Inside there, on the bottom."

There's a rush in my ears as I walk on wobbly legs toward the surprise. I can't imagine why Alton couldn't have given me the item in person, though it might have prompted another trip to the ER, since one of our last altercations involved me knocking his tooth out.

Better safe than sorry, I think ruefully.

I pull at the handle and open the door. There, at the bottom, is a blue box. Robin's egg blue. Tiffany blue. With a white bow, tied tight. Silver lettering.

When I turn and face Mama, I can barely breathe. With a shaking hand, I pull at the ribbon, letting it fall apart. I wiggle at the top of the box.

"Oh my gosh," I exclaim as the exquisite jewelry is revealed.

It's the Tiffany Soleste Yellow Diamond pendant I've coveted for so long. The one I'd practically demanded on our anniversary. I blush hot pink as I tilt the box, allowing the light to catch the brilliance of the teardrop-shaped pendant. The yellow diamond looks like pure sunlight, and surrounded by tiny white gems. The chain holding it is thick and platinum.

"He remembered," I whisper, offering the box to Mama so that she can admire the gift. I'm crying then, at the memory. How I'd behaved. How I don't deserve something so marvelous at a time like this.

"Alton said, and he wanted me to tell you this specifically," Mama continues, reaching to wipe away my tears, "that it was long overdue. And that you can keep it or give it away. Do whatever you'd like with it. He wanted you to have the one thing that was so important to you."

"I can't believe him," I laugh through my weeping.

The funny thing was, the pendant isn't important at all. I wasn't that girl anymore, though Alton probably had no way of knowing that at the time of the purchase.

If he had, though, it likely wouldn't have mattered. He would have bought it anyway. Out of principle. Because he could, because it would blow me away, and because it made him happy.

A lightning bolt hits me.

A solution.

"Mama," I say, thinking out my idea. "He said *anything*?" My breathing becomes shallow. My mind races with possibilities.

Her head tilts. "Yes." She reaches her hand for a small, folded piece of paper on her desk. "And he left this."

It's the receipt. I reach out my hand slowly and take it, then examine the numbers and fine print, shaking my head.

The pendant could be the answer to my prayers. The money for the shop. Freedom from Quinn Hillyer.

Inside, I wrestle with whether it's wrong.

"I can't return it," I say, almost relieved that Alton bought it from Tiffany more than 30 days ago, which makes a return impossible. "But there's someone who might love this," I say slowly.

Mama raises an eyebrow. "That's quite a sacrifice, Searcy."

I wipe at my cheeks. "It's not like I can wear it while I'm baking," I joke. "And if we don't have the shop, a seventeen thousand dollar pendant isn't going to do either of us a bit of good."

My mother watches me.

"Is it wrong?" I ask.

"That's not for me to decide," she replies. "If you're asking if I think Alton would mind, the answer is no. Especially if it makes a difference for your future. For everything we've worked for. He wants you to be happy, too."

That settled it.

"What time are you meeting Quinn?"

"Eight. At the shop."

"I'd like to be there," Mama says. "And before you protest, I've already mentioned it to my doctors. They've okayed a few hours, provided we come straight back tonight."

"No wild parties?" I grin.

She smiles. "It's important to me. It's my shop, too. And I may be able to lend some influence. Talk some sense into him."

"Ah, element of surprise," I say, winking at Mama. "I like it."

I hug my mother close.

"Go, see what you can do with the necklace," Mama urges me. "And pick me up around seven?"

"Deal." Carefully, I give one last look to the yellow diamond pendant. It shines so brightly that it almost blinds me. *How could anyone turn this down?* I close the box and retie the ribbon.

A shiver of anticipation courses through me.

"Searcy?" Mama calls out as I start for the door.

I stop and smile back at her.

"Good luck."

CHAPTER 38

Haley and Jimmy Richmond's house is a mansion overlooking Mobile Bay. Stately, with white pillars and a yard that stretches forever. The flowers, all in bloom, are perfectly manicured and placed. Wrought iron benches wait for visitors, and butterflies dance over azalea and camellia bushes.

I texted ahead, afraid that the family would be out of town, or at their beach house on Ono Island. As luck has it, I receive a message back in minutes.

"Come on over."

The Cadillac sputters and chugs down the driveway, managing to announce my presence with a backfire that seems to resound from Fairhope to Point Clear. It's then that I glance in the mirror.

I'm a total wreck. I haven't showered, or combed my hair. The wrinkles in my shirt and shorts are pressed in like someone ironed them in place. There's not a swipe of lip gloss or mascara left, and I feel like if I stopped moving, I could lie down on the driveway and sleep for a week.

My stomach contracts as I switch off the ignition, step out of the car, and close the door behind me. Box in hand, I begin the seemingly endless walk to the front steps. The driveway is paved with bricks, perfectly spaced. Waving hibiscus bend toward me as I walk closer, seeming to sense that I have something very important to do.

The huge wooden door swings open, and Jimmy greets me with a broad smile.

"To what do we owe the pleasure?"

"Hey there," I say, hiding the box behind my back.

We step inside the house, which is cool and airy. There are paintings everywhere, modern furniture, and colors that speak to aqua, blues, and silvers found in beach scenes.

"Come on in," Jimmy says, leading me further into the house. "I figured we could sit on the back porch."

I follow behind him, stepping carefully to avoid anything breakable or fragile. There are vases and expensive knick-knacks everywhere, perched on tables, balanced on shelves. And dozens upon dozens of pictures of Haley, everywhere I look. Haley skiing. Haley at a family outing. Haley in Paris. None, I note, have Jimmy. Or their two adorable children.

Pushing the thought aside, we cross over the threshold to an expansive back deck, where overhead, ceiling fans spin lazily in the summer air.

As my eyes adjust again to the brightness, I see Haley, bikini-clad, sunbathing next to the Richmond's pool. It's a lagoon like shape, with exotic plants draping near the edge, a waterfall in the center, and a hot tub to one side. I feel as if I've stepped into a Caribbean paradise.

Haley lifts her head briefly in my direction, doesn't speak, and lies back to continue absorbing the gorgeous weather.

"I-I came to speak to both of you," I say, projecting my voice so that Haley can hear me clearly. "It's rather urgent, actually."

Jimmy draws up a chair. "Shoot."

"I know you've both been so helpful and supportive with Mama. And the shop. I'm so grateful, which is why it's very difficult to come here today and ask this of you."

"Go on," Jimmy urges. He's interested, and shoots a look at his wife, who's pretending not to hear any of the conversation.

"You see, and I'm sure you're aware of the situation we're in at the shop," I begin. "Mama's illness caused her to get behind with bills and rent. It's all come due. Tonight. Quinn Hillyer's expecting it all. Needs it all."

"Or?"

"He'll revoke the lease. Close us down."

Jimmy sits back in his chair. "The fundraiser?"

"Huge success," I say. "Really fabulous. Great turnout. But we're a little short."

From the corner of my eye, I see Haley wince. She's listening.

"Let's cut to the chase. How can I help?" Jimmy asks. "Do you need a loan?"

I shake my head. "No."

By now, Haley is sitting up. She's pretending to slather on more lotion.

"It's this," I say, putting the Tiffany box on the table.

Haley perks up slightly.

With a swift movement, I untie the ribbon a second time and open the box.

Jimmy gasps. His wife is on her feet in seconds. I try not to notice that her body might as well be a supermodel's—all tanned and golden. She doesn't have an ounce of fat on any part. Believe me, the gold bikini she's wearing is small enough that I can tell, even at a distance.

When Haley ambles over, trying not to look the slightest bit interested, I clear my throat and hold it out for her to examine.

Her eyes graze the box, float over to Jimmy, then lock on me.

"Is this part of your "yard sale?" she asks, looking at me through mascaraed lashes. "Castoffs that you no longer want? Or can afford, I should say."

Her voice drips venom.

I struggle to maintain my dignity, feeling every ounce the idiot for expecting some sort of courtesy, being in the woman's home turf.

Jimmy licks his lips, and a sheen of sweat appears on his brow.

"It was a gift from Alton," I explain quickly, so as not to lose their attention. "I'd wanted the necklace for a long time. He remembered that from our last anniversary."

There's an awkward pause, and I continue.

"He left it with Mama…after I signed the divorce papers."

It sounds like a consolation prize, marking me a castoff. But Alton's not like that. I still believe that he's a good person. In many ways, I will always love him.

The gesture was in good faith. He wanted me to have it. And Mama said I could use it any way I choose.

I can tell Jimmy's on the verge of telling me to hush. His wife, on the contrary, is mesmerized by the story, locked in as if I've become Scheherazade in *Arabian Nights*, desperately trying to save herself by weaving a tale so wondrous and compelling that her new husband, the Persian ruler, Shahryar, keeps her alive for one thousand and one nights.

My story, however, isn't nearly as interesting as Sinbad, Ali Baba, or Aladdin. I'm just a girl with a money problem. A girl who needs a favor, or a miracle. Help from a friend. Heck, I'll take help from an enemy at this point, which is exactly what Jimmy's wife believes I am.

"So, I've come tonight to ask if you might buy the pendant," I say. "I'm asking five thousand dollars—only half of what I need to pay Quinn Hillyer" I pause and swallow. "The necklace, and you can check the Tiffany website, is worth more than three times that."

Jimmy's eyes grow huge. Even Haley can't contain herself. There's a hint of happiness under the glossy plastic surface of her perfectly formed face.

As I can't hold the box out any longer, I set it down on the nearest patio table. "I can give you a few moments to talk about it," I say. "Again, I am sorry to interrupt your afternoon."

"There's nothing to discuss," Jimmy says with a smile. "And there's nothing to apologize for. We're—"

"Not interested," Haley cuts him off. She steps in front of her husband, blocking his view of me. She steps toward me, teetering on her five-inch heels. I realize then, that she's drunk.

Her breath, as she gets closer, reeks of whiskey.

"You have some nerve, Searcy Roberts," she slurs. "First, you're not woman enough to hang on to a man like Alton. Then, you think you can move back to Fairhope and start your life over. And now, you barge into my house, and want to turn around and sell off a gift that your husband—excuse me—*ex*-husband bought you."

"It's not like that at all," I exclaim, backing away from her. I need an exit plan. Or for Haley to trip over her own stilettos so that I can escape with out scratch marks.

"You don't appreciate anything," she screeches, waving her arms in circles.

Jimmy puts a hand up to brace himself from potential blows, and tries to step in front of his wife. "Calm down. You're making a scene."

"I was just leaving," I say under my breath, straining to tiptoe around the woman and pick up the Tiffany box while Jimmy has her attention.

Then, from nowhere, his wife begins sobbing and collapses on a chaise lounge. I should say that she tries to collapse, and lands half on the pool deck instead. This makes her cry harder.

I walk faster, heading for the door without saying goodbye. In fact, I may never come back.

"I loved him," she sobs.

This makes me stop cold. Not thinking I heard her correctly, I look over my shoulder.

"That's right," she yells. "And I tried to get him to love me. I flirted, then I offered to sleep with him. I begged, I pleaded."

Jimmy's jaw goes slack. The poor man is genuinely horror-stricken.

"But noooo," she slurs. "It was Searcy, Searcy, Searcy." Her fingers wave as she wobbles to sit up straight.

"When?" I hear myself ask.

"Senior year, Christmas break," she says, trying to grin at me. Her eyes won't focus. "You were off at some cheerleading competition. Something ridiculous," she practically spits.

Jimmy and I exchange a long glance.

"I told him you weren't worth it." She smiles wickedly.

The jab doesn't hurt as much as I thought it would. I was ready. I anticipated that she'd say it. I smile back, sadly amused at the whole situation, and feeling a bit sorry for Jimmy, that he's married to such a horrible person.

"I also told Alton that you wouldn't make him happy," she adds.

"If you want the truth, neither one of us would have."

Haley narrows her eyes. "How do you know?"

This makes me laugh, and I start walking, again, toward the door. "You'll find out soon enough."

She's beside herself and tries to stand up. Jimmy forces her back down, and she slaps at him furiously.

I shouldn't play this game. I don't need to. But I've had enough. And I don't believe, after this performance, that Alton will mind at all. In fact, I may call him up and give him a play by play. In another month or two.

"Find out what?" she calls after me.

My hand grasps the door and I turn the knob and pull. I give Haley one last look.

"That Alton prefers men."

CHAPTER 39

It's five minutes to eight, and the sun is beginning to set over Mobile Bay. Just as I promised, I pick up Mama from the hospital, check her out temporarily, and wheel her down to the Cadillac.

Thirty minutes later, I have her arranged comfortably in the shop, propped with pillows. Though she won't admit it, Mama is nervous. Her hands won't still, and every five seconds, she glances out the window.

She hadn't said much about the altercation with Jimmy's wife, other than that the girl needed psychiatric help and a stint in rehab, followed by a "bless her heart."

"Do you think he'll be on time?" I ask, knowing that she'll answer yes.

Mama nods. "He doesn't miss an opportunity, especially when he thinks he has the upper hand."

"But I haven't told anyone we're short," I say.

"It doesn't matter," Mama says, shaking her head. "He's like a lion. He can smell fear a mile away."

"Was he always like that? Even in high school?" I finish brewing coffee, add cream and sugar, and carry the steaming mugs over to Mama and set them on the table. With a shudder, I suddenly realize that it may be the last pot of coffee I make.

"He was aggressive, sure. On the football field, on the baseball diamond. A standout athlete, broke all sorts of records." Mama goes silent, then, and stares at the ceiling.

"But?" I prompt her.

She sighs and smiles. "He has a temper. Always has. And it got him in trouble. Beat up some boy from Daphne so badly that it put him in the hospital."

"Really?"

"Another time," she continues, "in college, when he played at Ole Miss, he cut a man in a bar fight. He'd been drinking. The man pressed charges. It got ugly and ended his football career."

"And then what happened?"

"He came home," Mama replies. "Got a job in his daddy's business. Got into real estate. Almost married a girl once, but I think his depression got the best of him. He's been alone now for a long time."

A rap on the door makes us both jump. When I look up, Quinn Hillyer is standing outside the shop's picture window. Though we've been expecting him for hours, I'm still startled to see his stern expression.

"I hope he didn't hear us," I murmur to Mama as I get up to unlock the door.

She gives me an encouraging smile and waves me on.

"Good evening," he says gruffly as I gesture for him to come in and sit down. He doesn't notice Mama until he's halfway across the dining room.

"Quinn," she says, offering an elegant hand for him to shake.

I'm not sure what comes over him in that moment, but it's as if all of the rough edges fall away. He softens—the features in his face, his eyes—even the tiny muscles around his jawline.

"Maggie," he answers her, and approaches as if she's a china figurine that might shatter if he comes too close. "Are you—is that—a wheelchair?"

Mama pats the handrail and bats her eyelashes. "Oh, this old thing?"

"Are you all right?" He asks. "I didn't know that anything…is it serious?"

I almost feel as if I'm eavesdropping on their conversation. The talk seems intimate, familiar. As if there was a time and a place they knew each other well.

Which is impossible, I remind myself, because he's a mean man and a monster. My mother is only being polite. Her Southern manners are impeccable. It's how she'd treat anyone.

"…immune system," I hear her tell him. She mentions the hospital, Jimmy, and that she's taking medicine and hopes to get her strength back. In true Mama fashion, she downplays the seriousness of the illness. "I'm fine, really. Just a hiccup."

I cross my arms approvingly. He certainly doesn't need to know intimate details.

Finally, when they've exhausted all of the details Mama's willing to share, Quinn Hillyer seems to remember that there's business at hand, and I'm involved in it.

He clears his throat, straightens his tie, and takes a seat next to me at the café table. As he does so, the same cloud descends back over his face.

"We've worked hard to get you everything you've asked for," I say. "And I can give you everything…"

Quinn's face registers surprise.

"…except ten thousand dollars."

He doesn't look at Mama. "We had an agreement."

"It's your agreement, not mine," I retort. "Maybe you thought we were—"

"Searcy," my mother chides me.

Quinn shakes his head and rubs his chin with the back of his hand. "I have another couple who'd love to have this property. They're willing to pay more, quite a bit more than the rent I'm charging you."

I shrink away from him, not daring to speak. The idea that he's wheeling and dealing behind my back, behind Mama's, makes me so angry I could spit nails.

"So," Mama asks, "what will you do? We've been partners for nearly 20 years, Quinn."

"Partners?" his voice sounds strangled. "Is that what you'd call this?"

Mama tilts her head, but doesn't change her calm expression. "It's a mutually beneficial business situation. Is there another term you'd prefer?"

The color rising in Quinn's face deepens. "If it was mutual, then why didn't you tell me you were ill, Maggie?"

My mother doesn't answer.

"Is that the reason you couldn't pay the rent?" His voice grows stronger. "You could have come to me," he continues. "You could have told me. Asked me. We could have worked it out."

"Why?" Mama finally replies. "Would you do that for any of your tenants? Or just me? Because I don't need or want special treatment." Her eyes flash.

I look quickly between the two of them with growing anxiety.

"My health is none of your business."

Quinn frowns. "Then your pride will be your downfall."

"You would have wanted more."

I gulp and stare at my mother. *More.*

"Maybe at one time, yes," he agrees. "But I'm a grown man, now. Older and wiser. I learned a long time ago where I stand with you. And how easy it is for you to change your mind."

There's not a thing I understand about the conversation, and I brace for it to turn ugly. For Quinn Hillyer to yell, or Mama to ask him to leave.

"All you had to do was tell me, Maggie." He stands up to leave. "But if you can't trust me, if you won't give an inch, then I'll need you out by next Friday."

I gasp, not believing what I'm hearing. Tears spill out, over my cheeks.

He glances at me and then stares down at Mama. "I do believe that this business means more to your daughter than it ever did to you. Can't you see that?"

Mama lifts her chin. "I see that, Quinn," she replies, her voice barely audible. "But it's more complicated than you know."

A banging on the window makes all of us jump.

Jimmy Richmond is outside, gesturing with a thick envelope. The contents, I am guessing, are exactly what I've been praying might fall out of the sky.

"What in the world?" Quinn Hillyer mutters.

"Oh my goodness," I shriek and jump up. "Don't go anywhere."

It takes me all of ten seconds to retrieve my purse, fumble for the Tiffany box, and exchange it for the money. "Thank you," I breathe as I hug him close. I kiss him full on the lips for good measure, not caring that everyone and anyone in Fairhope can see, and will be talking about it for the next week.

I rush back inside and thrust the money at Quinn. "Here you are. Five thousand dollars," I announce with flourish. "I'll just fetch the rest out of Luke's safe. I'll owe you another five. I'll get it to you in a month. I'll figure out something. I'll sell the Cadillac," I say. Breathing hard, I beam at Mama.

"No," he says.

"What?" I demand.

"It's too late," Quinn says, with a flick of his wrist. He shows me the watch. 8:42 p.m.

"No."

We stare at each other.

"All because of my mother? And some lover's quarrel you had forty years ago?" I am yelling now, and stomp my right foot. "Well, get over it. Both of you."

Neither one answers.

"You're not going to take away the business that my mother started from nothing." My mind races as I come up with reasons to fight Quinn Hillyer. "I love this shop. And lots of other people do, too. I'll-I'll get them to sign a petition," I threaten. "I'll come up with hundreds of names. And if that's not enough, I'll take my case to the TV station. And fight you in court."

I fold my arms across my chest, daring Quinn Hillyer to argue.

"Besides, this town needs a pie shop. People like it. We're good for the economy. We employ people. What are they going to do for jobs?" I take a breath. "We have to stay open. And, I'll work out any details you want. Come up with the extra money. Make you any sort of pie you'd like on a daily basis. Heck, I'll even name a pie after you. Would that make you feel better?" I am shouting so loudly that when I stop, the windows reverberate.

Quinn blinks at me. Mama's mouth is open slightly.

"I don't know if I can argue with that," Quinn says, breaking out into a smile. He begins to laugh, a loud, booming sound that echoes across the tables.

My mother lifts a hand to her mouth. It's shaking. And there's a tear on her cheek. Another slides down, chasing the first.

I search her face and grip her hand.

"She's certainly your daughter, Maggie."

Mama smiles at me and takes a deep breath. She squeezes my fingers gently.

"Well, Quinn, she's your daughter, too."

His face registers shock. I almost faint.

"Daughter?" Quinn repeats. "Maggie…"

Is it true? How could she have kept this from me? From both of us?

I start to cry and press a hand to my lips. I can't take my eyes off the man in front of me.

Mama looks from me to Quinn. "Searcy, meet your father."

Epilogue

The pink chiffon looks like clouds above my head. I've draped silver streamers, as well, and hung hearts from every corner of the room. They sway back and forth in the breeze from the open door.

After pulling the heavy blackboard sign to the sidewalk, I letter the day's specials in red and white chalk. Cherry pie, raspberry tarts, and strawberry turnovers. I add a roasted red pepper and goat cheese quiche and a tomato and basil frittata to the breakfast selections.

It's so early that the birds have barely begun chirping. Though I can't really afford the time, I decide to lock the front door behind me, and take a short stroll down Magnolia Avenue, enjoying the cool February air. Behind me, the faintest hint of light begins peeking over the horizon, the rays hitting Mobile Bay, making the waves sparkle.

A few dedicated runners skim by the shore, their legs pumping in time with the beat of my heart. Further in the distance, a fishing boat trolls the shallow waters, thin lines cast like the edges of a bridal veil. Near the shore, a heron stretches his wings, settling in near a pair of egrets.

This scene is home.

Though I grew up here, it took leaving and coming back for me to connect with Fairhope's air, water, and land. To appreciate the perfection of my surroundings, the heart of the city's people. It's always been a part of me. I just didn't realize it was necessary to make me whole.

As I make my way back up the hill toward Section Street, I consider how far I've come, not only in distance from Atlanta, but in maturity, growth, and love. After all, the past year hasn't been easy.

It's been a complete shock to discover my father's lived in Fairhope almost my whole life, a secret Mama had sworn to take to the grave. They'd engaged in a torrid love affair after graduation from high school.

He'd been gorgeous and invincible, with dark hair that fell in his eyes and shoulders that appeared to be carved from marble. When it was time for Quinn to head to Ole Miss and play ball, Mama was pregnant with me.

Not about to ruin his life, Mama sent herself to my grandmother's farm for the year, cutting all ties without any explanation. She'd cried herself through the next nine months, all the while hoping for a baby girl.

After my birth, my mother moved back to town, rented a small house, set up her own little studio, and began raising me as a single parent.

When Quinn returned years later, his life shattered, and football career over, Mama refused to see him. My appearance only added to his hurt and confusion. He withdrew, became a shell of his former self, bitter and filled with regret.

How strange that five words can change everything.

Quinn, she's your daughter, too.

I pause and take a breath in front of the shop, smiling up at the *Pie Girls* sign.

I have a family. A mother, a real father.

Withdrawing the key from my pocket, I slide the metal into the lock and turn. The scent of brewed coffee and pastries tickles my nose.

It hasn't been the perfect transition. Mama, despite a valiant attempt to rally against her disease, is failing. When Jimmy gave us the news back in November, I smiled bravely, said something about my mother beating the odds, and tried to make her promise to outlive me. I was blathering, babbling nonsense, trying to sort out why our time was being cut short.

As only Mama can, she stayed serene, and right in Dr. Richmond's office, made me promise to live each day to the fullest. Work hard. Enjoy and celebrate each other.

I held it together for as long as I could, but after dropping off Mama at her house, I went straight to the bike shop. Without stopping or pausing for an explanation, I walked in the door and threw myself straight into Luke's arms, sobbing.

I didn't care that he was covered in oil and dust from a long ride. I only cared that he was healthy and breathing and that he loved me. After kissing away my tears in the middle of the store, he proposed.

"I love you, Searcy Roberts," he said, kneeling in front of me. "Marry me."

The entire shop erupted into applause. Customers, employees, friends.

"Yes," I whispered through my tears.

A month later, on Christmas, in front of Mama, Quinn, and Luke's sister, Sarah, I unwrapped tickets to Key West. We were leaving the next day. All of us.

"Tobi's husband promised to watch the shop," Luke said. "It's all settled."

We were married on the beach at sunset on New Year's Eve. I'd borrowed a white Carolina Herrera sheath from Phillipa, who overnighted me the dress, along with a topaz blue and diamond pendant, her gift to me for the wedding. My shoes were new—simple ballet slippers encrusted with a dusting of rhinestones and edged with thin ribbon. Mama gave me something old—my grandmother's diamond ring, which fit perfectly on my left hand.

Tobi stood in as my maid of honor, while Quinn served as best man. Phillipa, Mimi, and Luke's sister,

Sarah, were bridesmaids. Mama cried her eyes out, going through an entire box of tissues. Tears of joy, she kept insisting. We danced until well past midnight, until Luke picked me up in his arms and carried me back to the room. Laughing and kissing, we waved to Mama, Quinn, and Sarah.

Luke undressed me carefully, slipping the straps of the dress off my shoulders one at a time. His lips brushed my skin, sending shivers across every nerve ending in my body. Gently, he turned me around, running his hand from my neck to the small of my back.

"You are an amazing woman," he said. "And I love you more each day."

With a gentle motion, Luke unzipped my dress and let it fall to the floor. I undressed him then, first his jacket, then his tie. I unbuttoned his shirt, running my palms over his skin.

We fell into bed, exploring each other's bodies, dizzy with pleasure. When he looked into my eyes, I was transported. Never in my life had I experienced such complete joy.

For hours, we made love, until we were exhausted and fell asleep in each other's arms.

The sounds of waves crashing on the beach woke us the next morning.

We stayed three more days, snorkeling, playing in the water, and dining out. Pure bliss. Mama's symptoms even seemed to disappear.

When it came time to board the plane to come home, I was ready. It was time to start our life together.

I sigh and smile, bringing myself back to the present. Humming lightly, I busy myself filling the pastry case.

When I hear the click of the back door, Tobi calls out to me.

"How's Mrs. Nolan this morning?"

I blush, still enraptured in our honeymoon phase. "Lovely."

"Are we ready for today?" she raises an eyebrow. "You've been a busy girl." She takes in all of the pies and tarts with appreciation.

"Couldn't sleep," I admit with a grin. "Just excited."

"I think it's going to be huge," Tobi says, clapping her hands together in anticipation.

I smile.

We've been planning the event for a month. After much debate, Luke, Mama, Tobi, and I decided that Valentine's Day was the perfect occasion for our annual Free Pie Day. This year, the second annual, would kick off this morning at ten o'clock sharp.

The mayor is invited, the town council, television stations, and local dignitaries. The shop has become so successful that we decided that any tips or donations collected would go toward a scholarship we established at Fairhope High School. Each year, one senior who has been accepted to culinary school will receive the funds.

This May will be our first scholarship, and I'm giddy with anticipation at awarding the money to a lucky recipient. We've also begun an after school program for local students who are thinking about a career in restaurant management. Each afternoon, kids will work alongside Tobi or me, learning to measure, bake, and create.

It's my way of giving back after the tremendous support we received from the community.

Quinn, my father, has become the shop's biggest cheerleader. He's so proud of me, bragging to everyone he meets.

At nine thirty, customers begin trickling in the shop. By nine forty-five, it is standing room only, with people standing shoulder to shoulder.

Luke rushes in one minute before ten, brandishing a bouquet of pink roses. Two dozen. He kisses me and wishes me luck.

Tobi whistles for everyone's attention, clapping her hands for silence.

I walk carefully to the counter, smiling at all of the happy faces.

"Thank you all for coming today," I begin. "We're so excited to share Valentine's Day with you. We've come so far in the past year, and you've helped make it happen. You've supported the shop, bought our pies, enjoyed our coffee, and come back, day after day. I'm—we're indebted to you. We couldn't have made it this far without you."

Applause ripples through the shop.

"I want to say a special thank you to my mother, Maggie, who created *Pie Girls*, and my father, Quinn, who provided the location and backing to keep this venture going. I love you both."

Mama smiles. She's holding Quinn's hand, and the two look so happy.

"Before we get started—and believe me, there's plenty of free pie to be had by all—I have an announcement to share with you."

I motion for Luke to join me.

He hesitates, then walks over. "We have some exciting news," I begin. "And since you're all family, we wanted you to be the first to know."

Luke smiles down at me.

"We're expanding…"

There's a squeal of excitement from someone in the crowd. "A new store?"

"How about Foley?"

"Destin."

"We need one in Mobile," someone else comments.

Luke raises a hand. "Well, maybe someday. But this is a different way that we're adding to the *Pie Girls* family."

I hear Mama gasp. Luke's sister beams. Quinn jumps to his feet.

"We're pregnant!" I announce.

Cheers erupt, and Luke beams with pride. He slides his arm around me and pulls me close. The applause is deafening, and everyone is talking at once.

"Wait," I call out over the noise. "There's one more thing."

The room falls silent. Luke raises an eyebrow. He was out of town for yesterday's appointment and it's all I could do to keep it a secret until now.

"Tell me," he whispers, and the rest of the world melts away as he takes me in his arms.

I stand on tiptoes and whisper in his ear.

I wait for the shock to leave Luke's face. He's ecstatic.

"Twins!" he shouts, bending down to caress my face.

There's more applause and whistling.

"These little girls are going to be beautiful," Luke adds. "Just like their Mama."

I laugh. "And how do you know they're not boys?"

"Because the sign says *Pie Girls*." He cups my face in his hands and kisses me, long and slow. "And who am I to argue with success?

READERS GUIDE

1. Searcy is very much a spoiled-rotten Southern belle at the outset of the story. Does she have any redeeming qualities?

2. How do you feel about Searcy's shopping therapy to punish Alton for his absences? Is it a way for Searcy to get Alton's attention?

3. Clearly, Searcy and Alton's relationship lacks good communication. Is it okay for couples to keep secrets like Alton's surgery?

4. What does C.C.'s character say about Alton? How are they alike or different?

5. Did growing up without a father affect Searcy's decision to marry Alton?

6. Why does Maggie hide her illness from Searcy?

7. Did you ever have a high school nemesis like Haley?

8. In many ways, Tobi is the glue that holds *Pie Girls* together. Have you ever had a friend like Tobi?

9. How much does Searcy grow and change over the course of the story? Is that one reason Luke is attracted to her?

10. Searcy eventually forgives Alton. Should she?

11. Do you agree with Searcy's idea to save *Pie Girls*? Why or why not? What other ideas would you suggest?

12. How do you feel about the secret revealed by Maggie near the end of the story?

MAGGIE'S BEST EVER PIE CRUST

3 cups of flour
1 ½ teaspoons salt
1 cup plus 3 tablespoons shortening
9 tablespoons cold water

Mix flour and salt, cut in shortening until well mixed. Sprinkle with flour and stir with a fork or your hands until the mixture leaves the sides of the bowl and forms a semi-smooth appearance. Press into a ball shape, wrap in waxed paper, and refrigerate 30 minutes.

When you are ready to use, divide the dough in half and place on a lightly floured surface, Smooth with a rolling pin into a nine-inch circle. Place in pie pan, press lightly into the bottom and sides of a nine-inch pie plate, and trim any extra off the edges with a knife.

Makes two 9-inch bottom crusts or one bottom and one top for a 9-inch pie.

Searcy's Chess Pie

½ pound of butter
2 cups of white sugar
1 teaspoon of vanilla
8 egg yolks, beaten
½ cup of heavy cream or half and half
2 tablespoons of corn meal
½ recipe of Best Ever Pie Crust

Cream butter and sugar with a mixer; add yolks, vanilla, and heavy cream. Fold in cornmeal. Pour into 9-inch pie plate with Best Ever Pie Crust. Bake at 350 until medium brown on top, 45-55 minutes. Pie should be almost set before removing from the oven. Cool before cutting. Serves 8.

MAGGIE'S DECADENT CHOCOLATE PECAN PIE

1 cup of white sugar
1 cup light corn syrup
½ cup butter
4 eggs, beaten
2 tablespoons of honey (can substitute bourbon if preferred)
2 teaspoons of vanilla
¼ teaspoon of salt
6 ounces semisweet chocolate chips
1 cup of chopped pecans
½ Recipe Best Ever Pie Crust

Combine sugar, corn syrup, and butter in a saucepan and place over medium heat, stirring until butter melts and sugar dissolves. Let cool slightly.

In a large bowl, mix eggs, honey, vanilla, and salt. Whisk the sugar mixture into the egg mixture. Mix in the chocolate chips and pecans. Pour into 9-inch pie plate with Best Ever Pie Crust.

Bake for one hour at 325 degrees. Pie should be mostly set when removed from oven. Let cool before cutting. Serves 8.

Tobi's Lemon Sponge Pie

Grated rind of 1 lemon
Juice of 1 lemon
1 cup of white sugar
3 rounded tablespoons of flour
2 tablespoons of melted butter
1 cup of whole milk
2 egg yolks
2 egg whites
½ Recipe of Best Ever Pie Crust

Combine all ingredients except for egg whites. Beat the two egg whites with a mixer until stiff. Fold into the lemon mixture. Pour into 9-inch pie plate with Best Ever Pie Crust. Bake 30-40 minutes at 400 degrees. Top should be nicely brown and mostly set before removing from the oven. Cool before cutting. Serves 8.

Acknowledgements

To my wonderful sons, Patrick and John David, I love you! Hugs to Mom and Dad for offering endless encouragement. Mark, Peg, Josh, and Sarah—miss you!

I am indebted to my grandmother, Ruth Weirs, for providing Searcy and Maggie's recipes. They were passed down to my mother, who passed them down to me. I will treasure them always, and I hope you enjoy them, too!

Laura Pepper Wu, I can't thank you enough for the many hours spent discussing Searcy's story. Your insight makes every manuscript shine brighter!

My fabulous early readers include Maxine Kidder, Mary Steudle, Linda Moore, Jen McGee, and Tobi Helton. Thank you, also, to Tracie Banister, Karen Pokras Toz, Jen Tucker, Lisa Hirsch, Yvonne Edeker, Cecelia Heyer, Jana Simpson, April Sanders, Ted and Linda Hicks, Jessica Sinn, Valerie Case, Ron Wright, and the *Movie Mavens*. Love you all!

I am indebted to Damonza, who created the fabulous cover for *Pie Girls*. Hugs to the talented Caroline Steudle for her sharp eye and critical reading skills. Kudos to Christopher Moyer for making my pages look lovely.

I'm so grateful to the readers who've supported my books and recommended them to others! You have my heartfelt gratitude. I love hearing from you—reach out to me anytime in any of these ways:

E-mail: laurenclarkbooks@gmail.com
Twitter: @LaurenClark_Bks
Facebook: Facebook.com/LaurenClarkBooks
Web: www.laurenclarkbooks.com

If you enjoyed *Pie Girls*, please write a quick Amazon, BN.com, or GoodReads review. There's no greater compliment!

ABOUT THE AUTHOR

Lauren Clark writes contemporary novels sprinkled with sunshine, suspense, and secrets. A former TV news anchor, Lauren adores flavored coffee, local bookstores, and anywhere she can stick her toes in the sand. Her big loves are her family, paying it forward, and true-blue friends.

She is the author of several award-winning novels, including *Dancing Naked in Dixie*, *Stardust Summer*, and *Stay Tuned*. Lauren is a member of the Gulf Coast Writers Association and the Mobile Writers Guild. Check out her website at www.laurenclarkbooks.com.

READ ON FOR AN EXCERPT FROM

Dancing Naked in Dixie
Lauren Clark

Dancing Naked In Dixie
Chapter 1

"The new editor needs you, Julia." A stern summons from Dolores Stanley leaps over the cubicles and follows me like a panther stalking its prey.

"Just give me a minute," I beg with a wide smile as I sail by the front office and a row of hunch-shouldered executive assistants. Steaming Starbucks in hand, my new powder-white jacket stuffed in the crook of my arm, I give a quick wave over my shoulder.

I am, after all, late, a bit jet-lagged, and on deadline. A very tight deadline.

A glance at my watch confirms two hours and counting to finish the article. I walk faster. My heart twists a teensy bit.

I don't mean to get behind. Really, it just sort of happens.

However, that's all going to change, starting today. I'm going to organize my life, work, home, all of it. I'll be able to check email on the road, never miss an appointment, and keep up with all of my deadlines.

Just as soon as I can find the instruction manual to my new iPhone. And my earpiece.

Anyway, it's going to be great!

So great, that I'm not the least bit panicked when I round the corner and see my desk; which, by the way, is wallpapered in post-it notes, flanked by teetering stacks of mail, and littered with random packages. Even my voicemail light is flashing furiously.

Before I can take another step, the phone starts ringing.

In my rush to pick it up, I trip and nearly fall over a pile of books and magazines someone carelessly left behind. A thick travel guide lands on my foot and excruciating pain shoots through my toes. My coffee flies out of my hand and splats on the carpeting. I watch in horror as my latte seeps into the rug fibers.

"Darn it all!" I exclaim, snatching up the leaking cup and setting it on my desk. Other choice expressions shuttle through my brain as I catch the edge of the chair with one hand to steady myself. I frown at the offending mess on the floor. *Who in the world?*

Until it dawns on me. Oh, right. I left it all there in my hurry to make my flight to Rome. My fault. I close my eyes, sigh deeply, and the strap of my bag tumbles off my shoulder. Everything—keys, mascara, lip gloss, spare change—falls onto the desk with a huge clatter. Letters and paper flutter to the floor like confetti in the Macy's Day Parade. Just as Dolores sounds off again, her voice raspy and caffeine-deprived.

"*Now*, Julia."

My spine stiffens.

"Be right there," I call out in my most dutiful employee voice. Right after I find my notes and calm down.

As I start to search through my briefcase, a head full of thick silver curls appears over the nubby blue paneling.

"Hey, before you rush off," Marietta whispers, "how was Italy? Was it gorgeous, wonderful?"

"Marvelous," I smile broadly at my closest friend and conjure up a picture postcard of Rome, Florence, and sun-drenched Tuscany. Five cities, seven days. The pure bliss of nothing but forward motion. "From the sound of it, I should have stayed another day."

Marietta studies my face.

It's the understatement of the year. I hate to admit it, but the prospect of inhabiting an office cubicle for a week intimidates me more than missing the last connection from Gatwick and sleeping on the airport floor. Claustrophobia takes over. I actually get hives from sitting still too long. Most days, I live out of suitcases. And couldn't be happier!

I'm a travel writer at *Getaways* magazine. Paid for the glorious task of gathering fascinating snippets of culture and piecing them into quirky little stories. Jet-setting to the Riviera, exploring the Great Barrier Reef, basking on Bermuda beaches. It's as glamorous and exhilarating as I imagined.

Okay, it is a tad lonely, from time to time, and quite exhausting.

Which is precisely why I have to get organized. Today.

I sink into my chair and try to concentrate. What to tackle first? Think, think.

"Julia Sullivan!"

Third reminder from Dolores. Uh-oh.

Marietta rolls her eyes. "Guess you better walk the plank," she teases. "New guy's waiting. Haven't met him yet, but I've heard he's the 'take no prisoners' sort. Hope you come back alive."

All of a sudden, my head feels light and hollow.

I've been dying to find out about the magazine's new editor.

Every last gory detail.

Until now.

"I'm still in another time zone," I offer up to Marietta with a weak smile. My insides churn as I ease out of my chair.

Marietta tosses me a wry look. "Nice try. Get going already, sport."

I tilt my head toward the hallway and pretend to pout. When I glance back, Marietta's already disappeared. Smart girl.

"Fine, fine." I tug a piece of rebellious auburn hair into place, smooth my suit, and begin to march. My neck prickles.

I'm not going to worry. Not much anyway.

My pulse thuds.

Not going to worry about change. Or a reorganization. Or pink slips.

Focus, Julia.

The last three editors adored me.

At least half of the North American Travel Journalist Association awards hanging in the lobby are mine.

The best projects land in my lap. Almost always.

Well, there was the one time I was passed over for St. Barts, but I'm sure what's-her-name just had PMS that day. And I did get Morocco in February.

This last trip to Italy? Hands-down, one of the choice assignments.

I round the corner and come within an inch of Dolores Stanley's bulbous nose. As I step back, her thin red lips fold into a minus sign. Chanel No. 5 wraps around me like a toxic veil.

Dolores is the magazine's oldest and crankiest employee. Everyone's afraid of her. To be perfectly honest, Dolores doesn't like *anyone*, except Marietta—and the guy in accounting who signs her paycheck. And that's only twice a month.

Most of the office avoids her as if she's been quarantined with a deadly virus. "Good morning, Dolores," I say with forced cheer.

As expected, she ignores me completely. Instead, Dolores heaves her purple polyester-clad bottom up off the chair, and lumbers toward the editor's office. Breathing hard, she pushes open the huge mahogany door, frowns, and tosses in my name like a careless football punt.

I follow the momentum, shoulders back, hoping Dolores doesn't notice my shaking hands.

Stop it, Julia. No worries, right?

Dolores pauses and murmurs something that sounds like 'good luck.' *Wait. Dolores wished me luck?* That freaks me out completely. I want to run. Or fall to the floor, hand pressed to my forehead, prompting someone to call the paramedics.

Too late. The door clicks shut behind me. The office already smells different. Masculine, earthy, like leather and sand. I crane my neck to see the new person's face, but the high-back chair blocks my view; an occasional tap-tap on a keyboard the only sound in the room.

I fill my lungs, exhale, and wait.

Light streams onto the desk, now piled high with newspapers, memos, and several back issues of *Getaways*. A navy Brooks Brothers jacket hangs in the corner.

I gaze out the window at the majestic skyscrapers lining Broadway, a blur of activity hidden behind a silver skin of glass and metal. A taxi ride away, three international airports bustle with life. Jets ready to whisk me away at a moment's notice. My pulse starts to race just thinking about it.

"Not in a big hurry to meet the boss?"

The gruff voice startles me. My knees lock up.

"Sir?" I play innocent and hope he'll blame Dolores.

The chair spins around. Two large feet plop on the desk and cross at the ankles. My eyes travel up well-dressed legs, a starched shirt, and a red silk tie. They settle on a pair of dark eyes that almost match mine.

For a moment, nothing works. My brain, my mouth, I can't breathe. It absolutely, positively may be the worst shock-of-my-life come true.

"David?" I stutter like a fool and gather my composure from where it has fallen around my feet.

The broad, easy grin is the same. But the hair is now a little more salt than pepper. The face, more weather-beaten than I remember.

"I told them you'd be surprised." David's face flashes from smug to slightly apologetic.

I say nothing.

"They talked me out of retirement," David folds his arms across his chest and leans back. "Said they *had* to have me."

"I'll bet," I offer with a cool nod.

His face reveals nothing. "Not going to be a problem, is it?"

Of course, it is! I dig my fingernails into my palm, shake my head, and manage to force up the corners of my mouth.

"Good." David slides his feet off the desk and thumbs through a pile of magazines.

I stand motionless, watching his hands work. The familiar flash of gold is gone. I glower at his bare finger, incensed to the point of nearly missing all that he is saying. I watch David's mouth move; he's gesturing.

"...and so, we're going to be going in a new direction." He narrows his gaze. "Julia?"

I wrench my eyes up. "A new direction," I repeat in a stupid, sing-song voice.

David frowns. With a smooth flick of his wrist, he tosses a copy of *Getaways* across the desk. He motions for me to take it.

"The latest issue," he says.

Gingerly, I reach for it. And choke. *That's funny.* I purse my lips. *Funny strange.* The cover story was supposed to be mine. My feet start to tingle. I want to run.

Instead, I force myself to begin paging through for the article and stunning photos I'd submitted—shots of the sapphire-blue water, honey-gold beaches, and the lush green landscape.

With forced nonchalance, I search through the pages. *Flip. Flip. Flip.* In a minute, I'm halfway through the magazine. No article. No Belize. No nothing. My fingers don't want to work anymore. I feel sick.

"Julia, what is it? You seem a little pale," David prods. He leans back in his chair and stares at me with an unreadable expression.

I continue looking. *Where* is my article? Buried in the middle? Hidden in the back? More pages. I peek up at David, who meets my dismay with a steady gaze.

What kind of game is he playing?

I yank my chin up. "No, nothing's wrong," I say lightly, "not a thing."

Inside, I'm screaming like a lunatic. *There must be a mistake.* My bottom lip trembles the slightest bit. I blink. Surely, I'm not going to…lose my…

"It was junk. Pure and simple," David interrupts, the furrows on his forehead now more pronounced. He jumps up and folds his arms across his chest. "Bland, vanilla. The article screamed boring. It was crap."

Crap? Don't mince any words, David. He might as well toss a bucket of ice water on my head. I shiver, watching him.

"Let me ask you this." David stops walking back and forth and puts his fists on the desk. "How much time did you actually spend writing and researching the article? Just give me a rough estimate. In hours or days?" David's finished making his point. He sits down and begins glancing through a red folder.

My mind races. Last month? Right. Trip to Belize.

Focus. Try to focus.

I fidget and tap out an uneven rhythm with my shoe. Excuses jumble in my head, swirling like my brain is on spin cycle.

David clears his throat. He opens a manila envelope, thumbs through the contents, then gazes at me with the force of a steam-driven locomotive. "Are you taking care of yourself? Taking your ... prescriptions?"

The words cut like a winter wind off the Baltic Sea.

I grope for words. My thoughts fall through my fingers.

My attention deficit isn't exactly a secret. Most everyone knows it's been a problem in the past. But, things are under control ... it's all been fine.

Until now.

I start to seethe. David continues to gaze intently and wait for my reply.

What are you, a psychiatrist? I want to spout. *Not to mention all of the HR rules you're breaking by asking me that.*

"I'm off the medication. Doctor's orders. Have been for several years," I answer, managing to give him a haughty *the-rest-is-none-of-your-business* stare.

David backs off with a swivel of his chair. "Sorry. Just concerned," he says, holding one cuff-linked hand in the air. "So, *exactly* how much *time* did you *spend* on the *article*?" David enunciates each word, stabbing them through my skin like daggers.

"Five hours," I blurt out, immediately wishing I could swallow the words and say twelve. "Maybe seven."

David makes a noise. Then, I realize he's laughing. At me. At my enormous fib.

My face is scarlet, glowing hot.

Head bent, David flips through a set of papers. He pauses at a small stack. I recognize the coffee stain on one edge and the crinkled corner. My article.

"Let me quote verbatim to you, Ms. Sullivan," he says, his tone mocking. "Belize offers the best of both worlds, lovely beaches and a bustling city full of good restaurants. Visitors can find fascinating artwork and treasure hunt for souvenirs downtown."

He stops.

Surely, my article was better. He must have the draft. Oh, there wasn't a draft. Oops. Because I hadn't allowed myself much time. Come to think of it, I banged most of it out on the taxi ride from the airport. I accidentally threw away most of my notes in a shopping bag, which wasn't really my fault. I was late for my plane. And then...

"So, I killed it." David ceremoniously holds the papers over the trash can and lets go.

I watch the white papers float, then settle to their final resting place. Maybe I should jump in after them? My legs start to ache. Why did I wear these stupid Prada boots that pinch my left heel?

"But, all is not lost," David says dramatically. "I'll give you a chance to redeem yourself." He drums his fingers on the desk. "If you can up the caliber of your writing. Spend some time. Put your heart into it."

I don't say a word. Or make a sound. Because if I do, I'm sure to sputter out something I'll regret. Or, God forbid, cry. *Redeem myself? Put my heart into it?*

Deep breath. Okay, I can afford to work a teensy bit harder. Give a tad more effort here and there. But, the criticism. Ouch! And coming from David, it's one hundred times worse. The award-winning super-journalist who circled the globe, blah, blah, blah.

David cracks his knuckles. "Look, I know it's been tough since your mother's illness and all." His tone softens slightly. "Her passing away has been difficult for everyone."

I manage not to leap over the desk and shake him by the shoulders. *Difficult? How would he know?* My blood pressure doubles. *Stay calm. Just a few more minutes.* Doesn't he have some other important meeting? An executive lunch?

David drones on like he's giving a sermon. I try to tune him out, but can't help hearing the next part.

"Julia, it's affected your writing. Immensely. And look at you. You've lost weight. You're exhausted. I want you to know I understand your pain—"

"You *don't* understand," I cut in before I can stop myself. My mother died two years ago. She was sick before that. I still miss her every day. *Damn him. Get out of my personal life. And stay out.*

We stare each other down, stubborn, gritty gunfighters in the Wild West.

"Fine," David says evenly and breaks my gaze. "So, as you've heard, the magazine is going in a new direction. The focus group research says …" He glances down at some scribbled notes. "It says our American readers want to see more 'out of the way' places to visit. Road trips. A Route 66 feel, if you will."

Focus groups. I forgot all about that obsession.

David pauses to make sure I'm listening. For once, he has my undivided attention.

"According to the numbers, they're saturated with Paris, London, the Swiss Alps. They want off the beaten path. Local flavor. So, we're going to give it a shot. We'll call it something like 'Back Roads to Big Dreams.'"

What a horrible idea. I swallow hard. Our readers don't want that! Who did he interview in these focus groups? The Beverly Hillbillies?

David continues, immensely pleased with the concept. "The emphasis is going to be on places that offer something special—perhaps historically or culturally. But the town or city must also be looking toward the future. Planning how to thrive, socially and economically. It's going to be part of a new series, if it turns out well." David puts emphasis on 'if' and shoots me a look. "What do you think?"

Is he joking? He doesn't want my opinion. Does he honestly think I like the idea?

David pauses. Apparently, he expects a response. An intelligent, supportive one.

"Sounds ... interesting," I manage to squeak out and shift uncomfortably. I predict that I'll be spending a full day spinning half-truths. I'll likely be offered a lifetime membership in Deceivers Anonymous if I don't die first.

David snatches up his glasses. *Glasses?* When did he start wearing glasses?

"I know you're our token globe-trotter, but I'd hoped you'd be more enthusiastic." He taps his Mont Blanc on his desk calendar and then points to the enormous wall atlas. "I'm thinking Alabama."

Something massive and thick catches in my throat. My head swivels to the lower portion of the map. I begin to cough uncontrollably.

Ever so calmly, David waits for me to quit.

When I catch my breath, my mind races with excuses. The words stumble out of my mouth, tripping over themselves. "But, I have plans. Tickets to the Met, a fundraiser, a gallery opening, and book club on Monday." I don't mention the Filene's trip I'd planned. Or the romantic date I've been promising Andrew, my neglected boyfriend.

David waves a hand to dismiss it all. "Marietta can handle the magazine-related responsibilities."

From the top drawer of his desk, he produces an airline ticket and a folder with my name on it. He sets them on the edge of his desk. Something I can't decipher plays on his lips.

I keep my voice even. "What about Bali?" I had planned to leave for the South Pacific a week from Friday. "It's on my calendar. It's been on there…"

David shakes his head. "Not anymore."

The words wound me like a thousand bee stings.

"Alabama," David repeats.

I swallow, indignant. He's plucked me off a plum assignment without a thought to my schedule. My new boss is sending me to who-knows-where, and he looks perfectly content. I narrow my eyes and fold my arms.

"Seriously David, you're sending me on an assignment to…Alabama? *Alabama*?" I sputter, searching my brain for an appropriate retort. "I'd rather—I don't know—*dance naked* for my next assignment than go to Alabama!"

The announcement comes out much louder than I intend and reverberates through the room. Dolores probably has her ear pressed to the door, but the phrase bounces off my boss like a cotton ball.

David smothers a chuckle. "Suit yourself."

"It's a done deal, isn't it?" I finally manage, my voice low and uneven. The answer is obvious. The airline ticket and folder are within my grasp. I don't move a centimeter toward them. For all I know, the inside of one of them is coated with Anthrax. For a brief moment, I picture myself, drawing one last ragged breath, on the floor of David's brand-spanking-new office carpeting.

"It's your choice." David swipes at his glasses and settles them on his nose. "Deadline's a week from today. That's next Wednesday. Five o'clock. Take it or leave it."

I stifle an outward cringe at his tone, and the way he's spelling it out for me. Syllable by syllable, like I'm a toddler caught with my hand in the cookie jar.

Take it or leave it.

Not the assignment. My job.

It's your choice.

David's fingers hit the keyboard. Click-clack. "Oh, and leave your notes on Italy with Dolores. I'll write the article myself."

That's it. The meeting's over. I'm fuming. Furious. I want to rip up the papers an inch from his face and let a hailstorm of white scraps fall to the carpet.

Take it or leave it.

I start to turn on my heel and walk out like we'd never had the conversation. David will come around, won't he?

Then, I stop. It's a joke. An awful, terrible joke. Do I have other job prospects? Do I want to change careers? What about my apartment? What about the bills?

Fine. Okay. Have it your way, David.

I catch myself before I stick my tongue out. He probably has surveillance cameras set up on a 24-hour loop.

David knows I'm beaten.

So, I bend, ever so slightly. In one quick motion, I reach out to tuck the folder and ticket under my arm. In slow motion, the papers slip through my fingers like water between rocks in a stream.

Damn! The clatter of David's awkward typing stops.

So much for a smooth exit.

On the ground lies a square white envelope and matching note card. I swoop down to gather my mess.

Though I'm trying not to notice, I can't help but stare at the delicate pen and ink lines on the front of the card. There's no lettering, just thin strokes of black that form the outline of a majestic mansion and its towering columns. Before I can stop myself, I flip open the note card, expecting a flowery verse or invitation. Some event I'll be expected to attend for the magazine? A party?

There are only a few sentences inside, barely legible, scrawled in loopy, old-fashioned writing. *David, Please help*, I can make out. Underneath, a scribbled signature. An *M*, maybe?

Hmph. There's no end to what people will do to get a story. Gifts, money, flowers, I've seen it all. Traded for a snippet of publicity.

I refold the note and hand it across the desk. It must not be particularly important, because David takes the card and sets it aside without glancing at it.

Necessary papers tucked securely in the crook of my arm, I straighten up, flick an imaginary piece of lint off my skirt with my free hand, and begin to walk out. My feet brush the carpet in small, level steps.

I reach for the doorknob, inches from the hallway.

"Have fun! Don't forget to check in," David calls after me. "Oh, and send a postcard."

I scowl. His voice is ringing in my ears.

That's low. Lower than low. He knows I collect postcards. Make that *used to*. In my past life. I want to stomp out—have a proper four-year-old temper tantrum. Be in control, I tell myself. Keep your chin up. Walk.

David can go to Hell!

I make the most horrible, gruesome face I can think of. Surveillance cameras be damned.

Visit www.LaurenClarkBooks.com to
purchase your copy of *Dancing Naked in Dixie*.